CROWBAIT

DAVID RAE

Books by David Rae

The Sun Thief trilogy
Crowman
Crowtower
Crowbait

CROWBAIT

Book Three of The Sun Thief trilogy

DAVID RAE

Milton, Ontario

This is a work of fiction. All of the characters, events, and organizations portrayed in this novel are either products of the author's imagination or are used fictitiously.

Brain Lag Publishing
Milton, Ontario
http://www.brain-lag.com/

Cover artwork by Catherine Fitzsimmons

ISBN 978-1-928011-92-7

Library and Archives Canada Cataloguing in Publication

Title: Crowbait / David Rae.
Names: Rae, David, 1962- author.
Description: "Book three of The sun thief trilogy."
Identifiers: Canadiana (print) 20220484449 | Canadiana (ebook) 20220484473 | ISBN 9781928011927
(softcover) | ISBN 9781928011934 (EPUB)
Classification: LCC PR6118.A32 C75 2023 | DDC 823/.92—dc23

Content warnings: Abuse (implied, sexual), death, violence

This book is dedicated to my family and all of their patience and support.

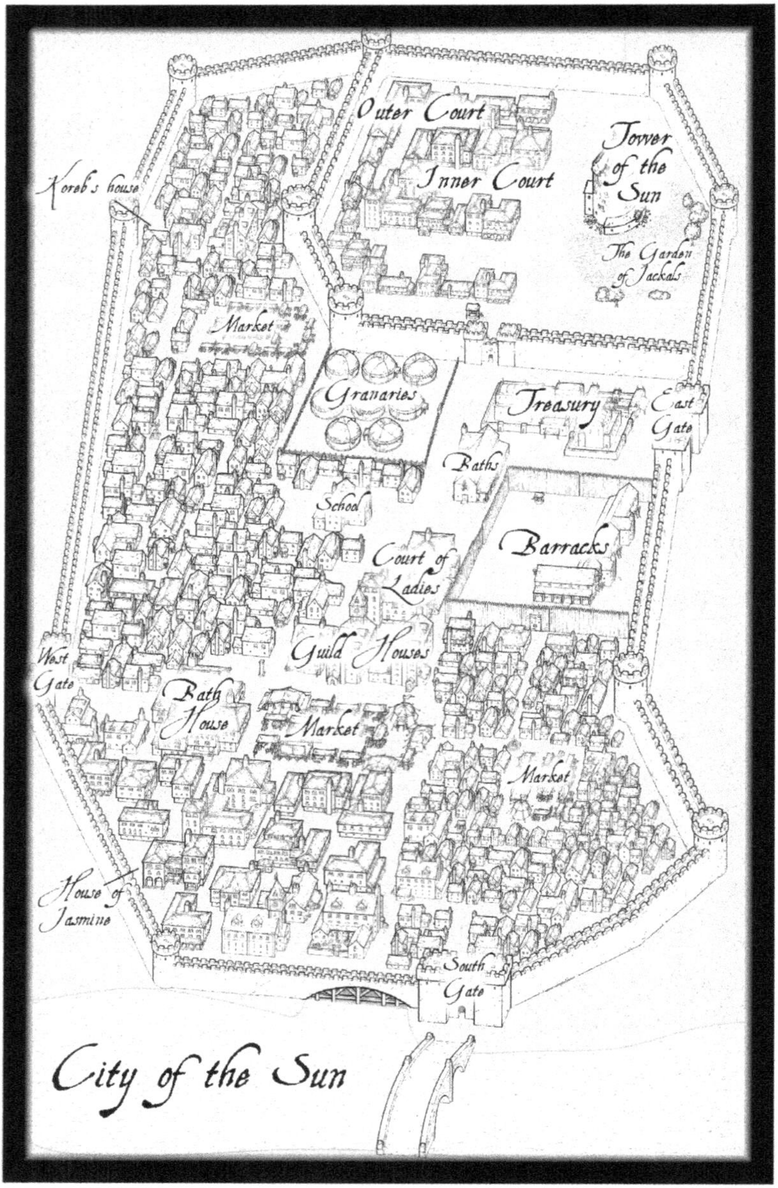

City of the Sun

Outer Court
Inner Court
Tower of the Sun
The Garden of Jackals
Koreb's house
Market
Granaries
Treasury
East Gate
Baths
School
Barracks
Court of Ladies
Guild Houses
West Gate
Bath House
Market
Market
House of Jasmine
South Gate

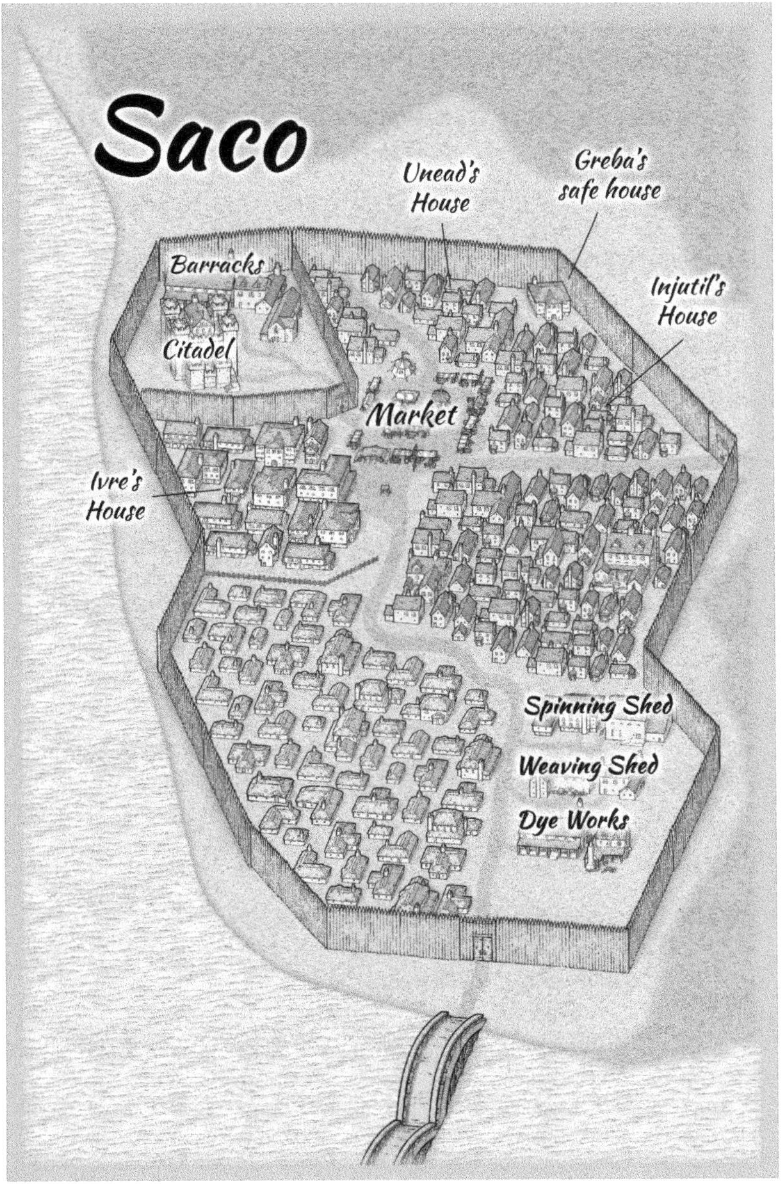

Saco

Unead's House
Greba's safe house
Barracks
Injutil's House
Citadel
Market
Ivre's House
Spinning Shed
Weaving Shed
Dye Works

Prologue

Vatu stands and the twelve cower before him. Erroi: his body hangs from the gibbet. Vatu has made him pay for his treachery. He has tortured him and slain him. He has killed his wife and child before his eyes. But Vatu is not finished with the high priest yet. He is not finished with the rebel.

"This is my world and no one will take it from me. No one can escape."

Vatu reaches out in the night to capture the spirit of Erroi. He will drag him back to be reborn. He will drag him back to hell. Over and over he has dragged Erroi and all the twelve back. It has been so since the moon first turned around the dark land.

This where they belong. They cannot rebel against him. He is master of the dark.

But when he reaches for Erroi, I stand before him and will not allow it.

His rage is terrible. A tempest of darkness and fire.

"You cannot take him from me. He is mine," Vatu says. "You have no place here. This world is mine."

But I am the Whisperer. I cannot be silenced and everyone will hear my voice. And those that heed my voice are mine.

Chapter One
The Garden of Jackals

Greba

When you arrived I was waiting for you. How angry you were, there in the Garden of Jackals. You were surprised to see me. Why? Did you not think I would be here? I am everywhere.

You rushed to her side. She lay there broken, and yet almost perfect. Her long dark hair covered her face. Her robe spread out, covering her limbs.

"It is too late," you said. "I am too late." As if it could be otherwise.

I said nothing while you cried and moved to touch her. It seemed as if you were afraid to see her body. I do not blame you. I have seen it. I have seen everything. You steel your nerve and brush her hair back. It is not pretty, her skull has been smashed in the fall. You shrink back. Do not blame yourself. What did you think you would find? Did you think you would hold her in your arms? One last kiss? There is only blood and pulp.

"I am sorry," I tell you. And you turn to me. You do not shout, and for that I am glad. Who knows what your calls would bring. There are worse things than jackals. Worse things for you.

You cannot bring yourself to speak. Should I speak for you? Should I say the words that you cannot? But you find your voice. Keeping it low, you hiss. "You could have saved her."

I will not deny it. I could have, but I did not. His words roll towards me like mist.

"You could have saved her."

I breathe the night air. In the darkness, I see the stars in the heavens above. There is no moon. Around us, I see the pinprick light of the eyes of beasts.

"I cannot leave her here," you say. Now you touch her robes. "I cannot let the jackals take her."

You are angry, but you are right. She is your daughter after all.

"I can do this for her at least." You have brought a shroud. You lay it down beside her and roll her gently onto the cloth. Now her hair has fallen back. You wrap the cloth over her so that you can no longer see. I listen to your sobs. I know how much you loved her.

"She was happy," I whisper to you. "For a while she was happy."

You nod, but cannot say anything. I place a hand upon your back. Do you take comfort from it? You do not shake me away.

"This is your fault," you say. "You could have saved them. You could have saved my daughter."

I do not know what to say. It is true. And so I say nothing. Instead, I open my cloak and hold forth what I had hidden. "I saved this."

A child cries in the darkness. No, not darkness. The infant shines with the faintest of glows. She is alive. You turn and stare. Your eyes are wide. "How…"

I do not say how. That is not what you want to know. "She is your granddaughter. She is alive. What will you do with her?"

It is a test. Will you pass? I can see the shadows of your thoughts flicker behind your eyes. What will you choose?

"How is this possible?" you say again. You open your arms and reach to hold her as you held her only a few hours before. Up there at the point of justice in the tower. You held her and then passed her to Kong. Still, I let you take her from me. She is yours now, yours and his.

"What will become of her?" you ask as if that is up to me. As if I should tell you all that will happen in a child's lifetime.

"You should dig two graves," I say. You have brought a shovel to bury your daughter.

"Two graves? But she is not dead."

"Two graves. Make a small one for the child, but make it shallow. When they come to look, they will think the jackals have dug up her body and taken her."

I can see you want to ask me more, but instead, you hand me the child back and begin to dig. I had forgotten how strong you are. You dig quickly with sharp cutting thrusts into the soil and lift out clumps of bone and mud.

"How many people have died here?" you ask me. I can hear the reproach in your voice.

"You blame me?"

"Did you not make this world?"

Are you right? Am I to blame for the horrors of this world?

"I think you are responsible for many of these bones," I tell you.

You look up from digging. "Did you not make me? And Vatu?"

You think to blame me for all of this. How cowardly.

"I have made many things."

You grunt and return to your digging. When you have dug a hole higher than your waist, you stop. You clamber out and move next to the body. I can see how reluctant you are. It is too late now to change things. She is dead.

"You could have saved her," you say again.

"I did," I reply, "I saved her from this." And I gesture around, indicating the darkness. You spit onto the upturned earth. I can see anger knot inside you. Do you not wish to be free of the dark?

Anger is useful, you take your anger and with it, you steel yourself to cast your daughter into the pit you made. It is a lie, a red rag that you can cover your thoughts with. In a mindless rage you drag the corpse to the edge of the grave and let it, let her slide in. And then your rage fails you and you fall to your knees weeping. As you should.

I let you cry for a while. I should let you cry forever, but eventually, you stop.

"Now dig the other grave," I tell you. How heartless of me. But it must be done. You dig the hole for your granddaughter. It is only a few shovel widths wide. You dig it down to the depth of your knees. And then I tell you to stop.

"No deeper. If you dig deeper the jackals will not dig it up."

"They won't dig it up if there is nothing in it anyway," you say.

"Here," I reply and hand you a cloth covered in blood. "The smell of blood will attract them."

But they are already here. I can hear their cackling call and see the light of their eyes. They are padding just out of sight, but close, very close. They are crunching on old bones. I wonder if they will attack us. But they wait. They know they will find something to eat soon. There is always something for them in the garden. Justice keeps them well fed. They will wait until we are gone.

You take the cloth from me and place it in the hole, then push the soil down over it, and press it flat with your shovel.

"Now the other one," I say. I am cruel but it must be done. There are some things that must be faced.

"I cannot," you say. But you find the strength. You let the earth drop from your shovel onto your daughter's body. It makes a thudding sound as it lands on the matting she is wrapped in.

"If she had never met him, she would still be alive," you say. "He is to blame for this. I will kill him."

"Is he not already dead?" I ask and think of his body hanging from a dark gibbet above us. You cannot kill him. "Besides, it is not his fault any more than it is your fault for having a child."

"I protected her," you say. "I kept her secret."

You do not understand what I am trying to tell you.

The grave is filled, both graves are filled. Now it seems it is time to leave. You cannot do it. You cannot walk away. "Would you have me say something? Words of comfort, a blessing?"

You nod.

"From the darkness to the light." The words of heresy. You flinch when I say them but I see that they comfort you nonetheless.

"Has she truly gone? Has she really escaped?"

"Yes, that is my promise."

You look and I know what you wish to ask.

"Not yet," I tell you. "But soon."

"It has been ages," you say. "Age after age, life after life. When?"

"Not yet but soon."

I still have the child. Would you like to hold it one last time? You shake your head.

"Let me just look at her." And so I draw the cover from her and hold her. The faintest of glows.

"She is beautiful."

"Yes," I agree. I have made so much beauty even in this world.

You do not ask where I will take her. If you did I would not answer. And where I take her you cannot follow. I will give you more reason yet to hate me.

"She will be safe," I tell you. "For a while at least."

"She was safe, for a while too."

"Yes."

"And then what?"

I turn to go and do not answer. You shout after me. Cursing. But I am not listening. And I will not smite you down.

Chapter Two
A Meeting of Heretics

Koreb

Some things must be. Even I am bound by the word. I, who know all things, do you think I will do other than what I must? There is a power higher than mine, most certainly.

You are waiting for me. In the city. I walk through the dark street until I am there. I enter and in the room, there are nine people. You are praying and do not look up. You do not know who I am. I have walked amongst you so many times unnoticed. I do not mind, in fact, it is for the best.

"Join us," you say to me. And I sit on the mat while you make the sign of heresy. You bless me. And I join in the prayers. Afterwards, bread is brought and we sit and talk about faith.

"How do we know he hears our prayers?"

Do I hear your prayers? Yes, of course. I hear all of your prayers spoken and unspoken. The pleadings of a million people begging to be set free. And other prayers too. Have faith. Believe in me.

"It is not him that must listen to us, but us that must listen to him," you say. I have made you very wise, and I nod my head. But others are not convinced.

"How many prayers must we say before he will listen to our pleas?"

"If he will listen to your prayer, none is needed. If he will not then none is needed."

"Then why do we pray if he will not heed us?"

"Through prayer, we can become one with him, and through prayer, our wishes and desires can be aligned with the divine purpose."

Again you are wise, but you think you can take your wisdom and give it to the others here. Have you not read that you cannot put old wine in new bottles? They listen with their ears but their hearts are elsewhere.

"What is the purpose of the divine? What does he wish for us? And why does he suffer this to be so?"

See, they do not understand. None can comprehend. They see only the smallest glimpse of things and think themselves wise. You know you are a fool and that is your greatest wisdom.

You look around and your eyes dwell on me for a moment and then move on. I am eating bread.

"Each has our own purpose in him, that is what he wishes for us, and he suffers this that we might be as he wishes."

Is that correct? I think on your wise words, and chew the flatbread that you have shared with me.

"There is a purpose in everything, everything is arranged as he wishes. All of us here tonight are here because he wishes it and by being here we fulfill our purpose."

You turn to look for me again, but I am gone. Where I sat there is a bundle. Will you fulfill my purpose? You reach over and unwrap the child, the gift I have given you. The child smiles at you, and my work is done.

"Who is this?" you ask. The others now crowd around you. As you say they are also here for a purpose. No one speaks. Three of you prostrate yourself as if to worship the child. I am not angry. I do not live for praise. Nor do I grudge it for others.

The child's glow is strong enough to be visible under the lamplight. One of you, Ennet, a woman, reaches out to touch her. You are afraid and gesture to Ennet to move back.

"Do not touch her." But Ennet does not listen. That is her purpose. She reaches out and takes the child. She holds her to her as a mother, a foster mother. The child's mother is dead. You buried her in the garden of jackals.

"She needs fed, and cared for." That is right, Ennet. You will feed and care for her.

"Where is he?" you ask. I am everywhere. You look around but cannot see me.

"He's gone," says another voice. "Did anyone see where he went?"

"Who was he? Who is this child?" You know the answers.

"I can take her home with me," says Ennet. "She cannot be seen.

I can care for her."

You are angry, but to care for the child, to be her nurse. That is not your purpose.

"We must think on this," you say, but there is nothing to think about. It is done. She will go with Ennet and she will hide her in her chamber, for a while at least.

The moon will rise soon. You should leave and return to your homes. You make the sign once more in the air and say the blessing. The others bow their heads as you speak. One by one they depart to new purposes. Soon there is only yourself and Ennet and the child.

How you long for her. How you long to take her. You feel as if I have cheated you. And there it enters your heart and I hold my breath and wait. I could take her, you think. I could make her mine. You are strong and Ennet is not young. You could kill her and take the child, the glowing child. The child of hope. You could make Ennet's purpose yours, or so you think. You could defy me. I would not stop you. And I understand. How could anyone not wish to possess the child?

In your mind you see yourself with the child, keeping her safe. You would love her, and she would love you. She would be yours, so you tell yourself.

Such a small thing and on it so much hangs. Will you blot out my purpose or would you obey my will? But it does not matter, either way, I will win. You cannot cheat me, you can only cheat yourself.

What are you thinking? I can see into your very heart, but can you? Can you see that your heart is full of love and goodness? Can you see that you do not wish to steal or murder or to raise yourself above others? Will you be blinded by the tempter? You are shaking. You are imagining Ennet dead. You are thinking how you would do it. Could you choke her to death? Could you wrap your hands around her frail neck and squeeze the life out of her while her eyes looked at you pleading and betrayed? Could you do that? Just because your pride is hurt and you think that I have betrayed you. I have a purpose for you. Do not doubt it. But this is not it.

I have described this instant and yet there is more and more I could say. One heartbeat. Each and every heartbeat holds as much.

I have made you wise and I have made you kind. What more could I have done? You reach out. But it is with one hand only and you make the sign above the child. You have listened to your own words.

"Take care of her, Ennet," you say.

"I will, Koreb, and you must tell me what we must do with her. She is not ours, she does not belong to any of us. We must find his purpose for her. You must find it." I have also made Ennet wise and kind.

"Yes," you say, and there is both sorrow and gladness in your voice. You see my hand in this, you have glimpsed the divine.

"Go in peace."

When she is gone, they are gone. You turn off the lantern and lay in the darkness. There is another reason for prayer and that is why you pray now. And of course, I forgive you. There is nothing to forgive. A man is judged not by his thoughts but by his deeds. Dark thoughts haunt all of us. My grace unto you.

Chapter Three
A Search Begins

Greba

Look at you, Greba, the Whip, the so-called hard man of the twelve. You are broken. All your pride has failed. All your strength is gone. What now? Will you go into the darkness and begin again? You are thinking about it. You are in your chambers alone thinking about death. Even that is denied you. Vatu will bring you home again and you will start anew, having forgotten everything. Perhaps that is a gift. Oblivion.

But it is not oblivion. You will have to start again and you will make the same mistakes over and over. Tell me this, Greba, what would you change if you could?

You are still too proud to call to me. But I am there, and I am not too proud to come uninvited.

"Why are you here?" Your voice is hard and brittle. I have pity for you, Greba. More pity than you have shown, in this or any other life. But you do not have to earn my pity. You only need to accept it.

"I am everywhere," I tell you.

You wish to argue. "Vatu is everywhere. This is his world."

I will not debate with you. There are things that you cannot know. That you will not understand. That you will not see.

"But I am here and he is not." Make of that what you will, Greba. You cannot deny it.

"You cannot save me. You could not save any of them. You cannot save anyone."

You are wrong. And I will save you too, Greba. I will let you save yourself. I will let you set yourself free and I will let you come to me. And you, Greba? Could you not have saved them? You could not even raise your voice to protest and now you blame me. It was not me who cast your daughter and granddaughter from the tower.

"Your granddaughter is alive."

"And my daughter? And them?"

What do you wish me to say; she is in a better place? Would you listen to me if I did? I think not. You are not ready to hear what in your heart you already know. Did you think she could live forever? She is not like you. Vatu will not drag her back to the wheel of this life. Her time is done and she has moved on and left you behind as she always would.

"They are both alive," I tell you. And that causes hate to rise in your heart. So be it. It is better to let blood flow from a wound until it is clean. I can see the hate in your eyes. Even in the darkness of your chambers, I see everything. I know everything.

"How can they be alive? How is that possible?"

How is anything possible? It is because I say it is. For the author of all things, nothing is impossible.

"I will find them," you say. Still so angry.

"And what then?"

"I will kill them. I will make them pay."

"Have they not suffered enough? Do you think that is what she would want?"

But you have stopped your ears. My words make no change in your heart. You call for one of the secretaries who comes rushing in and bows low. He can sense your anger and prostrates himself. He does not wish to feel the lash of your rage. The secretary's face is to the ground, but even so, I would not let him see me. He and I, we shall have our talk another time.

"The high priest, has anyone been to his chambers?"

The secretary is confused and afraid. I rest my grace upon him and his heartbeat slows and he finds the calmness to speak.

"No, great one, none have dared to enter."

You consider his words. You know it is a risk and you know all the twelve are cowards, only you are brave enough to take the risk. If Vatu is angry then you will endure it or perish. But you have set yourself upon a path.

Ignoring the slave, you rise and head out into the tower. Outside there is stillness and heat. The fear of Vatu's anger hangs over the tower. No doubt the rest of the twelve are cowering in their quarters. You will not cower. You will not be afraid. You stride through the darkness. The slave follows at your side. When we arrive at the door to the High Priest's chambers, you stop.

See, you are afraid. Fear is a natural thing, it is only your anger and pride that keeps it away. And now fear rises, but you will not let it conquer.

The doors of the tower are not locked. In the place of darkness, there is no need to keep anyone out. You push the black slab of glassy stone forward and it pivots to allow entry.

"Light the lamps," you say. But the slave stays at your side. His fear of the darkness is greater than his fear of you and he is not foolish. You walk forward and light them yourself. You are not afraid, you lie to yourself.

Your eyes adjust to the light. You have been here many times before when the high priest called to you. You have stood here while he instructed you or worse. You go to the table where he would sit. There are tablets sitting there. You sit and read but you do not find what you are looking for. Do you even know what you are looking for?

The secretary asks the same question. "What are you looking for?"

"Where is his secretary?" you ask.

"I will fetch him," the slave says and leaves. Now we are alone again. We wait in the darkness but you will not speak to me. Have you forgotten I am everywhere?

A short man enters. He is alone. The other slave has gone.

"What is your name?" you ask. Such a question.

"I am called Henoi," the short man replies.

"And you are the high priest's secretary?"

"I suppose." The slave is not afraid. Perhaps he has not heard of his master's fate.

"He is gone."

"Yes, he is not here."

"Where?"

Henoi shrugs. "I cannot say. I am only a scribe. I write what I am told."

"And to who does he write?"

"No one, everyone. He writes the business of the court. As you know, great one. You have worked with him also. You and Hilketa are the two he writes to most."

You think about that, and you know it is true. You were as close to him as any and yet you know nothing.

"The woman that was here? What became of her?"

The short man, Henoi, shakes as he answers. Utas had hoped to keep it secret, but there are no secrets. "She is gone."

"Where?"

"She was given to Vatu on the day of the Sun. The high priest kept the tablet here." And Henoi points out the tablet.

The woman Algria is to be prepared for Vatu. She is to be given to him as is custom.

Short and to the point. That is like him.

"Tell me about her."

"Great one, she was here for a time and then moved to the cells. She died as he commanded."

You know so little.

"Why was he interested in this one?" But you know the slave will not answer. You have asked the wrong question.

"Why did he move her to the cells?" A better question.

"He did not say."

"I did not ask what he said."

The short man shrugged again. "He got tired of her, perhaps. Or maybe he did not like it when she was got with child."

See, I told you it was a better question.

"Child?" you ask. "There is no mention of a child." You point to the tablet.

"The child was gone, taken," said Henoi. "The twelve have no children. You know that, great one."

"And yet."

"And yet what, great one? The high priest would not defy Vatu. Did not defy Vatu."

But it seems that he did, you think to yourself. And you have defied him too. Are you going to still defy him?

You know that he has defied Vatu. You know that the child lives. What will you do now? Still so angry. You dismiss Henoi. You will deal with him later. You will find out all he knows and all that he has not told you.

Chapter Four
Ennet's House

Koreb

Ennet is holding the child, your child, and she is thinking of another she held not long ago, the child you seek, and of another child she held long before that. Do you know what happened to that child? The one that she bore in her womb for nine moon turns? Do you wish me to tell you of how she bled and screamed as it pushed her way into the world? And of how she held it for a while.

Ennet's master was kind. He did not let her keep it of course. But he let her keep it for a while. A girl child is not worth much, but it is worth something. It is certainly too valuable for a slave to keep. Even if Ennet's master is the father.

Such a hollow word. Father. It means nothing if you are a slave. Ennet's master cared nothing for the child or for Ennet. But he was kind. Let her keep it and nurse it. The child is worth more once it is weaned. Once it is older it is easier to sell, but it means Ennet's master will have to pay to feed it. And so Kind Master lets Ennet keep the child but only for a while, only until it is well enough to sell. She can keep the child only long enough to fall in love with her daughter and to cry every day after she is gone.

But you do not wish to hear about that. It is not Ennet's child you wish to know about. It is this child and the other one. The children of the great ones are of more interest to you than the fate of some poor slave girl. If she is pretty she will be in one of the women's houses. But if not she will be serving somewhere. Ennet is not pretty, nor is her kind master handsome. Her child will not be in the house of women. She will be serving somewhere. Ennet is skilled with a needle and thread. Her master was a tailor, although she is a free woman now. Perhaps Ennet's child is also skilled. Or perhaps she is dead. Who knows what the child's new master chose to do with her? Ennet does not know, but she holds this child, this girl child, Alaba, to her and sings to her. As she does, she wonders where in the world her own daughter is, or if her daughter is even alive.

There is a knock at the door to Ennet's shack. It could be someone coming with work for her to do, but when she opens the door it is not. When she opens the door it is you standing there.

"Please come in, Koreb," she says and bows.

"No need to bow, sister," you tell her but enter. "How is the child?"

"She is well," Ennet replies and takes Alaba from her hiding place and passes her to you.

You hold the child and marvel. How can this be? A child from nowhere, a child brought by the Whisperer. A child that glows with light.

"What can it mean?" you say.

"I don't know," says Ennet, but it is not her you are asking.

"She looks stronger."

"I have been feeding her rice water. She has also taken a little rice. I will try to get milk and perhaps oats. She might eat a light gruel."

You are not listening. Let the old woman babble. You are thinking about the child and what it means. But you are not listening and anyway, it does not matter. I would not have told you, and if I had you would not have understood.

"We cannot keep her here." You are correct.

"We could send her away. We could send her where we sent the boy."

You shake your head. This one cannot hide. The light from her skin betrays her. A city set on a hill cannot be hidden, neither do men light a candle and hide it beneath a bushel.

"It is a sign," you say. But you cannot think what it is a sign of. Nor can you think what candlestick it should be set in. Nor do you ask.

Chapter Five
By the Wagon

Utas

You are filled with tears. You are lying on the ground. You wish you would die. I will not let you die. You are too weary to be angry but you plead with me over and over.

"Why are you punishing me?"

I am not, but you cannot see that. You think I am angry with you for your sins and they are many, but I am not. You wish me to forgive you and I have. You wish me to help you, and so I do. I have healed your body and given you strength. Now you must heal your mind and your soul. I have blessed you greatly.

Still, you plead for death. As if I would take your life, or as if it is I that stops you from taking a knife or a rope. Can you not see that you want to live and that even now in all this life is sweet? Do you forget the sweet kiss of air in your lungs or the soft melody of your heartbeat, the caress of wind upon your skin, the majesty of your thoughts? Life is beautiful. You should not seek to lose it so lightly. It will be gone soon enough. There will be some summers yet and then the pages will close on the book of life.

You have far to go, things to do, people to meet. I am not done with you yet.

You crouch down and begin to gather twigs. You have a flint and start a small fire. See, I knew you wanted to live. You reach your hands to the flames to warm them. It will be a while before the moon rises. Ah, now you are remembering, you are thinking of a house where once you lived with Irid. You have left it days ago and will not go back. You are thinking of the tower. You know that to go there is certain death. How strange that you plead with me for death but you will not go to the tower. Perhaps you think something worse than death awaits you. In that you are correct.

Now you are hungry. So many ways to live. You look through the wagon and find flour, salt and water, you mix an unleavened dough and cook it on a stone by your fire. When it is ready you eat. Afterwards, after you have eaten and rested, you cry and once more beg me for death.

"Why do you not answer me? I have lost everything." It is true, but it is not true. It is you that have thrown away what you had. I will help you find what you have not lost. I will help you live again.

"I cannot feel him." You reach out to your other self and feel nothing. "He is dead."

But he is not dead, his ghost stands before you. You reach towards your ghost and now you realize that all along you were one.

"Why are you here?" you ask.

"Where else would I be?" Then you see that he is not one ghost but a thousand. He is the ghost of every life you ever lived. You try to count them but you cannot. How many times has the moon sailed across the sky?

"I am sorry. I failed." The voices of a thousand ghosts echo.

"I have failed," your voice among them.

"They are dead then?" and the ghosts do not deny it. They do not deny it. "She is dead," they tell you. You start to curse me, and all other gods. I understand and I am merciful. I will not smite you because of your words, but I cannot speak for the other gods. Neither they nor I am guilty of what you claim. The guilt lies elsewhere.

Erroi, the last of your ghosts, comes and sits by you. You offer him some of your bread and he eats.

"What now?" you ask.

"You are asking the wrong person," Erroi replies.

You feel rage burning within you. "Are you not angry?" you ask.

"Ghosts cannot feel anger," he tells you.

"You cannot feel anger, but you can eat?"

"Yes," says Erroi, "that is what I said."

You look into his eyes, your eyes and you realize that what he says is true. "It does not matter," you tell him. "I have enough anger for both of us."

"Anger is not what we need."

How galling you find it, the ghost of your own wisdom echoed back to you. "And what do we need?"

"Food," says Erroi, "and rest."

You lie down and the images of the past flood your dreams. You see again, Vatu the dark spirit possesses you. You see again you sacrificing Algria, your love, to Vatu, after taking her son, your son, and hiding him. Hoping that will be enough to save Irid and Alaba. You see Vatu possessing you and finding your secret. You remember hunting for your other self, for Erroi, and taking him and Irid and Alaba to the tower. You remember Vatu killing them while you were helpless to stop him. You recall begging me to save them. You are too blind to see that I have.

As you sleep you have other dreams, darker. I will not speak of these. Not now. But remember I am graceful and have forgiven you. Now you must find grace and forgive yourself.

When you wake Erroi has left you, for a while at least. "Was it just a dream?" you ask, and I answer, no it was not. It was real. I whisper the words to you.

"So you have returned," you say with bitterness.

"I have never left you," I reply. "I am with you always."

I raise you to your feet and breathe life into you. You will live. You will grow strong again. I help you to the wagon and at my word the horse, still hitched to the wagon, moves forward.

"It is all you can do," I tell you. "Move forward."

Eventually, you sleep again. This time your dreams are peaceful. You dream of the cottage in the woods and of moths in a cage. You dream of children playing. You dream of life. I watch over you. I have always watched over you. I place my hand on your brow. It is hot, not with fever but with anger. So much anger. Erroi is right, it is not what you need. It will not help you. It never has.

Chapter Six
The Moon

Greba

You are not the only one who is angry. Vatu is angry too, calls all the twelve to him. He draws you to the chamber, and you cannot resist. Nor do you ask me to save you. They are there; Kong, Hilketa, Irruzura. All of them are here. And of course, I am here. I am everywhere.

I pity you. I watch as Vatu flays you and holds you naked in the dark. Burning and bleeding before the black sun of his rage. You howl and your howls are drowned by the howls of the rest of the twelve. Shall I tell you of the agony? Will I remind you? Or have you put all that behind you? How long did you hang there? I could tell you. What did you beg for? I could tell you. I saw it all.

At last, his rage burns out. At last, he is satisfied. He releases you, and the other priests of darkness. You slink away like a dog with your tail between your legs, except…

Except you smile to yourself. Your secrets are still yours. The dark one had no interest in your secret. He does not think that any of you would ever keep anything from him. Why would he?

You smile, but it is a bitter smile. You have lost so much already. You fan your anger and once more you will have revenge.

You go to your chambers and wash. How exhausted you are. You lie on your bed and look into the darkness. I know your secret. I know all about you. But you do not call me. Instead, you rise and dress. I follow you again, but I know where you are going and who you wish to meet. He is there. He is waiting for you. He knows you will come.

He is sitting in the pavilion watching the moon.

"Welcome," Hilketa says. You reply to his call and sit next to him. The moon is full. Hilketa is sitting, staring at it. He is always looking at the moon.

"You must tell me everything," you say.

"Everything?" Hilketa laughs. "What makes you think I know everything?"

"Then tell me what you know."

"About what? I don't think you have come here for an astrology lesson."

"About them, I believe they are alive."

"Impossible," Hilketa says. "Why do you think that?"

You shift uneasily. You do not want to say, because the author of all things told you.

"If they were dead, then Vatu would send us to find the reborn high priest. He must be alive."

Hilketa continues to look at the moon.

"Yes, I suppose you are right. That must be why Vatu is so angry."

"So tell me, where will they be?"

"Looking at the moon," Hilketa says.

You are angry at his words. You think he is mocking you. You never did have time for subtlety. You clench your fists. How you want to beat him to a pulp. That will do you no good. Hilketa rises, even though he is younger than you he seems ancient.

"I am not mocking you," he says. "I only know they are under the same moon as us."

"But you suspect much, I am sure."

"I am not certain. He had a child, a boy. He may be with the boy if he is still alive. But I am not certain he is. I have only your word for it. Less than that. Your guess."

"He is alive," you say with certainty.

Hilketa pretends to doubt you. But he is also certain. "Why do you wish to find him anyway? We are better off without him."

"I wish to kill him."

"You cannot kill him," says Hilketa. "Not that way."

"He can die. He has died many times."

It is true. He has, and you have killed him many times. A knife in the back, drowning, poisons, suffocation: so many ways he has been killed, and all the twelve have killed him. Killed him many times. But always Vatu has brought him back, as he has brought you back, and each of the twelve back, time after time.

"I will kill him," you say again. "But first I must find him."

"I do not know where he is. Do you think I could keep that secret from Vatu?"

Hilketa is afraid. He thinks that you may try to kill him here on the tower. He wraps his cloak around him as if he is cold. But it is never cold at the tower.

"How beautiful the moon is," he says. "Will you sit and watch it with me?"

You should do as he asks. There is much to learn from watching the moon.

"How many times has the moon travelled over these skies?" he asks. But there is no answer. There is a number but it would mean nothing to him or to you and to whisper it in full would take an age to tell.

"Who cares about the moon?" you say angrily. But you are thinking of a time and a place and a person. She sat with you looking at the moon and whispering words of love in your ear. Now she is gone. You sent her away to keep her safe. You look at the moon and wonder if somewhere she is looking at it too and if she is thinking of you as you are thinking of her. You think of her daughter, your daughter who you buried in a pit of bones to keep the jackals from tearing her flesh. You think of Unead again. How you wish she was near you. You put her out of your mind. "I have no time to look at the moon."

"Nor do I," said Hilketa, "and yet here I am."

"You will say nothing of where I can find him?"

"No, I do not know where you might find him."

"There was a child, another child. Where is he?"

"Dead, most likely. There must be as many dead children as the times the moon has turned. We do not permit our children to live. Vatu will not allow them to live."

And now Hilketa is looking at you. He knows your secret. That is why he is afraid. He thinks you will kill him.

"I think he sent the child away. I think he tried to save him as he tried to…" Now your voice trails off. You cannot think what to say. As he tried to save his daughter and your granddaughter. As you tried to save your daughter.

"Even if he did, the child will be dead. He will have paid some courtier to take it away, and the courtier will have killed the child and kept the money."

You know he is right. You are certain he is right. That is the harsh truth. It is why you could never send Irid away. And yet you do not believe it. He would find a way.

"The child is alive. I am certain. And he will go to find it. That is where I will find him. I must find the child and then I will kill him."

The full moon is sailing across the stars. The brilliant light floods the pavilion. The full face of the moon is lit and glowing.

"How will you find the child? Even if it is not dead."

"Who has left the service of the tower? Who left when the child left? It will be written. Nothing happens except it is written. You are master of all this. You keep all the records. You know who has left and when. If you do not tell me then it is because you are hiding it from me. You know what is written. If you do not tell me, then I will kill you."

Hilketa stands up. He is still facing the moon. "He will kill me if I tell you."

"Then you have spoken of this."

"No, he is more subtle than that. He did not need to tell me. As I say, the child is most likely dead."

"You should fear me more than you fear him."

"Fear. You think I fear him."

"I think you should fear me."

Hilketa twitches, and you wonder what trick he has concealed in his robes. Perhaps some powder or other poison.

"I would kill you before you could use whatever you have up your sleeve."

"And then you will never find the child." Hilketa raises his arms to the heavens and lets the sleeves of his robe fall back. "I have nothing up my sleeves." His arms and wrists are thin and slender. There is no bracelet with poison or strapped dagger, but it does not mean he has no weapon concealed. You do not trust him and are wise not to do so.

"Will you tell me where the child went?"

Hilketa shakes his head. "I do not know, but I will tell you this. He spent a great deal of time with that girl, the mother of the boy, and a heretic. He spent a great deal of time reading about the heretics. Every record we had about them, he has looked at."

Ah, see. Hilketa knows nothing but guesses much. Do his guesses sound good to you? Where better to hide the boy than amongst the believers? They at least will not kill the child and steal the money that Utas has given them.

"I will have those records sent to you," says Hilketa.

"There are heretics here?" you ask.

"There are heretics everywhere," replies Hilketa and makes the sign in the air.

Chapter Seven
At the Tower

Hilketa

Do not think I have forgotten about you or any other. You think that I have deserted you. You think that I have cursed you simply because I have dragged you to hell. I have given you what you wished for. I am graceful to those that call on me.

I watch as you sit looking at the moon. I know your thoughts. Always so curious, so eager to know. But you cannot know.

You make the sign in the air again as you made it before. You think it is some kind of incantation and because you have made it you bring me to you.

"Are you there?"

"Yes," I reply. "I am always here."

"How is that possible?"

"Is that what you wish to ask me?"

"No, that is not why I have called you here."

"I have told you, you did not call me here. I am always here." Still, you do not understand. But it does not matter. I did not expect you to, nor do you need to understand. There are greater things than knowledge.

"So the sign is useless after all." No, it is not, but that is not its use.

"You will understand one day," I tell you.

"Why not now? Why will you not tell me?" But I have told you. I have told you over and over. A sign is like a word. It enables you to speak, but like words, it is useless unless you mean what you say. Still, you do not understand.

"Why did he come? What does he want?" You are speaking of Greba.

"He is angry and wants to punish someone."

"Is he correct, does the High Priest live?"

"Yes."

"How is it possible? We burned his body and placed his ashes in the grave."

"One of his bodies. Utas cheated Vatu. When Kong brought him to the tower at his last incarnation, he brought someone else and let Utas go free. Vatu is deceived. Utas lives and Vatu has discarded him."

"So the other one is dead?"

Always you need to know more.

"His ghost is here."

"I don't believe in ghosts," you say.

"You don't believe in gods either. And yet here we are."

"This is just some trick of my mind. You are just my imagination. You have not created me, I have created you."

Such pride, such arrogance. Do not worry, I will make you humble.

"What need have I of humility," you demand. "I am a priest of Vatu. He is the god of this earth."

"I thought you did not believe in gods," I say.

"I believe in him and his power. I believe what I have seen with my own eyes. He has given me everything and raised me up. He brings me back from death time after time. How many times have I sat looking at the moon?"

"Does it matter how many times, if you have not learned what it will tell you? But you have not called me here for an astronomy lesson."

"Clever, to use my own words. To pretend you were there when Greba spoke with me. But you are my imagination, I remember my own words."

"If you do not believe in me then why do you ask me? If you believe in Vatu, why do you not ask him what you seek?"

"Because he is a god and does not listen to us."

"I am listening. I am always listening."

Hilketa, how many times have we spoken just like this? How many lives have you struggled to believe?

"The child, does she live?"

"Both children live."

"How is that possible?"

"Because I am mightier than Vatu. And what I will stands."

"Nonsense, Vatu is the god of this earth."

"This is no earth," I tell you. "This is hell. And he is not the god of it. Even if he was, there are other worlds, he is not the god of those."

"I will not believe," you say again. "I will not believe he is alive. What will Greba do?"

"He will seek to find Utas and his child and he will seek to kill them."

Now you have stopped to think. You believe this at least. You are thinking how you can use this to your advantage.

"Greba also has a child or had one. The woman that Utas married, one of them, she was Greba's daughter. The one he watched cast from the tower. That is why he hates him so and will have his revenge."

You stop and look at me. For someone who does not believe you can hardly take your eyes from me.

"Impossible."

"Not at all. All things are possible."

You are thinking to share what you know with Vatu and with the rest of the twelve. You think you can destroy Greba.

"I will not allow that," I tell you.

"How can you stop me?"

I reach out my hand and stop the blood running to his brain. He falls clutching his head. He thinks I will kill him, but I am merciful. He rises and glares at me.

"It is a trick," he says again. "It is a trick of my mind. See. I am sick. You are just a figment of my sickness. You cannot be real. You cannot."

"I will not let you harm Greba. Not now. I have put you in this hell, and I will put you in a worse one if I must. I am gracious and forgiving, but I will not be thwarted. I have plans and I have plans for you. They are gracious and kind, I will lead you from this hell."

"I do not wish to go."

"No, not yet."

Chapter Eight
Ghosts

Erroi

"Am I a ghost?" you ask me.

"Do ghosts eat and drink?" I pass bread and wine across the table.

You think for a moment. "Yes, they do. They eat and drink and feel cold."

I laugh and put another log on the fire. "Perhaps we are all ghosts."

"Are you a ghost?" you ask. And when you say these words, I realize that I am.

"I am all things," I tell you.

You nod and take a bite of the bread. You are a hungry ghost, but you are not just a ghost, you are Erroi.

"So once you were like me." Always so clever, Erroi.

Yes, once I was like you. Once I was flesh and blood. Then what have I become? Am I a ghost now? Surely more than a ghost. More than just a ghost. I am a ghost and a man and the Whisperer all at the same time. Which am I? I am them all.

"I know everything," you tell me.

"That is good. Then there is no need for me to tell you anything."

"I mean I remember everything. All of it." You are speaking of your past lives and before.

"It is almost done," I tell you. "Only a little bit more."

"I know who I am," you say.

"You must keep that a secret."

"They will know. Eventually."

"Perhaps," I admit.
"What will they think?"
It is a good question.
"It does not matter, it will be too late."
You nod your head.

Chapter Nine
Tablets

Greba

There really are heretics everywhere. It is just as Hilketa told you. When you see the tablets that he promised you, you are amazed at how many there are. How is it possible for people to believe in the Whisperer right here in the City of the Sun? Right here at the centre of Vatu's power they doubt him and turn elsewhere.

It is clear that Utas was keeping this from the twelve and from Vatu. None of the reports were acted on. You would have known if there had been even a fraction of the arrests that should have happened. How could you have been so blind? Here, for example, you read:

> *Great one, we followed the suspect and found him making the sign of heresy in the dust before his house. A number of the lower classes, freed slaves, and menial servants entered. It seemed to be a gathering of heretics. We entered but did nothing as you commanded and there he taught the heretic faith to the gathered. The man's name is Koreb. We await your instructions.*

But no instructions came. Heretics are like weeds. If you cut them down they spring forth again tenfold. Why did you let them flourish unchecked even here? There are over a hundred of these reports. You find that slaves have stitched the sign into their clothes, that children draw it in the dust. That heresy is taught by weavers and seamstresses. Maids whisper heresy into the ears of their mistresses. In the market you can buy little tokens of heresy made of brass if you make the sign in the palm of a merchant's hand. All this and more. And yet nothing is done.

"What is your plan, Utas?" you ask aloud. But it is not his plan, it is mine, and I do not tell you. There is only one thing you can do. You rise from your chair and go and remove your robes of priesthood. You don a homespun cowl and cape. Even so, you cannot imagine that you will not be recognized Do you? Your proud bearing is still evident as you walk out of the tower and into the inner court. No one will mistake you for one of the penitent. You are strong and powerful. It will take more than a change of clothes to disguise the darkness in your heart.

And then as you leave the inner court, you slump and I see how fine an actor you are. I see that you have been only acting as a priest of darkness. Now you change into what you truly are; a grieving father and husband who has lost everything he loves. Now I see how you managed to hide your secret for so long. Only Utas discovered it, and then Kong.

"Kong did not," you protest. "He discovered Utas' secret, not mine."

"That is true," I admit. "And he also lost much. Lost everything."

"He ruined everything he touched."

"Darkness ruins everything," I say but I do not think you understand. And I should have said evil, not darkness, but then you definitely would not understand. It is the darkness in your heart I speak of. Do not let it ruin things. Do not let it ruin you.

You know where the house is, but you do not go directly there. You know that the house is only used as a gathering place when the moon is resting, making a dark passage across the sky. You know that this man Koreb will trace the sign in the dust and then the faithful will gather. You wander through the alleyways of the city. It seems as if you are aimless but you are not. Eventually, you stop, you are certain that you are not followed. You are followed by no one except me. You double back to check. There is a couple coming down the ally, but if they were agents of the court you would have known their faces. If they had been you would have killed them. You consider killing them anyway to be sure.

"You can never be sure," I tell you. "Trust me. Let them live."

"Is life so precious to you now?"

You are still bitter because I did not save Irid.

"All life is precious. It is my gift and it is only mine to take."

"You did not take Irid. That was him."

No, that was Vatu, and yourself, but I let it pass. You will see eventually.

"In the end I did. In the end, I was with her and took her to me."

"And if I killed them you would take them too."

"Yes, yes I would."

"So what difference does it make? In the end, you will come for us all."

"No," I reply. "I do not come for all. I will not come for you or any of the twelve." Not yet anyway. Not until you have lived as many lives as once you took.

"That is because Vatu comes for us."

You say the words with pride, but in your heart is bitterness and anger. So much anger. Even after a thousand lifetimes, it has not petered out.

"It is because I am not done with you yet," I tell you.

At any rate, you let them live and I am grateful. I am in your debt. I thank you.

We are outside the house now, and you pull your cowl over your face. You watch a few people enter and then think you should enter too. It is why you have come. If you will find Utas and his child by Algria, then you will find them amongst the heretics. There is nowhere else they can hide.

Are you afraid as you push the door open? I think you are. Not afraid of heretics, but afraid that you are recognized. Then you would have to kill them all. None of my pleading would stop you. Then you would have to start again. You would need to look elsewhere. You are afraid that you will not get your revenge.

You are not recognized. Or if you are it makes no difference to them. They do not shy away.

"Come stranger, a soldier can believe as much as a slave," says a tall man. Perhaps he was a soldier, you think and note his broad shoulders. "We all have a tale to tell." And the rest of the followers gather around you. "What is your tale? How has the Whisperer brought you here?"

They look at you and wait for you to answer. They are seated on the floor. And so you lower yourself down to the rush matting.

"What has the darkness taken from you?" A quiet voice from a young girl.

"Everything," you say. "Everything. Once I had favour and so I married and had a child. My daughter I cared for and protected. I married her off to a minor official. I had a granddaughter. But then the darkness came. They took my wife from me and my daughter and granddaughter were cast from the tower. They lie in the Garden of Jackals. I have lost them and now I have nothing."

They are real tears that fall down your face. You are not lying. You have lost everything you loved.

"Why could he not save them?" No hand reaches to hold you, nor arm wraps around you to give you comfort. None, except mine.

"I loved them. I protected them. But the darkness found them and took them."

They are silent. They do not intrude upon your grief. It is a story they have heard a thousand times before. Each of them carries a story of their own.

"Is this how the Whisperer brings us to him? By taking everything from us?"

Still, they do not answer. It is a question each of them has asked.

"If he is merciful, why does he not show mercy? If he is the creator of all things, why did he create the dark? Why did he create pain and hate and murder and death? Why did he create these things?"

You think they will argue, that they will protest. You think they will defend me. But they sit silently.

I whisper to you, and I answer as I answered each of them; why did I create love? Why did I create kindness? Why did I create joy? Why did I create you?

They wait for you to say more, but when it is clear that you will not, they make the sign. "Peace be unto you and unto us."

It is over. They rise from the ground and depart one after another. You rise up to go. What a waste of time, you think, I have found nothing. They know nothing.

You do not wish to leave just yet, not while tears are still on your face.

"You are welcome to stay for a while," says the tall man. "I must go and remove the sign. But you can stay here."

He walks out to brush away the sign in the dust and leaves you alone in his house. It is not a grand house, but is modest and clean. A single room, but a large one and with a chest and charcoal brazier. The owner is not rich, but he is not poor.

When he enters, you ask him his name.

"I am Koreb," he replies.

"Were you a guard too?" you ask him. He shakes his head.

"I am a clerk at the treasury. A minor clerk. My mother taught me to read and count. And so I work at the treasury."

"Would you not have been better suited to work as a guard?"

Koreb laughs. "Because I am tall does not mean I am strong. I was ill as a child. My father said my mother should have let me die. But I did not die, but I lay sick and alone for many months. Even now I am not strong."

And you look again. You should have noticed his leg is twisted. He has had bone fever, an abscess on the bone which should have been cut out. His father was correct. He would have done better to have died. He should have died; even with the bone cut away, few recover. It must have been an agony. And yet here he is alive.

"I have food if you wish? And some drink."

You sit once more and bow your gratitude. Koreb fans the brazier to a flame and sets two skewers of some kind of meat over the coals. He takes a bottle of rice wine from the chest and two cups.

"I am honoured," he says and bows.

"No, it is I who am honoured," you tell him.

He pours two small measures into the cups, and motions to drink. You move the cup to your lips and take the smallest sip. It is sour and bitter. It's cheap rice wine, but then what should you expect? Clearly, Koreb is not rich. It has been a while since you drank such gut rot. You sip again and it brings back memories of when you first met her. When Unead worked in that cheap tavern, and you pretended to be a guardsman. Despite everything, you smile.

"I apologize," says Koreb. "It is cheap wine."

"No, not at all. I was just thinking, just remembering," you say.

"Good memories."

"Yes, good memories. But bitter also."

Koreb takes the bottle and pours more wine.

"Next time I will bring wine," you tell him.

The two skewers are ready now, and he hands one to you and starts to eat the other. You do not ask what is on the skewer, it is probably better not to know.

Chapter Ten
Filthy

Arraio

Arraio loves you. He is thinking of you. He has taken your skull from the pyre and hidden it in his room. He is a great artist. Even you acknowledged that. He has taken your skull and built layer after layer of clay over it until it seems as if you are there in his room. It is beautiful in its way. He holds it in his hand. It is no longer your skull but something else entirely. It is his now, and a part of you is his forever.

He thought he loved you. He holds the skull and limps around the room. Even now the wound you gave him pains him.

"I should have saved you," he says.

Can you believe that he loved you? I know full well that you despised him, and with reason.

Does Arraio understand love? Does anyone? I am not asking you to forgive him, only not to hate him. He is as damaged as any of the twelve.

His shuffling footsteps echo in the dark. The light of his lantern flickers across the room and he holds the head that he moulded up to the light. He is still not content. He kisses the lips as he longed to kiss them when you were alive, but there is no warmth, no sweetness to the kiss. It is as if he has taken flesh and turned it into stone.

"When will you return to me?" Arraio asks. And in his head, he imagines you were once his, and that once you loved him. In all his lives and yours, do you think that you ever loved him? Poor Arraio. Shall I tell you? Not once did you love him. Not once.

His is not love, you say. You talk of how he forced himself on you and abused you. You know full well he does this time after time and not with you only. It is not love, it is abuse. But what is the difference? He is driven to that by the same impulse that drives others and is called love.

"I do not forgive you," you whisper to him. If your clay-formed lips could move, that is what they would tell him. Do not worry, he hears your words. He hears them every day.

"I do not love you." You do not need to say these words either. They are etched in his heart. Poor Arraio, perhaps this hell is cruellest for you. Over and over you must quest for love and do not find it. And do not understand it.

"Will you forgive him?" you ask me. Foul, pervert, there are no names low enough for him. The most despised of all the twelve. Surely there is no forgiveness for him. Do you shudder when you think of his crimes?

But even he knows me. He knows I am here. He knows I am ever with him. "Surely I am beyond forgiveness."

He places your skull back upon his desk. He has work to do. Shall we follow him and see his sins? They are many, they are as many as yours. What a fool he is, to think that his crimes are acts of love. To love someone is not to force yourself upon them.

And who does not love a child? It is what we do with that love that is the crime. A crime he says is love but is not.

I do not need to show you it all. But I am everywhere. I see everything and know everything. I do not blink. I follow him.

He is going to the outer court, to the house of women. You do not need me to tell you what kind of house it is. He pushes his way into the house, and silence descends. The sitar player halts in mid-stroke. Half-dressed men pull their clothes over to cover themselves. If Arraio has come here for love, even for feigned love, he is disappointed. The scent of fear is thick in the air above the scent of attar and incense.

Can you see his face? What glints in his eye? It is not anger, it is pain. They know who is his. He can never hide what he is.

He gestures and the matron of the house comes forward.

"What can I do for you, great one?" She bows low and does not look him in the eyes.

"A chair," Arraio says. And one is brought straight away. He seats himself and looks around. But what he is seeking is not here. Does he even know what he seeks? Does he think he can fill the emptiness with wine and flesh? How weary he feels. How unloved and alone. Even here, and surrounded he is alone.

I whisper to him but he does not listen. This is not the way. The way to find love is to love. It is kindness that will mend your heart and your soul. It is the things that you do that will save you. Be kind, be merciful. My words fall like seeds on stony ground. They must be watered with tears. Your tears, Arraio.

And yet I have hope and will not stop. I will not abandon you nor will I desert him. Is that not love? I whisper, “Can you not see that you are loved? Even you are loved. Is my love not enough?”

Arraio looks over those who await his commands. His eyes halt on round, dark flesh. He thinks of flashing dark eyes, and deep dark curled hair. There are all things here, except what he seeks.

“Some wine,” Arraio says.

The matron bows and scuttles away, her silk gown trailing on the ground as she rushes out as quickly as she dares.

Arraio looks at the women. Each turns away at his glance.

“Look at me,” he commands. And each turns to stare at him; in their eyes, there is only fear.

Chapter Eleven
Rice Wine

Greba

You stop at the market and purchase a bottle of rice wine. It is a better vintage than the gut-rot that Koreb served you but not too much better. You do not want to shame him. The vendor wants four shillings for the bottle, you haggle him down to two shillings and four pennies. You feel pleased with yourself even though you could pay four shillings a thousand times over. It is what you would do if you were really a retired guardsman on the way to visit a friend.

The smell of pastries comes from a nearby stall. You are tempted. Despite yourself, your mouth waters. It would be good to share pastries with Koreb.

"Two please," you say. The baker takes two and wraps them in paper. They are still warm. You head straight to Koreb's house, walking through the narrow alleyways by the light of the moon. You do not wait for the next dark moon, and for the meeting of heretics. You know the house now. There is nothing remarkable about it now, no sign or clue.

You call out to Koreb and wait for him to invite you in. He opens his door and bows.

"Welcome, friend."

You are pleased that he is in. You thought perhaps he would be at the courts working or at the market, or on some other business. He ushers you into the room, and even better, he is alone. You hold up the flask of wine and smile.

"I promised you something better than that poison you served me."

"Words are cheap, we shall have to test it and see." Koreb laughs as he says this. "Do we need something to soak up the alcohol?"

"I have brought these," you say and hold up the pastries.

"They smell good. Where did you get these?"

"Never mind that," you tell him. "Get the cups and let's get drinking." Again Koreb laughs and gets two cups out of his chest.

You sit together by his brazier, and he stokes it up. It is not cold, but still. You stretch your hand out to the flame while he pours out two glasses.

"To us," you say, and take a sip.

Koreb tastes the rice wine and makes an approving look with his eyes. Clearly, he seldom has good wine, or perhaps he is just being polite.

"It is good," he says, "much better than the bottle I shared."

Now you wonder if you have brought too fine a wine. You do not want to shame him.

"It is the least I could do," you reply. "I..." and here you hesitate.

"You want to ask me?"

"Yes, I want to know. I want to know everything."

"I don't know everything. If you wish to know that then you must ask someone else." And he makes the sign. He means you must ask me.

"Tell me about him, about how you came to know him."

"I told you. When I was a boy I had bone fever. When I lay in the room alone, he came to me. My father was like you, a guardsman. When I first saw you, you reminded me of him. There was something about you. The way you moved, coiled like a whip as if he was ready to spring and fight."

"I suppose we all look like that," you say. "It is what we are trained for."

"I suppose," Koreb agrees, "but not like my father. I have never seen anyone that looked so angry. It was as if he was angry all the time."

"I am sorry," you say. "I hope he was not too hard on you."

"No, not at all, even although he seemed so fierce, he was always kind to my mother, and to me. When I was ill, he said I would be better off dead. But he still sat by me for hours. He was very gentle with me. I think you also have that gentleness."

You laugh when says that. "If only you knew," you tell him. If only indeed.

"I am sure you have much that you regret," says Koreb, "as do we all. You must let that go."

"So where is your father now?" you ask.

"He died many years ago. He died when I was five summers old. Or so I think. He did not stay with us but came when he could and then stopped coming. Mother went to the guardhouse to look for him. But they told her there was no guardsman of that name. It is possible that he was moved to another posting. Who knows? I have forgiven him. The Whisperer asks us to forgive everyone. And who knows, perhaps there is nothing for me to forgive. Perhaps he is dead. Surely he is dead. That was fifty summers ago. Fifty-four. Mother was certain he was dead. She was certain he would not leave us."

"Woman are often deceived," you reply.

Koreb takes a bite from his pastry and a mouthful of wine. He nods.

"You do not think so," you say.

"No, I think he died. I think he died when I was a child. Yes, sometimes that same anger that he had is in me, but I remember him and how he stayed with me while I was ill. I do not believe he would do that if he did not love us."

"You can love something and still desert it," you say.

"Did you love something too?"

"I told you, those that I loved are dead."

"So you did not desert them."

Now it is your turn to hesitate. You look away so that he may not see what is in your eye. And you wait until you can control your voice.

"Did I? I do not know. I do not know what else I could have done to save them. I should have found a way. I did not desert them, but if I did not then I failed them. Is that not worse?"

"You remind me so much of him," says Koreb.

"Except I did not die fifty summers ago." Or did you?

"No, but I do wonder, perhaps we are brothers. It is possible."

"You think I am like him so much?"

"Yes, yes I do."

"Fifty summers is a long time. The mind can play tricks."

Again Koreb nods, and then rises from the floor and collects something from his box. He comes and sits with you again. He is holding something.

"What is that?" you ask and try to keep your voice calm.

"I have not told you everything I know about my father," says

Koreb.

"Perhaps you should not."

"I think I must," he continues. "There are things I need to know."

Even if it costs you your life, you think. You do not say it but Koreb knows.

"Yes, I think I must show you this." And he hands you a bronze medallion. On the medallion is a face that you know only too well. You have seen it many times and never. You have glimpsed it in pools, and mirrors and nowhere.

Chapter Twelve
Father - Brother

Greba

"It is like you," you say.

"A bit," admits Koreb. "There is something of my father in me."

You look him over, and you see it is true. Koreb is stronger than he looks, and if he has not spent a lifetime learning to fight and kill, still he is powerful.

"I do not know my father," you say. "We might be brothers."

Koreb looks away. "Perhaps." It is a lie.

You had never thought on that once. You see now why the twelve do not keep their children. You reach out to touch him and think on a time before you were born. Did you hold him in your arms the way you held Irid? Did you love him like you loved Irid? Did you love his mother the way you loved Unead?

You know who he is. And he knows who you are. When you look at him you can see he knows. That he loves you the way that once you loved him.

"Do you know who I am?" you ask.

"I have always known," says Koreb. "I have always known, Father."

"I should kill you."

"I am ready to die. The Whisperer will take me with him."

"Why did you not send me away? Why did you bring me in? Why do you let me know?"

But you know why. Because from the first he loved you.

"The faith is for all of us," he says. "Even for the twelve.

Perhaps especially for the twelve."

He is right, Greba. Listen.

"How can the faith be for us? We are Vatu's servants."

"In this hell, you are the chief sufferers. The rest of us escape, but not you. You are brought back here time after time. There is no escape for you until this hell is finished."

"Why?"

"He does not tell me everything. There are things you must ask him yourself."

"What have I done to deserve this?"

Koreb is now sitting with his head down and with his neck exposed. If you will kill him you should kill him now, quickly and painlessly. You rise to your feet and still he does not move.

"Will you betray me?" you ask. But he does not answer, nor does he plead for his life. Did you once love him? Does that love still lie within you? Is that why you hesitate?

"You must tell no one who I am." But still, he does not answer. He will make no promise to you. It has taken you long to find him. Years.

"If I let you live, what then?"

Koreb bows silently.

How many times, you wonder, have you stood in this place or another and faced the same choice? If Irid had lived, would you have found her when you were reborn and faced the same choice? But you already faced that choice and failed her. You let them take her and cast her to the jackals. Why show mercy to Koreb when you showed none to Irid? But then you tell yourself that this is not true. You had no choice. There was nothing you could do to save Irid. All you could have done was die with her.

"It is not fair to make me choose again," you say. You let that same rage that is always in you rise up. It would be a small thing to strike this man dead.

"Anger is not the answer," I tell you. And I make my presence known. I stand beside you and whisper in your ear.

You turn towards me, and I do not retreat.

"Why have you done this to me?" you ask.

"To save you," I reply. "I have turned away from no one. Not even you."

So much anger within you. And yet it is not enough. It is not enough to make you strike your own child dead. You cannot do it. You have found something greater even than your rage. Something that halts you and sends you storming from the house. You will not slay Koreb.

"I will be back," you say. As if it is a threat.

When we are alone, I lift Koreb to his feet. So much goodness and faith.

"Whisperer, what now?" he asks.

"That will be seen soon enough," I tell him. "But I am always with you."

"Will you not take me from this place?"

But I have already faded from his sight. I have heard his plea and will answer in my own good time.

He lifts the half-drunk bottle of rice wine and replaces the stopper before putting it away, then he takes the two cups and rinses them in water and places them on a shelf. He is still afraid. Greba could send soldiers to kill him and all the heretics. But he is also glad and at peace. And in his heart there is love.

Chapter Thirteen
At the Library

Greba

Arraio accompanies you to the library. Only the twelve are allowed there. He holds a lantern while you look at the shelves.

"What do you seek?" he asks you. Do you even know?

"Hold the light higher."

There are so many tablets on the shelves. What is it that you seek? You will know it when you find it. You run your fingers over the tablets. Why so many tablets? What do they signify? Each of them means nothing. Accounts of stores, and purchases. Censuses of distant cities. Records of troop movements and recruitment. Here, what is this? It is an account of a trial and execution. So many pointless records. Why? Do the scribes believe these things will not happen unless they record them? So much nonsense. Nothing matters. It is not important. You take a tablet from the shelf and cast it into the void, into the space that leads down and down. I wait and listen. At last, I hear it clatter and break on the floor far below.

Arraio holds the light but says nothing. He shrinks back from you. He is afraid that you will cast him over the balcony to fall to his death.

"How deep is this hall?" you ask.

"I do not know. No one does. No one has gone down for many generations. Perhaps no one has ever gone to the end of these shelves."

"Why?" Are you asking me?

"I have been to the end of these shelves," I whisper in your ear.

"I have read every tablet and every volume. There is nothing hidden from me. There is nothing I have looked away from. I have seen it all. I have been where even the twelve will not go."

You hear my words and shudder. Arraio rushes forward to offer you a cloak. He thinks you are cold. Here in the tower, it is never cold.

"That is not what I seek," you say.

"No, and you will not find it here."

Nevertheless, you still root through the tablets. "Tell me, when you first left the care of the twelve and returned to your quarters after being reborn. What is the first thing that you found?"

"I am not sure what you mean."

"When I first entered my chambers that had been shut for twelve years, when I came into myself, I felt lost. As if none of that place belonged to me. I felt there must be some mistake. I thought I could not possibly be reborn because I knew nothing."

"You were mistaken. You are Greba. You are one of the twelve that is always reborn."

"Still, I walked through my chambers and felt like I was a grave robber or a thief. It felt as if I did not belong there, or as if the chamber did not belong to me."

"But it did."

"You are right. I walked through those rooms and there on a stand there was a sword, double-edged and straight."

"Not the one you wear now?"

"No, not this one. This sword was white as a snowstorm. I reached for it and held it in my hand, and I knew that I had held that sword before."

"As you had."

"Yes, I had held it before. It fitted my hand and as I practised with it, so all that I knew about the way of the blade was taught to me again."

"And by the high priest," says Arraio.

"Yes, and by the high priest. But this was different. This was something the high priest could not ever know or ever teach me."

"So perhaps it is this sword that you seek?"

"No," you say. "I have learned all that the sword will teach me, and I know where it is. But recently I have considered that there may be other swords and other things that I must learn."

"Then should you not look in the armoury rather than the library?"

You laugh. "You always did take things too literally."

Arraio looks down, you have shamed him.

"I have no sword," he says. "But when I first came to my rooms there was something there I had left behind from before I died and was reborn. I knew I had left it for me to find."

"What did you leave for yourself?" you ask.

"A picture."

Now you are interested. You had thought of Arraio as only filthy and disgusting and beneath you. There is more to him than you thought.

"A picture of what?" you ask.

"I wish I can show it to you. Words will not explain it. It was hidden but I found it. When I saw it, I knew I had to copy it. I took brush and ink and painted the same picture. With each brushstroke, I knew myself more. It is when I knew who I was. It is when I became myself."

You grunt.

"What did you do with the picture?"

"I hid it, I put them both back where they are hidden."

"Why did you hide it?"

"I did not want anyone else to see it."

"So why are willing to let me see it now?"

"You have told me the story about the sword. I see that we are alike."

You wince when he says these words, and you think about killing him. We are nothing alike, you want to scream. But perhaps he's right. All of the twelve are alike. All of us are alike. Those things that he has done, you could do. The thought revolts you. Surely you are better than him. In your mind, you want to ask me. And I know what is in your heart. Creator of all things, do you not love me more than that creature? Am I not better than him? But my love is not for you alone, nor can it be measured. If it could, then it would not be a perfect, endless love that can overcome all things. Yes, his sins are greater, he may make me weep more than you. Does that give you comfort? Perhaps Greba, you are too proud as well as too angry.

"How are we alike?" you ask Arraio.

"We are both lost in the darkness," he replies.

"We are servants of Vatu, we are servants of the dark." Even you do not believe your words.

Chapter Fourteen
Visits

Erroi

You are going about my business. You have brought yourself to the City of the Sun. You go first to the garden and stand by her grave. I can feel anger rise within you.

"Now I see that ghosts feel anger as well as the cold."

You sit and listen to the sound of bones crunching in the distance. Irid is buried too deeply for the jackals to dig up. They are not her bones that are broken and lie strewn across the killing ground, but they are someone's bones.

You say a silent prayer for them. For all of them. A prayer for the dead. But it is the living that need your prayers, and it is the living you have come for. You would stay here if you could but you cannot. There is much for you to do. You rise and look upwards to the top of the tower. Does Hilketa sit above you watching the moon?

"It is not time for that," I tell you.

"You could stop it now," you say. And you are right, but I will not.

"Let us write what must be written," I tell you.

In the dark, you can hear the soft footpads of the jackals circling around you. They are getting nearer. You wish to lash out and kill them. See! You are human still.

You let the jackals approach. You shift your weight. You will kill them if you must. But the wind rises. I raise it. And your scent drifts towards them. They smell blood but they smell more than that. They smell your anger and your hate and they slink back into the night.

Are you still cold? Cold even here at the Tower of the Sun? Why else do you pull your hat low and wrap your cloak around you? You send your mind into the night. You are searching for him. But he is not here, he is far away.

"I could kill them all," you say. "All twelve." I do not doubt it, but to what end?

"It is not them you must defeat."

"I could defeat Vatu. I could slay the dark one. I could stop it all."

"No," I say. You could not slay Vatu, and why would I wish that? "I am not the destroyer."

"What are you then?"

You do not expect me to answer. And so I say nothing. But one day I will tell you without words.

"Come, there is work to do."

You follow me and I lead you into the city. There is so much to put right.

"I cannot do it all," you tell me.

There is another place you wish to see. You wander through the lanes that you first walked dressed as a scribe and you come to the place. It is empty and the door is barred with nailed wood. Still, locked doors will not keep out ghosts. You walk into the courtyard. The house is empty. All empty. And yet full.

The scent of jasmine drifts through the house. Moths flutter in the light of the streetlamp that spills over the wall and onto the cobbles. The pavilion still stands but the cloth is torn and billows in the wind. You sit. And she is not there.

"Here was my greatest foolishness."

"Yes," I agree, "but what came of that foolishness?"

"What indeed. And what became of it?"

"Good things, I believe. If you had not fallen in love, where would you be now? Not here."

"No," you agree, "and not with you. I would be free."

You are wrong. You are free now. You are freer than you have ever been. You pick up a birdcage that has fallen to the floor. It is empty. The bird is long gone. You toss it aside. Do you recall how the bird sang for you as you lay in her arms? She was like a bird. Her song was sweet, but she was trapped and sad.

"She was free. You set her free."

"For a while," you agree. "Now she is dead."

"Now she is free."

I leave you to your thoughts for a while, for a short while. I still have much for you to do. I can only leave you for a while and then I return.

"It is time to go."

Chapter Fifteen
Leaving

Ennet

Koreb has arranged for the child to leave. Ennet, how sad you feel. It fills you like darkness. It is as if your child is being taken from you all over again. You pray to me for strength and I come and whisper in your ear.

"Why don't you go with her? There is nothing for you here." I wish to bring joy to your life which has been so hard.

You look around the single room of your shack. This is what your life is. You are alone and your home is meagre and empty. Not so, I tell you, it is filled with love. But love you can take with you wherever you go. You count your little hoard of coins. It is small. You have saved it for when you can no longer work. A penny here and there. It is not enough. You will starve when your eyes fail and you can no longer sew. As it is you earn barely enough to feed yourself.

"How will I earn my keep if I go with her?" you ask me.

"Have faith."

Faith, it is such a big thing and so often betrayed. I sense your fears, and I understand. I have a plan for you and for everyone, but if you will not trust me, then how can my plan come to be? I will not force you to go. And it is not just me that you have faith in. Your brothers and sisters, the heretics will not let you starve surely. You have faith in them, even if you do not have quite enough faith in me. I look at your handful of coins. Should I multiply them in your lap so that they overflow? But what then? Then you would have a new challenge, the curse of being rich. Would that make you bitter and mean? I do not think it will. Yours is not the love of money. But I do something, I take a gold coin and place it in your lap, and when you return the coins to your purse you see it. A single Royal. More money than you have ever seen in your life.

"How…" You take the coin and stare. "It must be a mistake." Your first thought is who it might belong to and if you can return it, and how much trouble it will cause you. See, even small miracles are a burden.

I hope I have not placed too much upon your shoulders. Your thoughts do you credit but even so, you should not spurn my gift. You realize that you must keep the coin, and now you place it in your purse, burying it deep amongst the pennies and shillings.

What will you do now? Now you know you will not starve when you can work no more. Or perhaps you could buy your own silk and sell the gowns you make. All of this you think on and more. It is good to think on these things, to know what you are giving up when you decide to leave with the child. It is right that you consider. But I have faith in you, Ennet. I have faith in your goodness and your love for the child. I know you will do right.

"The child will need me," you say.

"Her name is Alaba," I whisper to you.

"Alaba," you repeat. And you turn to the light shining in your home and the source of love. "I will never leave you."

That last, I do not seal upon you. I have work for you too, Ennet. But this I grant, that I will never leave you.

Now you are making a bundle with your belongings. Your clothes and your money. What else? You have the rag doll you made for your daughter. They would not let her take it when she was taken from you. Your needles, perhaps they will be of use. Your lamp. You would take your brazier but it may be too heavy. What of your pots and pans?

There is a knock on the door. They have come. Rise and open the door. Koreb is there with another man. Outside is a wagon.

"Come in," you say, and they enter.

"This is the child," says the man you do not know. And he bows low to the ground. Awestruck by the glowing infant.

You rush over and lift her in a blanket. "I want to go with her," you say.

"I cannot allow that," says Koreb. As if he is in charge and not me.

"Who will care for her?" Such an obvious point. You look at Koreb and the stranger. Two men. As if men know how to care for a child.

"She is right," says the stranger, he is a good man and not a stranger to me, nor I a stranger to him. "She will need someone to care for her. Children take a lot of caring for."

Koreb is struck silent for a moment. But he too is a good man and I do not need to correct him. "Very well then," he says. "What do you need to bring?"

"I'm ready," you say, and smile at Alaba, holding her up and kissing her softly.

"We haven't much room," says the stranger. "We can take your pack, but you will need to leave your pans behind. We have pans in the wagon. Can you cook?"

"Of course, I can cook," you reply almost laughing.

"What's your name then?" says the stranger. "My name is Bidann."

"I am Ennet and this," you say holding Alaba, "is Alaba."

"Pleased to meet you Ennet, and you too Alaba." He holds out a hand and Alaba grabs his finger. He is smiling and happy.

Poor Koreb, he thinks I have forgotten him. How he wishes he were going also. He wishes he could be with the child and surrounded by love. He is surrounded by love, by my love.

"Here," he says and fumbles in his purse, and then passes his whole purse to Ennet. "You will need this."

It is kind and thoughtful and to his credit. But Ennet shakes her head. "I have enough, and the author of all things will provide what I lack."

Now Koreb is sad. "Perhaps I should go too?" But he knows he is not needed and would just be another useless mouth to feed along the way.

"I need you here," I whisper to him. "I have much for you to do."

The others do not hear, because my words are not for them.

Chapter Sixteen
Keep Going

Utas

The moon is rising. It is rising in Capricorn. It is almost full, just past. The light falls on your face. It is time to rise and to travel. You have far to go.

"What is the point?" You are asking yourself, not me. But I answer.

"You will see."

You swear at me, but I am not offended. I can see your heart and I know that load you bear. It will take more than a curse to chase me off. It cannot be done. I am everywhere. I see everything. I hear everything. Still, the sound of the curse dulls your hearing, so that you can barely hear my voice. But nothing, not the loudest roaring of the sea, not the howl of the storm can drown me out.

In spite of your complaint, you rise and stretch. "I am hungry," you complain. And then continue bitterly, mocking me. "Man does not live by bread alone."

Have I not fed you already? Have I not placed fruits in the fields and in the forest? Have I not given you the birds of the air and beasts of the land and the fish in rivers and oceans? What do you hunger for? Do you thirst for blood? Do you long for the fineries of the City of the Sun? You will have to settle for the oatmeal in the back of the wagon.

"Why should I bother going on?" you ask. "I have lost everything."

You have started a fire and begun to cook the oatmeal. You go on because you want to go on. Life is worth living. There is salt in the wagon for your oatmeal, but no milk nor anything else. You let it cool and then sup it, careful not to burn your mouth. I have nothing to tell you for now, only that you must go on. Things will be made clear in time. You must be patient. Think of it like a book or a song. Each word and each note must be in the right place, not too soon and not late. And then eventually it is all clear, everything is revealed.

The moonlight warms you just enough. It is bright enough to see around you. The forest is thick and the ground is covered with moss. You slept well on the tufted, mossy cushions. Your strength has come back to you. Although you are still sore. Vatu used you most harsh.

When Vatu took you and made you track down the missing child, you knew everything he did. You know what food is in the wagon, and what gear and where Vatu hid the coins. You know the names of the horses and their natures. They feared you when Vatu resided within you, but now they do not shy away. You approach and they let you brush them down, and lead them to the traces.

"Is it done?" you wonder. Has Vatu set you free? It seems you are of no concern to him now.

"I was never really the high priest. I was a fraud. Erroi was the high priest. Vatu has forgotten about me."

You pack up your blankets and kick out the fire. It is time to move on. But to where? There is no track and the forest seems endless. The Tower of the Sun is to the east. You fear to head that way, but you also know that is where you are more likely to find a town or even a city. Eastwards. You could go back to the house that Erroi built for Irid, the cottage in the woods. You could live there safe. But what good would that be? If you still know one thing it is this: that you do not want to be alone.

"I am with you," I remind you but I know that is not enough. Why should it be? A child does not wish to sit on its father's knee forever.

"Eastward," you agree, "but southeastward. For now at least."

You let the horses have their head and you track your course by the pole star. They move at a gentle pace, and a part of you wishes to spur them on, while another part wishes to slow the horses to a stop. Still, eventually, you cross a road. You ease the wagon onto the track. It runs northeast to southwest.

"Which way now?" It is not a hard choice. Northeast would lead closer to the City of the Sun and to the dark devil that is Vatu. Southwest you head. You try to remember the name of towns in that quarter. No cities in that direction. It is further from the Sun and harvest there is poorer. You try to remember the maps that once you pored over with Hilketa. You cannot think of them. You cannot recall.

"Kota," I whisper.

Ah, you remember now. "Kota, Stane, Allet."

The names of places of exile. Places to send those who displeased you, but did not displease you enough for you to kill them.

"Perhaps someone there might recognize me," you think and stop. But then who would imagine that the high priest would be a vagrant traveller, aged and broken? No one will recognize you, my friend. You nod your head and agree. Then you flick the reins to set the horses trotting.

"What do I do now?" you ask.

Heal, my friend, heal and be made well and whole.

Chapter Seventeen
Bribes Worth Nothing

Hilketa

The delegation has arrived. They enter your office and fall to the floor.

"Praise the darkness," they say. You rise and your footsteps echo in the hall as you step forward. The tribute lies in front of them. You can barely take your eyes off the gold as it glistens in the lamplight. They have brought all that they can. There is not enough, not nearly enough. There is never enough. So greedy. It was your greed that caught you and brought you here.

"What brings you here?" you ask. You motion for them to rise, and the aged merchants and officials rise. You let them get to their feet and let the groans and creaking joints settle before you continue. "Well?"

"Great one, it is a disaster," says a plump man wearing a purple robe. And he brings forward a jar of grain. It is sealed and he motions for the clay top to be removed. No words are needed. You can see why they have come. The black mould covers all the grains of rice and they are soft and stinking. You take a handful and then place it back in the jar. A slave runs forward with a cloth and water for you to clean yourself.

"It is all like this, great one. The whole rice harvest has been lost in Saco. Our city will have no rice."

"What will you have me do?" you ask.

"Send us rice."

If only that were possible. Saco is not the only city to have a spoiled harvest.

"If I give with one hand, then I must take with another. There are many this year that wish for aid. We cannot aid them all. The City of the Sun must eat too."

"Then let the Sun be opened and let us harvest again."

Yes, that is what they want. They are greedy for the Sun. Everywhere and everyone wishes the same. Let the Sun out and let us harvest again.

"That…" You let the words trail off. If you refuse outright, then they will take their gold with them.

"It has been done before."

Yes, it has, but only when the high priest begged the dark one to do so. Now there is no high priest.

"It is not a simple matter," you tell them. "And…" You point to the tribute and let them see on your face what you are thinking. "The dark one has no need of gold, but…" Again you let your voice trail off.

You can see the disappointment on their faces. "Can it not be done?"

You know it cannot. Kong will never be able to face Vatu and beg him to open the Sun before the due season. Even when the high priest was here, it was hardly possible.

"I will see what I can do. But I make no promises." There are no promises in this life.

They know that you are lying to them. But they do not challenge you. Rumours have spread. They know there is no high priest, but what else can they do? Where else can they go? They want to beg you, they want to prostrate themselves and cry to you to show mercy. The plump one is already trying to lower himself to the ground. It is the last thing you want. Six old men lying on the floor moaning and crying while you have work to do.

"There may be a solution," you tell them. "I will need to speak with the twelve. You should leave your tribute with me. Come back tomorrow. I will have a solution. I will find a solution."

Now they are bowing and smiling. They believe you, or they want to believe you.

"Thank you great one, thank you." Their thanks are almost as irritating as their pleas for mercy. You smile and place the tribute on your desk.

"I will keep this safe for now. And I will speak with you tomorrow. When the moon is in the south."

"Thank you great one," they say again as the servants usher them from the counting hall. "You are merciful."

Now they are gone. Merciful, you think to yourself. The dark is not merciful, it is just. It has no place for mercy. There is no mercy in you or in any of the twelve. Mercy is the gift of the heretic. It is the doctrine of the Whisperer. It is my doctrine.

"What has mercy to do with me?" you say.

"My mercy reaches even you," I tell you.

"What will your mercy do? What good is it to me?"

But I tell you that my mercy is worth more than all the gold in the world. I tell you that it reaches even you, and it will redeem you from the darkness and from your sins. And when you find mercy for others in your heart, you will treasure it greater than jewels.

"The dark has no mercy," you repeat. "Vatu will not help them. There is only one kind of mercy he will show."

But this is not about Vatu or the darkness. It is about Hilketa and what you find in your heart. Will you not help them, and if you cannot help them, will you not pity them? I will judge you not just by what you do, but also by what you wish to do. You can take their gold, steal it if you will. In a thousand lifetimes have you not stolen enough gold? Is it not time to find a new path?

You try to ignore my words, but you have heard them. You can stop your ears with wax and clay and you will still hear them. I cannot be drowned out or stopped. I am the Whisperer and my voice is in the ears of the faithful and the unfaithful. Let the darkness do as it will, Hilketa.

"And I know what must be done, what will be done."

So you will do the dark one's bidding but not mine.

You cast your stylus down. And stand up and leave the hall. But I follow you everywhere. I will not leave you. I have not left you once in all of your thousands upon thousands of lives. My love and my mercy are with you always. There are tears in your eyes as you leave. I see everything. I see the tears in your eyes and see the start of mercy in your heart.

Chapter Eighteen
A Hard Choice

Greba

The three of you stand by the empty throne. Kong will not sit in it. Only the high priest can sit on the throne and only when possessed by Vatu. When the high priest is still a child, no one sits on it. It is Vatu's throne and no one else's. Hilketa is holding a tablet. He has called this meeting.

"What is the problem?" Kong asks. Anything that keeps him from his pleasure is a problem.

"It is the granaries," says Hilketa.

"What of them?" Kong is bored.

"They have been infested with mould. In Saco. Almost the whole harvest is lost."

Kong still looks disinterested. He is fiddling with something up his sleeve.

"They will starve," Hilketa says.

Kong is sitting now, not on the throne but on the steps. "Then let them starve." Kong was always slow to pick things up. But you are not. You know exactly why Hilketa has brought you here.

"You must speak with Vatu," you say. Kong looks up, he is startled. And you see he is afraid. You are not surprised. Kong is a coward, but you would not relish going into the darkness to speak with the dark one. "You wear the high priest's amulet."

His hand drifts up to the black-jet necklace. The symbol of the high priest. But Kong is not the high priest. He is a weak, snivelling coward. He thinks only of himself. The amulet may as well be a trinket. It is a symbol of nothing. In all his many lives he is still thinking only of himself. He still thinks he can cheat the darkness, and cheat me.

"This has nothing to do with Vatu. The dark one has no interest in this."

"He could open the Sun on Saco and let them harvest again," says Hilketa.

"Have they sent tribute? Vatu will not do so without tribute."

"Yes, they have sent tribute. Saco is not the only city to send tribute begging for the Sun to open."

"Then I must have my share, you cannot keep it all." Kong does not even pretend that he will speak with Vatu.

You wait. Let Hilketa be the one to say it.

"If the Sun does not open then they will starve."

"Let them starve then."

"Thousands and hundreds of thousands of people will starve and may die."

Still, Kong is uninterested. Or so he appears. Even he is not beyond me.

"What do I care?"

You wonder if Kong was always this stupid. Yes, in every life I have seen him, he is, but he is also tricky and cunning. You would do well to remember that.

"There is another way," Hilketa says. "It is the usual way."

Now Kong gets Hilketa's meaning. "What is the point of that?"

"It is quick and painless," Hilketa says. "It is merciful." There is that word. "It is just. It is the dark one's will."

"Then you go and ask him," says Kong. "If you are so merciful."

Now you speak. You have wasted enough time and enough words. "A starving peasant is a dangerous peasant. Famine is a breeding ground for heresy. And for rebellion." Now you turn to Hilketa, he at least understands. "How many must we cull?"

"About a hundred thousand," Hilketa replies. "If we wipe out Saco that should be enough."

"Wipe out Saco," says Kong. "What are you saying?"

Poor, stupid Kong. If he read half the tablets that cross his desk he would know that this is nothing to what we do every day.

"A hundred thousand. Will Vatu kill them for us?"

Hilketa turns to you. "He will not kill them for us. He has never done anything for us. Only the high priest can ask him. And there is no high priest."

"I am high priest," shouts Kong, but neither you nor Hilketa are listening to him. He is nothing. He wears the robes and the amulet, but the blackness is only on the surface of him. The darkness does not live in him.

"Vatu will not open the Sun early. If we can persuade him, then he can cull the dark land and there will be enough to stop the famine from starting."

You know that none of you can do that. "So if we cannot persuade Vatu to help us?" you ask. But you know full well. That is why you are here.

"There are heretics everywhere," says Hilketa. Kong looks startled. He thinks you are talking of him.

"I am no heretic," he says. But he is, you are all heretics and are disloyal to the dark. In your hearts, you are all mine.

"I have other things I need to attend to," you say. Even you balk at the thought of murdering thousands.

"What can you have to do that is more important than stamping out heretics?" Hilketa challenges you.

"There are others you can send." And then you hide your feelings with outrage and anger. "Who are you to think you can command me? You are not the high priest."

"But I am," says Kong. "And I can command you. If I command you then you will obey me."

You turn to Kong and let your anger show. He quails at the sight of your eyes. He fears that you will take his throat between your great, powerful hands and choke the life from him. You have done it before in other lives. You have throttled him until his face turned purple and his eyes bulged. You could kill him now. But see, mercy, even you have found mercy.

"He does not deserve to live," you tell me. And I do not disagree. If mercy is deserved, it is not mercy. It is justice.

"I… Let me live," he begs and prostrates himself. "I… do not command you, as you say, we can send another. I dismiss you." Now that he knows that you will not kill him, he is back to his old self. You will not kill him. He is a fool. But when you turn to Hilketa and see him looking quizzically you wonder if you should kill him. You do not want him to thwart your plans, even if you do not know yet what these plans are.

"Keep your nose out of my business, runt," you snarl as you pass by him. "Keep your nose out or I break it off and ram it down your throat." He also is one that you have slain many times in your past lives. Both of them have slain you in your past lives using tricks and poisons. This life the twelve have is one big round of murder and more murder. No wonder you are all tired of it and wish to die. "Send another, or let them live. I don't care. I won't do it."

Chapter Nineteen
Concerns

Greba

As you leave the chambers, a thought comes to you. A gift. If they start hunting down heretics, then Koreb is in danger. It was not hard to find him.

"Why should I care?"

But you have asked the wrong question. You do care. Why do you care?

"He is not my son." Is he not? He is your son from a past life. There must be a way to warn him. He should be careful. He is in danger. And if he is in danger, then what of your granddaughter? Why could Hilketa not manage the granaries better than this? You will warn him.

"Yes, I will." One of the guards looks up when you speak, but does not say anything. They know better than that. They have learned never to question you or any other of the twelve.

You stride through the corridors of the tower and down to the dungeons. There are twelve prisoners in the cells. Five are single cells and the others are huddled together in the hole. You have not inspected them yet. A guard hands you a tablet with the list of new arrivals.

You do not have time for this, and you feel anger. Do not take your anger out on the prisoners, I whisper to you.

You motion for the door to be opened and when the battered oak swings wide you enter. All of your anger has returned. You glare around, and the prisoners shrink down against the walls. They are mostly old and poor and female. It is strange how the guards always find that women are to blame for most crimes. Still, justice is not your concern. That was the responsibility of the high priest. Now it is the responsibility of Kong. In your experience, no one is ever innocent. All of them will die. It is only your job to keep them alive until Kong calls for them. And to stop them escaping. The thought of it makes you laugh. How can anyone escape from Vatu? And yet you think of Utas. How did he escape? Why has the dark one not sent you to find his reborn soul in the body of a child? It troubles you, as it should.

"Are you looking to me to answer?" I ask you. You pretend not to hear and kick an old woman back into a corner.

"Stay away, I don't want to catch your disease." Not that you would, or if you did, then Hilketa would have a cure. Some ointment to rub on any sores or pustules that form. But you do not want to take the risk. You will have Hilketa look at the old hag. You do not want her to die before Kong calls for her. Nor do you want her spreading her pox on the other prisoners. You see that each has water and bread. There is a muscular looking man in one corner. Sometimes you need to show them that they are no longer strong, but are weak as children. But this one looks away when you approach.

"Were you a soldier? You look like a soldier."

"No, great one. I was a porter. I carried goods around the city."

"You do not look like a porter."

"I am a porter, great one."

You do not believe him, but it does not matter. You are not the judge. You cannot always tell a man's crimes just by looking at him. Or a woman's.

You grab the man by the hair. "If I say you are a soldier, then you are a soldier."

"Yes, great one."

See, he is broken already. You do not need to watch this one.

"Take the poxy old hag to a cell. The rest can stay here. Get the doctors to look at her. The last thing we want is a pox outbreak."

The guards hurry forward to obey your command. They too are wary of touching her skin. But she is old and weak, and she makes no effort to resist. Sometimes they do. Then you must force them to see that they have no choice. In jail or out, freedom is just an illusion. All must serve the dark, willing or not.

The rest are still as mice when the hawk hovers overhead. Or as children hiding in a shelter when they hear the drone of engines in the sky. The thought takes you back. Even after a million lifetimes, you will not forget. And if you do, I will remind you.

"I thought you wish to redeem and to forgive," you say.

"Yes, yes I do. But I do not wish to forget."

You try to run from me. You leave the chamber and run along the corridors. You cannot escape me. I am everywhere. Still, I let you run. What will you do? In some lives, at this moment, you have cast yourself down. But even then, not a hair on your head is harmed unless I will it. I could take you in my hand and pluck you as you fall from the tower. I could set you down as a man sets down a feather.

"I do not believe it," you say. Try me, I reply. Tempt the lord of all things.

"So now you lay claim on this world." You are trying to make me angry. But I am not. Anger is your thing, Greba. It is the tool that you have used.

"Why me?" you shout angrily. Angrily, is that allowed? Yes. I allow it.

"What will you do to me?" you ask. But I have already told you.

"I will save you."

"I don't need saved. Except from you."

But you know that you do. Still, after all these lives you will fight me. Still your anger burns.

You think then of the day we first met. How happy you were.

"You tricked me."

"I did not."

"You think I could have done anything different."

"Yes."

"You should have told me. You should have told me that this is the price. And why me. Why am I here? There are plenty others, many worse than me."

"I agree. This is not the only hell I have created."

"So they all rot in the same hell? Lifetime after lifetime of torture."

"Not all of them, some have left it behind."

"Then why can't I? Why can't I just leave this hell?"

"You can, you all can," I tell you. You do not believe me. You think I am a liar. I am not a liar.

"There is no way they can be forgiven."

I say there is. I say that even you can be saved. I am not here to torment you. If this is torment then it leads to freedom.

"Some things cannot be forgiven." You are wrong. My love is deep enough even for you. Deep enough for you all.

Chapter Twenty
Travelling

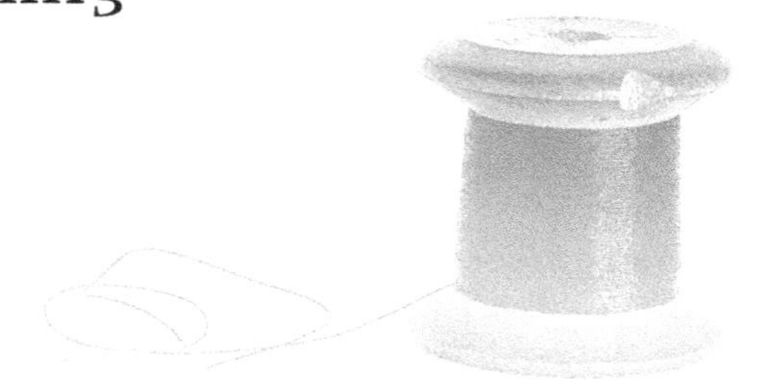

Ennet

I watch over you both as the wagon passes through the dark land. You sit in the back with the child. You cannot take her and sit with Bidann in case someone sees her glowing.

"Are you an angel?" you ask the child. But of course, she is too young to speak. Instead, she looks at you with those eyes.

"Everyone is an angel," I whisper to you. And you hear my voice and hug Alaba to you tightly.

Bidann pulls up the wagon. "Time to stop," he says. "The moon will go down soon so best to rest for now."

He clambers back into the covered section. He looks at Alaba and watches you hold her.

"It is a miracle," he says. "What can it mean?"

"It means we must keep her safe," you tell him. And you are right. Think on what needs done for now. And what needs done for now is to start a fire and cook. You hand the child to Bidann.

"Here, hold her for a while and I will start on the fire."

"I can do that," says Bidann, clearly uncomfortable holding a baby. You do not laugh, but you want to. That would be unkind.

"You hold her for now. Don't be afraid. I'll get the fire started and cook some rice."

You take the smouldering box and blow. A small flame flickers and you tease it to life with threads of cotton, then the kindling.

"I can get firewood," says Bidann.

"We have enough for now. You can get some after you've eaten. You must be hungry."

"No, not too hungry."

"Hold the child," you say and now you are laughing. "Honestly, men and children. They are more afraid of them than of a sabretooth."

Bidann grins. "You would not say that if you met a sabretooth. Besides, I'm not afraid."

"Good. Now come and sit by the fire and warm up."

"I'm fine, and I should be looking to the horses. Here, take her back."

"Just put her in that basket and set it over there. I've too much to do just now. She should sleep anyway." And as if on cue, Alaba yawns.

"See, sleepyhead."

Bidann places her in the basket. "She sleeps a lot."

"For now," you tell him.

Bidann goes to loosen the traces and walk the horses, then tethers them for the night. He has some grain for them to feed on.

"What will they do with her?" he asks.

"What did Koreb say?"

"Only to take her to Saco. There may be someone there willing to hide her."

"How can you hide her? Anyone seeing her will know who she is. Or what she is. Or… Well, they will see her."

What is she? You wonder what Alaba is. You do not know what she is or why she glows. Not even Koreb could say why Alaba shines like the moon.

The rice porridge is almost ready. You take a bowlful and pass it to Bidann.

"Thank you," he says and bows his head to say a prayer of thanks. Bidann is a good man, you think. If you had a son, you would have wished him to be like him.

"All men are good," I tell you. But you do not believe me. That has not been your experience. But it is true, even a devil can do good.

You have been with Bidann for almost a week now.

"I do not think we should go to Saco," you say. And Bidann startles.

"Why do you say that?"

"I do not know, but there is something nagging at me. It is as if there is somewhere else we need to go."

"I have to take the wagon load to Saco. After that, we'll see."

You know he is right, and yet you know he is wrong. That unease falls upon you again. "West," I whisper.

"Do you not feel it?" you ask Bidann.

"Yes," he says. He also hears my voice. "I'm not sure what it means though." He hears it only faintly.

"I'm not sure either," you say. "I wish I knew what it meant."

"Tell me," says Bidann. "When did the Whisperer come to you?"

Once more you tell him the story of your lost child.

"So that is why Alaba means so much to you," he says.

"Perhaps. I like to think she would anyway. But you are right. If the master had kept my child, I would have stayed with him. Maybe I would never have listened to the whispers. Then would I be taking this child now? I do not know."

"The past is the past and cannot be rewritten, but you are a good woman and I think you would be a good woman no matter what."

You are not so sure. There are many things that could be different.

"Thank you. How did the Author of All Things come to you?"

"Sometimes I am not sure that he has," says Bidann. "I travel alone in the dark carting goods backwards and forwards. I have seen the full horrors of this land. Alone I have heard his voice in the dark, or so it seemed to me. Sometimes I am not sure. But I hope I have heard him. I hope he has a place for me."

"I am certain he has," you tell him. "The Author of All Things has a place for us all."

"Sometimes I wonder," Bidann says. And then he looks at the light coming from Alaba as she sleeps in the basket. "Sometimes I think, how can I doubt? But then why does he not make himself plain for us all?"

The sense of unease keeps rising within you. How much plainer do you wish me to make things? And you Bidann, is it not plain to you too?

"We should not go to Saco."

You think that Bidann will argue, but he does not. Instead, he screws his face up and sits by the fire.

"I think I must go," he says. "Even if you and the child do not come with me, I must go. Otherwise, my master will seek for me. He will think I have stolen from him."

You see the sense in his words.

"All right," you agree, "but I do not think we should stay there."

Chapter Twenty-One
Learning

Hilketa

"Why does the moon shine?" you ask. "Even when the Sun is locked away, the moon still shines."

"Because I am graceful," I reply. "Because I give you light even in the darkness."

You know better than to ask more. And you would not understand. You want to me to show you calculations and charts with orbits and rotations. That is not how it is done. You think you are wise. That was always your weakness.

"I do not understand," you say. But you do not have to understand. You think that if you do not understand then it cannot be, but there can be things beyond even your understanding.

"It does not matter."

It does not. You have other things to think about. You wonder who is going to feed the cities now that the harvest is spoiled.

"If Greba will not lead the armies then who will?"

You still think that to take the lives of a hundred thousand or more to save the lives of a million is a bargain. You still think that some lives can be placed on the scales and weigh more than others. You still think that you are the judge that decides the value of a soul. How can you ever know the worth of a man? Can you look into his heart and decide? I say that you cannot.

"Perhaps Kong will lead the army," you say. But you know full well that Kong is too afraid to leave the tower, even with an army. He will think that you or one of the others will seek to take his place as high priest. He still thinks that to be high priest is a blessing, not a curse.

"Perhaps I could lead the army," but you know full well that you will not. You never did like getting your hands dirty. You like to at least pretend that others are to blame and not you.

"You should trust me," I tell you. "Not a sparrow falls but I allow it." But that is not your way. That is never your way. You wonder how you can bend Greba to your will. How can you make him your slave?

When you think those thoughts, is it any wonder that Greba has murdered you so many times? Or that you have also murdered him?

"I will not let it happen." You think it is a virtue. To murder so that others can live. Can you not see that this is not so? This is your crime repeated again. I have tried to save you from this. I will save you from this. My love will make you see and stay your hand. You will find mercy, and you will find it within yourself.

"This world," you complain. "Why have you made this world?"

"Because I am merciful," I tell you.

"Mercy." Your voice is heavy with scorn. "What good is mercy? It is bread that people need, not mercy."

This is true, but it is not just bread that you need.

The moon is sailing across the sky. It is not in the quadrant of Libra. It is the full moon, so the light it shares must come from Aries. But there is no sign of it. It is caught in Vatu's dark casket.

"Look," you say, and you point to Aries. Low on the horizon, there is a patch of darkness. It is like a black sun. The stars are blotted out. "I have watched that darkness travel across the sky many times. As often as the moon. How can a box hold the Sun? This whole world is ridiculous."

I do not disagree.

"Is there nothing to be done?" You arise. If there is something to be done, then you must do it. You walk the dark corridors. If Kong is too afraid to face Vatu, then you must do it.

Chapter Twenty-Two
Wisdom

Vatu

The devils also believe and tremble.

"I am not afraid of you."

And yet you hide in your cavern beneath the dark tower. Do you think that I cannot see you? I see you and know your mind. There is nothing hidden from me.

"You cannot take this from me. You gave it to me. You made it and gave it to me. It is mine. You are a thief. You will not steal it away. It is mine."

I have given you so much. And yet what have you done with it? Have you not heard the tale of the unprofitable servant? The one who took what I gave him and buried it in the earth. I have given you everything and what have you done with it? You have kept it close to you for fear of losing it. And in doing so lost everything.

"It is mine," you say again.

But you still hide in a dark hole. You still fear. What use is it to you? Even you can be set free. Can you not see that this is a trap you have made for yourself?

"You will not take it from me."

But you cannot see that it, even now, is not yours.

The door to the cavern is pushed open, and you seek the intruder. You fear it, and then you see it is one of yours. It is the clever one. How easy it was for you to trap him. Now he is yours you say, but he is not. He is mine.

His voice echoes in the dark. He is praying to you and repeating the words that he has said in a million lifetimes. He has come to beg you for aid.

"Great Vatu, hear my prayer. Great Vatu, hear my prayer."

You have no choice but to answer him. That is part of the bargain you made.

"I hear."

"I ask you to send death. I ask you to cull the land. I beg of you."

"Death." The word sends you into a quiver of delight. "Yes, death."

Is that the answer to your fears? If you kill, kill thousands, then will that not make you safe? If they are dead then they cannot steal from you. I tell you it is not.

"Death," you say again and find joy in the word.

"Great Vatu, send the darkness to take from this world. It is a mercy."

O Hilketa, you who upbraided me and scorned my mercy, would you use that word for what you will do? How often we wrap our crimes in virtue. Does that make our crimes virtuous, or does it make our virtues a crime? You cannot have this. You cannot murder and call it good. It is a crime and nothing more. It is not virtue. When you try and pull that cloth over your crime, you will find it has become something else entirely. Mercy. For the greater good. Necessary. Can you not see it is a lie? It is the first and greatest lie. No evil is necessary. There is no greater good. It is not a mercy.

"Great Vatu, go forth and slay the people, do not let them starve."

"Death." Again you say the word. It is sweet to your lips. Perhaps, you think you should slay them all. You think you should slay everyone. That way you will be safe. Then no one will steal what is yours. How afraid and weak you are.

"I could slay you."

Hilketa shrinks when he hears these words. "Great Vatu. If I have displeased you, then do as you will."

"I should slay you."

Hilketa is afraid now, and not afraid. The twelve no longer fear death. They have been reborn too many times to fear it.

"If that is your will." He lies on the stone ground of the cavern surrounded by darkness and waits. I do nothing because I have already done what I will.

"No," you tell him. "I will not release you. I will have you serve me. You are mine. And they are mine also. They send me gold and treasure. They are mine. I will not let them go."

And as I knew you would, you let your greed and cruelty conquer your fear.

"I will not do it."

Hilketa lies in the darkness listening to your voice and despairs. He is crying. Can he not see he is fortunate? I have saved him from this crime.

In his mind thoughts run backwards and forwards. He is seeking a way. There is no way. You must trust me. I whisper to him and seek to calm him. Even here in the chamber of Vatu, I am here and you hear my voice.

"You have thwarted me," he answers. "You have stayed my hand. Would that you had stayed my hand once before."

"Would that I could have, but that was in another world and at another time."

"There were others as guilty as I was."

"Yes," I agree.

"What of them?" Hilketa asks. "What have you done with them?"

Would it comfort him to know? Would it make his suffering less to know that others suffer too?

"I could not have done it alone. I only made it possible."

Indeed that is true but is that not crime enough for one man?

Chapter Twenty-Three
A Light in the Forest

Ennet

When the arrows come I blow them to one side so that they land, three dark feathered shafts in a tight bunch, barely a foot away from you. You startle and grab Alaba, holding her tight to you and turning your back to where you think the arrows came from. As if you could save her by giving up your own life.

Bidann looks around. He has been held up by bandits before. He drops to his knees immediately and holds his hands high. "We surrender," he says.

But you do not surrender. You have something more valuable than a cartful of wine to protect. You rise and make to run.

"Stop," shouts Bidann. "They will shoot you. You cannot save her that way."

Another arrow flies towards you and I let it drift just past your ear. I will not let them harm you, but now you know this is serious. You turn and walk slowly back to the campfire.

"Wise choice," says a voice. Of course, to shoot arrows in the dark is never a sure thing, but they would not shoot unless they had you surrounded. Now at the edge of the firelight, you see the shapes of men coming towards you. They are armed with cudgels and staves and bows. You see now that you could not have run off. They would have caught you. You say a prayer to me and I listen. I will keep you safe.

The foremost of the bandits is a tall man. He is clean and well dressed. In spite of his height, he looks more like a lawyer than a bandit. He is thin and slightly balding. He is carrying an axe. It looks too heavy for him to swing.

"What is in the wagon?" he asks.

"Wine," says Bidann. He knows full well that the cargo is not worth his life.

"Wine," repeats the bandit.

"Yes, from the Valley of the Sun. A good vintage."

"Show me." The bandit gestures for Bidann to get to his feet. He leads them to the wagon and draws back the awning. There are stacks of amphora in the wagon.

The bandit sucks his teeth. The cargo is very valuable, but it will be hard to sell. Perhaps they will keep it and drink it themselves. Certainly, they will not be able to just take it back to their camp. They will need to take the wagon. Bidann has kept his head bowed. He is hoping that the bandits will take the wagon and leave him. Leave him and you and Alaba. It is the best he can hope for.

With his toe, Bidann is drawing a pattern in the dust. It is the sign. He is hoping that it will be a prayer to me. But something else happens. The bandit looks down and sees what he has drawn.

"So you are a heretic."

Bidann seeks to deny it and rubs out the pattern with his foot. "No, sir. I am no heretic."

The tall man laughs. "Are you afraid we will hand you over to the magistrate? What do we care about heresy? We have our own troubles. Still, maybe we should punish you anyway. We do not want the wrath of Vatu to follow us."

Bidann sinks to his knees again to plead for his life. The bandits have gathered around him and are laughing. One cuffs Bidann on the head.

"Heretic, eh? It's because of the like of you Vatu lets us all go hungry."

You think then that you can run to the trees with Alaba, but when you look around there is another bandit watching you. You know that you cannot escape. Then inside you, you find that you are brave. There is no point in hiding. You step forward and raise Alaba in front of you. You let the cloth slip back from her face and hair. You say nothing but the light from the child shines. It shines brighter than the fire and brighter than moonlight. The brilliant light causes the bandits to gasp, and then to drop to their knees.

"Who is she?" You look around and the bandit by your side is also kneeling. Their eyes are averted from Alaba as if she were too holy even to look on. You step forward.

"Who is she?" It is the bald one that is speaking. He has raised his head but has turned away as if he were too afraid to look at her.

"You can look at her," you say. "She will not burn your eyes out. Do not be afraid." You say that last bit in mocking tones, and the bandits look towards the child, muttering angrily.

"We are not afraid," says the bald man.

"She was brought to us by the Whisperer," you tell them. "He came to us and placed her in our care." When you say these words, you are struck at how strange it is that you should be trusted with this child. "Do you wish to harm her? Or us? Do you wish to defy the Whisperer?"

One of the men spits. Is that out of anger, or to avert harm? "No," says some while others ask, "Who is the Whisperer? Who is the Author of All Things?"

Now you wish that Koreb was here. He was always better with words than you were. He would not be struck dumb and speechless. Who is the Whisperer? How can you possibly answer that?

"He is come to save us from hell." It is Bidann that speaks. "He will redeem us and take us from the dark one's grasp. He will set the captive free and feed the hungry, he will clothe the naked and heal the sick."

Bidann has risen to his feet. "Stand up," he says. It is not a command. He does not demand it. His voice is soft and gentle. "His is the better way. Will you follow him?"

"Never mind about him," says the bald man. "What about her? Why does she glow?"

And you, Ennet, realize that you do not know why she glows. Does it matter?

"Does it matter?" Bidann says. "She glows because the Whisperer will bring light to the world."

That seems to satisfy them. They stand up now.

"Very well, come with us," says the bald man. He sends two of the bandits to lead the wagon. Where is he taking you, you wonder and then walk to Bidann and take Alaba back from him. He hands her to you and you kiss her gently on the forehead, then hold her tight to you.

You and Bidann follow as the wagon is led off the road and into the trees. At first, the ground is rough and you stumble a couple of times. Each time you do, Bidann takes your arm and stops you from falling. As you go the forest thins out and the ground is easier to walk on. But it seems as if you walk for hours. No one speaks to you, or to Bidann. It seems that you are prisoners. For all Bidann's words, you are prisoners.

“Where are we going?” Bidann asks.

“Be quiet,” says the bandit that is walking behind you.

“The old woman can’t keep this up much longer. She will need to rest.”

You snort; old woman, indeed. But you are old and he is right. You will need to rest soon.

“I said be quiet.” And the outlaw, a bulky man, strikes Bidann. He turns and looks at the man. You can see that he is thinking of striking him back. You pray to me that he does not. But Bidann does not listen to you or to me. He punches the man full in the face and sends him reeling and falling onto the ground.

Immediately, four other bandits surround Bidann. They are armed with cudgels.

“I warn you now,” says Bidann. “If you hit me, you’ll get the same. I’m not afraid of you.”

Pride is his undoing. He cannot hope to fight all five of them.

“Stop,” you say and walk between them. “We are coming as you asked. There is no need.”

The man punched by Bidann rises to his feet. His mouth is bleeding, and he glares at Bidann.

“Enough.” It is the bald man that shouts. “What’s going on here?”

“He struck me,” says Bidann. “He just got what he deserves.”

“I told you to bring them, not to beat them,” says the bald man.

“He hit me, Condito,” says the bleeding man.

“Count yourself lucky I don’t hit you, Gaesta,” says Condito, the bald man.

“This isn’t over,” Gaesta says to Bidann.

“No it isn’t,” says Bidann calmly.

“Put the woman in the wagon,” says Condito. At least he does not call you old woman. Besides, you would be happy to rest in the wagon.

“What about the big fella?” someone asks.

“Stick him in the wagon too,” says Condito. “The last thing we need is more trouble.”

“It’s not me causing trouble,” says Bidann.

“Really,” says Condito. But he cannot hide a glimmer of a smile. You see it cross his face. And it seems that Gaesta is not that popular with the other bandits.

When you are seated in the wagon, you turn to Bidann and say, “You should not have done that. They might have killed you.”

“They might have, but at least now we are in the wagon. Besides, if I hadn't hit him back he would have kept hitting me and most likely hit you too."

You wonder if he is right. And even if he is right, is it not your place to endure all things?

"What is a beating in the big scheme of things?" you say.

"It's a big thing," says Bidann, "and it would not be just the one beating. Most likely he would have continued until one of us was dead. The bald one knew it. That is why he never took Gaesta's side."

You do not think he is right, but do not argue. You know that is not the way. But what other way is there?

Chapter Twenty-Four
The House of Jasmine

Greba

In the City of the Sun, you walk through the alleyways. You know I am with you. You know I am near you. You want to go to a certain place but you hesitate. Why?

You are caught up in your mind. You are not as careful as you should be and you do not hear them following you. Now you hear them, and you are glad.

You let them get close to you and then you walk into a dark narrow passage. They think they have you and follow. You listen to the sound of daggers grating on stone. They do not speak. They have not come to rob you but to kill. Kill first, rob later. That is a good plan. But in this case not good enough.

You halt and turn and stand tall. You let them see that you will not run. You give them a chance. But they do not run. So, if they will not run then they must die. All you need to do is wait for them to close with you and it will be over. You will not even need to draw your blade.

What makes you duck just in time? A bolt misses by inches. This is why they did not run. They are only a decoy. They are running now. And at first, you think to run after them. But then you realize the archer is still a danger. Perhaps if you follow, that also is a trap. This trap is sprung, and now you must prise it open. You will find that archer and kill them. You trace a line back from where the arrow is embedded in the timbers of the passageway. He is on the roof of the house to your left. He is not running. If he were, you would hear the sound of footsteps on the tiles. You are tight against the wall now, so that the archer cannot get a clear shot without leaning over the roof. You have a dagger in your hand now, a light, well balanced blade for throwing. It might not be enough. The wall is high and even you might not be able to throw a blade straight and true so high. Why is he not moving? And then a corpse falls. It is the archer. He has taken his life. Whoever sent him against you took no risk. Dead men tell no tales, they say. Not unless Kong or Hilketa use their witchcraft.

But there are other things they can reveal. You walk carefully towards the body. It is still warm and you can smell the scent of bitter almonds. It is poison such as Kong would use, or any other of the twelve that wished you to think that Kong sent the assassin. And you realize that there is nothing to learn from the corpse because you already know. All of them wish you dead.

But it shows how slack you have been, how distracted. Your mind has been on other things. You have been thinking of Unead. You know you will never see her again. You can search the whole of the dark lands and you will never find her.

"She is lost to me forever," you say, and once again you wish to go back to that house and that place where, for a while at least, you were at peace.

It is true that when she, your wife, and family were discovered, they did as you planned. They left without delay. They may even be dead for all you know. There is no way for you to find them, or for anyone else to find them.

"She is not dead," I tell you. Is that a comfort?

You are standing outside the house that you lived in with her. As once you did before when you were too ashamed to face her. She had forgiven you. What could you do except let the High Priest have his way and marry your daughter? But there is always a choice. You tried to kill them and set them free. But you could not. You loved them too much. No, your daughter is dead, and your wife long gone.

You look up to that pavilion where Unead would look at you, her face begging you to return. But there is no face there now. In the years since she left the place has become desolate, a place for ghosts.

You know this full well, but still, you enter. How you wish that Unead's ghost will come to you. Have you loved in all your lives so deeply? You wonder. You must ask Koreb next time you meet him. In the empty courtyard, there is still night jasmine flowering. The scent drifts in and out. Now stronger and then fainter and each breath brings another memory of her. And of your daughter. You recall her laugh and her weak singing voice. She was beautiful, but she was more than that. When you looked in her eyes always a smile hid there. She was vain and greedy and sometimes foolish, but each of these flaws only made you love her more. You can picture her sitting in the courtyard with you. Always dressed so fine. As if she were afraid you would leave her if she were anything less than perfect for you. But also she knew that whatever she did, you would love her.

And did she love you too? She said she did. But what else would she say? Men trap women, and you trapped Unead. She had no choice but to love you. Or else you would have cast her onto the street to starve, or to sell herself. And yet, you know this is not true either. She could have found some other man to care for her and to set her up. One to visit her when he could. Just like you. You find you have regrets, many regrets. But your main regret is that you did not come more often when you could. Now you will never see her again.

"Will I ever see her again?" You ask me that directly. As ever, you know I am near and hear your voice.

"Not in this life," I tell you. But you already knew that, and it is not what you ask. "Perhaps in another."

"This is the last time I can come here," you say. "Now that someone knows, it is too dangerous. Kong knows about this place, of course. But why only try to kill me now? Someone else must know. I have been careless. I thought that because they were gone from here they would be safe, but now I know they are not. Even if it is only their memories that are in danger, I cannot come here again."

You turn and face me directly. "Promise me," you say. "Promise me that you will keep her safe."

I consider your words. "And in return?"

You have fallen to my feet and are begging me.

"I can do nothing for you," you say. "There is nothing I can do that you cannot do yourself. Please, I am begging. Have you not punished me enough?"

And still, you do not understand. I reach down and lift you up.

"I can do nothing."

"Enough, I will keep her safe," I promise, "until the end."

"Will you be with her?"

"I am with everyone."

"But you do not keep everyone safe."

"Yes, yes I do. In the end, I keep everyone safe."

You cannot say the words you wish to say, but they form silently on your lips. It does not matter. I hear them. I hear everything.

"Yes," I promise, "even you, I will come for in the end."

Chapter Twenty-Five
The Spinner and the Weaver and the Cutter

Unead

Where did they think I would find you, proud woman? They had not thought to find you here. They remember you so proud and vain. All of the servants feared you and well they should have. How you would fly into a rage if any of them so much as spilt water. Every day by your mirror while the maid brushed your long black hair and then wound it into a plait. Each day spent looking in that mirror sighing over a new wrinkle, or worse a grey hair. How you feared getting old. One day, you were certain, he would look at you, and in his eyes, you would see pity and not love. At least now you will be spared that day, should it ever have come. He will always think of you the way you were then. What has happened since, he does not need to know.

It gladdens your heart to think of him. To know that perhaps he is thinking of you. But you smile and tell yourself that he is not. He is still strong and he will find someone else. He will be happy now. And somehow that gladdens your heart still more.

"He is not such a fool." You say the words out loud, but no one is listening. Except me. Besides, no one can hear you above the clack-clack of the looms. The noise is loud enough to drown out any talk. You watch the shuttle fly between the warp, and then shift the threads before sending it on the return. Who would have thought? A weaver. It is enough to keep you alive, and if your hands are no longer soft then at least your stomach is not empty.

You know how lucky you are to have this job. And you touch the little carving on the loom. The Spinner and the Weaver: the gods that you pray to now. You are glad for that too, even if you don't believe in them. It is better to believe in something rather than nothing, or worse, to put your faith in the dark devil Vatu.

The Weaver and the Spinner bow to me as I enter the weaving shed. But I do not stop them in their work. There is plenty of room in this world for many gods. I am not jealous. The Weaver takes my hand, and the Spinner kisses my cheek. The Cutter does not look up.

"What can we do for you, Author of All Things?" they ask.

The Spinner turns elegantly, showing her figure in the light that falls from the lantern. The Weaver throws a cloth in the air as if she would dance. Motes of dust, or is it threads of silk, float in the air. Their dance is the dance of both the Weaver and the Spinner, they are both dancing.

"I have made a promise," I say. And when I look I see the hall is filled with women, each weaving silk.

"A promise just for her?" asks the Weaver.

"Have you none for us?" asks the Spinner.

How beguiling they are.

"What do you want from us?" they ask.

"I want you to spin the threads of this tale, and to weave them together, not losing any stray threads."

"And this thread?" they ask, pointing to you.

"Keep it safe," I say.

"Yes," they agree, "but in the end, the Cutter comes for each thread."

"In the end," I tell them, but until then.

They fade and return to where they came from. I settle beside you. And when the foreman strikes the block three times, you like all the others rise from the loom and go to leave. I follow you out of the shed. As you go you talk to a friend. How strange it is to see you dressed in coarse-spun. You who wore only the finest. And now to see you working to make that same cloth. Not one of the weavers will ever dress in silk.

What are you laughing at? Sometimes it is better not to know. Your friend has her hand over her mouth in an expression of feigned shock.

You walk together past a stall, and purchase some root vegetables. You do not dine on fish now. You sit with your friend in the square and enjoy the last of the moonlight. It fades below the rooftops, and the stars dim. The lanterns light up, but soon they will go dark too. You must be home before the curfew. A nod to your friend and you rise to your feet. You are surprised to find that you are happy in this new life. All this is just as I promised. You are safe and well and the only things from your past that you miss are Irid and Greba.

As you walk, you think about Irid. You wonder if she is alive or dead. You know only that she left with Erroi to escape the City of the Sun. You wonder if you are a grandmother. You smile at the thought that once would have horrified you. Being old is not the horror that you thought it would be.

You take a small token from a pocket, the token of the Weaver, and make a small prayer.

"Weaver of all threads, weave my grandchild's thread with mine."

You have said the prayer, and the Weaver listens.

You make the sign of the Spinner.

"Spinner of threads, spin for me a thread twined with my daughter and my husband."

You say the prayer and the Spinner listens.

They smile and dance, they will weave a grand pattern of coloured threads.

But you make no prayer to the Cutter and she is silent. She does not dance but sits waiting and holding the scissors.

Chapter Twenty-Six
The Other Child

Unead

There is another child that we must consider. The boy. Have you forgotten about him? Then let me remind you. He is the son of Utas and of Algria. Utas sent him far away without even giving the child a name. As soon as he was born, Utas took him from his mother. He thought he was being kind. If he could not save Algria from her fate, then he would save the boy. Nameless, that child is in this world. Where has he been sent? Greba, you have forgotten him, and that is good. Did you think that to slay a child would make you feel better? Revenge they say is a dish best served cold. But I say it is a poison that you should not eat.

Will we give the child a name? It is a big responsibility.

The Spinner holds the child's thread and passes it to the Weaver. The Cutter holds her scissors. One snip, then there is no need to name the child. They look to me. All is silent and still.

"Mukito," I say. There, it is done. The Cutter takes her scissors away and the other two sisters dance. Their eyes are full of mischief. But it does not matter. His fate is his now.

You are walking in the darkness and almost trip over the box. You curse loudly. You hoped to be home before now. You kick at the box and from it comes a weak cry. A moaning sound. It is a child. You sigh. You are sensible. You know you cannot save every starving child. The world is full of starving children and this one will soon be gone. Let the Cutter come for the child. Let her end this thread. Let her save the child from the dark. You walk on and then stop. The child has not cried out again but there is another nagging sound inside your head. You think of the prayer you just gave to the Weaver and the Spinner. They have dropped a thread at your feet, should you not pick it up?

You know that it is nonsense. You do not believe, not really. But you do not need to believe to do good things, nor do you need to believe to be kind. The child will die, but what is the harm in comforting it while it departs the dark world for the next? No child should die alone. You turn back to the child.

Can you hear me? I wonder. Perhaps you are not so far from me. You lift the box, a packing case, was it meant as a cradle or a coffin? It could be either of these things. You open the box and lift a boy from it. If it were a coffin, he is free of it now.

"A boy," you say. And you cannot help yourself. You smile and that most ancient of magic begins. Two threads are intertwined. There is nothing else for it. You take the child with you to the hut. It's late now to leave it and you are too tired to take it anywhere else.

"I have nothing for you to eat," you say. The child is thin and malnourished. He is light in your arms as you carry him. The child still does not cry, but it seems as if he is fading away in your arms. So be it, you think. It is better if the child dies. But if that is so, why does it hurt so much to think on it?

In the hut, you place the child on the floor. I will boil the roots, you think. The child can drink some cooled water from the pot. It is too weak to eat the roots, even mashed. And so you boil the roots, and take the water and let it cool. Then you take the water and spoon it into the boy's mouth. The child takes every drop that you give him and then suddenly it is all gone. Now you take the roots which are soft now and pulpy. You eat one while the child lies on the floor. It would have been better to eat them while they were hot, but you eat them anyway. You are hungry and when you are finished, you take the child and lie down on your bed. No doubt he will be dead when you wake in the morning. The thought disturbs you and it might be better to let the child sleep on the mat. But you cannot leave him alone. You hold him tight and sleep. He is warm and still, and when you awake, he is alive. What am I to do with you? you ask yourself.

The early moonlight comes slipping through the window. You hold the child up to look at him.

"You're a handsome boy," you say laughing. Because he is not. His features are even enough and he has the dark skin of so many from the Valley of the Sun. But even so, he is thin and scrawny. He looks like a drowned rat.

"So what is your name?" you ask.

"His name is Mukito," I whisper to you.

"Mukito," you say. "How are you, Mukito?" And the boy smiles.

But what are you to do with him? Some of the women take their children to the weaving sheds, those without older daughters to care for their children, or without mothers at home too old to work. But the sheds are dark and noisy and the air full of dust. Few children thrive there. Still, there is no other choice. You wrap up Mukito in a homespun shawl and walk out into the moonlight.

"Who is that?" asks a neighbour.

"A child I picked up on the street. I thought he would die and wanted to ease his crossing, but it seems he wants to live."

"They say no good deed goes unpunished," says the neighbour. "Here, let me see him."

You hand the boy over to your neighbour.

"His name is Mukito," you tell her.

"Mukito," the neighbour says, and starts crooning to the boy. "You cannot take him to the weaving sheds. Leave him here with me."

"Thank you, grandmother," you say.

"He's certainly ugly enough to be my grandson," says the grandmother. "No wonder they deserted him. Maybe you should do the same."

And even though you know your neighbour is right, and even though you know your neighbour speaks half in jest, an anger rises within you.

"He's not that ugly," you say.

"Leave him with me," says the old woman. "If he's ugly, then at least he's no uglier than I am."

"All right," you say, reaching into your pouch to pay the grandmother a few coppers.

"No need," says the grandmother. "I doubt the child will eat more than a few spoonfuls of rice."

"Thank you grandmother," you say again. And utter a silent prayer to those gods in whom you do not believe that they will keep the Cutter from the child's thread.

"Grandmother. I'm barely older than you. Call me Canna."

"Thank you Canna," you say and once more utter a prayer as you hurry off to the weaving shed.

Chapter Twenty-Seven
With the Bandits

Ennet

Even though you have been seated in the wagon, you are tired when you arrive. Where am I, you wonder. You are stiff and sore as you dismount. How you long for the mattress in your old home. I should not have come, you think. But still, when you look at Alaba you are glad that you did. You look around at the camp. It is bigger than you expected and better organized. There are huts made of timber set in a row. There are even pens for goats and chickens. You think there is a grain pit and there are some women grinding corn. There is water too, a stream runs a little way from camp.

The wagon is set and Condito comes to speak with you and Bidann.

"Are we prisoners?" you ask him. What else would you be?

He scowls and says no, but what else would he say? He calls to one of the women grinding corn.

"You are not prisoners, but you must earn your keep," Condito says.

"We were earning our keep until you took us prisoner," says Bidann.

Condito ignores him.

"You must help the women," says Condito to you. "Ezena will tell you what to do."

"And the child?"

"What about her? Take her with you."

You bow and follow the sullen-eyed woman who has come at

Condito's call.

"Ezena? Is that your name?" The woman does not answer but just looks at you, then walks back to the quern stone.

You place Alaba on the ground and begin to turn the heavy stone. Ezena pours more kernels into the hollow centre. You sit facing each other both with a hand on the turning rod and grind the corn. Ezena's face shows no emotion. All she does is turn the grindstone and from time to time feed more kernels into the hopper.

It is hard work. But once you find a rhythm the work goes well. When you are exhausted, another woman takes your place. Then Ezena swaps her place. Eventually, all of you have had a turn, and you think that you will have to grind again. But instead, the meal is gathered up and divided among the women. To your surprise, you are handed a small bag of meal.

"Thank you," you say, but still none of the women have spoken. The women leave, each going back to the huts. Now you are alone. You look around for Bidann. But you cannot see him.

All your life you have heard tales of the fearsome bandits in the forest. They do not look like the bandits in the story. They look like poor and broken men that have been cast out and must make their own way in the world. They look pitiful to you. And they are pitiable to me. I pity them.

Condito is coming towards you.

"You need to put up a tent. There's no room for you in any of the huts."

"Where is Bidann?"

"He'll be here soon. He's been cutting wood to make a hut. But it will be weeks before it's ready at the rate he's going. Here."

You take the offered rope and waxed canvas.

"You'll be best to put it up over there." Condito points. "That's probably where your son will build the hut, so you may as well set up there."

"We have somewhere to go," you tell him. "We cannot stay here."

"Really," says Condito. "You think we are just going to let you go on your way? You and that shining child. The girl is ours now, and you and Bidann. You do what we say."

"Who is we?"

Condito laughs. "You're right. I should have said, 'You do what I say.' Is that clearer?"

"So we're slaves?"

"Yes, if you like. You're my slave. Now get on with it. You have meal so you better cook something or you'll go hungry."

"We have food in the wagon."

"No, you had food in the wagon. That's mine now. I gave you corn. You should be grateful for that."

"Can I take my pots from the wagon? And my stuff? It's all in one chest."

"Bring it here and let me look through it."

You go to the wagon and tug at your trunk. You put the baby down and use two hands to lift it from the wagon. It is still too heavy, and you think of the little bag of coins that you have hidden in the box. No doubt Condito will take that from you. Still, it cannot be helped. You pull again at the box, and this time, unseen, I lift one end and the box falls to the ground. You pick up Alaba and with one hand drag it to Condito.

"You could have helped an old lady," you tell him.

"I could have," he says, "but I never."

He opens your chest and looks through your clothes. Blankets, clothes, a rag doll, a sewing set, pots. He takes each item and throws it to the ground. You protest.

"You're going to get everything filthy." But he just pushes you away. Soon the box is empty.

"All right," he says. "There's nothing there that I want. You can keep it." He turns and walks away, his filthy boots tramping through your belongings. You rush forward and begin to repack your belongings. Alaba is awake now. She has begun to cry.

"Hush, darling," you say, and let the cover fall from her face. The light shines, but she still cries. You pick up the rag doll, the one that was your daughter's, and let Alaba hold it. She stops crying as you shake the doll in front of her.

"Well," you say. "I guess this is yours now."

Chapter Twenty-Eight
Father

Koreb

You are not surprised when he comes to your house once more. You hoped he would come. You have never had a family before and now you have him. When you open the door you see he has brought rice wine again.

"We still have half of the last bottle," you say to Greba.

"But this is better than that," he tells you. And you can see that it is expensive. It is not a wine that a guardsman can afford, but then you know that Greba is not a guard. You have tried to hide it from yourself, but you know who he is. It seems he is no longer trying to hide it from you either.

"Is this some kind of special occasion?" you ask.

"Yes," says Greba.

"And what is the occasion?" you ask as you settle on the floor and bring two glasses.

"It's a farewell."

You startle when he says that.

"Where are you going?"

"I'm not going anywhere; you are. But stop, let's not get ahead of things. I'm not here to cause you trouble. I know who you are."

"And who do you think I am?"

"I can't tell you that, not without telling me who I am first."

"I already know who you are."

"Do you?" Greba laughs. "Who do you think I am?"

You hesitate. Words once spoken cannot be unspoken. Must you say them? Yes, you suppose you must.

"You are many things," you say. "But mostly you are yourself. I will tell you who the world thinks you are but remember there is more. You are firstly my friend. Also, you are a heretic like me. You believe in the Whisperer. You are more than what I will say next. You are more than what the darkness wishes you to be."

"And what is that?"

"You are one of the priests of Vatu. You are his servant. You are reborn at his command. And also you, or one of you that died and was reborn, was my father."

Greba does not speak for a while. You are afraid, but at least he does not kill you.

"Some of what you say is true," he says at last.

"Have you come to kill me? Is that where I am to depart to?"

"No," says Greba, "here, drink up. Look." He spreads his hands wide. "I have brought no weapon."

But you know he needs no weapon to kill you. Still, why pretend? It seems he is truthful.

"You will have to leave the city," Greba says. "I have enemies and I cannot keep you safe. You must leave."

"You have enemies, but you are one of the twelve."

"The twelve are my enemies. And I am theirs. We are all enemies one to another. I have other secrets, and they have been discovered. If they discover you, they will either seek to use you against me or kill you. It is no longer safe."

"It was never safe," you say.

"I suppose not," he agrees, "but it is more dangerous now. The fact that you are a heretic is one thing, but to be close to me is to bring death."

"Are you really my father?"

"I do not know for certain. Probably yes. Look at us, I am your double. I'm certain when I am your age I will look just like you. Have you…"

"Have I what?"

"Have you any children of your own?"

"Why do you ask?" Now you are angry. How dare he ask that question?

"I only wanted to know if I could help them. Listen, I will tell you. I married in secret. The twelve are prohibited from having children. To marry is not forbidden, but it weakens us. If the other of the twelve know who we care for then they will use that against us. But also if we have a child they must die. That is the will of Vatu. If you are still alive, then I, your father, must have kept you secret."

"I see. I must die and any children I have must die also."

"No, that is just it. You must not die, and neither must your children. It is your children that will set us free. I have a wife and daughter. When they were discovered, they fled. My wife is somewhere I do not know, but my daughter they caught and killed. And my granddaughter…"

Greba's voice trails off.

"What of her?" you ask.

"She is dead too," Greba replies. Can you hear the lie in his voice? You are not certain. Why would he lie to you now?

"So I am discovered and must die."

"No, not yet, but you could be. I have already lost so much and now I must lose you also."

Greba rises and walks towards you. You finch as his arms wrap around you and for a moment, you think he is going to kill you after all. But he does not and then you realize that he is crying.

You think then how cruel Vatu is, and most of all how cruel to the twelve. What great crime have they committed, you wonder, to deserve this torture? But it does not matter, the Whisperer will come for them too.

"I cannot go," you tell him. "My place is here. I am needed here."

"But I need you to live," he tells you.

"I am old," you remind him. "I will not live for much longer. Perhaps the guard will take me for being a heretic. Perhaps I will catch the black cough, or perhaps I will just die lying in my bed."

"Nonsense. You are as healthy as I am. You must go, leave here before the guard takes you or something worse happens."

"I cannot leave. I will not leave." And you think of how not so long ago, you were desperate to leave and follow Alaba. How you sent her away to safety just as Greba is trying to send you. His arms are still around you. Now he rises and pours more rice wine.

"I can make you leave," he says. "I can put your name on a piece of paper and exile you from the city. I can make you go."

"You must do what you must," you reply. "But I do not think you will. If you do, people will ask why you did it."

Greba shakes his head. "No one questions the priests of Vatu." No one except the other priests.

"I have had a child," you tell him. "But I do not know where they are. I never married. But I had a lover, once. I thought then that love was nothing, not a real thing. So when she was with child

I sent her away. She had a daughter that was not mine, and then I don't know what the other child was. I sent them away. Perhaps they are dead."

"Have you no way to find them?"

"No, I think she died. Probably the children too."

"Perhaps it is for the best."

"If they have gone to the light then it is for the best, or so I tell myself." You bow your head ashamed, but remember, none of us is without guilt and I am here for you too.

Chapter Twenty-Nine
One Word

Hilketa

So now you know everything, Hilketa, or so you think. Thoughts come back to you, and you remember that time before time started in this world. Did you never think about it? Did you just hide from it all these years?

"I am not guilty," you say. But you are. We are all guilty. Now you walk to the library. You know where you have hidden it. It is a tablet of clay that you take. It is old and broken. You wrote it years and years ago. Now you will write it again on a new tablet, but the words will be the same. You look around the great library. Here is all the knowledge of the world in one place. It is so great that nothing can be found. Everything is hidden.

"To hide a tree, grow a forest."

And here is a forest of books and scrolls. What is hidden here? It is like an old man. The secret is here but he cannot find it. It is safe. You have taken that knowledge and hidden it here where you do not need to think about it.

But now, it seems it is time to remember and to re-write those things.

"Are they not better forgotten and hidden?"

"No, they are not," I answer you.

"I could cast the tablet into the void and let it fall. There are many cast down, or so I believe. There they can never be retrieved."

If only it were so simple. To take it and hide it and then everything is made well. But it is not.

"And how would that help you?" I ask.

"I have not thought on this for a long time," you tell me. "I have not thought on this since I wrote it. What good is it to think on these things? I am guilty and I am punished. The guilty are not always punished. Why should I be? Why should I bear the guilt? I am not alone."

"The guilty are always punished," I tell you.

"It does not seem so," you reply. "Not even in this world, and not in the world you brought me from. I have seen them. They sleep well and go about their business. Guilt does not trouble them. They are rewarded for their crimes. They are rich."

"What you say is true, and all the worse for them."

"How so?"

"Do you think that others know how you suffer?" I ask.

And here you droop. It is as if the weight of it has come upon you all at once.

"You have made me suffer," you complain.

We walk to your chamber and there you place the tablet on a table. Other tablets are sitting there. You walk back and forth. You do not wish to write this.

"I will not die for years yet," you say and it is true. You are still young. You could live for another forty years. You are healthy too, perhaps longer. "I have always lived longer than the others."

That is true, usually.

"I am more careful. They have killed me many times but I am craftier than they are. They will not kill me easily."

It is as if you think this is a game. Who can kill who? You think there is a score kept, a tally. And you think that if there was then you would be leading it. How would you score that game, Hilketa? How many points for murder, and how many for a death avoided? I do not keep that score. I keep a different one, and it is not a game.

"What would you win in such a game? What prize would you like me to give?"

I can see you thinking. You would like to say 'knowledge,' but you wonder if there is a better prize on offer.

"Am I winning the game?"

"There are no winners in this game. Or if there is, then there is a prize that everyone can win."

You make a face. The thought does not please you.

"So I am no better than the others, what you will give me is just the same as you will give them."

"You do not even know what I will give you. Yet all you think is that whatever I give, you must have more. It does not work that way."

You go now and sit at the desk. The crumbling clay tablet is in front of you.

"When did I write this?"

"It is not as old as you think," I reply. "It is only just over a hundred years old. You wrote it at the end of your life before the last."

"And I did not rewrite it in my last life?"

"You did," I tell you, "but you did not hide it there."

You run your fingers over the indentations.

"I should write this on brass, then I will not need to rewrite it. Not ever."

"You don't need to rewrite it."

You look down at the tablet again and read.

"I am not to blame. He came and told me what to do and so I did it. He promised me a world of my own to share with him. When I asked about those that would die, he said it was only just. And I pretended to believe him. Besides, I didn't believe in devils, not then at least. Things were not going as well as was hoped, and they were going to replace me. And they were going to take my security level away. We could detonate static installations. But now we needed to find a way to fire them remotely. A way to transport and deliver and then detonate. When he showed me how then it was so obvious. I should have thought of it myself. I would have, I am sure. Perhaps he stopped me from thinking about it. I asked him what he wanted in exchange. 'Nothing,' he said. 'I have everything I need. You'll be helping me. It's only fair that if you do this then I reward you.' I knew he was lying. No one ever gives anything for nothing. I lit a cigarette and pretended to think about it. 'How does it work again?' I knew how it worked of course and it was such an obvious solution. He ran over it one more time, even writing it on the chalkboard."

You stop. There are tears in your eyes, but they are tears for yourself.

"I am not to blame," you say. "They would have solved it anyway. They did. They found another way. Besides, it was the right thing to do. I am not guilty. He tricked me. He said we would share this world forever."

"Do you want to rule this world? What is it you want? If you are not guilty then why are you so sure this world is a punishment and not a reward?"

"What was I supposed to do? What choice did I have?"

"I already told you there are no winners. There is no right answer. Everyone is guilty."

"If everyone is guilty, then how can anyone escape? How can I escape?"

"First they have to wish to escape. Do you?"

"Yes, yes I wish to escape."

"That is only the first step."

You look long and hard at the clay tablet. You take a fresh tablet and place it before you. You pick up a stylus. You are holding it in your hand. Once more you go to copy the tablet, to rewrite the same lies over again. Just because something is written does not make it true. Have I failed again?

You write only one word on the clay, pressing each shape. It is a word you have never written in all of the lifetimes you have lived. Now you put the stylus down. Again there are tears in your eyes, but they are not tears for yourself. You say the word out loud. That word that you fought for so long and would never say. One word.

"Guilty."

Chapter Thirty
The Moonstone

Utas

You are travelling when you first see it. My gift to you. It is lying half buried in the ground. It is rough and pitted. The crescent moon is as high as it will rise, barely visible in the southern sky. How you grumble about the light. But still, you press on.

"What use is the crescent?" you complain but it is useful enough that you wish to make use of its light before the moon drops below the sky line, when there will be no light. "Can you not give me a better light than this?"

And that is when you see it.

Of course, you stop, and you think of her. Alaba. You get down from the wagon and start to dig. The rock is about the size of your head, and it is heavy. You have nothing to dig with except your hands and again you complain. But for all your complaints you manage to dig the boulder out. It is only the top of the boulder that shines. But it all seems to be made of the same stuff. When you roll it over, again only the top shines, and when you put it in the wagon, it stops shining altogether.

You take the blanket off the stone and once more it shines on the top. It is very bright. Even in the full moon, it would be bright. It is as if a piece of the moon has fallen to earth, it is so bright.

You take the stone and place it next to you on the bench seat. It is bright enough to light your way. So you head off on your way. Your path is lit by a magical stone that shines in the darkness, and you do not think to thank me.

When the moon drops behind the horizon, the stone stops shining.

"I knew it was useless," you say. "I knew it was too much to ask for." Had you hoped the stone would light your way forever? You are angry and I think you would throw it away if it was not so heavy. You go to roll it out of the wagon. But the stone is hot. You draw your hand back quickly and complain some more. So many complaints. The stone is hot enough on the top to cook on. And so you make a dough of flour and cook flatbread. More complaints. You are tired of camp fare. You wish that you had rice or beans. Or wine. Wine would be nice. Poor Utas, with no wine. There is a stream behind you and you go and fetch water. It is cool and refreshing but I do not turn it into wine. Water is better than wine. You are refreshed somewhat, but you are also tired. It is time to sleep. You do not need to light a fire. The stone gives off a heat. You set your bed near it. Perhaps you are too hot. I send a breeze to cool you. The sound of gentle rustling leaves calms you, although you pull your blanket tight around you.

"Sleep well." And now your soft breathing mingles with the sound of running water and the breeze. It is peaceful. What do you dream of, Utas? Your sleep is broken and you turn over and over. What is haunting your dreams? Are you thinking of all that you have lost or all that you have done? Still, you sleep soundly and do not wake at the sound of padding footsteps. From the edge of the woods, eyes shine in the darkness. But do not be afraid. I lead the wolf pack away from you. I have spared you but must give them something else to feed on. I take them on a hunt into the hills where they scent the smell of deer. They will feed and you will be safe, and your horse. He has smelt the wolves and is shifting. The sound of him wakes you.

"What is it?" you ask. You rise and soothe the horse. You bring him some hay to feed on. The moon will not rise until the next moonrise. You must stay here in the dark.

You go back to the moonstone. It is cooler than before. You cannot use it to cook food now. And so you go out into the wood to collect firewood. The trees are mostly pines, so the timber will burn well, even if it will spit and crack a little. There is a good log lying and you drag it back to the camp. You sned the branches, leaving a straight log, but your little axe would take too long to split chop the log.

Once your fire is going, you make a thin porridge. You wish there was salt in the wagon. Or better still, bacon. The smell of the porridge is good though and it is filling. You sit and eat, and then to your surprise, the moonstone starts to glow again. It shines only from the top, and when you touch it, it is warm again, not as warm as before, but it seems to be getting warmer.

"I don't understand," you say. But even so, it shines brightly. "What is this? Is this a piece of the moon fallen to earth?"

"In a way," I tell you. But not in the way you think. You put your hand on the stone and think how strange it is. It is not like a normal rock at all. It is all angles and hard geometric shapes.

"How did it come to be here?" you ask. Your curiosity overcomes you.

What can I tell you? That the moon and this earth are not as ancient as you think? They are ancient, yes. But in the eternities their age is as nothing. Once the moon was part of this earth. And then in the ages long before any life walked this land, the moon burst from the earth's surface, and now orbits around in an endless cycle that will end one day. Uncountable is not the same as infinite. It is only uncountable to you. To me all things are countable. This is not part of the moon fallen but part of the moon left behind.

"Why does it shine when the moon does not?"

"The moon is shining. The moon always shines; it is just that you cannot see it."

"But this does not always shine. Why is that?"

Once again you lift the glowing rock and place it on your wagon. When you lean over the rock the glow dims in your shadow. What is it that you are shading the rock from? You look to the sky and can see nothing.

"Hilketa says there is a black moon that travels across the sky. I could never see it when he took me to the moon viewing platform. He said it was a ball of darkness that blotted out the stars." And you think the black moon must send a black light that touches the white moon. And then the white moon turns the black light into white. Not quite white, there are touches of yellow and green and blue and even red light coming from the stone.

"I should have asked Vatu when I could," you say. But he would not have answered you. You hitch the horse up and clear the camp. Then you travel onwards like the wandering moon.

Chapter Thirty-One
A Meal of Rabbit

Ennet

Bidann has nearly finished the hut. You think it is a good job, and you are impressed. It is bigger than you expected with two rooms. One for you and Alaba and one for Bidann. He has worked hard every day. But so have you. You worked twisting ropes or grinding corn or cooking and most of all looking after Alaba. She is no trouble, you say. Except, of course, she is. All children are trouble of some sort.

How big she is getting. Now she can walk on her own. Her hair is growing in, and her teeth. She is such a sweet child. Here amongst the bandits, there are very few children. Just one other girl. But now they are used to seeing her walk around, most of them pay no notice. A glowing child, you would think it was a miracle and it is, but they do not bother with it. How quickly we get used to miraculous things. The whole earth is a miracle and yet no one bothers.

She is starting to speak now, and you listen to her call you mama. How hard it is to hear and how wonderful. Each time she says it, your heart leaps and then you think of your daughter. Where is she? That is another story for another time. I will not take you to her. I will not bring her to you. But I have told you she is well and I do not lie.

Food is the biggest problem at the camp. The bandits—they are not really bandits, just people cast from ordinary life—have no stores. They can only eat what they can find or steal. The camp is growing. Although there are few children, new arrivals come. They are mostly runaway slaves. Condito makes them promise allegiance to him and sets them to work. But they never bring food. It is always more mouths to feed.

Bidann is on hunting patrol. It seems he is a good hunter. It is not something you expected, but most days he comes back with meat or fish. Who would have thought it? You forage for fiddlebacks and roots. And there is some grain. If you go and grind at the quern stone you can have flour. Even so, you are hungry most of the time, and you are thinner than ever. Bidann is thinner too, and Alaba is thin. She does not cry or complain, but she is not getting enough food. You can see it. The other child has come to play with Alaba. Her name is Sifyre and she is a little older. She seldom talks, and is dirty and sucks on stones to whet her appetite. Her eyes are gummy.

You watch as she helps Alaba walk, taking her hand and walking across the mossy ground. If you were still in the City of the Sun, you would not have let your own daughter play with such a child. Still, this is not the city and perhaps you should be kinder. It is not the child's fault.

"Come here," you say, calling both children over. You have a basin of water and you tell Sifyre to sit while you take a cloth and wash her. Her hair is matted and you wash it and then you take a comb and run it through her hair. Sifyre struggles, but you say, "Hush now, I am making you pretty," and so she sits. Is she smiling? Once you have untangled her hair you put it into plaits. You cannot help yourself and you begin to sing an old song to her. One that you sang to your own daughter.

"Stand up and let me look at you," you say, and Sifyre does as you ask. "Turn around." Again she is obedient.

You have an old mirror of polished brass. You hold it out to her and she takes it in her hand.

"You look very pretty," you say.

"I am pretty," Sifyre says and there is delight in her voice. "Nearly as pretty as Alaba."

You look at the glowing child. Sifyre will never be as beautiful as her. At least not in your eyes.

"Yes," you tell Sifyre and give her a hug. "Take Alaba for a walk. Not too far, and make sure she does not get dirty."

Sifyre nods her head. And takes Alaba's hand again. You wish you could watch them forever, but you have work to do. Bidann has brought you a rabbit. It is skinned and gutted and quartered. It's not much to feed three. You have a skillet and braise it in oil with some onion seed. Then you put it in a pot with roots and water and let it boil. You have made flatbread with the flour.

Bidann has come out from the hut to sit with you.

"That smells good," he says.

You slap his hand away as he tries to steal a flatbread.

"Wait until it's ready."

Bidann sits.

"Thank you for the rabbit," you tell him.

"No, thank you, for cooking it."

"It is kind to share it with the two of us."

"Not at all. I'm only sorry that's all there is."

You bow to show your appreciation. Bidann could have cooked and eaten the rabbit by himself. It would have made only a small meal for one. Shared between them, there will be only a little. You will only eat a few mouthfuls, you tell yourself, and Alaba will hardly eat any.

Again you bow.

"What's with all the bowing, old woman?" Bidann asks. "It's not like you."

"I have a favour to ask."

"Well then, you better ask it."

"May I share the rabbit with Sifyre? May I ask her to eat with us?"

Bidann looks right at you. What is he thinking? Why did you ask anyway? It was a stupid thing to ask.

"Yes," he says. "She can eat with us."

Sifyre has come back with Alaba. They are laughing together.

"Come," you say to her. "This good man will share his meat with you."

Sifyre looks wary.

"It's all right," says Bidann, "I won't hurt you."

She comes into the hut and looks around. You have put four bowls out. Bidann has taken his.

"Thank you for this meal," he says. You do not know if he is thanking you or the creator. In a way, it is the same thing.

"Thank you for this meal," Sifyre parrots. You know that she is hungry. Everyone in the camp is hungry. There is not enough food to go around. She takes a sip of the broth and then fishes out one of the chunks of root to eat.

"Here," you say, and pass her a piece of flatbread. She dips it into the broth. Then she eats in silence while you feed Alaba. Your own bowl is untouched.

When you finish feeding Alaba, you see that Sifyre is sitting. Her eyes are on your bowl. You are hungry too, but somehow, you know that you cannot eat it. You have lost your appetite.

"Why don't you eat that too," you say, and push the bowl over to the child. You know you will be hungry later, but you know that if you eat it, then what? There are worse things than hunger.

"No thank you," the girl says.

"Please," says Bidann. "If you do not eat it then it will go to waste."

You are thankful for his words and Sifyre takes the bowl and eats. It is still scant enough provision.

The glow from Alaba seems to shine brighter for a moment.

"She is happy," says Sifyre.

"Yes, she must be," you agree.

Sifyre rises and bows then leaves.

"Thank you," you say to Bidann.

"Don't thank me," he replies. "I didn't do anything. Besides…"

"Besides what?"

"Nothing," he replies.

What can he mean? It is clearly not nothing. You do not ask though. It is not your business.

Chapter Thirty-Two
A Tangle of Threads

Unead

Canna watches Mukito every day while you go to the weaving sheds. You pay her a few coppers and for that she feeds him and when you come home, there is food ready for you to eat. Canna is always waiting for you, holding the boy when you come home. He has grown and it seems that he will not die. For that you are glad. And more. Mukito is always happy when you come home. His face lights up with joy and he reaches for you. That moment is worth all of the coppers you pay to keep him.

Canna lives by herself. She is grateful for the coppers. And if she takes some of what she cooks for herself, what of it.

It is sensible that she should move into your hut. There is no point paying the overseers for two huts when one will do.

Now she sleeps with Mukito on the floor and you sleep over on the bench.

The soft glow of moonlight wakens you. It is time to rise. You light a lantern and Canna rises to start the charcoal burner and boil water to make tea. There are rice balls and you pass one to Mukito. Now you are dressed and ready to go.

"Take care, little one," you tell Mukito, and he reaches for you.

You head out to the weaving shed, the overseer comes and unlocks the shed, and you go over to your loom.

As you weave you listen to the chatter of the women in the shed. They are talking mostly about their children and their menfolk. But also about the cost of food.

"Can you believe how much it cost me for those radishes?" says your draw girl as she sets up the heddies.

"How much?" you ask. You have to re-thread the shuttle. Your draw girl holds up three fingers.

"Three coppers?" you ask. "For how many?"

"Only four."

"Three coppers for four radishes." You put the shuttle to one side. "That can't be right."

"I'm telling you, every day food gets dearer."

"But still…"

"My husband was so angry when I told him."

"Men are like that," you agree.

"Are you married?" the girl asks.

You sigh. Why is it that when two women speak their conversation always turns to men? Most men are not even that interesting. You have had to listen to the weaver girls talking endlessly about their husbands. It is as if they exist only to keep their husbands content. Surely women exist to do more than just serve men. Or to have babies. That is another topic of endless conversations.

You have the shuttle ready to start, but when you look up, the draw girl is looking at you.

"Are you married?"

"Let's get started," you say. You are paid by the length. Standing around talking is not going to make you any money. "Let's see if we can earn enough to buy radishes."

The girl pulls the heddies and sheds the weft. You send the shuttle flying across the threads. The looms are all running now and the clatter of shuttles is too loud to speak. Above you, the Spinner hands the Weaver a new thread to weave into your tapestry. Up and down goes the heddies. You have three shuttles, each a different colour. The new thread, the one just threaded on the shuttle, is black. A fine glossy back.

You send the shuttles backwards and forward. Then you comb down the weave with the baffle. It is a beautiful silk you are weaving; a pattern of golden chrysanthemums against black that shines in the moonlight that slips into the shed.

When the moon is at its height, you stop. It is time to eat. Your draw girl has a radish and you have some bread. You sit by the loom and begin to eat. A foreman has sent a girl round with water.

"So do you?" asks the draw girl, after you have both taken a drink. "Do you have a husband?"

Again you wonder why that is so important. Why can the girl not talk of something else?

"No," you tell her. "Not now."

"So you did have a husband. Did he beat you? Is that why you left him and came to the factories?"

"No, he did not beat me. He…" And somehow this has become painful to think on. You have tried not to think of Greba.

"So he's dead then," the girl says. "A man would not leave a woman as pretty as you. Even if you are older."

Now you are offended. "I'm not that old."

"Yes but…" and here she makes a rude gesture. "Men always like younger women."

Now you are angry, but, when you look, you see the girl is laughing. She has been teasing you.

"If I slap you with the paddle it wouldn't be enough to give you sense," you complain. But the draw girl is still laughing. "I hope you choke on that radish. Then those three coppers will have been well spent."

But you are glad that you do not have to think of Greba anymore, or Irid. It is enough to think of weaving and Canna and Mukito and of the cost of radishes.

Soon, you are back at work sending the shuttles through the threads. How slow it is, one thread at a time that the cloth grows. But it does grow and you wind the cloth on. You and the draw girl have worked well today. When the whistle for the end of the shift goes, you are pleased. You have made more than your yardage. And when you run your hand over the cloth, it is flawless. The overseer comes with his yardstick to measure, and then hands you some coppers. Twelve coppers for the draw girl and two silvers for you. You smile and put the money into your pouch. You still have all the money you got when you sold your wagon. Hidden in your hut below the fire pit, there you have your treasure. It would be enough to buy your own loom and more. Perhaps you should set up on your own. When Mukito is older, he can be your draw boy. You can teach him to weave. That way when you are too old to weave, he can keep you by weaving, and old Canna if she is still alive then.

You take your silvers and head for the market. You will get some rice and pickles to take back to the hut. There is still some moonlight in the streets, shining off the cobbles of the market. The baker's stall is open and you go to get bread. Now it is older, but hopefully, you can get it for cheaper. When you get to the stall there is only one loaf left.

"How much for your last loaf," you say. "I'll take it for nothing if you're just going to throw it away."

Sometimes that works. Sometimes the baker will give you it for nothing. But today the baker is not listening.

"How much then, for a stale old loaf? I have a few coppers. I can spare one for the loaf."

"I'm taking it home," says the baker. "My family need to eat too."

"You're feeding your family on an old, dried-up loaf like that?" you say.

"The cobbler's children have no shoes," says the baker. "We eat what we must."

"Well, what about a poor old woman like me? What can I eat?"

"I can't let my children starve," says the baker. You are pretty sure the baker has no children.

"No doubt your wife will have rice or even meat. I've never seen a starving baker yet, and by the looks of you, you could do with starving for a bit."

"It's not for sale," says the baker, but he does not take it and wrap it up, nor does he close up his stall.

"Well then, I suppose I better be on my way," you say.

"I suppose you better."

"I do like a bit of bread though. What will you say? Half the loaf? A half for me and a half for your children?"

"Six coppers."

"Six coppers, for half a stale loaf!"

"Six coppers."

"I guess I better move on then. Six coppers for half a loaf."

"I guess you better."

When you go round the stalls, the other bakers are closed, and when you come back to the first stall, he is closed too. Six coppers for half a loaf. Now you have to go back with no bread. There is no stall open selling pickles either. You will just have to eat whatever Canna has left.

When you get home, Mukito comes and climbs into your arms.

"Have you been good today?" you ask.

"He's always good," says Canna.

"I'll bet he is." When you hold Mukito, it is as if something that has been missing has been found.

"There is not much to eat," says Canna, and hands you a small bowl.

"There was nothing to buy at the market," you say. "Most of the stalls were closed. And the baker wanted six coppers for half a loaf."

"We're hardly halfway through winter. There should be plenty of food. It's still five moon turns until summer."

"Maybe a shipment was late, or perhaps bandits intercepted it. No doubt tomorrow the market will be open. I'll leave you some coins and you can go early. I was late getting out of the weaving sheds. The overseer wanted to look over my yardage. I'd done a fair bit over the quota, and he wanted to make sure I still had the weave tight. You know how it is. They are always thinking you are trying to cheat them."

You lie Mukito down in the basket next to where Canna has set her mat.

"Goodnight," you say. You are also tired. You hope you are right about the market. When you were with Greba, you never needed to worry about these things. And even now, for all your complaining you could spend six coppers or more on half a loaf. You have the money, even if you could never actually make yourself spend that much. Six coppers. It makes you laugh as you lie on your bench and blow out the candle.

Chapter Thirty-Three
Shame

Koreb

When he asks you, you know that you should not answer. Is this what he was waiting for?

"Did you come here to find this out? Is that what this is all about?" You want him to say no. But he does not look away or seem ashamed.

"Yes, I know that the child was brought here. We have records in the tower. It is why I came here in the first place. I need to know."

How much pain you feel. You thought that there was something more. You thought you had found a family. Instead, you have found a betrayer.

"What if I don't tell you?"

He leaves that question unanswered. For a moment.

"Should I call the guard? I warn you, if I take you to the tower, you will not come back out. This is better, is it not? All you need to do is answer my questions."

"I don't know what you are talking about."

"Yes, you do." Now Greba pours you a drink. "A boy, barely six months old, he was brought here a few months before the last Sunday. He was left with you. So he's about a year old now. Coming up for two years."

"As you can see, there is no child here." You do not take the offered drink, nor can you hide the hurt in your voice.

"If he was here, I would not have to ask you about him."

"Who is he? Why do you care?"

"Why do you care?" Greba replies.

"Because the Whisperer cares."

He is shuffling next to you. "I should have you taken just for saying that name."

You want to tell him to take you. You are old and have not long to wait until he comes for you.

"I will be dead soon enough," you reply and hope there is no fear in your voice.

"Not if I take you to the tower," says Greba. "No one dies there until we say so."

"I will not tell you."

"Yes, you will. In the end, everyone tells us. It's not worth it. It may make you feel better for a while to think that you have defied me. But later when I have you and you are screaming what you know it will be worse."

You look around for a knife or something sharp.

"I've already taken the knife," Greba says and holds it up. "I've had a look round, there is nothing else sharp. I take it you were thinking of killing yourself. To be honest," and here he tosses the knife up and catches it, "I would be too quick for you even if you had a knife. Do wish to try?" And here he offers you the knife handle.

"What if I don't know anything?"

"I'm sure you don't know much. But I'm not looking for much. I'm just looking for the next name. Where did he go next? Who came for him?"

"No one, he died. He was ill and did not survive."

Greba chuckles. "So then tell me who would have come for him. If he's dead then it does not matter what you tell me."

"I don't remember."

"All I need is a name. I'll do the rest. No one will know it was you that told me."

No one except you.

"What will you do to them?"

"Nothing, I promise. I want to find the child, the boy, and that is all."

"He probably is dead. What do you want him for anyway? What can a child do?"

Now you wish that you could hear his thoughts. What is going on in Greba's mind? Shall I tell you? You have asked the right question. What will you do, Greba? What will you do if you find the child of your enemy? Do you think that you can get revenge? And will that soothe your soul? Be careful. There is more, Greba, that is tied to this than you can think on.

"What will you do with the boy?" you ask again. "Will you kill him? I thought…"

"You thought what? That I am better than that, and that your homespun teaching has changed me? I am one of the twelve. I am Greba, I am the Whip. I am a servant of Vatu, a priest of darkness."

"If that is true, then why do you seek to spare my life? Why do you not just take me and torture me until I speak?"

Again, what is going on in Greba's mind? You can see thoughts spinning behind his eyes. It seems like ages until he speaks.

"I am not weak. I am not afraid of hurting you. I am not doing this for your sake. If I take you to the tower, then there are others that will know what I am doing. It would be better if they did not. Better for both the boy and for me. And of course better for you too. You can tell yourself that you are doing this to save the boy. It is better for him if he only has me to deal with."

"How is it better if you kill him? How is better for you if you are a child killer? How is it better for me if I am to blame for his death?"

Now you think to say a prayer to me. You ask me to take your life. Take me now, you say in your silent plea. And of course, I could, but I do not. You think that it is better to die than to be guilty. Perhaps you have forgotten that everyone is guilty. You have told yourself that you are better than Greba, and perhaps you are. But that is not the bar that you must pass.

"I…" and then you stop. You see that you have weakened.

"See," he tells you. He puts down the knife. He puts it between you both. He is tempting you and teasing you. "Have that drink. It is sitting there for you. Don't let it go to waste."

You take the drink and sip it. Not because you want it, but because for a few more seconds you are not guilty. For a few more seconds you hold out.

"I am a coward," you say.

"No," says Greba, "or not any more than anyone else."

"If you were me what would you do?"

Again Greba's eyes flash. What is he thinking of? He is thinking of when Irid stood at the place of justice and he did nothing. He is thinking of Alaba being cast from the tower and he did nothing. He is thinking of his daughter, raped by Kong, and he did nothing.

"I too am a coward," he says. "I would tell everything." And from the shame in his voice, you know that he is not lying.

"Promise me you will not harm the boy."

"I cannot promise you that."

"Or that you will not harm anyone else."

He shakes his head. "This is no bargaining here."

"Will he suffer?"

"I… I don't know. I have still to decide, there are many things still to decide."

"And what will you do with me?"

Greba considers for a moment. "I will let you live. If you send notice to warn them, it will only make finding the boy easier."

"As I said, he may already be dead."

"Then all of this will have been for nothing." And here Greba gestures with his hand.

"I don't have a name."

"So what do you have?"

You breathe in and let your shame take you. You have not even been beaten and you will tell him. "I have a place. I know where he was sent to. I don't even know if he made it there."

"Then tell me."

Tears are in your eyes, but still, you say the words. "Saco, he is in Saco."

There, it is done. Greba stands and goes to leave. Then he turns and hands you a bag of silver.

"I did not do it for this," you tell him.

"Then what did you do it for?"

He is gone now, and the knife is where he left it. You think to take it and to end your shame. I will not stop you, but I whisper in your ear, "There is a better way. A way to make things right."

Chapter Thirty-Four
Outcast

Ennet

Sifyre's mother is young and has no husband. Many men visit her, even men that have wives of their own. The other women hate her. They will not let her sit with them, nor will they let her grind corn with them. Once Ezena beat her badly when her husband visited the mean shack that Sifyre and her mother live in. But often the woman has bruises that the women have not given her.

And what of you, Ennet? Do you hate the woman? You do not even know her name. You are angry with her because she neglects her child. If you had been given the chance to keep your child, you would not let her go dirty and hungry. She is not your child but you do not let her go hungry.

"Someone should do something," you say, but who? You have done your best. When she comes you make sure that she has something to eat, you wash her and comb her hair. But every day, she comes back dirty and hungry. She is like a bird that once fed, returns over and over.

How troublesome it is. But also how wonderful you think.

"Am I doing your work, Whisperer?" you ask me. "But if I am, why do I have to do it over and over again? What more do you want from me?"

Sifyre is here, and she is playing with Alaba. They have a loop of string and she is showing Alaba how to play cat's cradle.

"Where did you learn that, child?" you ask as she makes the spindle, and then the loom, and then the scissors.

"My mother taught me."

Your good-for-nothing-mother. What else will she teach the girl? Nothing any good, that's for certain. You have decided.

"Stay here and watch Alaba for me," you say to Sifyre. And you go out into the moonlight into the village. That's what it is now: a village. It is a poor and mean huddle of huts and shacks but it is a village. And on the outskirts of the village are those not truly accepted. Sifyre's hut lies away from the others. You continue to walk there. And when you arrive you knock loudly on the door.

At first, no one answers, but you know that she is in there. So you continue to knock until she opens the door just the slightest and looks out.

"Who is it? What do you want?"

"It's about Sifyre," you say.

The door opens a fraction wider, and you see that she is not fully dressed. There is noise from behind her. The woman turns and says something. And then a man pushes past you without a word. You do not look at each other.

"What has she done?"

"Nothing, she's fine."

"Then what?"

"You need to take better care of her," you say.

The door is open now and you see that she is thinner than worn cotton, she needs to take better care of herself.

"What has it to do with you?"

"She comes to my house every day looking for food."

"I will tell her to stop."

"No." No, that is not what you want. You do not want to lose Sifyre.

"Then what?"

"I will keep her. I will look after her."

"You want to take my daughter? I won't allow it."

"She'd be better with me. I can feed her, and besides…" You do not say what, but you both know what you mean. "She should not have to end up like you."

When you say the words you wish you could take them back, even if they are the truth. For a moment, the woman's dark eyes flash with anger. "I am her mother."

You choke back your reply. You bow your head and let her anger burn itself out.

"I am sorry," you say. You wish you knew what words would stop her anger. But her anger does not last long. It is a slight, frail thing that burns out in a moment. You stand and realize that her life is not the one she wished for.

"What is your name?" you ask. "I am Ennet."

"Dova," she replies.

"That is a nice name."

"It was after my grandmother."

"Sifyre is a nice girl, she helps me with Alaba."

"You mean the shining child?"

"Yes, she is very helpful. I don't know how I would manage without her. She plays with her while I grind corn or if I am cooking, drawing water. Sometimes she helps with that too. I'm too old to carry water from the stream, she is a great help."

Dova's face brightens with pride. "She is a clever girl."

You would not go that far, you tell yourself, but then you think, why not. She is clever. She is good at playing and making Alaba laugh, and when you show her how to do something, she learns quickly.

"She is," you agree.

"It is all right for you," says Dova. "You have a man to look after you. The women dare not spit at you or take your corn."

"No, they don't," you agree, and you realize how fortunate you are that Bidann has let you stay in his home.

Dova is crying now and cursing yourself as a soft fool, you reach out to her. She draws back.

"Sifyre can come as often as she likes. I will feed her what I can when she helps me."

"I have nothing to give her most of the time," says Dova. You wonder then what the men bring to her in exchange if she has nothing to eat. But you do not ask. It would seem the oldest profession is not the most lucrative. There is a scent of cactus mescal. Is that what they bring you? Is that what makes you open the door to them? You have seen it many times. A woman that will do anything for alcohol, and men too. It is just that they do different things, otherwise, it is the same. You understand a little better now.

"Yes, that would be good. I would have no problem with that."

"She can stay overnight sometimes," you continue. "There may be times that it is better if she is not here. It will just be sometimes."

Dova stiffens.

"It will be for you to decide what is best. But if you think that you do not need her here, then she can stay the night. It would be a big help," you say.

"And what of that man?" Dova says, looking you in the eye.

"You mean Bidann? The cabin has two rooms. He does not sleep with us. It will be quite safe. Quite respectable."

"He comes here too, you know."

You knew. You did not know for certain, but you knew.

"He is not my son," you say. "He is free to do as he wishes."

"What is he like?" Dova asks.

"Bidann, well, you probably know more than I do. You've seen him. He's big and strong and a good worker. He built our hut and did a really good job. He's a good provider. Most days he catches something, even now when game is scare. He'll get something for certain. Like I say, you've seen him. I suppose he's handsome enough. He's a bit impetuous, a bit idealistic."

"He says he wants me to be his woman." That comes as a bit of a shock. But when you think about it, that would be like Bidann.

"Did he?" You can think of nothing else to say.

"Yes, he did. He asked me if I would move into his cabin, or if I wanted, he would build a new cabin for just me and him. He said if I was his woman, he'd make sure I got corn and rice like the rest of the women."

"Really."

"Yes, really. I said no. If I had said yes, then he would have had to fight all of the others. Some wouldn't bother. But Gaesta would. Gaesta would want to fight him. One of them would get killed."

"I think Bidann could take care of Gaesta," you say, thinking of Bidann. You cannot see him losing any fight.

"I think so too," says Dova, "if it was a fair fight. But I know Gaesta. It wouldn't be. And if it wasn't a fair fight then maybe Bidann would be killed."

Now Dova is shutting the door. "I told him no anyway. " And you are relieved not because you think Bidann would die. You have seen those that need to drink. Dova would betray Bidann for a flask of wine or mescal.

"What about Sifyre," you ask as the door closes on the sad woman.

"Send her home tomorrow, after midmoon."

Chapter Thirty-Five
The Camp

Utas

Erroi has joined you on the wagon. "What is this?" he asks you and points to the moonstone. It is now glowing brilliantly.

"I do not know," you tell him. "Can you not tell me?" But Erroi is no longer interested in the glowing stone. If he knows, he is not going to tell you, and when you reach for his mind, you cannot find it.

"What do you want?" you ask him.

"I want to help."

"Help do what?" you ask.

"I don't know. What do you want to do?"

"I…" But you do not know what you want to do. Why are you still going?

"I want to find my daughter."

"Our daughter," Erroi says. It does not matter.

"Yes, our daughter," you agree. Ahead you see a cluster of mean looking huts. "Why have you brought me here?" you ask, but when you look, Erroi has gone.

You can hear a shout coming from the huts, and men come running. They have bows and clubs. You would turn away if there was a way to escape.

"Who are you and what is that?" a thin, bald man asks.

"My name is Utas."

"Utas," the leader of the men repeats. "What do you want here, Utas?"

"I want nothing. I will be happy to go on my way."

"I'm sure you would," says the bald man. "But I don't think that is going to be possible. Why don't you come down and let us have a good look at you? Then we can decide what to do with you."

He is not making a request. And you feel your muscles tighten. In your mind, you count the bandits and weigh up your chances. Once it would not have been a consideration. You would have killed them all without a thought. Once you could have, now with old bones and the darkness gone from inside you, you are not so sure. So you tie the reins and clamber down.

The bald man is taller than you thought, even if he is scrawny.

"I'm sure there is no need for all of this," you tell him.

"Gaesta, check the wagon. And see what is going on with that stone."

A broad-shouldered man walks forward and climbs onto your wagon.

"Be careful," you protest. But he ignores you. You can hear him climbing over your goods in the back, and then he comes out.

"Cloth," Gaesta says. "Bolts of cloth."

"We could use that," says another bandit. And it is true, most of them are dressed in rags.

"Any food?"

"Some," says Gaesta. "There's a barrel of oats, some flour, and a bag of apples. Not much."

"Get it unloaded," and two more bandits go to help Gaesta take your belongings.

They carry the food away first. One of the bandits sticks an apple in his mouth, and Condito shouts, "Hey! None of that. That's going into the stores so no helping yourself. That apple is coming out of your share."

Two other bandits have cut the traces on your horse and are leading it away from the wagon.

"Don't take my food," you protest. "Don't take my horse."

"We're just making sure everyone gets what they need," says Condito. "You'll get a share too."

"I need to be on my way," you protest.

"To where?" asks Condito. And you realize that you do not know where.

"I am looking for something."

"Oh yes? What are you looking for?" He turns and looks at you.

"I am… I am looking for my daughter."

"Your daughter. Where do you think you will find your daughter? Where is your daughter?"

"I think she is at the City of the Sun," you say.

"So that's where you're heading, is it. Do you have a pass?"

"No. I..." What? You don't need one? There may have been a time when that was true, but not now. You are no longer the high priest of darkness. You will need a pass. Or even a pass might not be enough. They might kill you, Vatu's guards might kill you if they know who you are. And the bandits might kill you too. You could die here in this mean bandit village. Or die on the trail of starvation if they drive you out. "I don't have a pass."

"Where did you get that stone?" Condito asks.

"I found it," you say truthfully.

"Where?"

"It was buried in the ground, and I could see it shining. I dug it up and took it with me."

"What is it?"

"I don't know. I really don't. If I was guessing I would say part of the moon, but how a part of the moon gets to be buried in the forest, I don't know. And it does not shine at the same time as the moon, or not always. And if you cover it over, it stops shining. I've never seen anything like it before." No, nothing, not in all of your unremembered lifetimes.

The stone has been moved from your wagon, and now sits just in front of Condito. "I've never seen anything like this either," he says. "It must be valuable." And he is correct.

"You may keep it if you wish. You may keep it as payment for letting me go on my way." You know that you cannot give up on the child. You must find Alaba.

Condito looks at you as if you are mad, and then someone strikes you hard from behind. You fall to the soft, springy moss. Count to ten, I tell you. It will do you no good to rise again and fight. "Must I suffer this too?" you ask me. It seems that you must. All that is really injured is your pride, and you have told me that you have none.

"What is that for?" you ask.

"I do not make bargains," says Condito. "Everything you have is mine now."

"I ask only to go on my way."

It is Condito that kicks you. He is stronger than he looks and the kick is hard in your midriff. It leaves you breathless.

"You are mine too. Do you think I will let you wander off and set the guards on us? You could tell them where we are camped."

"I would not," you protest. But your words are met with another blow.

"There is only one question," says Condito and he smiles at you, showing his teeth. "Are you worth keeping alive? We do not need another mouth to feed."

"I only want to find my daughter," you say.

"Perhaps she is already dead. If we kill you then we might be sending you to her." He reaches down and grabs your hair. He puts a knife to your throat.

It is too much you tell me, and you reach up to his arm, then throw him to the ground and take the knife and then you stop. It would be so easy to kill him. It would be over in an instant. He deserves it. You feel anger and hate and fear build within you. But I have laid my hand on yours. Stay your hand and show mercy, I beg of you.

"He deserves to die," you say. Yes, but you do not deserve to be a killer. Have we not put that behind us?

You climb to your feet and then toss the blade aside. It is all so quick that the other bandits have had no time to react. They rush forward and then hesitate when you turn towards them.

Condito raises himself from the ground and spits. He is angry too. And then he laughs.

"So, you can fight at least. That is something. You need to teach me that trick."

"It's not a trick," you tell him. But then you think perhaps it is.

"Where did you learn that? Are you a soldier?"

"I am nothing but a poor traveller," you say.

"Poor travellers can't do that," he says. "No lies. Tell me who you are."

No lies. Is that even possible? What is the truth anyway?

You open your mouth but no words come out. Who are you? You do not know anymore.

Suddenly, there is a woman by your side. You have never met her before but she is standing beside you.

"He is a servant of the Whisperer," she says. "The author of all things has sent him to us." Then she turns to you and asks, "What is your daughter's name?"

"Her name is Alaba," you reply and then you see her. She is walking towards you. Has it really been so long, now she can walk? How many summers? Three perhaps? A taller girl is holding her hand. The other girl is about ten and very dirty. But you can look only at Alaba. She is alive. Alaba looks at you but does not know who you are. That is good. If she knew all of your sins, how could you find it within you to face her? She is glowing with a soft light, and when she gets nearer, you fall to the ground and begin to cry.

Chapter Thirty-Six
The Hall of Shrouded Mirrors

Greba

In the darkness, you stand. Around you, you sense but cannot see the mirrors that line the walls. They are old and almost forgotten. But you have not forgotten. The twelve do not forget. There are a hundred mirrors; each one has never seen the light. Each one is paired with another far away. Long ago Vatu made them. He took the darkness and split it in half. He placed one half in one mirror and the other in another. Then each half mirror was sent around the dark lands, one to each province. All that is needed to travel is to step through the mirror and go from one darkness to another. How easy is that?

You have never been through the mirrors. Not in this life at least. No one goes through them now. People hesitate to use them. What is so important that you need to travel in an instant? The mirrors are scarcely used. And anyway, only one person can use them at a time.

In the dark, you find the mirror linked to Saco. Has it ever been used? Not in your lifetime. Perhaps none of them have. If you step through you will find yourself in Saco. But what will you find?

Why do you hesitate? You are not afraid of the dark. If you step through the mirror, then you can be in Saco without any of the others knowing where you have gone. You can step through but what then?

"You should let it go. Your granddaughter is alive. Let the other child live too."

"But she has been taken from me."

"She is being kept safe."

"I have lost everything."

Yes, you have. But what have you done to deserve what you had? What did you do to keep it? In the end, you made your choice, and now you must make another choice. Now you should let it go.

"And what if I do not? Will you stop me? Will you punish me?" How angry you are. But no, I will not stop you. I will not force you. You must be redeemed by your own will.

"I will not stop you."

"Will not, or cannot. It seems there is much that you will not do. You would not save my daughter or my or her child." You will not goad me to do something I have no wish to do. "Show me your great power." You try to tempt me.

But my greatest power is the power to change hearts. And bit by bit I will change yours. When you come to me, you will find me waiting for you. I have given you my word and I will wait a thousand lifetimes or more. I will be ready when you come.

You step towards the mirror. Your anger is stronger than your fear. Now you do not hesitate, and you step boldly forward. Straight through you plunge into that pool of darkness and step into the other side.

How does it feel to step through? There is no physical sensation. Your stomach does not lurch nor does your head spin, or your heart stop. But it is still strange to pass from one place to another.

What did you expect? You find that you are still in darkness. Is this a store cupboard? Has the dark portal been put away next to unused furniture and boxes of old clothes? You feel around with your fingers and find the wall of the cupboard and following the wall, you find the door. It is locked. But that will not stop you. You put your shoulder to the door and push. It cracks and bursts. Outside you are still in darkness, but you can see light coming from the end of the corridor and head towards it. The noise of breaking the door has not brought anyone to you, but when you reach the end of the corridor and turn there are two guards.

"What are you doing here?" one says, and they both hold out their spears. You want to kill them. You are not sure why. It is the anger that rises within you. You know that if you kill them, you will just have to find others to take you to the governor. So instead you step into the light.

"I am the Whip," you say. And one of the soldiers drops his spear. You are slightly impressed that they did not both drop them.

"What is your name?" you ask the soldier who still holds his spear.

"Caester," replies the soldier.

"Do you know who I am?"

The soldier nods. "How did you get here? How can we help you?"

You do not answer his first question, but to the second, you bark out a command, "Take me to the governor of this town."

The guards say nothing, but turn and walk along the corridors. It does not take you long to arrive at the offices of the governor. There are more guards, and they whisper together. They think that you cannot hear them. There is so much fear in their voices. The other guards are reluctant to allow you access, but they know that they cannot keep you out. But it is unheard of for one of the twelve to turn up unannounced. A messenger is sent to the governor, and then he returns with more questions. In the end, they let you enter. What other choice do they have? You could have made them let you in before now, but you are patient. You do not need to hurry.

"Please come with me, sir," the clerk says to you and bows. At least this one has manners.

He leads you into the brightly lit office of the governor, who rises when you enter and then abases himself.

"Rise," you say. And the governor does as you command. He stands with his head bowed and does not speak.

"What is your name?" you ask. Not that it matters.

"Perdona," he replies. "How may I serve you?"

"I require information."

"Yes, great one. What information do you require?"

"It concerns heretics."

"We have no heretics here, great one."

You consider smiting him for contradicting you. But let it pass.

"I believe otherwise. I am not saying you are to blame. But I know there are heretics here. Or suspect heretics at least."

"In the cloth sheds, there are some who believe in the Weaver, the Spinner and the Cutter. It is there that you will find heretics."

"None that believe in the Whisperer?" you ask.

The governor looks up in shock when you say that word.

"No, great one. That would not be tolerated. No one can believe in him and live." And yet here you are, and here I am. You believe in me, or at least acknowledge that I am. You hear my voice, just like the others. They all hear me calling to them, even you and even Perdona.

"I am looking for a child," you continue. "I believe he was brought here by heretics."

Now on solid ground, the governor calls to his clerk. "What date was the child brought?" he asks you. "If it was brought here then we can check the records." He does not say no one can live in Saco without being on their records, everyone knows that.

"A boy, about three years old now. Brought from the City of the Sun. Maybe two years ago, perhaps less." Has it really been three summers since that day?

Perdona motions to the clerk who rushes off to the archive.

"Do you wish refreshment while you wait?" Perdona asks. And you sit on the couch that the governor ushers you to.

The wait is longer than expected. Perdona has provided wine, but you do not drink it. "Water is better."

"Of course."

When the clerk returns, he looks worried.

"Great one, there are no records of any child coming from the City of the Sun to settle in Saco."

"What of children coming from other places?"

"There are five names. But the records indicate they are older and two are not males."

"So," you say, "the child is here but not recorded. He must be hidden. What about older people coming from the City of the Sun?"

"Many have come to trade, or on other business. We produce much of the finest silk. But few settle here."

"But you have looked?"

"Yes, of course, great one. I have looked. No children. No families. One settler, a woman aged forty who works in the weaving shed. That is all over the past three years."

"And from other areas?"

"Over the last three years, we have admitted four people other than the woman. We admit few to Saco. Our weaving sheds are full, and very few new workers are needed. If you wish, we can have them all brought here."

"No," you say. "Give me the list and I will deal with the matter. You have been helpful." With that, you rise, and so too do the clerk and the governor. "I have the information that I need," you tell them. "Please forget about my coming. Tell no one. Do nothing."

"It will be as you say." You are handed a parchment. You leave and command the guard to stay. You trace your way back to the mirror and once more you step into darkness, through darkness and out of darkness. Once more you are in the hall of mirrors and you carry the scroll back to your room. There you light a candle and read the list of names. There at the very top of the list, you read and for a moment your breath stops. You read it again and again: "Unead." You have not found the child but you have found something better and something worse. You have found the wife you sought to protect. The one you hoped to keep safe and hidden even from yourself.

Unead. The thought of her fills you with joy and with fear. You think of her dark hair and soft touch. You think of her laugh and of all the life that has passed between you. How you wish to go to her, but you are afraid. What darkness will you bring with you? What darkness will you bring upon her? What have you done?

Chapter Thirty-Seven
A Picture

Arraio

You find painting relaxing. It makes you think only of the moment, of the process of putting paint onto vellum. There is the craft of it, mixing colours, preparing hides and stretching them on frames. All of that takes your mind off things and off the past. There is also the art of it. The skill of making your hand form what your mind has conjured. The consideration of line and contrast. So much beauty. The feel of the brush as you drag it along. It is more than relaxing, it is ecstasy and it is torture.

And there is that other thing too. It is also an art. It is the art of seeing. Of looking. All your lives you have been an observer. Even in that first one long, long ago. You can barely recall it. The darkness keeps you safe from the thought of it. And what did you do that was so wrong? Nothing, all you did was look. All you did was observe. And measure and record. It is just like painting. It is about seeing. You see what no one else has seen. And you have made a picture, a story. If you had not then the story would not have been told. Dispassionate. That is the role of the observer. You could not think of them as people or as children, and not as victims. You could only think of them as objects to be observed.

Why does that make you guilty? The Whisperer has erred in bringing you here. But it is not the Whisperer that came to you all those lives ago and made a deal. It is not the Whisperer that lied to you and brought you to this hell. The darkness took your guilt and hid it. There are no secrets from the dark, but the dark contains many secrets. The darkness has hidden your guilt and the guilt of all the twelve. But now that bargain is beginning to unravel, and you do not know if you are happy or sad. Afraid certainly.

Here is your secret, this picture that you paint. You have painted it in every lifetime and it is always the same. How odd everyone looks in that picture. Especially you. You are wearing a white coat. It is as if you were a priest of light and life instead of a priest of darkness. How strange that once you thought you were the opposite of what you are.

You still see them. What is seen cannot be unseen. Even the darkness cannot change that. You see what has been done to them, the children and the others. You make pictures and sketches. You measure with calipers. You make them stand naked while you measure and observe.

You paint those faces now. Little gnomelike creatures with swollen heads or shrunken heads or with growths disfiguring their faces. Some are twisted. It is as if they have been melted and reformed, but reformed by hands clumsier than God's. They have been reformed by men's hands.

You can see the fear and worry in their faces. You have captured a perfect likeness of it. What a skilled artist you are.

"I should not be doing this," you say. But you cannot stop yourself. You have to do it. Each brush stroke is a caress of those creatures, you cannot bring yourself to call them children. It was not a crime. It was a service. With this knowledge, men are armed for the future.

You move your eye behind the children and paint the cherry blossom and the trees. The blossoms are falling through the air like a pink rain. They are flying in the wind like a thousand tiny cranes. Fluttering like scraps of paper.

"I did nothing wrong," you say again. "I did what I could to help." Which was nothing: you did nothing to help. Dispassionate, an observer. You did nothing. And when they stood naked before you, as counted and measured and weighted, did you not see what you did to them? Could you really think of nothing to do for them? What thoughts did go through your mind?

When you counted and measured and weighed, did you not see that it was your own soul that was being measured? Found wanting. Found to be short.

"I cannot be responsible for everyone." And so you became responsible for no one. So you became responsible for nothing. You took your secret knowledge and kept it. You gave it only to your masters. You licked their feet like a dog.

“I could not have saved them.”

You step back and look at your brush strokes. The picture is almost complete.

Chapter Thirty-Eight
A Dream

Unead

What a dream you had, and at your age too. It was as if he came to you. And you took him in. Why would you not? Besides, you are not that old. Greba, his name is sweet in your mouth. When you wake, you turn towards him but he is not there. You let your hand drift over the coverlet to an empty space. Most nights he spent away from you anyway, so why now is it that when the moon is down, that is when you miss him most? It's almost time to rise anyway. Canna and Mukito are sleeping. The stillness interrupted only by their breathing. You say a silent prayer to the Weaver that she will weave a pattern for Greba and keep him safe. Then you think how silly it is to pray to one of the small hidden gods to save the priest of darkness. As if the Weaver could do anything against the power of Vatu. Or that the Weaver should reward Greba more than his master. Vatu will take care of his own. Or so you have always been told.

You blow on the embers of the fire, but they will not light. A quick prayer to Motoni, the master of the hearth, and to your delight the embers glow red and spring to life. Soon you have enough heat to put the kettle on the flames.

The flames spread a flickering light across the room, and Mukito rises first and runs to you. He hugs you tight and once again you are glad that you did not let him die when you found him abandoned.

"Good moon to you boy," you say, trying to hide the love in your heart.

He is looking at you but says nothing. What a quiet child he is.

Now Canna is rising.

"Here, let me take that," she says and tries to take over.

"I can make tea," you protest.

"Hmm," says Canna. But settles back down. "You always make it too weak."

"You always make it too strong. It is better if you can taste it without the flavour overpowering."

Canna shrugs. She is thinking that you are too used to drinking tea when there is something for the flavour to overpower and not when it is the only flavour that you have. She says nothing. She does not want to let on that she knows that once you were rich and that you have never known hunger.

Even now, when food is scarce and costs so much, somehow you always find a little extra to buy what you need. Canna does not want you to know she has seen the hidden purse of coins in the rafters. She does not want you to think that she might steal it and cast her out. If you have secrets, then she is happy to let you keep them.

"Sleep well?" she asks you. And instantly you wonder why she is asking.

"Yes, very well," you say. "Why?"

"No reason. Just usually I'm up first."

You say nothing but drink your tea. "I should be going soon." The horned moon is rising. It is time to go to the weaving sheds.

"Have some bread," says Canna. But you know there is not enough, and if you take it then Canna and Mukito will go short.

"No, I have enough."

"If you go hungry and cannot work, then we will all starve."

"I have enough," you say again, and pull a wrap around you. The crescent moon sheds only little heat. Then you head out into the street. Mukito shouts after you, and even though you do not turn back it makes you smile.

In the town, you think you can smell him behind you. You almost turn to check, but you know that he cannot be there. There is no way that he can find you. There is no way that he should find you. But always you think of him. If he were here, he would carry your work bag. It is not heavy, and you can carry it fine. But you think of those times you went to the market together and he carried home the things that you bought. He did not need to do that, he could have had a porter bring them later. There were so many things that he did not need to do, but he did them anyway, and when he did you were glad.

As you walk to the sheds, you hear a voice in the shadows. For just a moment, you think it is him. But it is not. It is one of the foremen.

"Hurry up Unead, you do not want to be late. They will dock your wages."

You are not late, nor will you be. Still, you bow your head and turn to rush on.

"Wait up," says the foreman. "You can't get in until I unlock the sheds."

It would be impolite to rush on, but you wish that you could. You feel uncomfortable now. Aware that he is just behind you. And now beside you.

"That looks like a heavy bag."

"No, not heavy," you tell him.

"Want me to carry it?"

"Thank you, it is not heavy. It is fine."

How long has it been since a man made you afraid? And he is just being kind. You cast your eyes around looking for someone you know and shout over to your draw-girl.

"Hey Injutil," you shout and hurry over to her.

"What?" says the girl when you arrive. "What has set your treads in a tangle?"

You say nothing but Injutil looks over to Brau and laughs. "He's harmless," she says, "and about your age too I would think."

But her words do not make you feel better. They make you feel worse. And above unseen, the Spinner is spinning, the Weaver is weaving and the Cutter is holding the scissors.

Chapter Thirty-Nine
A Guest

Ennet

There is a deal of commotion outside. You are not quite sure what is going on. There is always some trouble in the bandit camp. Why should you bother? You are washing and mending Sifyre's clothes. They are still too small and her arms and legs stretch out past the hems of the skirts and sleeves. You should make her new clothes.

"I will, in time," you tell me, "but she needs something to wear in the meantime."

You are sitting by candlelight threading a needle. It is taking you longer than you thought it would. Your old eyes are not what they were. Unseen, I breathe upon your eyes and now you can see just well enough to thread the needle. You take the thin material and start to sew a rip closed.

"Is it worth it?" you ask. But then you look at Sifyre sitting wrapped in a blanket. She is staring at you with those eyes full of hope and gratitude. You sew quickly with neat little stitches. The cloth holds the thread at least, but there are other parts where you will have to patch over.

"It won't take me long," you tell Sifyre. Alaba is walking around the room. "Come here and stand by me," you say. And in the glow from her skin, you can see much better.

The noise is getting louder. You are nearly finished.

"What is going on outside?" you ask, and look over at Bidann. But he does not take your meaning. Instead, he sits thinking. You wonder what he is thinking and you hope it is not what you fear.

You hope he is not thinking of Sifyre's mother.

"What's on your mind?" you ask.

"Nothing," he replies.

"I spoke to Sifyre's mother," you tell him.

"Oh yes?"

"I've agreed to look after the child. She'll be staying here mostly from now on."

Bidann looks at you. "Why?"

"Because the child needs looked after and Dova can't look after her."

"Dova's all right. People should leave her alone."

Now you put down your sewing. What can you say? Dova is not all right.

"I wonder how she ended up the way she is," you say.

"What do you mean?"

You look at Sifyre. "Here child, that's as good a job as I can do." You hand her the dress. "Why don't you take Alaba outside into the moonlight?" You do not want to talk ill of her mother in front of the child. Although looking at her, you realize she will not be a child for much longer. That is another reason that she should stay with you.

When the children are gone, you turn back to Bidann. "No woman starts off wanting to be a whore."

"Don't call her that."

"If you like. I can see that you like her, but be careful."

"If you knew what she's been through," said Bidann, "you would not be so quick to judge."

But you do know what she's been through, or you can imagine.

"I'm not judging her," you say. "But things are as they are."

"This is my house," says Bidann.

"I am grateful," you say. And you are. "I am grateful for all you do for me and for Alaba."

Bidann nods.

"I must go and speak with her," he says.

Now you are holding your breath. So he will ask her.

"She would be welcome," you tell him. "But you must be careful. She will not change. And there are other men."

"Do you think I don't know? She tells me everything. She has no choice. She needs to eat."

There never seems to be a choice, you think. There is no point in saying more to Bidann, he will not listen.

Sifyre comes to the door. "Grandma, you must come and see

this." And glad of a reason to leave Bidann to his thoughts, you follow her out into the street.

There you see it. A stone that shines like the full moon. Its light is brighter than the weak shine of the crescent that floats above the sky. What is this, you ask me. And I whisper in your ear.

You see a knot of bandits around a man. They are angry and they have their bows drawn. You think they will kill him. You are not wrong, and I tell you to hurry. You gather your skirts and run. I hold your hand to make certain that you do not fall. You push your way through the crowd. Where does that strength come from? What is it about you that makes the bandits fall back?

"Stop," you say, "do not kill him." Even Condito wavers. But then the man falls to the ground weeping. And when you turn you see that he is looking at Alaba.

"She is my daughter," he says.

"Get out of the way, old woman," says Condito. He is angry, but you must not let him kill the stranger.

"The Whisperer will not let you kill him," you say. "He is here, and he will do what is needed to protect this man."

"The Whisperer," says Gaesta, and spits. "This is what I think of the Whisperer." And he swings his club down towards the stranger's head. Almost effortlessly, I take your hand and use it to catch his. We stop the blow inches from the stranger's head. If you had not stopped him, then he would have caved the stranger's head in.

Gaesta looks at you in anger and amazement. The other bandits laugh.

"Can't beat an old woman, Gaesta."

Angrily he swings the club at you, but I trip him and he falls to the ground.

"Sober up, you drunk. You need to spend less time drinking mescal with that whore," the bandits jeer.

The stranger has now risen to his feet. Condito is looking him in the eye.

"I am the leader here," says Condito, and turning to Gaesta continues, "You're lucky you slipped, if you'd killed anyone without my say so then you'd have been next."

Gaesta picks himself up. "I'm not drunk," he protests.

"So." Now Condito is speaking to you. "What does the Whisperer want us to do with him?"

You consider. "I suppose he wants something to eat."

"Don't we all," grumbles one of the bandits.

"I won't give you more food for him," says Condito.

"That is fine. We will make do."

"All right, but until we're sure, he'll have to wear these," and he tosses a set of manacles to another of the bandits, who puts them on his arms and legs. The stranger does not resist. But even chained he looks dangerous. What are you doing Whisperer, you ask me.

"So, you'll be responsible if he tries anything."

"I will," you reply and lead the stranger back to your hut.

"My name is Utas," says the stranger.

"Pleased to meet you," you say and bow. "My name is Ennet."

"Where is this place?"

"It is just a bandit camp."

"But you are no bandit."

"No, I am a prisoner, like you."

Bidann is waiting by the hut. He has seen everything. He looks threateningly at Utas. "This is my house," he says.

"Are you a bandit?" Utas asks.

"No, he is a prisoner like us," you reply.

"I'm not a prisoner," says Bidann.

But if you are not a prisoner then what are you? You are not a bandit for all your posturing. And bravado.

"I am Utas," the stranger says to Bidann and bows. That seems to satisfy Bidann.

In the hut, Alaba comes and hides behind your skirts.

"Who is that?"

"Someone is coming to stay with us," you say. You fire up the wood burner, no charcoal here, and make tea.

"Can you hunt?" asks Bidann.

"Not in these," Utas replies, holding up his manacles.

"So what can you do?"

Utas seems to think for a moment and then says, "I can fish. Once I was a farmer, but that seems long ago now."

"They should start to farm. I have told them. They have barely enough food."

"It is still a long time until Sunday," says Utas.

"That is why I hunt. There is not enough food to go around. The others think they can hunt, but they can't. There is more to it than just being able to fire a bow."

"I'm sure there is."

Utas crouches down on the floor. He does not want to antagonize Bidann. So again he bows his head. You forget how young Bidann is.

"You should have spoken to me first," he says to you. And you bow.

"Yes, Bidann."

Now he feels stupid. Well, you think, that is because he has been stupid.

"Tell us about yourself, Utas," you ask. "Where do you come from? How did the Whisperer call to you?"

Utas looks at you.

"The Whisperer," he says. "He has spoken to me all my life and all my lives."

"Lives," says Bidann. "Only the twelve and the high priest of Vatu are trapped here for more than one life."

Utas has bowed his head. "I am not one of them," he says. "Not anymore."

There is silence for a while, but silence never lasts. Perhaps there is no such thing, you think. The fire still cracks, the kettle hums, the wind blows through the crack in the door. You wait for him to continue and when he does not, Bidann speaks.

"But you were? How can that be? How can you escape Vatu?"

"With the Whisperer, all things are possible." It is your voice and my words.

"But even so," says Bidann. "If you are the high priest of darkness, then we should..."

But Bidann does not know what he should do.

"Kill me perhaps?" asks Utas calmly.

"Yes, kill you," says Bidann. "I could do it." But it is bravado.

"Have you killed any before?" asks Utas.

"No," admits Bidann. "But I could do it. It would be just like shooting a squirrel or a rabbit."

"It would not," says Utas.

"And you would know? You must have killed hundreds of people."

"Yes," Utas agrees. "Many hundreds just in this life."

"And you think that makes you better than me."

"No, it makes me worse. I am reborn over and over, but consider, each of my lives did not start one after another. I am reborn before I died, before I was born. I am reborn as a man or as a woman. I am reborn as a priest or as a slave. I am reborn as a beast and a bird. Everything I am reborn as."

"What you are saying makes no sense."

You interrupt. "It is not what the Whisperer teaches. When we die we do not stay here, but go to another life."

“That is correct,” says Utas. “And is that not a rebirth? I have been reborn as you and as Ennet. I have been reborn as everyone that ever lived, and they have been reborn as me.”

“I do not believe that,” Bidann says.

“You do not have to,” says Utas, “but when you harm someone, when you kill them, you are harming yourself, yourself reborn. Each and every one of us is you, and you are each and every one of us too.”

“That sounds like superstitious nonsense,” Bidann protests. And then looks at you.

“I don’t know,” you say. “I don’t suppose it matters. The Whisperer did not reveal anything like that to me. But he told me to be kind to everyone. Even if they are not part of me, it is what I have been asked to do.”

“That is what I have been asked also,” says Bidann. “Sometimes I forget. It is hard. He did say we are all his. That we have a part of him in us. Maybe that is the same thing.”

“Maybe,” says Utas. “I am not a priest of the Whisperer, only a follower.”

“They are not followers of the Whisperer here.”

“I know.”

“They don’t even pretend to be. Some of them worship the small gods. But most of them have given their hearts to darkness.”

“He will still redeem them,” says Utas. I whisper the truth of it to you and to Bidann.

Bidann laughs. “If he can redeem the high priest of darkness, then he can redeem a bunch of bandits, for sure.”

“Bidann,” you protest.

“You will need to keep who you are secret from the bandits. Otherwise, who knows what they will do.”

“I have told them I was a farmer. There are plenty of poor farmers scraping by in the wilderness. Besides, it’s not a lie. I used to work with a shop owner collecting food and selling it in town.”

“You look more like a farmer than a high priest, that’s for sure,” says Bidann.

Chapter Forty
Talking

Utas

Bidann's words please you. And you think of Huneko, your stepfather. The man you lived with until you, another you entirely, killed him. You were hiding from yourself. Living an easy life with Huneko and his wife Tandan, your foster mother, and Nino, your foster sister. But you found yourself, and would not let yourself be at peace. If the Whisperer had not come you would still not be at peace.

"I will take that as a compliment," you say. "I wish I was a farmer."

"Perhaps you will be. You do look like one, especially with those chains on."

"I've been demoted to field hand," you laugh. But then you feel ashamed. Even when you lived with Huneko, you had no sympathy for those slaves. Even when you thought you were free there was still darkness within you.

"There are worse things to be," you say. "Where is Alaba? Where is my daughter?"

"She is playing. She will be back soon. Why does she glow?"

"I do not know. It is a miracle. It is the work of the Whisperer."

"But why? What does it mean? Why has he done this?"

Ennet hands you a cup of tea as she asks you the question and you take a sip. It is warm and refreshing. You thank her.

"Who can say?" you reply. But I can say. I can tell you if you ask. I could tell you that every child glows with an inner light. Each and every one. But I have changed you so that you can see that light. Everyone can see the light within her. It is the light within you all. But you do not ask me, and I remain silent.

"It is a sign," says Bidann.

"A sign of what?" you ask.

"It is a sign that the world is at an end. It is a sign that Vatu's reign is over. It is a sign that the Whisperer walks among us and will help us."

"Help us do what?" you ask.

Bidann smiles. "His work."

But what is his work, you wonder.

Ennet rises. "I have work to do," she says.

"May I help?" you offer.

"He could help me get firewood," says Ennet. "If he's going to stay, he may as well help."

"All right," agrees Bidann. "I suppose I better go looking for game, now that there are two extra mouths to feed." He gathers his bow and leaves.

"Come on then," says Ennet, and leads you out into the moonlight. Your stone is shining in the clearing. It is almost as bright as day but much colder.

"This way," Ennet tells you and hands you a sack. Together you head out to the forest edge. Ennet is holding a short hatchet. It occurs to you that you could take the hatchet and break the manacles. But then what? It is here you want to be, with Alaba.

In the forest, there is lots of fallen wood. It is dry and brittle. It will burn well. You bend down and start to fill your sack. Ennet also is collecting wood but she is too far away to speak to. Eventually, your sack is full.

"Do you need help?" you call over to Ennet.

"No, I've got a full bag, thank you." You gather your sack and walk towards her.

You have gone deeper into the forest than you think. When you arrive by Ennet's side, she motions you to crouch down and puts her finger to her lip. You hear someone approaching. You see the bandit that put the manacles on you. Is he here for you? Or for Ennet?

You watch and then you see approaching, Bidann. He has been successful in his hunt. He is carrying a brace of hares. When he sees the bandit, he stops.

"Not like you to be out hunting, Gaesta," he says. "Run out of rice wine?"

"I'm not hunting," says Gaesta. "Or at least, not animals."

Bidann laughs. “Just as well then, you’d scare them all off.”

Gaesta does not laugh. “I want you to stay away.”

“From what?”

“From her. She’s mine.”

“Yours,” says Bidann. “Really.”

“Yes, mine.”

“You better tell her that.”

“Oh, she knows. I’ve made sure of that. She’d forgotten for a while. But I reminded her. I brought her here. And I give her what she needs.”

“And what’s that?” Bidann has let the hares fall to the ground. He is standing with his hand on his bow.

“She works for me. And you won’t take her away.”

“And how will you stop me?” asks Bidann. “I am not afraid of you.” He moves to walk on, but Gaesta stands in his way.

“I will kill you.”

Bidann looks at him coolly. “You could try.” And then with startling speed, he cuffs the bandit across the face, sending him sprawling.

You move to stop the fighting, but Ennet puts her hand on your arm and shakes her head.

Bidann collects his catch and walks off. Later, Gaesta follows him. When he has left, you rise and go back to the village.

“What was that about?” you ask.

“A woman, what else,” she replies. What else indeed.

When you arrive back at the hut, you see Alaba and the other girl. You stack the timber while Ennet goes into the hut, and then you follow her in.

The two girls are in the room. Ennet is sewing. In your hand, you have a piece of twine from the sack. You tie it into a loop.

“Here,” you say to Alaba. “Let me show you.”

You put the loop over your fingers and think back to when you played this game with Nino. You make the blanket and hold it up to her.

“How did you do that?” she asks you.

“I can show you.” The two girls sit with you, and you take turns making shapes with the string. Ennet puts her sewing down and comes to sit with you.

“I used to play that game,” she says. “Here, let me show you.”

When she takes the string from you, she makes the sign.

“Where did you learn that?” you ask.

“I learned it long ago,” she says. “Now I am teaching it to these children."

"I learned it once," you tell, "but I had forgotten it. Thank you for reminding me."

Ennet cuts a length of twine for each of the girls and hands them over. The two girls go and play together.

Later, Bidann comes to the hut. He is holding a hare.

"Look," he says, holding up the animal which is almost as large as a small child. "I've been lucky today."

Chapter Forty-One
Anger

Koreb

There is no point in waiting. You may as well get on with it. You hand your papers over to the gatekeeper and he lets you pass. Outside the city, the road is busy with travellers. It is a long way to Saco. Perhaps you should have waited for Bidann to return and to travel on his wagon. But you could not wait. You had to get away. You had to make things right. You have to make up for your betrayal.

How long will it take you? A moon-turn? Two moon-turns, the rest of your life? Maybe you can do nothing to make up for what you did, but you will try.

The road is clear, and you set off. It is the first time you have ever been outside of the city. You have brought a sack with provisions, but it will not last the whole journey.

The thing that strikes you most about travelling is how dull it is. Step after step. It is a long way and you cannot wait until it is over.

It is not the arriving, it is the journey. Or so that saying goes. But it is a journey in the dark. From time to time someone passes you, or you pass them. The moon travels around and changes twice from dark to bright. And then you arrive. You are here.

You present your papers to the guard. He looks them over and then motions you inside.

You have a name. That is all you have. You ask the guard if he knows where they live, but he waves you away. You know that Bidann carried wines on his wagon, and you go to the market looking for a wine-seller. There you find one.

"Do you know this man?" you ask. "Do you know a man called Ivre?"

The wine seller points you in the direction of a warehouse. You arrive at a battered wooden door and knock. When the door opens you ask, "Are you Ivre?"

"Who wants to know?"

"I am Koreb."

"And?"

"I am looking for someone. A boy about three years old. Brought here by a man called Bidann."

"Why?"

"I am supposed to take him." And here you make the sign.

"I see. Sorry, the boy died."

"What?"

"He died. He got sick and he died."

You are shocked to hear these words.

"But…"

"He died."

"What did you do with the body?"

"Burned it."

You know he is lying, but you cannot find the words to challenge him.

"This can't be right."

"It is right."

You look at Ivre. He is cold-eyed. The death of the boy is nothing to him.

"When did he die?"

"Right after he arrived."

"Did you?" and then you see it. Ivre killed the boy. "You did." And in a rage, you force your way into the house, holding Ivre by the throat. "You killed him."

In a rage, you are pinning him to the stone floor and throttling the life out of him. Go on, you hear a voice that is not mine. Kill him. He deserves it.

Where did this strength come from? Where did this killing rage come from? Never before have you felt such strength flowing through your body. This is what you were made for: to kill.

But my voice is also there, even if it is only a whisper. Let him go. You can barely hear it. And how can a whisper hold back this rage that fills? The man is a murderer, he killed an innocent.

Do it, the other voice says.

Ivre is making short gagging sounds. His eyes are bulging and his hands are beating against you. But you are too strong. It would be so easy to squeeze the life out of him. To give him what he deserves.

Once more I whisper to let him go. And your grip loosens. You stand up while Ivre rolls on the floor choking.

"Stand up," you command. "Stand up. I should kill you." But you will not.

Ivre rises. You see now that he is thin and for all he is well dressed, he smells of brandy.

"Why did you kill him?"

"I never killed him," Ivre protests. Then he flinches as you move once more towards him.

"I promise. When he came, he had no permit to live here. It would cost me to get one."

"You could have sent him to one of the farms outside the city. They would have taken him. You could have even sold him."

"No, not at that age. No one would take him. There was a food shortage, there still is. No one would take another mouth to feed."

"You could have kept him. You have plenty to eat."

"I couldn't, not without getting a permit. They would notice. And even if I did, if someone came looking for him, they would find him here. It would not be safe."

"So what did you do?"

"What everyone does. What happens to every unwanted child? I left him in the street. He was still young enough to pass as a newborn. He would die in the street."

"You left a child in the street. A child we sent to you to take care of. You just left him to die."

"What other choice did I have?"

"You could have cared for him."

"It was not safe."

"And what of the girl? What of the girl that Bidann brought? The one we sent last time? Did you abandon her too?"

"What girl? Bidann has not been here since he brought me the boy. He was supposed to bring me wine, but he never came."

"So you have not seen Bidann? Or a woman, Ennet?"

"No, I promise. No one else has come."

You sink to your knees. You wonder briefly if Ivre will take the chance to attack you but he does not. It seems as if your betrayal was for nothing. Greba will find neither the boy who is dead nor the girl that shines. Perhaps she is dead too. Perhaps Ennet, Bidann and Alaba are dead, just like Mukito.

What a long way you have come for nothing. For no reason. Why have you brought me here Whisperer, you ask. And as you do there is another knock at the door.

"Open it," you say. And Ivre opens the door. A man pushes his way in. He is thickset and strong, just like you. You look up and see. It is Greba. He is here.

"What do you want?" you ask him. "Why are you here? You are too late anyway."

Chapter Forty-Two
Sharpness

Greba

When you read the name, you go to turn back. But you know you should not. Unead, her name forms in your mouth and it is as sweet as a first kiss. In your room, you lie thinking of her over and over. She is lost to you. She is lost forever. Or she was. Now there is a second chance. You could find her. Perhaps, there is a way. But it would mean danger for her. If the others of the twelve should find her, then what would they do to her?

"What should I do?" you ask. But it is not me you are asking. There must be a way. But then you think again of how Utas used your daughter and how Kong endangered both your daughter and your wife. You cannot take the risk.

You take the paper and burn it. But it is no use. You cannot burn the list from your mind. They are all on there and cannot be erased. Over and over the names run in your mind.

"I must speak to Hilketa," you say. And rise. Even though the moon has set, you know where he will be: in the moon viewing pavilion. And you are not wrong.

"What brings you here?" Hilketa asks without turning around.

"I have come to speak with you."

Now he turns around. "What about?"

"You are right. We should cull the peasants. I will go to Saco and carry it out."

"It is not a cull we need," says Hilketa. "You will need to exterminate them."

"Perhaps," you agree, "but mostly these famines are caused by the peasants hoarding food. I will go and kill a few. Raze their farms and search them for food. It will be enough. And if not then we can wipe them out."

Hilketa nods. "Good, when will you leave?"

"Soon."

"How many men will you need?"

"None, not at first anyway. I'll go and use the guard that is there. It should be easy."

"I think you will need more men."

"Maybe," you say, thinking it better to agree with Hilketa than to set him thinking. "If I do I will send for them. If I have to wait for you to organize a division, it will hold me back."

"Why the rush?"

"No rush. The sooner started the sooner finished."

"Well," says Hilketa. "You do not need my permission."

You forget how young he is, and how clever. You wonder if you should kill him. Does he suspect why you have agreed? It would be easy. But if you did, you would need to find his reborn body. It would take too much time.

"Have you spoken with Kong?"

"I do not need his permission either," you say. And the thought of Kong raises anger within you. There is one you would be happy to kill.

"No, I suppose not. I suppose you don't need anyone's permission. Except Vatu's permission."

"I serve the darkness in my own way," you tell Hilketa. "Vatu will not wish to be disturbed by trivial things."

"A hundred thousand lives. Yes, I suppose Vatu would think it trivial."

"That is not what I mean," you say. "Besides, it was your idea."

"I have changed my mind."

"That's up to you. As you said, I don't need your permission."

"So why have you come to tell me?"

"I thought you would be pleased."

"If you are doing this to please me, then don't."

"I'm not. And besides, if I'm right then I won't need to kill anyone, or not many, a few perhaps."

Hilketa looks at you. "How many people have you killed?"

"In this life?" you ask, and then begin to count, making a rough reckoning. "Do you mean by my own hand?"

"No, I mean in all your lives, and in the first one."

Now you see what this is. "I don't remember," you say. "The

darkness has eaten my memory and my guilt."

"Has it," says Hilketa. Now you are glad that you have not killed him. Now you watch him suffering and you are glad.

"It has," you say and turn and leave him.

Back in your room you still cannot sleep. How many people have you killed? How many by your hand? You do not know the answer. It is impossible to count. Besides, the darkness has swallowed your guilt. That was the bargain that you made. The bargain that I will unravel.

In your room, the sword is shining in the lamplight, resting on its stand. What a beautiful sword, very very old. You look at it, but you do not pick it up. It is made of iron, shiny with black etching on the blade, and the hilt is of bone. It is edged on both sides, but the edge is notched and worn from use. Still, the sword is polished to a brilliant sheen. It looks as if it is too ancient and frail to touch. But you know that it is not. You have held it in your hand and it reaches out to you, begging for you to touch it. How deceptive it is. But you know what memories it will bring. Sharp and deadly.

You reach to touch the blade. It is so beautiful you cannot resist. Your hand wraps around the hilt, a perfect fit as if it was made for you. Such a perfect weight. The balance, so fine. You swing the blade in a circle, and it cuts through the air.

In your mind, you hear the sound of throbbing engines humming as they drive the propellers. You are there again when you shut your eyes. It is as if the engines are singing.

Mine eyes have seen the glory of the coming of the Lord. As you sit in the cockpit flying through the early hours of the morning, you can hear the sound of the propellers cutting through the air. It seems to you as if their low drone is like voices singing. To the sound of the engines, your mind forms words that seem to fit with the harmonies of the propellers. He is trampling out the vintage where the grapes of wrath are stored.

There is a tight knot in your stomach. He hath loosed the fateful lightning of His terrible swift sword. But there is no danger, you are flying too high for anyone to reach. By the time the great black cloud rises you are far away and safe.

It is justice, you say. How many people will you kill? It does not matter to you. It is just. Besides, you will not see the faces or the fear as the bombs fall. You do not see the firestorms or the sickness that follows. Who can say which bomb will cause death and which will fall harmless to the side? That is not your concern. You are doing your job. If not you then it would be someone else.

There is no blood on your hands. Anyway, the darkness hides what you have done. There is a blinding light and then a cloud of darkness.

You put the sword down, and let the pictures fade from your mind. The bargain holds. You turn away.

Chapter Forty-Three
Flute Music

Greba

There is a knock at the door.

"Enter," you call. The door is opened and a servant hands you a report. You dismiss him and then take the tablet and read.

> *Koreb has left and heads to Saco. We will continue to follow him. He does not know he is watched. We will keep him safe on the road. There are reports of more bandit activity. He may be linked to this group.*

The tablet is not signed and you erase it. No one else must know. It is as you thought. If you scare him enough he will reveal what he knows. You knew he had more information.

You allow yourself a smile.

You will travel there now. As you say, you do not need anyone's permission.

And Unead? If there is danger, then it is better that you are close. You have decided and once decided, you will not change your mind.

You will travel to Saco, you will find Koreb and he will lead you to the boy. Then you will kill the child. The son of Utas and the slave girl he kept in his chambers. You will be avenged. You will give him pain, whatever pain you can. It will be as nothing to the pain that he gave you.

You kneel and bury your head. Let your anger cover your pain. That is what you wish to do. You wish to blame him for all of this, or me. But you know you are to blame for this too. I put my arm around you and you shrug it off. You will not be comforted.

"You will find no comfort in revenge," I tell you.

"There is no comfort to be found anywhere."

"If you cannot find comfort, then find faith. I have promised you."

"I will not believe. This is madness. I am mad. You are not real and all your words are empty imaginings. The Whisperer, as well to call you the meaningless sound of the imagination. The hope of the weak and the weak-minded."

I will not argue with you. Nor will I remind you of the past.

Now you rise again. You will leave tomorrow. Alone you will travel. You do not need any help. Nor will you share your vengeance. It is yours you say.

Always leave for a journey on the horned moon. That is what they say. The light is weak, but each night it will get stronger. If you travel quick enough then you will get to Saco before the moon rests.

When you reach the gates, you show your sign. The guard lets you pass. He does not know it is you, but you have given him the sign of those in your service. He will not question or tell any other. You have taught the guards well. They value their lives and say nothing. You are waved into Saco without a word. Now you must find those that are yours. You will not let the governor know you are here. It is not his concern, you have told him already.

You go to the house and knock. It is opened and a servant girl leads you to a chamber. It will do you now. You sit and wait. An old woman enters and bows.

"He has not arrived. He will arrive tomorrow. If he comes through the gates. It is possible he will go to one of the farms. There are many more heretics outside the gates than in them."

You know this is true. The poor always love the Whisperer, while those in the city, the rich love only themselves. Those in the city fear Vatu, those outside fear everything, and he is only one among many fears. There are many ways to die, especially if you are nothing.

"Is there anything I can do while you wait?" the old woman asks. "We have rooms ready and blood."

"These rooms are fine," you say. You think about food. You think about blood and milk. But you wish to keep your presence secret. You will not bleed anyone. A drained body might let someone know you are here if it were to be found. "Some fruit, bread and wine will be sufficient."

"As you wish," she replies.

"And bring a flute," you say. The words surprise you. What do you want a flute for? You have not played it once since he left you; since Utas left your training. You taught him many things, and in return, he taught you to play. Why now? It is to pass the time, you think.

It is brought to you and you play. You are not skilled, and it has been a long time since you held one. With your thick hands and stiff fingers, it is difficult and you stop and slide it through the palms of your hands. You are such a poor player, but you appreciate music. Utas was very talented. Perhaps the finest player you ever heard. You think back to when he hid behind a screen and played to you and Unead in the darkness. You should have known it was him. Only he could have played so well. But you were too in love with Unead to think of anything else. You were with her in the moonlight while the flute played and nothing else mattered.

"Love was always my weakness." And you think of Unead and the daughter she gave you.

"Love was always your strength," I tell you.

"If I had not loved her, Unead would be safe. If I had not loved Irid, she would not have died."

"You are wrong," I tell you.

"If you say so," you continue and put the flute down. The moon is sinking in the west. And there is a small window in the chamber that faces that direction. You rise and look out. It is very beautiful as it sets in low clouds. You let your memories of Unead rise up again. And knowing that somewhere she is near, you turn to me and ask.

"What will become of her?"

"She will be well, for now. She is thinking of you."

"I doubt it. She is still attractive. She will find some else."

I do not argue.

"Does she know about Irid?" you ask me.

"No," I reply. "She fears for her but does not know."

"I wish I did not know that Irid is dead. It would be better to have hope. She would be ashamed of me if she knew that I did not try to save our daughter. Not that I could have. I could only have died with her. I wish now that I had. I should have jumped after her. I should not have let Vatu murder her."

"It is in the past," I tell you. "And you could not have saved her. Do you think Vatu would have let you die? He would have called you back again as he has always done for the twelve. And for him. She forgives you, and so would Irid."

"I am not so sure," you say. "She must never know. If she knew, she would hate me."

Now you are pleading with me. You are kneeling in the last of the moonlight begging like a dog.

"Please, do not let her know that I let our child die and did nothing."

How can I refuse; I promise that I will not tell her. But that means that you must.

"Then she will hate me."

And it is true that she may for a while. But love and hate can reside in the same heart, and when the hate cools, then the love remains.

"I cannot see her. I will not see her. I cannot face her." And you hold the flute in your hands. You are thinking of the times that you would stand outside the house after Utas had taken your daughter. How ashamed you were. You could not face her then. You thought she would despise you for your weakness. But she did not, and when you found the strength to face her, she made you welcome.

"I cannot see her," you say again.

Chapter Forty-Four
Love

Ennet

When Bidann brings Dova to the hut you look away. You do not want him to see the worry in your eyes.

"She will sleep with me," he says. There is boastfulness in his voice. Dova also is looking away. But you can see she is afraid, not of Bidann surely. But if not him then who?

"Sifyre can sleep with me and Alaba. Utas sleeps mostly on the porch. We can make room."

"Good," says Bidann. As if that is all settled, and in a way, it is. "Go and help Ennet make dinner." This last to Dova.

She comes over to sit beside you next to the fire. Still not looking at you. Is it you she is afraid of?

"There is no need. I have things just about ready." Now she looks at you and you can see it is not you that she is afraid of.

"Let her help," says Bidann. You do not argue. What good would it do?

"Go get firewood," you say to Utas, and the old man rises in his chains and leaves. Bidann has gone through to his room and the girls are outside playing.

"Welcome," you say to Dova. And she looks in surprise.

"Thank you," she says.

"You will be safe, he is a good man," you say. You are hoping to make her at ease.

Now that you see her close up, you realize that she is pretty. The mescal has not rotted her teeth, and her hair is dark and glossy like yours never was no matter how you tried to make it so. You have long since given up trying. She is dirty and her clothes are ragged.

"Do you have anything that you want to bring from your hut?" you ask her. But she shakes her head. You cannot imagine that Gaesta allowed her to have much there anyway. You point to the water jug and say, "Why don't you wash and get ready to eat."

She shuffles away and leaves you stirring the congee. It is ready. You wish you had some fish paste to add to it.

But you also want to know about Bidann and Gaesta.

"Did they fight?" you ask. And Dova shrinks down even more. You would not have thought it was possible for her to make herself smaller. She looks at you. She is wiping the dirt from her face. She makes to speak and her lips move but no sound comes out.

Utas returns with firewood. You wish he would take longer. Perhaps there is some other errand you can send him on.

"Are the girls out there? I hope they have not gone too far. Did you see them? Did you tell them to come and eat?"

Utas replies, "They are coming. They will not take long. But you should keep them in afterwards."

"Why?" you ask.

Utas looks at Dova. She shakes.

"She has not told you?"

"No."

"Gaesta is dead. Dova's hut is burning."

"He set it on fire. I was in there with Bidann, he blocked the doorway, and set the thatch on fire."

You hold your tongue. You have so many questions. You look into those frightened eyes. Yes, her clothes are covered in soot. You are looking towards her, but she does not speak.

"Are you all right?" you ask. And she nods her head.

Perhaps you should go to Bidann and make sure he is all right.

"I should sit on the porch," says Utas. "If someone comes. They will have to speak to me."

You wonder what Utas can do if someone comes while he is in chains.

"I have a key for the chains," you say and rise to walk towards him.

"There is no need mother, I can take care of things."

You should be angry that he has called you mother when you are no older than him but have too many other things to think about. You let it pass.

"If someone comes, let me know," you say as Utas walks out onto the porch. As he does, the two girls enter. Alaba comes running to you.

"Is there rice?" she asks.

"Yes, it will be ready soon," you tell her, but it is ready now. "Sifyre, bring the bowls over."

The bowls are made of turned ash wood. Bidann has made them. You hold one in your hand and wonder how someone so clever can be so stupid. And you think how when you were young, no man would have risked his life for you. No man would have been so stupid. Are you jealous, you wonder? But jealous or not, you know that you are all in danger. You fill a bowl with congee and hand it to Sifyre.

"Take this out to Utas and come straight back."

"Yes Ennet," she says. And you think again what a good child she is. All children are good, you say. Why is it that all of us are not good when we are older? Am I good, you ask yourself? You try to be, and that is all that I ask.

Bidann has come back into the front room. So you hand him a bowl.

"Thank you, little mother," he says, teasing you. How can he be so calm?

You hand bowls to the two girls.

"Let them eat in the back room," says Bidann.

"As you wish," you reply and motion for the girls to leave.

"Come and sit with me," says Bidann to Dova, and she hurries over.

Now you see him you see there is a cut on one arm. He has covered it with a cloth but there is still blood.

"Would you like me to look at that?" you ask.

"In a moment," says Bidann and then looks as if he has forgotten something. "Let's eat first."

"As you wish."

"Where's your slave?" he asks.

"He's not my slave," you reply. Although you are not quite sure what Utas is. "He is guarding the door."

"Good."

"He says Gaesta is dead."

"Yes."

You think he will say nothing more, but he puts his bowl of congee down.

"I killed him." You could have guessed that. "He never gave me much choice. He came at me with his axe. I told him I would kill him. That very first day, remember. When we came here and he tried to beat you. That's when I told him. I would kill him if he tried to hurt us."

You remember.

"What else did the slave tell you?"

"He is not my slave," you say again. "The believers do not have slaves. The Whisperer does not allow it."

"Whatever, what has he told you?"

"That Gaesta set fire to Dova's hut. While you were in it."

Bidann nods. "Yes, I was…" You can imagine what Bidann was doing and wave him on. Why else would a man be at Dova's hut?

"Anyway," he continues. "It's not what you think, or what he thought. We were just talking. About this. About coming here. I told Dova that she could come and stay here and that we would look after her. You're already looking after her daughter. So she might as well stay here too. The other men can go elsewhere. There are more women arriving every day. They can find someone else. There are probably plenty other girls who will work for Gaesta. Or would if he was still alive.

"Dova was not sure. She was worried about what Gaesta would do. She said he was crazy, and how right she was. We never got a chance to say much else because we started to smell smoke. When I tried the door it was jammed shut, but I had my axe with me. I was going to try and fix a hole in the wall of the cabin, so it was short work to cut a way out. Probably just as well that Dova's hut was so ramshackle. Gaesta built it and it was almost falling down all by itself.

"When we got out, Gaesta was there. He had his axe and was swinging it about. He was drunk of course. He came running up to me shouting, telling me that he was going to kill me. I laughed at him and dodged out the way, but he kept coming. Then he told me that he would set my hut on fire while I was sleeping. I told him he was welcome to try, and if he did he would get what was coming to him. And thanks for the warning. But he still would not back off.

"Then he asked me where I was going with his woman. She's not your woman, I told him. But he said that she was. He said that he had bought and paid for her and that she was no one's woman but his. He started to grab at her, and then he came at her with his axe. Said that if he could not have her then no one could. Said he was going to kill her.

"I knocked him down a couple of times, but he just kept coming. In the end, I had no choice. It was easy. I hit him on the neck with my axe and he fell down bleeding. He was serious. He just would not stop. You can see that I have been cut where he caught me on the arm. It was his fault. You can ask Dova and she'll tell you the same. It was his fault."

Now he stopped speaking. You notice that he has not eaten any of his congee.

"Are you going to eat that?" you ask.

"I'm not hungry," he replies.

You have no words to add. What can you say? You can see that, for all his talk, Bidann is upset. Has he ever killed anyone before? You think not, you hope not. But what do you know of these things? Nothing. There is nothing you can say to him. You sit beside him, on the other side from Dova. You have brought silk thread and a needle. When you unwrap the wound, it is deeper than you expected.

"Let me see," you say and bring it to the light. You wish that Alaba was there to light the room, but candlelight will have to do. "We have rice wine, we can clean it with that." And so you do before threading your needle.

One, two, three, four, five, six stitches you sew, drawing the flesh closed. You tell yourself that it is just like sewing cloth. But when you are finished, you realize that you have bitten your lip. Silly fool, you call yourself. Then you wrap the arm up tight.

"That is the best I can do for you."

"Thank you again, little mother."

"You are welcome," you reply. And you say a silent prayer to me. Whisperer, heal this man. He has been a faithful follower. Even in this he is blameless. He had no choice but to take a life. Forgive him as you forgive all of us. Even Gaesta. Forgive him and take his soul to you.

I hear and I forgive. But there are others that you will need to plead to, they may not listen.

You stand up and put your sewing things away.

"Thank you," says Dova.

"What for?"

"For helping Bidann."

"It was nothing," you say. "I did nothing." And then you excuse yourself. You can hear the girls playing in the next room.

"I will get the bowls," you say. Dova starts to rise to help you. "Get the bowls from the girls if you like. I will get the others." And with that, you move out to the porch to sit with Utas.

Chapter Forty-Five
Trouble

Utas

When you sit out on the porch, you cannot see far. Clouds have covered the moon. Even that sliver of light is denied you. I sit beside you because I am always with you. You are troubled. A death always brings trouble. How odd that you who have killed so many should think so now. But you are not wrong.

Over at the centre of the camp, the moonstone is glowing. There is a fire there too, and you can hear voices raised in anger. You cannot make out what they are saying. But you know full well it is about Bidann and Gaesta. You can hear footsteps and two bandits appear just at the edge of the light of your lantern. They stop there and do not speak.

"Hey there," you call to them. But they do not answer. Instead, they nock arrows to their bows. So you stand up and walk forward.

"Stop there," one of them calls. "Don't come any closer."

"Why?"

"Because I say so."

You decide to let it go, for now. You go back to the porch and sit.

Ennet comes out and sits with you. "What is happening?" she asks.

"Nothing yet," you tell her. And you point out the two bowmen. "They are just here to make sure that no one escapes."

"Bidann will not leave," says Ennet. "That man is a fool. Look at the trouble he's caused. Dova is not worth it."

But you chide her, "The Whisperer says all of his creations are worth caring for and helping."

"I think it had more to do with helping himself," says Ennet. "There are other girls in the camp now. And more coming every day. He could have brought one of them to stay here."

You know that she is right.

"Who can understand the mysteries of love," you say.

"Love?" She laughs at that. "This is not about love, this was about showing Gaesta that he could not tell him what to do. Why do men fight over women? They would be better letting the woman decide who she wants to be with."

You laugh, you know she is right, but also wrong. "Letting a woman decide: what kind of world would that be?"

"A better one than this, I would think," Ennet says. "But you're right. That would mean that a man would have to listen to a woman. And anyway, there are plenty of women who like men fighting over them."

"What do you think will happen?" you ask.

Ennet looks at you. You can see that she is worried. "They might kill him," she says. And you nod your head.

"That is what I think too."

"No one liked Gaesta," Ennet says. "But even so, he was one of them. They will not allow it to go unpunished. And if Bidann is killed, then it will be worse for us. They will likely drive us out of the house. They might kill us too."

You notice then that Ennet is holding something in her hand.

"What have you got there?"

She holds the key to the manacles and pushes it into your hands. "In case I am killed, you can free yourself and run for it."

"I won't leave Alaba. She is my daughter."

"Then take her with you, and take the other girl, Sifyre. She deserves a better life."

You can hear the shouting at the moonstone getting louder and angrier.

"It seems they can't come to a decision," says Ennet.

"Not yet, but they will."

"What will they decide?"

More bandits come to the cottage. You can see about ten now. Perhaps there are more just out of sight.

Eventually, you can see the crowd from the moonstone turn towards the cottage. They are coming.

"Perhaps you should go inside?" you suggest, but Ennet shakes her head.

"I'd rather see what is coming. I'd rather know."

Dark shadows flicker across the light coming from the moonstone. They are here. Condito, the tall, bald leader walks forward and a guard of four bandits close around him. The others have drawn their bows and formed a line around the house.

"Where is Bidann?" says Condito when he gets close.

"Inside," you reply. Keeping your eyes down.

"Then fetch him, and Dova. Bring them out now."

Ennet rises and enters the house. While she is gone, you count the bandits. There are too many.

Bidann comes out, but only Ennet is with him. "What do you want?" he asks.

"Where is the woman? Where is Dova? I told you to bring her out too." This is directed to Ennet, but it is Bidann that replies.

"If you have something to say, then say it me."

Condito turns to Bidann. "I will have plenty to say to you." And he motions one of the bandits forward. "Bring him."

Bidann stares at the approaching bandit. "I wouldn't," he says. And the threat in his voice is clear. The bandit looks back to Condito.

"Don't be stupid," says the tall man. "I could have you full of arrows in an instant." But even so, the bandit stops and waits.

"What do you want?" asks Bidann.

"I want the woman, I want Dova."

"Why?"

"Because she belongs to me, to us. She works for us."

"Get someone else to work for you. She's mine now."

"Don't be stupid. Give her up and we'll leave it at that. Otherwise, we'll have to deal with you as well."

"For what? Dova was Gaesta's girl. Now he's dead, she is mine. If anyone else wants her, then they can fight me for her. The same way I fought Gaesta."

"Gaesta was drunk."

"Gaesta was always drunk. Now, if no one is going to fight me then clear off."

Condito's face twists in the lamplight.

"Are you going to fight me?" asks Bidann.

"I'm not drunk," says Condito. "You would not find me as easy."

Another bandit pushes forward. "I'll fight you," he says.

Bidann sneers. "If you like."

"Gaesta was my brother. You killed him and took what was his."

"A bandit is complaining about someone taking what was not theirs. I will fight you. And after I kill you, I'll take what's yours too. Isn't that the way it works?"

"I want the girl. You can keep Dova, she's a pox-ridden whore anyway. But the girl, her daughter. I want her."

Bidann pauses. The girl, Sifyre, is nothing to him. But he knows why this bandit wants her. "Men like you make me sick," he says. But the bandit does not flinch. Bidann turns to Condito. "You would let this happen in your camp?"

Condito looks ashamed. "It is nothing to do with me."

"Will you fight me or not?" says the bandit.

"I'll fight you," says Bidann. "You're as bad as your stinking brother. Worse."

The bandit looks outmatched. Bidann is bigger and stronger. But he is still dangerous. Bidann is not a warrior. He has not trained with weapons, he is simply a wagoner. The bandit has a sword. He takes it out and points it at Bidann. You are a good judge of men, to you, it seems that Bidann would most likely lose this fight for all of his bravado.

But Bidann does not back down. He hefts his axe. If he will die today, he will not make it easy. You know that you could save him. You know even with shackles around your hands and feet you could defeat the bandit. You consider offering to fight in Bidann's place. You could kill the bandit.

As you think, Bidann steps forward and so too does the bandit. They start to circle each other. The crowd draws close in anticipation of blood. You can see excitement in their eyes.

"Stop, stop," shouts Ennet, and pushes through the crowd. "The child is not his, she is mine. Dova gave her to me. If you want to take her it is me you must deal with."

The crowd laughs. The idea of an old woman fighting the bandit is absurd.

"Go back Ennet," says Bidann. "I will take care of this."

"Will you?" says Ennet. "By killing or by being killed? That's not the answer." And then she turns to the bandit. "Even if you do kill him. You will still need to deal with me. You may as well deal with me now. You will have to."

The crowd are now murmuring in confusion. It won't be much sport to watch the bandit kill an old lady.

"I could kill you in an instant," says the bandit. Even he is not sure about killing an old woman.

"I said deal, not fight. What do you want the girl for? She's too young to follow her mother's trade. And she's too stupid to be much help around your cabin."

"She'll grow," says the bandit.

"So," says Ennet nodding, "you want to use her for a whore. How much then?"

"What?"

"How much? How much to buy a whore? I'll pay for her. That's fair, isn't it? If you think that you're being cheated out of a whore, then how much to buy one?"

"More than you've got, old lady."

"Let's see, remember you need to feed and clothe her and provide a house. Now that Dova's house is burned down you'll need to build a new one for her. And if she grows up like her mother, she'll cost you a fortune in mescal."

"Don't try and bargain with me. I know how much a whore is worth, especially a young one. It's more money than you have."

But Ennet is not listening to the bandit. Instead, she has turned to Condito. "How much did Dova earn, a few coppers a day, and perhaps some rice or maybe half a rabbit?"

"Perhaps," agreed Condito.

"What was the most you've sold a slave for? And don't pretend. I was a slave once. I know the cost of these things. How much did you sell your prettiest girl slave for?"

Condito shifts uneasily. "A few silvers. Maybe six. A very young one like this one, at the right market? You could get perhaps ten. Ten silvers. If you have ten silvers then you could buy her."

"Ten silvers," says Ennet. "That is a lot."

"More than an old woman like you can have," says the bandit. "More than he's got for sure. Either give me the girl or let me fight."

But Ennet is walking forward and raises her hand. She lifts it high and you see what she is holding. A gold coin.

"This is worth far more than ten silvers," she says. She holds it high and shows it to the crowd. They have never seen a gold coin. It must be worth a hundred silvers.

"How much is this worth?" she asks. "Will you take this for the child?"

"I could take it anyway," says the bandit. But Condito steps forward.

"Let me see that," he says. And Ennet places it in his hand.

"It's real enough," says Condito.

"Why shouldn't I just take the coin and the girl?" asks the bandit.

Condito says nothing but cuffs the bandit across the face. "Why shouldn't I take them both?" he says. "I'm in charge here. You do what I say. You take the gold or the girl."

"And you'll still have to fight me for the girl," says Bidann.

"And me," you say and step forward.

Ennet has the gold coin again. She is holding it up and every eye is watching.

"Bring the girl out," says Condito. And this time, Dova, Alaba and Sifyre come out from the hut. "Come forward."

Sifyre walks nervously towards Condito. You realize just how young she is. The light from Alaba spills across the porch and out into the yard. In the light of Alaba, Sifyre looks younger still. She is clean and dressed in the new gown that Ennet sewed for her.

"So, choose now," says Condito. "Choose now, Garra. There will be no changing your mind. The coin is a fair price for both the girl and the woman. More than fair."

The bandit, Garra, looks from the girl to the coin. There can be no doubt which has his interest. He sheathes his sword.

"Give it to me," he says. And Ennet hands the coin over to him.

Who would have thought it? An old woman with a fortune in gold. You must ask her where it came from and how she managed to keep it from the bandits.

The crowd begins to disperse. It is the end of it for now. No more killing. Not for now at any rate.

Chapter Forty-Six
Pity

Vatu

I pity you and why should I not? I made you. I formed you from darkness and placed you in a hole. I gave you a world of your own. But it's not enough. I should have given you love. Do you think that I do not love you?

I will redeem each of you. Even you. Because I love all of you. I am the balm that heals your poisoned mind. You cannot turn me away and in the end, I will be there. I will take you from the depths of hell, even that hell that you have made. I will save you from that.

Did you think that this existence would last forever? It will not, even the mountains will wear to dust and the oceans dry. The rocks shall melt with the Sun. But I will still be there. My love will still be there.

Do you think that nothingness awaited you? Did you think that there was an escape in not being? There is more than that. I promise. But I will ease the pain and you will find joy.

I watch as you hide in the depths of the earth and think that you can keep all that you want to yourself. Do you not see how worthless these things are?

You turn to me, and you scream at me. You call me a thief and liar. You will not give up what you have. You seek to blot me out. I am nothing, you say, I am not real. How many times have you said those words and yet here I am. I am still speaking with you. You still hear my words.

You hold tight to what you have. It is everything and nothing. It is what keeps you here in the dark away from me. One day it will be gone and then what? When I am all you have I will still be here. I will still love you.

"I will destroy everything," you say. But even that will not be enough to stop me loving you. How afraid you are.

"I know what you are doing," you say. "I will stop you. I will take those that you love and destroy them. You will not take this world away from me."

Cannot you see, I can only take you from this world if you let it go? You must trust me, there is a better place.

You lash out, but you cannot hurt me, so you will hurt others instead. You will hurt yourself.

"I will not let you take what I have."

Can you not see that what you have is nothing? I have given you the whole world. I have given you the Sun and everything under it. You have taken that and buried it away like the unprofitable servant. It shall be given to another. What has it profited you? Has it brought you joy? It has brought you no joy. None whatever.

"You did this to me."

No, I did not. You did this to yourself. I have made a world so bountiful for you to share. It is not too late for you to find that joy.

"I will not give it up."

In the end, you will have no choice but to give it up. I will never leave you. And in the end, you will see this is nothing. It is worthless. You will see that you are alone, that only through giving can we find joy.

"I will take everything from everyone."

But that will give nothing. You cannot fill the emptiness within you with gold. Not even the whole earth can fill that void. Not even the Sun and the Moon and the Stars can fill the emptiness. Only love can fill your heart.

"I do not love anyone."

That is why your heart is empty. You think that you cannot love. You think that you are unable to love. But nothing is impossible. Nothing. You will find love. Even you. You will find my love.

"I do not love you."

You must find love there within you. It is like a seed that grows from nothing. It is like water seeping into the desert. It is like ice in sunshine. You will find it within you. You will find that you love even yourself. You are not undeserving of love. Even after all you have done or failed to do, you are deserving of love. I bring love to you. It is love that will heal you and love that will set you free. I am the love, I am the way to freedom. I bring hope to the prisoner, even to those that are prisoners of themselves. I have brought hope to you and it will not perish no matter how you may seek to trample upon it.

In the darkness, you hear my words. You tremble knowing that all you have built will fail. That even you must go into the unknown. That even you must take my hand. That even for you my love must be enough.

"It is not enough, I do not believe."

But it does not matter. There is a course set and an order to things. There is no changing, there is no escape. I will come for you in time. It will be enough. When the scales fall from your eyes and finally you see light. When you finally know who you are, when the heavens are rolled back, then you will know. You will finally know that you and I are one.

Still, you tremble in the darkness. Still, you rage, but anger will fail you. It will turn to cold ash. I will not be denied. I endure and remain. I am the Whisperer and the words I speak echo within you. I am the Whisperer and my words do not fade, they endure to the end.

Chapter Forty-Seven
Work

Unead

Your stomach is empty and it is hard to work when you are hungry. Still, at least you are not the draw girl and do not have to crouch above the loom. There is no chatter in the work shed, only the clacking of the shuttles as they go to and fro, but even that sounds subdued. Half-hearted throws across the warp. No one has the energy to rattle it over and over. The rhythm is gone. The work is slow.

But there is still plenty of work to do. Even if a day's work will barely earn you enough to eat. Injutil is slow and her face is sullen. You think to beat her to make her work faster. But you do not. Why should you?

Over in the corner, one of the weavers is beating her draw girl. The other weavers stop and crowd around watching, but saying nothing.

"This is what you get if you're slow," the weaver shouts. The girl is screaming and lying on the floor.

"Enough," says the foreman. "Get back to work."

The draw girl is still screaming. Then she gets up.

"Back to work, I said."

Reluctantly the girl goes back to sit on the gantry above the loom.

"Draw quicker," says the weaver, "and draw them right. I don't want any flaws." If there are flaws, then they will take money from your wage.

Injutil looks at you. "What good is a wage if you can't buy

anything?"

"It is nearly summer," you say. "When the Sun comes out there will be food for everyone."

"It is three moon turns until summer. What do we do until then?"

You are not sure. When you lived in the City of the Sun, you did not have to worry about the spring famines. Greba made sure you never went hungry. But now you are worried. You cannot remember the famine starting so soon. Usually, there were only a few moon rounds, one moon turn at most.

"Perhaps great Vatu will open the Sun early," you say. Injutil's face shows clearly what she thinks of that. "Get back to work," you continue.

But you know she is right. The hunger is just beginning.

Injutil is still slow. But when you look at her lean face, you know that she is doing all she can. If you beat her, it will only make her slower and weaker.

You have said a prayer to the weaver gods, perhaps you should pray to Cera and she will fill your flour bag. You laugh, who would have thought you would have turned into such a superstitious old woman. You do not believe in the gods. You believe only in Vatu, and even then only because you have no choice. At this rate, you will become a full-blown heretic. After all, so many of the weavers are. There are as many believe in the Whisperer as believe in the Spinner, the Weaver and the Cutter.

You touch the sign of the Weaver that is carved into the frame of the loom. You did not carve it. But still, when you trace the lines dug into the wood you feel a certain peace. The Weaver has a pattern for us all. And the Cutter, may she stay long away from you.

Now is not the time for such thoughts. Instead, you send the shuttle faster and faster, trying to build the rhythm of the weave. Most people do not know that cloth is made by music. But Injutil will not pick up the speed. She tries but is too slow and falters.

Eventually, the blocks strike together three times. It is time to rest and eat. Injutil has a rice ball, and you have a crust of bread. It is not much. But you are grateful for what you have. Water is brought to you. At least there is plenty of that and you drink. It is dry work in the weaving shed but it is better than the spinning rooms. There the air is thick with drifting fibres that stick in your throat and lungs. You have much to be grateful for, you tell yourself. So very much.

Injutil digs you in the ribs with her elbow.

"What is it," you say and turn to her.

She gestures over to the foreman Brau. He is looking in your direction. “He’s watching you,” she says.

“No, he’s not,” you say. But you know he is.

“What have you got against him? Would not be the worst thing to have the foreman as a friend.” And she digs her elbow in your side again.

“I am married,” you say. “I was married.”

“What happened to him?”

“He… He is dead.” What else can you say?

“So now someone else is interested. He’s the nicest of the foremen.”

“But single,” you say. “At his age why is he single? Something is not right there.”

“His wife died. He’s a widower too. Just like you. I’m guessing this is fate, the work of the Weaver.”

“I don’t believe in that. Not really. I’m sure I’m not the only widow in the shed.”

“But you’re the only widow he keeps looking at. You’re much prettier than Igri or Mannan.”

“I should hope so,” you reply, thinking of the two plain old widows. And then you realize that you are the same age as them. Maybe it would not be the worst thing to have an admirer. As long as he keeps his distance.

“I’m not interested in that stuff.”

“Oh,” says Injutil, “I guess your last husband wasn’t much for—” and here she makes a rude gesture.

You slap her hand, but you’re smiling too. “None of your business, but yes he was.” And you allow yourself to think of Greba and his strong arms.

Before any more can be said, the blocks sound. It is time to go back to work. You are glad. The work keeps your mind from being hungry, and other things. Still, as you weave your cloth, you can feel that he is watching you. But it makes you feel safe rather than afraid.

Chapter Forty-Eight
Rice

Unead

When the blocks are struck it is time to end. You tidy the threads and cover, brush the weave. Then cover the loom. It takes a while to get the loom set. Injutil helps you, but even so, you are one of the last to leave. Brau is waiting to lock the shed.

"Hurry up," he says. You bow apologetically.

He locks the shed and then turns to you. "Hopefully there's still rice to be bought."

"I hope so too."

You head to the market with Injutil by your side. When you get there, there is only one stall open. There is a line waiting and you join it behind Injutil. The stall is selling rice. One bag only for each person. Even so, the line moves slowly. Brau joins the line just behind you.

"Switch places," you whisper to Injutil, but she refuses. "I should beat you more," you say. But she still does not switch places and you can see she is amused at your discomfort. You turn to the foreman. "Why don't you go in front of us? It is our fault that you are late. We were slow to ready the loom."

"No, I couldn't do that," Brau replies.

"I won't let you go before me," says Injutil.

"You'll do as I say," you reply to her.

"I'm fine where I am," he says again.

The rice is in bags. One for each customer and no more. There is a woman at the stall arguing that she needs more, but the merchant will not relent. Their voices are loud. The rest of the line starts to shout at the woman. One is all they will get and now she is taking too long. They all have homes to go to.

The merchant threatens to give the woman no rice. Now she is crying and telling him about her hungry children. But he does not care. Children are easily replaced.

"Have you children?" asks Brau.

What can you say? Your daughter is gone. You do not know where she is, or if she is even alive.

"I have a son," you say, thinking of Mukito. "A foster child."

"Her husband is dead," says Injutil.

"I am sorry to hear that," says Brau and bows to you. "My wife passed away, it was the white lung."

"I am sorry for your loss."

"It was some time ago." But there is still hurt in his eyes. "How did your husband die?"

"It was not very long ago."

"I am sorry, I do not mean to intrude."

After that, he leaves you alone. You wait in line and think of Greba. He is not dead. And even this feels like a betrayal, all the worse because a part of you is thinking of Brau and his gentle kindness. You realize that you still hope that Greba will find you. Even though you know that he is not looking for you. You hope he is not looking for you, and you hope he is. You miss him. You miss him so much. How many years has it been now? Three years. It has been so long and no time at all.

While you think of him, you come to the head of the line. The stallholder hands Injutil a bag of rice. The last bag. She pays and smirks at you, then leaves.

"Have you no rice?" you ask.

Stallholder shakes his head. There are angry murmurs from behind you. Injutil has disappeared and it is lucky for her that she has. Those without might have taken her rice from her.

The stallholder is boarding up his shop.

"Wait, what about us?" someone asks.

"There's no rice here. I don't have any rice."

"Not even some for yourself? You must have some hidden in there."

"No," says the merchant. "I have nothing. Now get on your way, or I'll call the guard."

You walk away. If there is going to be trouble, you do not want to be part of it. Brau is following you.

"Wait up," he says.

"What?" you reply.

"I have rice."

You turn and look at him. "You have rice? How?"

"I can't say, not here. But I can bring rice to your house."

You want to say no, but you think about Mukito and Canna. There is nothing to eat.

"Thank you," you say. "I have money. I can pay you."

"There's no need," says Brau.

"Please, it will make me feel better," you tell him.

"If you insist. I will not take long. I will meet you at your home."

You wonder how he knows where you live, but you let it pass.

"Thank you," you say, and bow before leaving.

When you get home, Canna is waiting for you. "Did you get rice?" she asks.

"No, maybe," you say. You take Mukito in your arms.

Canna looks with worried eyes but says nothing. Mukito is sucking his fingers.

It is not the end of the world to go without rice for one day.

But then he arrives. He is carrying a bag of rice. He bows and hands it to you. And when you fish out a coin from your bag he takes it gracefully.

"Thank you," he says.

"Thank you," you reply. "Do you wish to eat with us?" It is only polite to offer, and it is only polite of him to decline.

"Perhaps another time," he says.

"There may not be anything to eat another time," says Canna. "You should come and eat now."

He agrees even though he is uncomfortable. Canna takes the rice and begins to cook it. She leaves Mukito with you.

"Is this your son?" ask Brau.

You laugh at that. "I am too old to have children. He is a foster child."

"She found him in the gutter and took him in," says Canna. "And me."

"That is very kind of you," says Brau.

"Not at all. It is better than living alone. Just."

Brau says nothing and you remember that his wife has passed on.

"Do you have children?" you ask.

"No," says Brau. "We had a son once."

"What happened?" you ask before you can stop yourself.

Brau makes the sign of the Cutter. He is dead.

"The rice is almost ready," says Canna. And you are grateful for the interruption. Brau has taken Mukito from you and you go to help Canna serve the rice.

"So where did you get the rice?" asks Canna as she hands Brau a bowl.

Brau looks uneasy. But then he shrugs. "I was born on a farm outside of the walls. They sent me some. Farmers always keep some food back. Even if there is no food here, they will have some. I think I will leave here soon. They cannot have enough food and when everyone starts to starve there will be riots, and worse."

"What about your job?"

"The sheds will close soon. We have plenty of silk, but no one is buying cloth just now. They might even be locked down tomorrow."

"So, I am out of work tomorrow too?"

"I think that is likely. If not tomorrow, then soon."

"And how will I pay for rice then?" you ask. But you know that hidden away you have a fortune in gold.

"You should leave too. All of you. You should get out while you can. Once the famine starts, the plague comes soon after. You should leave."

"And go where?"

Brau makes a sign. It is the sign of the Weaver. "There is a pattern for all of us. If you wish to come with me, then that would be good."

You think then, does the Weaver want your threads entwined? And you know what Brau would want in return.

"I am not ready for that," you say. "I might never be."

Brau nods his head. "I understand. I thought I would never be ready either. Perhaps I am not. I am asking too much. But I will likely be gone tomorrow."

"I'm ready if she's not," says Canna. "I'll go." It is meant as a joke. But neither you nor Brau laugh.

"Where will you go?"

Brau leans closer to whisper. Mukito has toddled off to the corner of the hut, but Canna is watching.

"I can hear you too," she says. "You'll need to lean closer if you don't want me to follow you."

"The farm I grew up on is called Ridgefield. You should find me there if you change your mind."

"Won't it be dangerous to go there too?" you ask. "If there is no food in Saco, they will send out soldiers to collect more."

"They will," says Brau, "but most likely they will find the farm empty when they come. You cannot march an army through the country and not be seen. The people will be long gone by the time they come."

"So you cannot stay there either."

"There is a place," says Brau. "You will find it if you look."

He takes something from his tunic. It is a twist of wire in the shape of an arrow and he hands it to you.

For a moment you do not recognize it. "What is this?"

But then you see. It is the mark of the bandit, of the hunter.

"Why do you have this?" you ask.

"I am useful to them. I give them information when asked. They pay me. That is how I got the rice."

You think for a moment about what that means.

"And what did you give them in exchange for the rice?"

Brau is not angry at your words. "It does not matter, it was nothing."

And you think because Brau has spoken, someone will be robbed or beaten. That is the price of your meal.

"Take it," he says. "Take it and use it when you need to. They will show you the place."

The twist of wire is cold in your hand. "The guard will kill me if they find this on me."

"It is possible, but when the famine starts, the guard will kill you for a grain of rice, or a copper coin. Leave it if you want, but you should leave here soon. Very soon. When the famine starts they will close the gates."

"I'll take it," says Canna. "This one cannot see what's plain. We should leave tonight. Before the trouble starts. I've lived through famine before. You have the right of it. If there is no food, then outside we can at least look for roots and fern shoots."

Now she turns to you. "You took me in and kept me alive, and the boy. If we are going to still live, then we need to leave."

You know she is right. But it seems so sudden, so final. But then you knew you would be running your whole life once you left the City of the Sun. What difference does it make to run some more?

"If you are leaving, then you may as well come with me. I know what you said, about not wanting our threads entwined. But the Weaver is patient. And if we are not to be woven, then let us at least avoid the Cutter, and this is the best way to do that. For you and the others."

"And besides," you say, "you might come to appreciate Canna's charms."

“I might,” says Brau, but when he says this, his eyes do not move from you.

Mukito has come back to the fire and is crawling into Brau’s lap. He seems to like the big man at least. And children know. There is that at least. Brau is a good person or at least as good as anyone in this world.

“We shall need to pack,” you say. “Where should we meet you?”

“It is best to meet outside of the walls. I will wait until the next moon rises, but no more.”

Canna is already packing, not that there is that much to bundle up.

Chapter Forty-Nine
The General

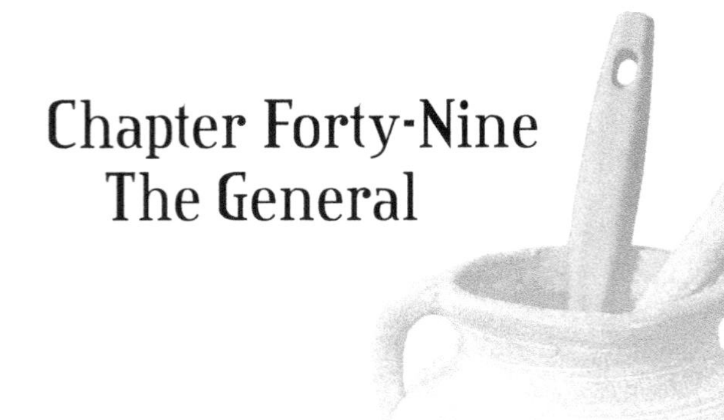

Hilketa

You are alone. It seems you are more alone than ever. But you are not alone. Here, even here I am with you. How restless you are. You pace back and forwards in your room.

With Greba gone, you find yourself alone too much. You have so much to do. The dark lands do not rule themselves, and it is always you that has to bother with the running of things. No one else cares. Each of the twelve will concern themselves with nothing but the darkness. How useless they are. Even Greba. Even when the high priest was here, all he did was follow what you said. Why did Vatu bother to bring the others, they are of no worth.

But now you feel alone, and anxious as you await word from Saco. And what then, you think. Why wait for word from Greba? You could march to Saco yourself with an army. But what good is that? Perhaps you are better out of this.

"What say you, Whisperer?" you ask. "How do I make things better?"

"Through kindness and goodness," I reply.

"People will starve, people will fight, people will die."

"Then how can you stop that?"

"I cannot."

And you are right. How can you stop what has happened a thousand times before? Famine, war, disease. They will all come. Again and again, they have come. They have killed more, many more than you have in all your lives.

You have sent the order to ready a battalion to send to Saco.

"Should I go with them?"

You have reports from Saco on your desk. You have read them many times over. The famine has started. Rice is now rationed. Even so, it will not be enough to last until the Sun rises. People are starving and many have left the town. Orders have been given to lock the gates. No one is to enter or to leave except by the will of the twelve. There are many pleas from the governor for food to be sent. The pleas have fallen on deaf ears, they have fallen on your ears.

Besides, there is a famine somewhere every year. It is how Vatu keeps things in check. Let the peasants die. They are unimportant.

"They are important to me," I tell you.

"I cannot save everyone," you say.

"I have not asked you to save everyone."

"Then what? What will you have me do?"

"What you can," I tell you. "Save those that you can."

But my words fall on the same ears that heard the plea of the governor. Deaf ears. They hear but do not listen nor do they understand. I will teach you. I will show you.

"I can save no one." And then you decide. The army is ready to march. You will go with them. You will lead them to Saco. You will make sure that the starving citizens do not escape to carry disease and violence through the land. If they will rebel, then they will die. You will not wait for Greba's word. He does not command you, and you do not need his permission. You will take the battalion and raze the city to the ground. You read the reports. The people are angry because they have no food. It is only a matter of time before they rise up. Already, they are openly praying to the other gods and worst of all to the Whisperer. That is enough reason to wipe the city clean. And you need no reason. You answer only to Vatu.

"And to me," I whisper.

"Then what would you have me do?"

But I have told you already, I would have you be kind.

"There is no room for kindness in this world that you have made."

You cast open the doors of your chambers. Outside a scribe is waiting.

"Call the general. Are we ready to depart?"

The scribe bows and runs off without a word. It is only moments before he returns. Behind him is the general. The general bows low but does not enter the chamber.

"Everything is ready, great one. We can leave at the moment you command."

You turn to the scribe. "Have a coach readied. I will go with them."

The scribe shows his surprise on his face but says nothing. You are pleased, otherwise, you would have to kill him. "You will come with me," you say. The scribe rushes off to follow your command.

Turning again to the general, you ask, "What is your name?"

Without rising, the general replies. "Espasa."

You see that he is young. He must be well connected to rise to the rank of general so soon.

"Stand up."

The general rises and you look him in the eye. His eyes are dark and there is no sign of fear in his eyes or on his face.

"Why are you chosen for this task?" you ask.

"I am the least of the generals. I will be the smallest loss to the city while I am gone."

Such humility in a general; it makes you laugh inside.

"But what if your talents are insufficient for my task? Perhaps I should have the finest at my command?"

"I am the least of the generals," he says, "but even the least of your generals will be more than sufficient to deal with any task. I am young but capable. I will follow your command in all things, and my men will follow mine. Whatever you wish of me, will be done. This I promise."

So, he is still ambitious. That is good.

"Whose man are you?" You think he will not betray which of the twelve has set him where he is, but you will find out.

"Your man," he declares.

And who else's, you wonder.

"I will follow all your commands, great one."

The scribe returns. "A carriage will be ready within the hour," he informs you.

"Good." You turn again to General Espasa. "Within the hour we leave."

"It shall be as you command," he says and turns to leave. His armour clinks in the darkness as he walks away. What fools soldiers are. No armour can protect you from the dark. It is better to go silently through the shadows.

"Go and gather my things," you say to the scribe. "Have them brought to the carriage."

And then you follow the general into the darkness.

Chapter Fifty
Forward

Hilketa

The wagon is ready. The horses are impatient and stamp and snort, ready to get going. There is only a half-moon risen, so there are lanterns set over the driver to light the way. The rest of the army stand ready. You will travel with the van. The general, Espasa, is mounted and waiting for you. It is as you expected. He is Greba's man. But he will do as you command. You motion to him, and he guides his horse forward but does not dismount. He underestimates you. You do not have Greba's gift for violence, but you have other gifts. He should take care not to offend you.

"All is ready," he tells you. "We await your command." He bows his head, but still has not dismounted. How confident he is in his own strength. But you could drag him from his horse and beat him. Why are you so angry? Why is it so important to you that he shows you respect? You have little interest in the army. That has always been Greba's concern. But your pride is pricked that he does not dismount. You will do nothing for now. If you humbled him here you would have to replace him. More delays. You are eager to be on your way.

"Very well," you say and turn your back on the general. You give him no sign that you are displeased but you will remember this.

The coach is a grand brake, sprung on leather straps. You enter and two scribes follow after you. Neither speaks. The general wheels off and the column begins to move out. The brake moves into line and you move out through the city down the main avenue to the gates. No one looks or watches. They turn away as you go past. The clicking of horseshoes on cobblestones and the sway of the cabin, the glint of moonlight through clouds. It is some time before you reach the gate. They are swung open and the column goes through without pause. The wagon moves only at a trot. Otherwise, the soldiers marching would be left behind. They march in line as if on parade. On the road, it will be harder to keep rank. The ground will be rougher and the road narrower. But for now, they march with stern faces and proud bearing. Soldiers always like to put on a show.

Outside of the city, it is as you thought. The soldiers move now at a slower gait and relax into an easier pace. You wonder if you should go ahead. But you decide against the idea. It is better to come with your army. That is what you told Greba you would do.

"How long to reach Saco?" you ask, although you know the answer well enough.

"We should be there by the time the moon is full," says one of the scribes. "If we travel without the column we can be there in half the time."

You could have stayed and left a few days later, but there is a message you wish to send. This is your army, your column, they are under your command.

For now, there is little more to do than to sit and wait. The column will not go far the first day. Espada has shown on the map each campsite. Once there were barracks on each roadway, a day's journey apart. But they are no longer in repair. In a lifetime long past you and Greba argued bitterly over the cost. It was a battle you won. You have read all of the records. How angry Greba must have been. The thought of it gives you pleasure, although now you wonder if your decision was correct. It does not matter. Of course, you were correct.

You look at the two scribes. One is familiar, the other is not. Neither looks at you. Both keep their eyes down. You should have chosen the two scribes, but you wished to see who would be sent and who would send them. You know who sent the familiar scribe. He is Kong's man. You wonder who has sent the other. They are like toys you will play with on the journey. You could slay them now. Both are here to betray you and to send word of your actions back to their masters. What fools the twelve are. They are all fools except you.

The cabin is lurching too much to make writing possible. Even reading would be difficult. More so in the poor light of the smoking lantern.

"Tell me your names," you say to put them at ease. They will not let their guard down, but you will play the game until you kill them. Neither will look up.

"Astani," says the familiar scribe.

"Andors," says the strange scribe.

But neither says anything else. You lie back and close your eyes pretending to sleep. But all the time thoughts pass through your mind. What, you wonder, are they thinking to themselves? They must surely know that you will kill them. That you will not let them betray you. It is pleasing to think that they are afraid. They will be more afraid before they die.

Chapter Fifty-One
The Storm

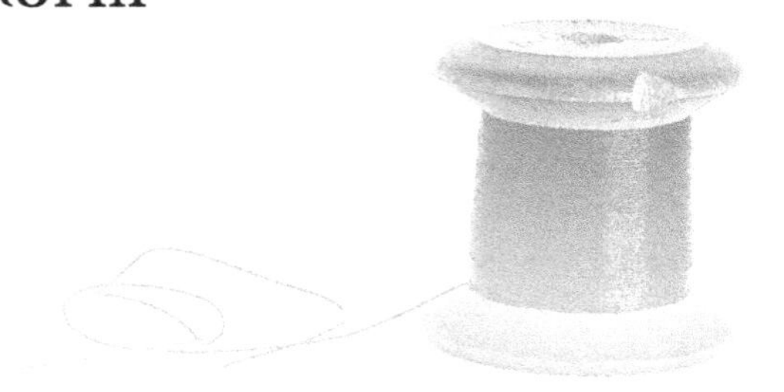

Ennet

When you get to the milling stone, Ezena and the other women are there. Some you do not recognize. There are more people arriving every day now. So many people have nowhere else to go.

There are two bandits by the grain hopper. There is another one down in the pit.

"There must be something," says Ezena. But one of the bandits pushes her back.

"Get back," he says.

"We need grain, otherwise we'll starve."

A man comes up the ladder. He is carrying a sack. "Here," he says.

"One sack," says Ezena.

"Condito says that is all. One sack today. There's not much down there."

"How is that going to feed us all?"

The bandit shrugs.

When Ezena turns and looks at the crowd, there is despair in her voice. The crowd pushes forward.

"Get back," says the bandit. "There's no more. There's not enough for everyone."

The women are complaining and pushing forward.

"That's all there is."

They reach out to grab the sack, but the bandit starts to beat them away.

"None today."

You watch as the women beg and plead but you know there will be none given. You are too old to push and fight for grain. Too old and too weak. You are hungry. If Dova had come with you, then she could have pushed through the crowd. But it would have done no good. The bandits will not give any more grain. You will have to do without. All of the women will have to do without.

You turn and head back to the cabin where they are waiting. When you get there you see Alaba smile and come towards you. Sifyre follows after her.

"Did you get anything?"

"No, not this time," you say. How weary you feel, and how hungry. Sifyre watches you and says nothing. "There is no grain and there is no flour."

No one asks what will we eat? Perhaps Bidann will be lucky today. When he comes back from hunting, perhaps he will have meat. But even that seems scarcer. It has been days since he brought back anything.

"Will we go and look for roots?" asks Sifyre. Unlike her mother, she is a hard and willing worker.

You nod. What else is there to do? You will have to walk far. Everything that is edible has been dug up or picked. Even the fern roots have all been eaten.

"Go and get your mother," you say. But Sifyre shifts uneasily. You can guess why she is reluctant to fetch Dova. "Well fetch Utas, he's got a good nose for mushrooms." And is more help anyway.

You shout over to the porch where Utas is laying on a mat. "You get a sack. We're going to look for food."

He rises up, still wearing his chains. "Someone should stay here."

"Dova can stay."

"I mean, someone should stay with Dova, and with the hut."

You know that he is right. There are so many people now, and all of them hungry and homeless. They will come and steal what they can from the hut. Dova cannot stop them, neither can the children. If Bidann was home, then you could leave them with him.

"When will Bidann be back? He should be back now, he's usually back before now."

Utas steps forward and stands beside you. "He will have had to go further to look for game."

You know that he is right. But still, you are worried. You are always worried now.

"I will get a sack," you say and enter the hut.

Dova is sitting. You can smell the mescal. Even when there is nothing to eat, there is still mescal. She looks up at you with vacant eyes. "Is he back yet?"

Why does she care? She has no love for Bidann. She is using him just like she uses everyone else. Just like she is using you. She cares for nothing, not even for her own child.

"There was no grain today," you say. "I will need to go and look for food."

"It's all right," she says, "I am not hungry." Her words make anger rise within you. You are forgetting my way. You are forgetting that you must love everyone.

"Sifyre is hungry, and Alaba," you reply. You have gathered a sack to put whatever you find in. You head to the door.

"Wait," says Dova, rising unsteadily to her feet. "I will come with you."

"If you like," you say. And push the door open. Outside there is light coming from the half-moon and from the moon rock. Dova follows you through the door.

"It's so bright out here," she says. Then she shouts to Sifyre who comes running over and takes her hand. "We're going to get food," she says.

"Look for food," you say. "We might not find anything."

"Bidann will find something," she replies.

You hope he does. You are not sure you will find anything.

"You stay here," you say to Utas. You would like to tell Dova to stay too but you know she will not agree.

"Yes," says Utas. "If you want you can leave the children. I will look after them."

Perhaps that is for the best. Sifyre has sharp eyes and nimble fingers. And you do not like to leave Alaba with anyone. Still, when you go through the forest, the light she brings makes it easier. If you leave her, then you will need to take a lantern. Besides, you do not fully trust Utas, no matter what I have told you.

"It is better if they come with me," you say.

He does not argue.

"Watch the hut," you say. And then you walk out away from the camp.

When you are out of the camp, the trees thicken and hide the moon. You follow a deer track through the trees.

"Look out for ferns," you say, "or mushrooms." Or anything. There are a few straggly stems here and there, but nothing worth picking. You will need to go deeper.

Alaba's soft light shows the path. Sifyre is walking ahead. She is singing a soft tune. You try to remember the words. Once you knew that song. Dova is struggling to keep up.

"There is nothing here," she says. And she is right.

"That is why we need to go in deeper."

"It is a lot of walking for some fern root."

You bite your tongue. She could have stayed at the hut. She will slow you down. And irritate you. Women like her always irritate you.

"It's not too late for you to turn back."

"But I have no lantern. I would get lost most likely."

Again you bite your tongue. Would that you should be so lucky. The wind has picked up and the dry clacking of twigs rubbing in the canopy sounds all around.

"I hope none of the trees come down," you say.

Dova comes closer to you. "Do you think they might?"

"Hopefully not," you tell her. But it does seem to you as if a storm is coming. You can feel the wetness in the air as it blows past you. And it is getting cooler.

"Call Sifyre back," you say to Dova. "We should stay closer to each other."

She does as you say, and her child comes skipping and glad back to you. She gives Dova a hug and then you too.

"I like the forest," she says. "I like the trees and the wind."

"Me too," you say. And you realize it is the truth. You had never thought on it before. How you like the majesty of the great trees or how you like the vaulted places underneath. The eyes of a child, how you wish you still had those.

Even the wind brings a restless pleasure. A sense of distant places, and a feeling as if you could leap in the air, and the wind would catch you like a falling leaf and carry you away.

"If the storm brings rain then it will bring on mushrooms."

"I like mushrooms," says Sifyre.

"Me too," you say.

"Me too," says Alaba. And you all laugh, even Dova.

"I like the big pale ones," says Dova. "Sliced and fried."

The thought of it makes you hungry.

"With garlic and lemon juice and fried in butternut oil," you add. If you are going to dream then dream properly.

"Garlic and lemon," says Dova. "Do we have any garlic? I know we have no lemons."

"No," you admit. "Not a bit. But maybe will find some in the wood. Or we could flavour them with pine needles."

"I've never been so hungry," says Sifyre. "Can you eat pine needles?"

"They won't fill you up," says Dova, "but if you chew on them, they taste a bit like lemon."

Sifyre gathers some and puts them in her mouth, then hands some to Alaba.

"No," you say. "She might choke on them."

"She'll be all right," says Dova. And you motion to Sifyre to go ahead.

It is true; chewing pine needles will not fill you up. But it does take the edge off your hunger.

"It is very quiet," says Sifyre.

It is not quiet. The wind is still up, but you know what she means. There has been not the flutter of a bird nor the call of a cicada. The forest is silent.

There is a fallen tree ahead of you. It is lying across your path.

"If it does rain," you say, "we could take shelter under the tree."

The wind is stronger now and is whistling over the trees.

"We can shelter from the wind at least."

You crouch down under the upturned roots. It forms a barrier against the wind and above you, the thick trunk offers some shelter from the rain as it starts to fall.

"It is a storm," says Sifyre. "Let's go home."

"Not now," you tell her. "It's safer here."

"I hope Bidann is safe," says Dova. "I hope he is home by now."

"He should be," you say, because you want him to be safe too, but also part of you wants to comfort Dova. It is a small thing to be kind. "The Whisperer will keep him safe."

Dova shrugs. She is not a believer. She does not believe in anything. Why, you wonder.

Now the rain is coming down hard and heavy. The wind whips the raindrops so that they fall and swirl around you. Your scant shelter will not keep you dry, and you hold your shawl over your head.

"Come here, girls," you say. "Come under the shawl and keep dry."

Dova has no shawl. She puts her arms over her head.

"Where did you get that shawl?" she asks. "It's very pretty."

You look at the shawl. It is nothing remarkable. You bought it in the market in the City of the Sun. But Dova has never been there.

"Take an end," you say. And she takes one end and you the

other. The two girls sit between you.

"How long will the rain last?" asks Sifyre.

"Not long," you say as much in hope as anything. Who knows how long the rain will last?

"Will we go back when it stops?"

"No," you tell Sifyre, "we still need to find food. After the rain, we should find more fern shoots and mushrooms. In a way, this storm is a blessing. We must thank the Whisperer."

"Who is the Whisperer?" Oh child, what a question. Who am I indeed?

You say to Sifyre, "He is the creator and the redeemer."

"What does that mean?" she asks.

"It means we must trust him in all things."

Dova is silent. You thought perhaps she would tell you to hush. She is not a believer. And what reason has she been given to believe? You have never asked for her story and she will not tell it. But you do not need to. You know that her life has been hard; harder even than your own. What reason have I given you to believe in me? But then you think of a thousand tiny kindnesses. You think of how I have blessed you in small ways. You think of Alaba and Sifyre. You think of the peace I have brought you.

"I trust he will keep us safe in this storm," Dova says.

"We will be," you tell her. "And if we are, will that be enough for you?"

"Perhaps if he feeds us too. Then I might believe."

Am I tempted to feed you? I will feed you, but not because of her words. I will feed you because I feed all things. You are in my care. Each breath and each morsel comes from me.

"We will find food somewhere," you tell her. "And when we do, I shall give thanks."

"I will too," says Sifyre.

The rain is still falling.

"How long will we have to stay here?"

The wind has changed direction.

"We should go to the other side," you say. "There will be less wind."

"But there will be no shelter from the rain."

The roots of the tree are leaning back, forming almost a cave.

"If we go in right under the roots we should be able to keep dry," you say.

Dova grumbles but stands up. The two girls follow you as you walk around the tree.

"I wish we could make a fire," says Dova. And you wish there was fire too.

In the cave of earth, the soil is fresh-turned and loose. It's soft to sit on, but you know it is making your clothes grubby. There is nothing else for it. Worms and grubs move through the soil, and your nose is full of the scent of leaf mould.

"I'm not hungry enough to eat grubs," says Dova. And neither are you.

"No, not me either," you say.

"I am," says Sifyre.

"No, don't eat them," you tell her. "You don't know which to eat and which to leave."

"Do you?" she asks.

"No. Not really." Although you have been so hungry you have eaten bugs before. "I think worms are OK. But you need to eat them quickly and not think about it."

Sifyre has a worm in her hand. She looks at it uncertainly and then casts it away. It seems she is not hungry enough to eat worms.

"It's a pity Alaba doesn't give off heat as well as light," says Dova.

"This is not the child's fault," you reply. "If we huddle close it will be warmer." Out of the wind, it is not that cold anyway. Alaba is restless and escapes from your arms. She walks around the little lean-to that the roots of the tree have formed.

"Don't play in the dirt," you tell her. But she does not listen. Instead, she gives a little excited call.

"What is it?" And when you look over, you see that she has found a cache of hazelnuts, perhaps the hoard of a squirrel or crow.

"Get those stones," you say and Dova brings them over. You crack one and hand it to her. Then you begin to pile them into your sack. It is a big cache. It is a good find. You crack a nut for Alaba and Sifyre and then one for yourself.

"At least we won't starve," you say.

Dova has taken a nut and broken it open herself. "No, we won't," she says. "But it will take more than a handful of nuts before I believe."

"Suit yourself," you tell her. "If a shining child and a piece of the moon are not enough to make you believe, then why would anything?"

"What have they got to do with him?" Dova protests.

You know better than to answer. Let her think what she will. If the Whisperer will not speak to her, then there is nothing you can do. And the words the Whisperer has for her are nothing to do with you. Let them have their own conversation. If she will not listen then that is up to her.

The wind has slowed to a steady whistle. It is still raining, but now it is a slow, steady downpour, not the torrents of rain that came before. The moon has fallen and the stars are covered by clouds. Alaba could light the way back, but it would be difficult to see ahead and you could miss turnings in the deer tracks and get lost.

"We should stay here until the moon rises again. And until the storm blows out. Then we should be able to get back."

"All we have to eat are those nuts," complains Dova. "And Bidann will be back. He will be worried about me."

"Utas will tell him where we have gone," you say. "It is better to wait here. And at the camp, we have nothing to eat. These nuts are all we have."

"Bidann will have brought game. And there is a fire. And a bed."

The last thing you want is for Dova to wander off on her own. She would get lost for sure.

"I said stay here," you tell her. "You only want to go back because you miss your mescal."

As soon as you say it, you regret the words. It is as if you have slapped her in the face. That is what you wanted to do anyway; slap her. It is what she deserves.

Dova looks at you. "You are just like the others. You hate me too."

She stands and moves to go and you grab her arm. "Stay. I'm sorry. I had no right to say that."

And now she changes again. She slumps. The way these women always do. "You had every right. It's true. I miss it. I need it. You don't know how that is."

But you do know. You want to tell her that you know exactly how it is.

"Lie down and go to sleep," you say. "Things will be better when the moon rises."

Chapter Fifty-Two
Breaking

Utas

The air is cold and you can feel the storm coming. Hopefully, Ennet has not taken Alaba too far and will get back before the storm breaks. You wonder if you should go and help them. The forest can be dangerous when the wind is high. But you should not leave the hut. You know that eyes are watching. It is a hard choice.

"She should have taken me with her," you say. You tell yourself that it will be fine. You know that Ennet is a capable woman. She will find somewhere to shelter if she cannot get back. That is the best thing; to ride out the storm and return later. You can be of no help to them.

But still, you worry. After all, Alaba is your daughter. How you want to go to her and make sure she is safe.

"Would I even find them?" you ask. You do not know which way Ennet left.

Before you can think more about it, there is a commotion at the moonstone. Condito is standing on top of it shouting and the rest of the bandits are shouting back. There is a crowd gathered. Nearly everyone is there. You decide to go. It might be important to hear what he is saying but you can guess, and when you get near you know that you are not wrong.

"There is plenty of food in Saco," he says. "And there are lots of us. We will raid the farms first and if need be we can take the town."

There is lots of shouting. Most of the bandits are waving their weapons in the air. Famine always comes to this. Those with almost nothing taking from those with even less. You look around. The crowd is armed with staves and rods. They will be able to raid farms and to beat farmers, but Vatu's guard would cut through them like a knife through butter. You know, you have seen it many times.

"We head out now," says Condito. And the bandits turn on the crowd and start to drive them forward towards Saco. They go willingly enough. The promise of food is enough for them. None of them think about what will happen if they meet the guard. At worst it will be a quick death instead of a slow one. You slip back to the hut and watch as they are driven like cattle onwards.

The moonstone is lifted back onto the wagon. And Condito sits by it and the wagon follows on from the rear.

You had not realized how many people are here. It takes over an hour for them all to leave the camp. You have hidden in the shadow so that you are not caught up with the rest of the starving people. You have no wish to fight or to see them murder the poor people of the country. It is not the solution to their problem. But then what is?

The storm has begun. The rain has begun to fall. That is another reason you do not wish to follow them.

You sit on the porch in the shadows and wait. Once they are all gone, the camp feels strange to you. Even sheltered from the rain, you shiver and pull your coat tight around you. And wait.

You do not have to wait long. He thinks that he cannot be seen. He comes stealthily, carefully. But still, you see him. You hear him and watch him.

When he is close, perhaps ten strides from the hut, he speaks.

"I have come for the whore, and the girl, bring them out."

He lights a torch. The message is clear; or else I will burn you out.

"She's not here," you say from your place in the shadow. "And Bidann would not like it. They were paid for, now they are his. Or the old woman's at any rate."

The torchlight flickers and you can see Garra's face. It seems as if he is possessed with rage. Has he kept his anger hidden all this time?

"She is mine, they are mine. I will deal with Bidann. Bring them out."

"They are not here," you say again.

"They are not with the mob," says Garra. Although how can he be sure with so many people heading out? "Nor is Bidann. If Bidann is there, then send him out. I will fight him now and kill him."

You are relieved to hear he thinks Bidann is in the hut. You had thought perhaps Garra had ambushed him in the forest, and that Bidann was lying somewhere with an arrow in his back.

"Bidann is not here. And if he was he would not be afraid to fight you." No, he would not be afraid, even if he should be.

"Either way," says Garra. "I either get what I came for or set the hut on fire."

"I can't let you do that," you say. "I am to keep the hut safe."

Garra does not answer. He thinks you are beneath even that. He lifts the torch high and walks forward. Now you rise and step out into the moonlight.

"Look at you," he says. "You are going to fight me with your shackles. What is this to you? All you are is a slave."

He is right, but you have reason to be grateful to Ennet, and to Bidann, even if he is a fool. He has drawn his sword in any case and is coming towards you. No doubt he thinks he can kill you with impunity.

"Condito will not be happy when he hears about this," you say. But he is not listening. In any case, Condito has left to sack the villages around Saco. Who knows if he will return. "You took Ennet's gold. It was agreed."

"And now I've come for more gold. And for the girl."

"Bidann will fight you."

Garra swings his sword at you, and your training takes over. He is not very skillful. It is easy to disarm him. You step and hold your arms apart so that his blow glances off the chains. Then wrapping the chain around the blade, you twist and snap the sword in two. The broken blade goes spinning and with a jerk, you strike the fleshy part at the base of Garra's thumb, causing him to release his grip.

He should back away. He should realize he is outmatched. Your manacles are weapon enough for you. Not that you need any weapon. You are the high priest of darkness. Or you were. What are you now? You hesitate. Once you would have killed Garra without a second thought. But now you step back. I hear you calling to me. What should I do?

It is enough for Garra to start again. Cursing you, he takes a dagger from his belt and approaches you more cautiously. The torch has fallen to the ground and lies guttering and flickering. You close your eyes. It is better not to have the flickering light distracting you.

"You should leave," you say. "If you go now, you can still live. There is no need for you to die."

"You're a cocky one. I'll grant you that," he says. And you can hear him coming closer. You can hear his breath and his heart beating. You can hear the rustle of his tunic against his flesh. And then you hear him breathe in sharply, and twist out from his onrushing blow. You follow his blow, pushing him forward and in front of you. This time it's his neck the chains wrap around. You should kill him. One sharp tug and his neck is broken. You should do it. The knife is still dangerous. It is still in his hand. It is what you should do. Again you hesitate. And he twists to slash at you. You brush his hand away, leading the blade in a looping circle that leads the point down and up and round and back. Your hand is on his wrist guiding him. He is yours and this time when the blade is turned to his throat you do not hesitate. The point of the blade slips just below Garra's Adam's apple, then turns upward neat as can be. You have cut his throat as neatly as a surgeon. Neater than most surgeons. You have not nicked a single cartilage. You have gone in and round and back out as neat as can be. And now there is a hole in Garra's throat and blood. Not a fountain of spurting blood, but an ocean of red pouring down and in Garra's lungs, drowning him. He drops the knife and you stand away. Next, he drops to his knees. His hands go to his throat. Even now, you think coldly it would be possible to save him. There is needle and thread in the hut. You are as skilled as any surgeon. Hilketa has taught you well. But you do not move. You hesitate.

"What have I done?" you ask me. "I only tried to protect myself."

You have killed so many times before; why are you so concerned with this one? I ask you.

"I have put that behind me," you say. "You have forgiven me for all that I have done."

So why do you think that I will not forgive you for this too?

"I will not, I cannot go back to this. I am not the high priest of darkness. I have left that behind."

Indeed, I tell you. The high priest would not give this man a second thought. You would have killed him and given it not another thought. How easy were all those thousands of deaths, and now how difficult is this one?

"I did not mean to kill him. He gave me no choice." But when you think over the short quick moments of the fight, you think perhaps you could have broken his arm. Or perhaps just taken the knife from him. It was too easy, too natural to kill. You had thought that was gone from you. The rain is falling heavier now. And the clouds have covered the moon. The shining stone is gone. Condito took it with him on his fool's quest. And Alaba is gone too. You are in darkness again.

"I have promised never to be that again," you tell me. You have fallen to the wet ground and you are calling out to me, promising that you will never again take a life. Is it a promise you can keep? I who know everything, whisper that I do not ask this of you. You think that you can be perfect in this world. That you can put all darkness from you. But you cannot, I say. Only I can take it from you. Only my love is great enough for you. And for Garra.

Chapter Fifty-Three
White Pale Things

Ennet

The storm is over. The clouds are clearing and you can see the stars, although there is no moon. It will rise soon enough, and perhaps it is better to travel in the dark.

"Come on, wake up," you say.

Sifyre is up and beside you almost straight away.

"Should I open some nuts?" she asks.

"No, we will get on our way. If we are quick we can get home in time for breakfast. Bidann will wonder where we are. It is best to get back as soon as we can."

Alaba is still sleeping. You could carry her. But then she awakes and smiles. That is worth more than gold.

"Hungry," she says.

"All right," you say and hand Sifyre a handful of hazelnuts. "Share these between you."

Dova is making a noise but has not sat up yet. "Come on," you tell her. And she turns and rises.

"My back is sore. I think a root must be under it."

You think something unkind, but keep it to yourself. I am pleased that you do. You are learning patience.

"Pack up," you say, although there is not much to pack.

After the girls have eaten, you have gathered the sacks. Dova is as ready as she will ever be.

"Which way?" asks Dova. The moon has risen now. You trace a line from the horns to the earth.

"That way," you tell them and head off back along the trail.

"Look out for mushrooms," you say. "After all that rain we should find some."

"I like mushrooms," says Sifyre. "I like the big white ones with no stem."

"You mean the giant puff-ball," you tell her.

"Yes, those ones."

"If we're lucky we will find a few."

"I like puff balls too," says Alaba.

"Then let's hope we find some."

The forest after the rain feels different. More alive. You can hear birds singing. And from time to time you can hear twigs snap. Deer are in the forest. They have come back to see what will spring up after the rain.

"If Bidann was here, he would catch us a deer," says Dova. "There will be meat when we get back to the hut."

It is likely, meat but no rice. Still, you can cut the flesh to strips and dry it. Then you can use the strips to make broth. It will last days. It is what you should have done with Bidann's kill from the start. But how were you to know there would be no rice or wheat? Your mouth starts to water at the thought of a broth. If you can find mushrooms then you can add them to the broth.

"Keep looking for mushrooms," you tell the girls. And they both skip ahead laughing. How you wish you were still young. But then you think about your life. You are not certain you would wish to relive it. There are too many things that are easier to forget than to live through again. And you think of your daughter. Where is she now, you wonder. Is she even alive? And you think of the man that owned you. Once he was kind but in the end, you were nothing to him.

"Here is one," you call to the girls, and head over to the puffball. Its white skin is almost luminous in the moonlight.

"It shines like me," says Alaba. Except Alaba shines if the moon is there or not. It is so strange, and Alaba is so ordinary. Just an ordinary girl.

"Can we have a piece?" asks Sifyre. "Just a little piece now."

You cut the mushroom from the ground and brush off dirt and twigs. "Why not," you say and trim a little for each girl.

"Can I have some?" asks Dova. Reluctantly you cut another slice and hand it to her. "I don't need all that," she says, and breaks the slice in two, handing you a piece.

"Thank you," you say. Thanking her for something that you gave her in the first place. But you are being too stiff. "Thank you," you say again, but this time you mean it. And anyway she is right. You are hungry, and the sweet white flesh of the puffball is a delight.

Alaba is nibbling her piece like a little mouse.

As you travel on, you find more. No more puffballs, but others that have just pushed through the soil. Mostly they are fresh and new. Very few have not been nibbled by something; slugs or mice or beetles. You find a stinkhorn. You smell it first, and there is a patch of them by the path.

"Ugh," says Sifyre, and covers her nose. Alaba copies her.

"You can eat those?" says Dova.

"I think you can. But I don't fancy it. What a smell. I'm not carrying that with me."

Dova laughs. "They're supposed to have certain uses."

You sniff. As if Dova needs that. Besides, it is hardly a topic to discuss in front of children.

As you travel, you feel a lightness within you as the moon rises. You are almost back at the camp. It will not be long now.

"Look, there is something over there," says Dova and points through the trees.

There is a white shape lying on the ground. It must be very big.

"Let's see what it is," you say and walk forward, but then you hold your hand up. "Dova, could you keep the children there?"

"Why, what is it? Not more stinkhorns?"

But it is too big to be a stinkhorn or a puffball. It is lying face down on the ground. The bare skin shining. The head is covered in hair. Two arrow wounds are in his back, but the arrows are gone. So are all of his clothes. He has nothing. It is strange how you recognize him even face down. You do not want to go near, but you know you must.

"What is it?" asks Dova. She has Alaba in her arms and is holding Sifyre's hand. You can hear fear in her voice. She knows. "I'm coming. Stay here, girls." She puts Alaba down and comes running. She runs past you. "Bidann!" she is shouting. "Bidann! Bidann," and then she is screaming. She is by the body trying to wake it, or perhaps she is trying to turn him over. She is pushing his shoulder. Alaba runs past you before you can catch her. But you catch Sifyre.

"Don't go," you tell her. "Don't look." And then you shout to Alaba to stop.

"What is it?" she asks.

But it is Dova that answers. "It is Bidann, he's dead. They shot him in the back and left him here."

At least they did not eat him, you think but do not say. Now you are afraid. Who will protect you now? Who will protect Dova and Sifyre?

"We cannot go back to camp," you say. Always thinking. Always knowing what to do. "Garra will be there waiting for us. For you."

But Dova is not listening, she has buried her face in Bidann's hair. She is sobbing and you do not know what to say to comfort her. What can you say? There is the sound of a twig snapping, and it is not a deer. They have come back.

"They are still here!" you shout. "Run!" and turning, you run as fast as you can. You hardly have time to turn and look. There are three men that you do not recognize One fires an arrow at you but it misses. You see two more coming from the side. "Run," you say.

Dova will not run. She is sitting by Bidann and will not move. Alaba is being held by one of the men, but Sifyre is by your side. "Go on child, run. Don't wait for me." She is running past you, but she is not running to camp. She is running at the two men. She is carrying a stick. They laugh at her until she whacks one. Then they stop laughing. They will not kill her because she is valuable to them. It is a short struggle but they catch her. Now she is being held. But it is enough for you to escape.

Chapter Fifty-Four
Calm

Utas

The storm is over. The clouds are clearing and you can see the stars, although there is no moon. The stone, even if it was giving light, is gone. Condito has taken it with him and his ragtag army. You are alone with the body of the man you killed.

How tired you feel! You fall to your knees. You do not think you have the strength to bury him, and now you wonder what will happen if Condito comes back and finds you have killed one of his men. You drag Garra's corpse to the stream which is now in flood and push it in. You hope the torrent will carry him away. If not, then it might look like an accident. Although few accidents result in a slit throat.

His body floats up. The air in his wet clothes keeps him on the surface of the stream. He is turning and is caught in an eddy. You will not go into the water to push him over the fall. The water is in full spate. It might take you and carry you downstream. With your manacles on you would not be able to swim. Is there a stick near? It will need to be strong so it does not break when you poke the body.

Garra is lying face down. When you get a suitable stick, you guide the body into the centre of the stream and away he goes. Let the river take him where it will.

Now it is time to go back to the hut and wait. The embers of the fire are still hot and you start a flame. Ennet would not want the fire out. It is only a small flame and gives little heat. The manacles mean that you cannot take your wet clothes off. And you do not have any others to change into. You have lost the key that Ennet gave you in the fight.

"Can you not set me free?" you ask.

The light of the fire flickers around the room. Bidann still has not returned.

That is why you are here. Because you want to save Alaba.

"Save her from what?" I ask you.

"From Garra at least. At least I have done that."

Now you are worried. What if Garra or someone else has found Alaba with Ennet? What if she has been taken? You should have gone with them and kept them safe.

"Where is she?"

She is with Ennet. But that is not enough. Still, you fret. You go outside to the woodpile and pick up the hatchet you use to make kindling. The manacles are not well made but are too strong to split easily with the hatchet. Even after many blows, the link holds. You will not get them off that way.

Then you think that a key will be in the hut, and go to look for it. All through the hut, you search until at last, you ask me to show you it.

Here, I take your hand and place it on the top of one of the beams. There it is. The manacles fall to the ground. You are free. Why did you not think to look there before? But what now? Should you go to look for Alaba? Would you find her? What if you go looking for them and they come back while you are gone?

You settle down to sleep, but cannot. You think about Alaba and worry. So much worry. And yet there is nothing you can do. All you can do is sleep and you cannot even do that. You are also hungry. But there is nothing to eat. You boil some water and sip it as if it were tea, it is better than nothing, not much better, but better. Now you are pacing backwards and forwards. It is nearly moonrise. When the moon rises you will go and look for them. If they are not back by then something must have happened.

Again you settle on the floor and wrap a cloth around you. Now at least you have taken your wet clothes off. Still your mind. Put all thoughts to one side. Imagine a pool of still water, calm and quiet. Eyes shut. Let the calm within you reach out to every part of you. The muscles in your neck and back relax. Imagine that still pool. Now the moon shines on it. Birds sing. Listen to only the song, see only the moonlight on water. Your breath comes in and out. Each breath takes you closer to sleep, each breath brings even more calm. Stop listening to the creaking of the house or the rustle of moth wings, or the crackle of the fire. Hear only the birdsong. Find peace.

You look at the pool again in your mind and deeper and deeper below the surface. Then you see it. Garra's face. His body rises to the surface and breaks the stillness that you have made. His eyes are open but lifeless. Now you sit up. You have not rested but will not sleep now. Your clothes are dry, or almost, slightly damp as you put them on. The heat of your body will dry them soon. Another stick on the fire and the flame rises and gives a little more heat.

Why do you see this face from all the people that you have killed? He is nothing to you. He would have killed you if he could. If you had not killed him then he would have set the hut on fire. You remember the first time you killed in this life. You do not even remember his name. But you remember his eyes bulging as you choked the life out of him. Even as a boy you had strong hands. How many other faces must you look at now? And of them all, how many names will you know? But no other faces come. Not for now. For that you are grateful.

"Must I pay for them all?" you ask.

But you have not paid for any of them. I have paid. I have forgiven you and paid the debt. You cannot pay for any of them.

"How can I stop seeing them?" You must forgive yourself.

"How can I do that?" It is the hardest thing. Rest now. You lie back down and listen to bird songs. Again you see the still pond. The moonlight shines like flickering silver. The calm returns. Still, you do not sleep, but you are rested. Now long you lie there looking at the picture in your head. The bird song follows a melody you remember. It is a song you played on your flute many times. You are finding peace.

Then you hear something else and rise. Someone is shouting at you. You open the cabin door and look out. You can hear Ennet's voice calling you. You start running towards the sound of her voice. You wish she would stop shouting. Who else can hear her?

"Utas, come help me!" she is shouting.

Where is Alaba? You cannot see her. You run as fast as you can. There is no one else in the camp. There is no light anywhere and the moon is still low. As you run, it casts shadows across the ground that seem to circle around you.

"Where are you?" you call. "Keep your voice down."

Now you can hear the sound of running feet. Even in the half-darkness, you can see her. She is alone. Where are the others? You catch her and she shakes as you hold her. You do not see blood. For that you are grateful.

"Where are they?" you ask her.

She has pulled away from you. She is looking around and her eyes are wild. She is afraid.

"Bidann is dead." You knew as much already.

"Where are the others?" you ask again.

She is sobbing. "Bidann is dead and they have taken the children. They have taken Dova."

You do not care about Sifyre or Dova. You only care about Alaba. "Who has taken them? Where are they?"

"I don't know. I don't know. I don't know who they are. They have taken them."

"Show me," you say, and Ennet turns back to the forest and starts running again.

"This way."

Chapter Fifty-Five
Knowledge

Koreb

Greba has bound the both of you. You and Ivre. Tied back to back with the murderer.

"You are too late," you say again. "He has killed the boy."

Greba is not listening. He is pacing back and forwards. What is wrong with him? He is muttering away to himself. Is he mad? But he is not mad, he is talking to me. Unless that is madness?

"I want the boy," he says again. There is murder in his eyes. He is mad. How did you not see that before? It would have made no difference, I tell you.

"The boy is not here," Ivre says. "I can show you where I left it."

It. Ivre does not even think of the boy as real, as a person. He was just some goods that passed through his possession. Less even than that. He would not have tossed goods out onto the street.

"You are scum," you say. But when you say those words, you wonder who you mean. Ivre is scum, a man who leaves a child in the street. Greba is scum, a man who will murder a boy just because of who his father is. And you? You are also scum. You who betrayed everyone.

I should tell you that my love is enough and that you are forgiven, but you have closed your ears to me. I am still whispering to you but you will not listen. Then you must learn a harder way.

Greba hits you in the face. He does not break the skin or dislodge teeth. He is holding his strength back. Why? He does not want you to be unable to speak.

"What are you doing here anyway?" It is as much an insult as a question.

"Trying to stop you," you say. "Trying to make up for what I have done."

"It's a bit late to find a backbone." He sneers.

"I should have let you kill me," you reply.

"I still might. Unless you tell me everything. I should have made sure you told me everything. I should have broken you into pieces. I should have had you beg to tell me all you know."

Yes, and why did he not? I know the answer. Shall I whisper it to you? The answer is love. You are the child of his other-self. The one before. He loves you as his own. To harm you is to harm himself. Love will always trump hate. That is why he will not kill you. Although he is thinking about it. He is trying to find a reason not to kill you. A reason other than love.

"I don't know anything," you say. And you smile when you realize that is true. There is nothing you can tell him that will help him find the boy. You cannot do anything more to help him.

"But he can," says Greba. He turns his attention to the warehouse owner.

"My men will be starting work soon," he says. "When they come they will set us free. They will call the guards. This is madness."

Can Ivre really be such a fool? Of course, he can. Can't he see that no amount of men or guards could stand against Greba? Does he not see who this is?

"Not for some hours yet," Greba says. "They will not start until moonrise. I have plenty of time yet. This will be finished long before that."

You can feel Ivre shudder as Greba speaks. And a chill also runs through you. How can he be so casual about what he is doing?

"What good would it do you to kill the child? How will that make any difference to you? The child is most likely dead anyway."

"The child is not dead," he replies.

"How do you know?"

"I would know."

"Why do you hate the child so much? He is only a child."

"I will kill him because his father is already dead, and I cannot be avenged upon him."

Revenge. It comes to you then. What is evil? The answer is simple. Revenge. Except it is not so simple. It is not as simple as that. How can it be?

"What did he do to you? Why do you hate him so much?" From

your mouth come the very questions that I have whispered to him. Again he hits you. And this time he still pulls his strength, but less so.

Even so, the punch is full in the stomach. It is painful, but you are also strong. You have not trained a lifetime in the arts of war, nor does the darkness fill you and lend you its power. Still, you are strong. You look at the ropes that bind you and realize you are strong enough to break them. All your life you have hidden that strength, kept it within you. You have never wished to use it, afraid that you might harm another. You look up at Greba wondering what you should do next.

"Hitting me will not help," you tell him. "I am not afraid of you."

"You should be." There is menace in his voice. But for some reason, you want to laugh. It is like a child. He is a child. He is a child that has never been loved.

The darkness does not lend you its strength, but I lend you mine. You flex your arms and brace yourself. The ropes snap. Not all at once, but one by one. Then you have to unravel them. You take the ropes from Ivre too. You stand up and walk towards Greba, your arms outstretched.

"Tell me what he did to you, I will listen."

Behind you, you can hear Ivre scuttling towards the door. Let him run. There is nothing he can tell you now anyway. You will not take revenge on him for what he did. You will let me deal with him.

Chapter Fifty-Six
Downstream

Unead

How cold it is! The moon is down now and you walk through the streets in the dark. The sound of clogs striking cobbles echoing as you go. Mukito is asleep in your arms. He is heavy but no heavier than the bundle that Canna is carrying on her back. Ahead you can see the gates. They are still standing open, and two guards are napping in the guardhouse. The rain has stopped at least, but water flows like rivers down and out through the gate.

"We should be home asleep," complains Canna. And part of you agrees. What is the point of this? Running away from the town and their life on the promise of some rice. But you know you cannot stay here. You know what happens when famine comes.

"Stop there, ladies," says one of the guards. "What are you up to at this time of night?"

"We're going to visit my cousins," says Canna. "We're taking the boy back to his parents."

You keep silent. If they hear your accent they will know you are from the City of the Sun. No one would believe that you have cousins on a farm outside Saco.

They are not interested in you, or the boy. "What's in the sack?" they demand. "Let's have a look."

Canna hands them her bundle and you pass over a smaller bag. The guards open both upon the wet cobbles. Cold water puddles around your feet.

They toss clothes and blankets onto the ground.

"Hey, you're getting it all wet!" shouts Canna and rushes to pick up the tossed aside clothes.

The guards laugh. But they do not find anything.

"Nothing to eat?" they ask. Even the guards are hungry.

"No," says Canna.

"What about the boy?"

"He has to go hungry like the rest of us."

The guard grunts in reply. They are wondering if they should search them. So far they have found nothing, but they are wondering if it is worth the effort. You keep your face down.

If you were young, then the guards would search you. They would make you take off your coat. Then they would run their hands over your clothes. They might have taken you to the guard room and made you strip. They would not rape you: only with their eyes, and their prying hands. You look down and shut out the memories.

But you are not young anymore, or perhaps these guards are better than those you met that time long ago. All that stopped when Greba took care of you. You are grateful to him. But that is over now. Now you are just an ordinary old woman. Why does that make you angry? You think of Greba. It would be different if he were here. With closed eyes, you can see his face. But would it be different? Would he see you or would he only see two old women and do nothing except walk past. Anyway, he is not here.

Canna is even older than you are. The guards have no interest in two old women. You are both relieved and angry.

"You'll wake the boy," Canna says. She can see the guards have not made up their mind yet. And then she coughs.

"Step back, old woman," says one of the guards. He is tall but ungainly. And his face is droopy around the eyes. "We don't want to catch anything from you."

It is just a cough. Surely Canna has just coughed to frighten them.

"All right, pick your stuff up and go." They have had enough. There is no fun to be had here. Without another word, they turn back to the guardhouse. Canna picks up her bundle and hands you the bag. Mukito is still sleeping.

"Thank you," you whisper to Canna, and to the Weaver. The Weaver tugs your thread, and you follow through the gate out of Saco.

Once you are through the gate and out of earshot, you sit down to rest. Canna has set a blanket over some dry moss, and you lay Mukito down. What a relief it is to lay down that weight. He is lying on his back snoring gently.

"How do they do it? How do they manage to sleep through anything?"

"I wish I could sleep," you reply.

"Me too. Still, we'll be able to sleep soon enough. If this Brau comes for us."

"He will." And somehow you are certain that he will come.

"I don't doubt it. I saw the way he looked at you."

But you don't want to talk about that. Why must Canna always talk about men?

"He should look somewhere else."

Thankfully, Canna does not reply. But you can tell that she does not believe you. Whatever. Let it pass. There will be time for all that later. What will happen when you refuse him? If he asks. If you refuse.

"Maybe he's more interested in you," you tell her.

"I doubt it," she replies.

"I should not have come."

"It's not too late to turn back." But you know it is. You know that you are lucky to have gotten out of Saco. You know that if you go back you will not be able to leave.

"How long until the moon rises?" you ask.

"Still a while yet I would guess."

But the sound of a cart comes from along the track. Then you see a lantern. He has come and he has come early. You can hear him groaning to himself as he pulls the cart along. As he gets closer and he can see you by the light of his lantern, he smiles.

"Hello, ladies, what brings you out here at this time of night?" And he stops. "Put your stuff on the cart and we'll get going." Brau's cart is almost full. But you do not have much. Once the cart is full, you and Canna take each end of the blanket Mukito is sleeping on and lift him on top of the baggage. He stirs in his sleep. Brau reaches over and strokes his body until he settles.

"Good with children, are you?" says Canna.

"I've had a few."

And you wonder how many. Why does it matter to you? It should not.

"Come on then," Brau says now that Mukito has settled. "We better be going." He strains against the weight of the wagon. He is strong, but not as strong as Greba. It is a pleasant night to go walking. The wagon moves easily along the trackway. The light of the lantern is enough to stop you from stumbling as you walk, but you cannot see far.

"Where are we going?" you ask.

"To a farmhouse. It will not take long. We should be there just soon."

The moon is starting to rise. The light slips across the dark ground. The air is fresh after the rain. You breathe it in. Ahead you can see barns against the moonlit sky. That must be where you're going.

"It is good to be out of the town," Brau says.

"Yes," you agree. And it is. The ground is wet but not too soft. The rain came heavy and fast but does not seem to have sunk in. There are puddles on the road.

When you reach a stream in spate, Brau says, "Sit on the wagon and I'll push you over. No point in us all getting our feet wet."

You and Canna sit on the cart while he takes off his shoes and hands them to you. They are leather shoes with leather soles. Not clogs.

He pushes the cart into the water. The stream is high and fast. It forms ripples and foams where it hits the wheels. Brau is pushing hard.

"We can help if you like," you offer.

"No, I can manage." How like a man. You can see it is hard work pushing against the flood.

In the moonlight, the water is so pretty. When you lived in the City of the Sun, there was a song about moonlight on water. How did it go? You hum a little of the tune in your head and watch the waters. The sound of the rushing stream is like the whisper of a ghost. And floating on the torrent, it comes towards you. A body.

"What is that?" shouts Canna. And the body bobs towards you. Canna slips from the cart and holds the body. You join her and together you steer the corpse to the shore.

Brau pushes the cart out of the water and then comes over to see the body. It is lying face down in shallow water. He turns him over and you can see that his throat is cut.

Canna takes your arm and steps back.

"Who is he?" But none of you know.

"What now? There is nothing we can do for him now. He is dead."

You nod your head. "Who could have done such a thing?" And then you realize you have taken Brau's hand and are clutching it tight. Even if you wanted to, you are not sure you could let go.

The corpse is facing upwards with an open mouth. Water is

pouring out the side and his eyes have rolled back.

Canna, practical as ever, says, "We should see if he is carrying anything." But she does not move forward to touch the body, now lying on the rush-lined edge of the river.

"Whoever did this will not have left anything in his purse, I think."

"Canna is right," says Brau, and he moves forward and checks over the body. In a bag, round his neck, he finds a single gold coin. It is more money than he has ever seen in his life. He holds it up in the moonlight. He looks at you slack-jawed. There is more money than that hidden in your clothes, but you gasp. It is important to keep up the act. No one must guess the truth about you.

Canna sits down. "We should go back to Saco and live like a governor."

But you know it takes more than a single gold coin to live that life. "No, we should go on. When the famine hits, the coin is worthless."

Brau nods. "We should keep this." And he hands it to you. "If anything happens to me, then you can use this. It might help you."

"What could happen to you?" Your voice is light and airy. As if you are making a joke. But the slit-throated corpse is right before you. Who did this? You wonder.

In the wet and cold you shiver. Canna is shivering too. She makes the sign to avert the Cutter. "Spinner and Weaver keep us from the Cutter yet."

But you wonder what pattern they are weaving now. It seems your thread is tied to Brau and Canna and Mukito. The thought makes you glad, and in your heart, you thank the Weaver. She has given you a new life.

"We can't just leave him here." But what else can you do? There is no room for a body on the cart. Nor is there anything to dig a grave with. "If we leave him here, the beasts will eat him."

There is only one thing to do. Together you roll him back into the flood and watch as he floats away.

"From darkness into light," says Brau. They are the words of heresy, but you and Canna echo them. And what else is there to say?

Now you can hear Mukito stirring. He is making soft groans. No doubt he will want fed but you have nothing to give him.

"There are some apples in the cart," says Brau.

"Apples!" says Canna. "Where did you get these?" She is rummaging through the cart looking for them. When she finds them, she hands one to the boy. "Can I have one?" she asks Brau.

"Yes of course," he replies, and there is a look of joy on Canna's face as she bites into the apple, even though it is old and the skin is wrinkled.

Brau fetches two from the bag. One for you and one for himself. He gives you the larger of the two and begins to eat. It is many hours since your last meal and days since you had fruit. The sweetness of the apple makes you moan with pleasure, and the pains in your stomach, that you had pretended were not there, subside.

"When this is over, I am going to eat until I am as fat as a courtesan," says Canna.

"Courtesans aren't fat," you protest.

"How would you know?" says Canna. "Courtiers like a bit of flesh. Or so I've been told. I've never seen a rich whore that doesn't end up fat. And good luck to them too. If I was rich, I'd eat buttered rice every day."

Let it go. If Canna wants to think that is the life of a courtesan then so be it. As she says, how would you know? The only way you can challenge her would be to tell her your secret. You smile. You are thinner than when you were Greba's whore. Perhaps Canna is right. What would Greba make of you if he saw you now? Ragged and scrawny. Not that he will, not that he ever will. He is gone and the only thing left is memories. Did he even love you anyway? He never said that he did.

Now Mukito is in your arms eating. He is looking at you with a happy face. Greba loved your daughter. Of that, you cannot doubt. And you remember him standing in the street below your window, too ashamed to come to you. That must have been love. Neither courtesans nor whores should find love. Is it possible you have found it twice?

"We should be going," says Brau.

"Let's finish eating."

"All right but don't take too long." What is the hurry? But you think again of the body floating down the river. It seems the dark lands are not as safe as they were. "When we get to the farm, there will be milk for the boy."

"How far is it?" You can see barns on the hill, silhouetted against the moonlit sky.

"You can see the cattle barns. We are about two hours walk from there. The farm is just down from the barn out of the wind. They are up there so the smell will carry away from the farm."

"Are you sure we will be welcome?" asks Canna.

"Yes," says Brau. "They know you are coming. It has been spoken on."

"It'll be good to get dry at least. Even if it is just before a fire of dried cow dung."

Brau laughs. "You must think we are all country bumpkins. The fire will be dried turf in the house."

"Whichever, I will be grateful for it."

"Me too," you say. "We are beggars now. And beggars cannot be choosers."

"You are not beggars," says Brau. "You are guests."

"Working guests, we promise," says Canna. You both know full well that mouths that do not work are unwelcome. "I know how to tend cows. I was born outside of Saco. Probably on a farm not so different to this."

"Do you still have family there?"

"No, they're all gone long ago. I don't have any family."

"What about you?" asks Brau. "Where were you born?"

Such a simple question. "I…" You hesitate. And then decide to tell the truth, or as much of it as you think is wise. "I was born the daughter of a courtesan. I was raised to be a courtesan. But eventually, I got my freedom. I learned to weave at the City of the Sun. But my old master would not leave me alone. I was not safe there. So I came to Saco. I have never worked on a farm, but I can sew and stitch."

Canna made a face. "And no doubt paint your face and pour tea in the proper way."

"Yes," you admit. Why do you feel ashamed? "And the other arts. But I also have run a house for my master."

"You won't be able to boss servants around here," says Canna.

"No, but that was long ago. You know I can work as hard as you or harder." And you hold your hands out. They are callused and worn from the weaving.

Canna nods. "I am sorry," she says. "I should not have said those things."

"It's time to go," says Brau. And he lifts Mukito back onto the cart, then pushes the cart along. The boy wriggles down and walks alongside you. You and Canna push from behind while Brau pulls the wagon along. What, you wonder, will Brau think of you now?

Chapter Fifty-Seven
A Reunion

Greba

Why did I not kill him? You ask yourself. I should have killed him. Instead, you have taken Koreb and put him in a cell in the fortress. He did not complain or resist. And when he looked at you with those eyes so similar to your own, there was no reproach in them.

"I know how you hurt," he whispered to you.

You told him everything. You told him how your daughter was taken from you. Stolen by him. By Utas.

"How can I not hate him?" you say. "He has taken everything from me."

You have gone to the rooms that you have in the house by the wall. There at least the governor will not bother you with question after question. Here at least you are alone. Or almost alone. I am here with you.

"Forgive him, and forgive yourself."

But even though you consider my words, you are not ready. Not yet. How can you forgive yourself, you wonder. And you think of all the blood and all the crimes. How can it all be made right? You cannot believe it.

"Have you not paid enough?" I ask. But you say that it can never be enough. That suffering can never end.

There is a knock at the door. Who dares to disturb you? If it is the fool of a governor, you will flay the skin from his bones.

You throw the door open. There are two guards there. Between them is a bag or sack. Something or someone is in the bag. They are crying. It sounds like a child, perhaps four or five.

"Be quiet," says one of the guards, and pushes the child. They enter the room, not waiting for your permission.

"What is this?"

"Sorry, sir. We think you need to see this." And with those words, they lift the bag from over the head of the child.

It is a girl child. As you guessed, about five summers. But that is not all. Her face is shining as if it were the moon in the sky. The room is filled with the light of it. It is her. It cannot be anyone else.

"A patrol brought her in."

"Give me the names of everyone besides you who has seen her."

"You mean seen her like this, or those that have seen her while she's been covered?"

"All of them," you say. It is better if they are all dead. Then no one can talk.

"Just us and the five lads on patrol. And the sergeant."

You think for a bit. "Does the governor know?"

"No sir, only us."

"Go fetch them all," you say, pointing to one of the soldiers. "You stay here."

The child is crying. There are tears on her cheeks. She is afraid. Can it really have been so long since you saw her? She is like her mother, but she has his colouring. You want to take her and embrace her. But not now. Not yet. You cannot do that. Instead, you say a silent prayer to me. Comfort my child's child. But I have already taken her hand. Already I give her my peace. She finds courage in her heart that I place there, and stops crying. She looks at you with eyes that do not flinch.

"Why did they kill Bidann?" she asks. But you do not know what she means. You turn to the guard.

"The patrol came across a bandit. He was dead when they found him and stripped." So how did they know he was a bandit? You wonder. But let the guard continue. "Then later they came across the girl and three others."

"What happened to them?" you ask. But you can hear footsteps outside. "Open it," you say.

There are five guards, the sergeant and two women. One is young, probably only twelve. The other is older and might have been pretty once, but you can see the lines on her face from too much mescal. The older woman's eyes are filled with fear, but the younger one, a child, is defiant. She walks over to your granddaughter and takes her hand.

The woman goes to speak, but one of the guards strikes her with his fist. "Be quiet and don't speak unless he tells you to."

Who are they? Why are they with your granddaughter? There are things to speak of here. But not with the guards present. It is simple. You know what you must do.

"Put the hood on the girl," you tell the guards. And when they have done that, you tell them to take you to where they were picked up.

Out through the passage in the wall and into the farmlands.

"It is about two hours from here," says the sergeant.

"Then we shall need to make good time," you tell him.

At first, you walk in silence. The pretty woman is crying. And the girl has not let go of your granddaughter's hand.

"What is your name, child?" you ask.

"Sifyre," she replies.

"And yours?" you ask your granddaughter. You do not even know her name.

"Alaba." A pretty name, you think.

"I am called Dova," the woman says. She has been trying to flirt with one of the guards. For a camp follower, she is pretty enough. She would find someone to take her.

The ground is wet. Even though the rain has stopped, the air is still cool. In the moonlight, mist lifts from the damp fields and fills each dip and hollow. Ahead the fields stop and the forest waits like a dark army of trees all standing to attention. Home of bandits and beasts, and runaways. It is not a good place to leave the child, to leave Alaba. But where can you leave her? You cannot keep her with you.

As the moon moves south, the trees get closer.

"The men would like to rest and eat for a moment, sir. Just a few moments before we enter the woods. We should probably tie the prisoners. They might want to try and run in the trees."

You agree. "Let the prisoners eat too. And no need to bind them. I cannot see them running." Alaba is hooded, and you can see that Sifyre will not leave her. The tart might run, but she would not get far.

"As you say, sir." But there is a tone of resentment in the guard's voice. He is angry that he will have to share his food.

"Take the hood off the child." Now that you are far enough away from the town, there is no reason to keep her hidden. When the guards lift the hood, you see her face again. Are you thinking about that day, the first day you ever saw her? She has changed. She has grown. That was the only time you ever held her in your arms. And when you did, you passed her to the other priests to cast her from the tower. Only I saved her. Do you think of that time after, when I came to you and showed you what I had done? Do you remember that hope raised within you? Have you given up on that hope?

I promise you that you can be free. I will not leave you in hell forever.

The guards give the children bread. One of the guards is teasing Dova, offering her bread then pulling it back. So she has found someone. Eventually, he gives her the crust. It is more than either of the children get. She does not share it with them.

The edge of the wood is close now.

"How far in do we need to go?" you ask.

"About another hour, sir," they tell you.

"Get ready then. We best be going."

You can hear the guards grumbling. Why do they all need to come? Why do they need to go to the forest anyway? What is it he thinks he will find?

But you know what you will find; a quiet place far from Saco where you can kill them all and leave their bodies. No one must know about your granddaughter. Not a one can be left alive.

Chapter Fifty-Eight
Paths

Koreb

"Are you just going to leave me here?"
"No, why do you think that?"
"Have I not done my part?"
But your part is never done. There is no end to it.
You rise to your feet and start to pace around your cell.
"Will he not have me killed?"
"No, he would have killed you before now if he would."
"Perhaps." A nod of the head in agreement. "Am I just to sit here and wait? Is that all I have to do now?"
What is it that you would have me do? I cannot direct your every move and tell you everything you should say and think.
"I should go back to the City of the Sun," you say. But then, "No, I need to find that boy. I do not believe you would let him die."
"If you think I keep him safe then why do you worry?"
You are pushing gently against the wooden door. It is locked. There is a window but it is high up and there are bars of steel. Look all you will, there is no escape here. The walls are solid and thick. The door, stout and banded with iron. The window is beyond your reach. You sit again on the pallet bed and put your head in your hands.
"What is the point? I am useless." The lamp flickers as you speak. "I can do nothing. He will not listen to me."
But Greba has listened to you, and your words have more weight than you know. You let your mind run over all that Greba told you,

about his daughter and his wife. How the high priest turned the things he loved most into a trap, a weight around his neck. And then how the high priest stole his daughter from him. How the high priest defied Vatu and the cost of that defiance. A cost that Greba had to pay.

How terrible is Vatu? You think of your own defiance. Would there be a cost too high for that? It is the cost of freedom and we all must pay it. If the cost is this, to be imprisoned and perhaps killed, then you will pay that too. You will not give in to the darkness.

"Whisperer, show me the way," you say.

And so I rise and open the door for you. It clicks on its lock and falls open. It swings wide. Beyond the door is the rest of the house that Greba took you to. At first, you are too stunned to move. How can this be happening, you ask yourself. The door was locked. You checked it yourself many times. Perhaps he is returned and come to speak with you. But there is no one there. No guards.

"I know you're there," you say. And lift your lamp high. It gutters in a draft of air. But there is no one there. No one speaks. The door begins to swing in the draft. It makes a noise like the corncrake as the hinges squeal.

You step forwards, still convinced that a guard or worse is about to jump out of concealment and take you. They are taunting you.

"Where are you?" Your voice is strong and echoes around the empty house. Bravely you step forward. Your cell is just to the side of a guard room. There is a desk and a rack of spears and shields. There is a half-drunk mug of ale and some crusts of bread. You drink and eat, not thinking about who has supped here before you. The spears are well made and heavy. But you have no training with weapons. You think you would be worse than useless with them. Besides, why would you want to kill anyone? Put them back. These things are not for you. There are two cells and only yours is open. The keys are on the bench. They are heavy in your hand as you go to open the other cell. No one speaks as you open the door. A man is lying on the ground. He is much younger than you. And he is naked. If you had not drunk the beer you could have fed him some. He is still breathing. It is hard work to make him sit up, and his head keeps rolling around.

"Who are you?" But he does not answer. He does not even look at you. You see that there are arrow wounds on his back. The wounds have been covered in tar to stop the bleeding.

"What can I do?"

There is a coat over one of the seats. You bring it over to him and place it around him. No doubt the man will die if you leave him. But his breathing is better now that he is sitting up.

"Can you stand?" A stupid question, the man cannot speak, nor can he even look at you.

"Wait here." As if he could even move. There is nothing in the guard room to help. If there was food then you could feed him. Taking the lamp, you enter the rest of the house. It is still empty. Where is everyone?

There is bread and water. You take it to him and dip the bread in water and push it into his mouth. At first, there is nothing, but then the man starts to chew and swallow. It seems life is coming back to him. You do not forget to thank me for that.

"Water," the man says. And you hand him a cup and watch as he takes his fill. It seems that he will live after all. At least for now.

"Can you stand? Here, let me help."

He rises to his feet with your help.

"We should get out of here." And then you recognize the man. It is the wagoner.

"How did you get here?"

"I don't know," says the wagoner. "I thought I was dead."

"You looked it for sure. What happened to you?"

"Later," says the wagoner. "Who are you?"

"I'm Koreb."

"The heretic? The Whisperer's priest? How did you get here?"

But the wagoner is right. That can wait for another time.

"Can you walk?"

"Maybe? Perhaps? I'm not sure. Can we get out?"

"I… I'm sure the Whisperer will show us the way."

"Are you? What makes you so sure of that?" says Bidann. Bidann, the wagoner's name is Bidann.

"Because he has shown us the way so far," you tell him.

Bidann fastens the coat around him. He looks around and finds a pair of boots. "Help me with these." He says. And when they are on, he stands. He lifts a spear, but he is using it as a crutch. "Lead on," he says.

Where now, you wonder. But I take your hand and his and lead you back to the kitchen. You gather up some food in a sack. It is not much, some bread and cheese and some dry fruit. Then I lead you to a door that opens at my touch. It opens out into a little hollow at the base of the walls. Unseen, we walk out of Saco.

"I need to go back," says Bidann. And now he is leading the way.

Chapter Fifty-Nine
Arriving

Hilketa

The governor awaits your arrival. Messages have been sent ahead. Now, he stands while you alight from the coach. He is nervous and keeps adjusting his clothes.

"Welcome to Saco," he says, stepping forward and bowing.

There is no sign of Greba. It would be too much to expect him to be here to welcome you, but you have had no communication from him. What is he up to? There is more to this than meets the eye.

"Thank you, Governor, please rise." A quick gesture of your hand. He stands tall. Looking him over you see that he likes to eat too much. But don't they all. He is young to have risen so high. No doubt he has some powerful friend in the Outer Court. Perhaps he seeks to join it one day.

"Allow me to show you to the citadel."

You nod and follow him to a chair. When you are seated, four guards lift it and lead the way through the streets. The governor walks beside you. All of the citizens have gathered along the way. They do not cheer, and many look away. Those that do not have hungry faces. Some are hopeful. They think you may have brought food. And you have, but not for them.

Saco, perhaps you have been here in another lifetime. Narrow winding streets, cobblestones. Low houses made of timber and thatch, and weaving sheds everywhere. The walls are in poor repair and the citadel looks neglected. Here and there the grander homes of silk merchants, but even they have a meanness to them.

The chair stops and you dismount. The governor leads you to the hall. Your scribes follow after him, and so too does General Espada with four of his guardsmen.

In the hall, the governor ushers you to the chair, and you sit. Your scribes on either side. One whispers the governor's name in your ear: Perdona.

Wine is brought to you, and some wafers with honey.

You say nothing but eat and drink. From the corner of your eye, you watch the governor and the general. You hand a wafer to each of your scribes. They bow and eat. The general is insulted. You can see anger in his face. Always so proud, these men of war and arms.

"Bring food for my general and let him approach."

A stool is set nearby and General Espada sits. He is brought bread and wine. He eats in silence, his eyes fixed on you.

When he is finished, you speak. "General, what news have you of the bandits that have plagued this province?"

The general stands. "We have reports of raids on wagons. These go back many months. We have reports of shipments of silk and wine and rice going missing. Farms have been raided. Cattle and rice have been stolen. Disloyal citizens have fled Saco and joined with raiders. There are claims of magic, heretic magic. A stone that shines, and child. There are many who have joined with this man. His name is Condito. He is a known runaway and murderer. He and all who join with him are sentenced to death by order of the Outer Court."

You motion for Espada to sit. He bows and sits on his stool, holding his sheathed sword across his legs.

The governor says nothing but looks at you in dismay. You motion him to approach.

"Great one," he says, but can think of nothing else to say. He is trembling. He thinks you will order his execution.

"Have you punished these heretic rebels? Have you sent guards to take this man and have him flogged through the streets? Does his head sit on a spike over the gates of Saco?"

He mumbles something.

"Speak up!" you command.

"No, Great One," he replies.

"So, you shelter and protect heretics and rebels?"

"No, no, Great One."

"Then what? Are you too lazy to do your duty? Are you too incompetent? Is this too hard a task? Must I come from the City of the Sun all the way to this backwater to do your job for you?"

"No, it is not like that. I am faithful, I am diligent. I am loyal to the dark." He throws himself on the floor. His fine silk robe will be dirty. It is a fine robe, it is woven with black and yellow silk. He is sobbing and protesting his loyalty. You raise a hand and he is silent.

"And yet here I am. Have I come all this way for no reason? Why then am I here?"

The governor remains silent. Perhaps he is not a total fool.

"General, take the governor and take him to someplace suitable. Somewhere in your camp. It will be better if he is safe. We do not know where or who the rebels are."

Two of the generals' guards lift the governor.

"I am doing this to keep you safe," you tell him. "I would not wish any harm to come to you."

One of the scribes whispers in your ear. It seems Greba is not in the Citadel. He has a safe house by the wall. Your men have searched it. It is empty. No one is there. It has been abandoned. It seems there is more to this indeed.

Chapter Sixty
A Choice

Ennet

How is that man able to walk so fast? You can barely keep up with him.

"Wait," you say. But he does not wait. And come to think of it, how did he get those manacles off? Has he found a key?

It is too late to worry about that now. Now all you can do is keep up with him and hope. What can he do against those five soldiers? Were they soldiers? At first, you thought they were bandits. You thought they were friends of Garra who had killed Bidann.

Was Bidann dead? He certainly was looked dead. He might be alive if the arrow did not pierce his lung.

"Wait," you shout again and run faster. "You do not know the way."

But it seems that he does. Every now and then he stops and checks the way. It is dark and so he has to bend and look closely. It gives you a chance to catch up.

Soon enough he is at the spot where the soldiers took Alaba and the others. But they are gone.

"Here! It was here," you call. "Here." And you point to where Bidann's body had lain.

Utas crouches low. There is a clear imprint in the moss. He waves his lantern over the site. There are blood spots.

"Not much blood," he says. Then he looks around. "Here," he says and points to where two saplings have been cut down. "They have made a litter to drag him." And then he shows you two parallel lines where Bidann's body has been dragged through the woodland.

"Why would they take the body?" you ask.

"It is strange," Utas says. "But it can mean only one thing. Bidann is alive."

"He was lying face down with an arrow in his back. And they had stripped him naked." You think of his body gleaming in the moonlight. You had always thought of Bidann as strong but then he had seemed as broken and feeble as any man. His pale skin showed that he had lived most of his life far from the Sun. "Why would they do that?"

Utas does not answer. Instead, he continues looking at the ground. He picks up an arrow shaft. "They were guards, you said?"

"Yes. I never thought so at the time. I was too panicked to think. But yes, they were wearing guard uniforms. I suppose they could have deserted. But why would they?"

Utas holds up the arrow. "This is not a guard's arrow. Look. The shaft is not very straight, and the tip is of glass-stone, not iron. And the fletching is different."

"So bandits shot Bidann after all?"

"Yes, and probably they stripped the body."

"I can't believe they left him alive. Surely they would have made sure he was dead? Surely they would have slit his throat?"

"My guess is that whoever shot Bidann was working alone." Utas is quiet for a moment. You think he knows more than he is saying.

"It must have been Garra," you say. "Who else had a grudge against him?"

"It could be," Utas says. "And then something distracts him. Perhaps he hears the soldiers coming, or maybe others. Someone scared him off and he left the body. Then the soldiers find him, still alive, and take him back with them."

"Why would they do that? Wouldn't they just finish him off and leave him?"

"Most would," Utas says. And again he is saying less than he knows.

"We should follow them," you say. It sounds like madness when you say it. What can an old man and an even older woman do?

"No need to do that," says Utas. "There can be only one place they would take him to."

"Saco. It's the only garrison near here. Even that is far. Why would they be so far?"

"I think that Condito has brought himself to the attention of the governor." Or worse. The unspoken words are clear even to you this time.

"You think that the City of the Sun has sent soldiers here? To take care of a few runaways?" But Condito's band is more than just a few runaways. Even if they are little more than a rabble, they are many and growing every day. The tale of the stone that shines has spread throughout the province. They are a rebel army now. And now they are marching who knows where. They had little choice. If they stayed at the camp they would starve. "Condito marches to his doom then."

"Yes," agrees Utas. "That is the most likely outcome. They may raid a few farms, but in the end, they will be crushed. It is always the way."

"We have to get them back."

"It is possible." Possible? How? "If they take them to Saco, then they will be put in the cells. We can free them."

It is madness. But even so, it is better to be mad than to give up. You want to go back to the hut and stay there. You want to go back and eat stewed mushrooms and perhaps a game bird that Bidann brings home. You want to watch Alaba and Sifyre playing together. You want to shout on them to come and eat and to be sure to wash first. You want to scold Dova for being lazy and not helping. You want to shout at Utas to get more wood for the fire. You realize now that you were happy there. Why is it we only ever realize we are happy when what we have is taken away?

"If we are going to Saco, then we should follow them. They will be going the quickest way back. If I can catch them, then it is better to take them there and then rather than trying to take them out of prison."

You look around and see that the soldiers have not taken your sack. "There are some nuts and mushrooms in the bag. You should eat something."

Utas picks up the sack and cracks some nuts. He hands some of the nutmeat to you. "Yes, we can eat as we go." Then casting the sack over his shoulder he follows the trail the soldiers have left. There is nothing else for you to do. You say a prayer to me and then start walking.

Chapter Sixty-One
Bodies

Unead

There are more bodies.

As you walk on pushing the cart, Brau calls to Mukito. "Come and sit on the cart, boy." He comes and Brau lifts him onto the cart.

"What is wrong?" you ask, and then you see it. That is the first of them. A group of six bodies are lying at the side of the road. You can make out six, but there may be more. Brau has stopped. "What do we do now?"

"Hide," he says and points to the mulberry bushes. They are covered in the thread of silkworms, like ghosts hanging in the air.

"I don't like this," says Canna. "We should have stayed."

"It's too late for that," you tell her. Besides, who knows what is happening there? Brau says that an army has arrived at Saco. That you got out just before they arrived. Now no one is allowed to leave.

The cart jolts and lurches as Brau pushes it off the track. "We should hide it and leave it here."

"Where can we hide?"

The light of your lantern shows a scowling face. He is troubled. Where can he go? "Let me go and look at the bodies," he says. "Once we know who did this then we'll have a better idea where to go."

"All right, but let me come with you," you say.

"I'll stay here with the boy," says Canna. "You should stay too. Some things are better not seen."

The air is cold now, and you shiver. But it is only the cold. "No," you say. "I need to see." You want to know. You want to decide.

"There are not footprints or signs of anyone coming this way," says Brau as you walk along the track to where the bodies lie.

"So whoever did this did not come from Saco?"

"I'm not sure. It may have been a patrol of the guard. We'll see. I'm glad you came with me. I would be fine looking at this myself, but this is better."

You reach out and take his hand. "Thank you for doing this. I am grateful."

He does not make a fuss. But you can see a smile on his lips. "It is nothing."

"No, I know what would happen to us. Two old women and a child. We would either starve or be murdered."

"You're not so old," says Brau. But you feel old. You feel every one of the summers you've seen.

"We are old, both of us."

"I'm sure I'm older than you."

The bodies are lying together face down. They are men. Perhaps young men.

"What happened here? Who are they?"

Brau kneels in the moss beside them. "Guards," he says. "See. They are wearing guard's armour."

"What are they doing here?"

"Patrols come from time to time. It's not that unusual to see patrols here. With the bandits getting bolder, they come out more often."

"So the bandits did this." You look around at the fields expecting a horde of wild men to come screaming out of them. It seems such a terrible thing.

Brau stands up. "I'm not sure this was bandits."

"Then what?" You make the sign of the Spinner. "Keep us from the Cutter," you mutter.

"Keep us from the Cutter indeed," says Brau and makes the same sign. "But there is not a wound on any of the bodies."

You step back, away from Brau and the corpses. He shakes his head. "Not plague. I don't think so. Each of them has a broken neck. That's not one of the symptoms. Thank the Weaver. They've been killed all right, but not by bandits or by a beast. Someone has broken each of their necks as easy as snapping a twig. And by the looks of it with hardly a struggle."

"What do you mean?" But in your heart you know. He could do

that. Could he be near? And if he is, what then? He could kill Brau in an instant. And Canna and the boy?

Now the thing that you fear is the thing you love most of all. How can he be here? Has he come for you?

The thought fills you with fear and thrills you. You love him. He loves you. He would do anything for you. And you? What would you do?

You open your mouth to shout his name. But nothing comes out. You are trembling. Is it fear or desire? He must be near. To kill six guards like that would be nothing to him. None of the other twelve could do that. The only other that could is Utas. Does that mean he is near? Is your daughter near? Is Irid here?

"I need to sit down," you say and sink to the roadside.

"We can't stay here," says Brau and tugs at your arm until you are back on your feet. He puts an arm around you and leads you back to where the cart is hidden.

"Who did this?" you ask again. And then turning around, there is a dull red glow coming from over the hill. "What is that?"

Brau stops and turns. The red light can only be one thing. Not the moon nor the stars, not the Sun. Fire. Beyond the hill, where the farm is, it is burning.

It is strangely quiet. You cannot hear anything. The farm is too far away. "What do we do now?"

Canna has come to stand beside you. She has Mukito in her arms. He is looking at the glow. "Pretty," he says. For a moment, you want to strike him. But he is only a child. He knows nothing. All he sees is a red light in the skies, like an aurora. Can you see sparks? Surely not at this distance. It must be a trick.

"Hush," says Canna, as much to herself as to the boy. "Is there somewhere else we can go?"

"I have to go," says Brau. "They are my family. I have to see what has happened. I need to go."

"Yes," you tell him. "But not now. Wait until the fire is gone. Then whoever did this will be gone too. It will be safer then."

"That would be too late. They could all be dead. I need to go." And now it is you that reaches and holds his arm, pulling him back.

"Wait until the fire is done. Then we can all go." If you go now, then all you can do to help is die with them. Those words are not spoken. They do not need to be spoken.

Brau sinks to the ground. He covers his face. You put a hand on his shoulder. "Let's go back to the wagon. I think we will have to stay here for now."

There is a smell of smoke now and there is ash in the air. The wind is coming from over the hill, a warm wind. Mukito is starting to fidget and Canna sets him on the ground. He runs around trying to catch the ash that turns to nothing in his hands.

"We should eat," says Canna. "And if there is no food then we should sleep. There is no point doing anything but waiting."

"There is food in the cart," says Brau. "But not much. If the farm is gone, then it may have to last us for a while."

He is right. But still, you are hungry. "Let's eat something," you say. It will give you something to do.

"I can make it," says Canna. She takes Mukito's hand and walks back.

"Come," you say. "There is nothing to do for now but wait."

Chapter Sixty-Two
News

Hilketa

Information is power. Everywhere you have eyes and ears. And your scribe speaks in your ear and tells you everything. So you know. You know before everyone. The rebels are on the move.

Espada has come to speak with you. He looks awkward and uncomfortable. How amusing.

"How may I help you, General?" you ask.

"I have come to report, great one." He bows. That same stiff reluctant bow. A scarce nod of the head.

"Thank you, General. Please tell me all of your success." That makes him blink, but he carries on.

"The rebels have come out of hiding and have sacked several farms to the south. They have set them on fire and taken any food stored there. The farms are empty. We have found the bodies of some farmers, but others may have fled or joined with the rebels."

"Or been burned to ash," you say.

"Yes," Espada says through gritted teeth. "Or been burned to ash."

"So we know the fate of only a few of the farmers. And we have none alive?"

"None, great one. I have sent patrols out to search for survivors. When we have some prisoners, we will interrogate them."

You already know this. And that several patrols have returned with nothing. And that several patrols have not returned.

"Where can they have gone, I wonder?"

"Into the forests most likely, great one."

"So have you sent patrols to the forest?"

"Yes, great one." The patrols have not returned. But Espada misses out on that information. You see that he is unreliable. You see he thinks more of his career than of telling the truth.

"And what of the rebels?"

"We have not been able to find them as yet. But we think they are most likely in the forest also. That is why we think the runaways have joined with them."

"And what of the town?"

The markets have not opened for days now. The citizens have tried to leave but have been turned back. There have been riots. Weaving sheds have been set alight. The guards have been called to protect the merchants quarter. As yet no one has approached the citadel. The general has killed many to keep the peace. Even so, rebellion is everywhere. When you are starving, you have no choice. You know all of this, but you ask anyway. You wish to hear what the general will say.

"The town is quiet, at least for now. We have sufficient guards to keep the peace. We have let no one leave since we arrived."

"What of the other farms?" you ask. "How many are still intact?"

"The majority are untouched. We have put guards at each. And have set up garrisons that can move quickly to support any farm that is attacked. If the rebels approach we will deal with them."

"And have you taken an inventory? What stores are there? Remember it is still moon-turns until the Sun will come. We will need food before that."

"We have secured sufficient for the army but have no surplus."

"Then how will they eat? Who will be left to plant and grow when the Sun does return?"

You are taunting him. You know all of this. When the Sun comes, the army will be forced to plant and harvest. Not many others will survive. You know that soon Saco will be rioting again for food. Perhaps as soon as moon-down. It will start again.

"I will have the army plant if there are no farmers."

You know full well that the farms have food hidden. Or if they have to, they will kill the last of their livestock to make it through the long night. But where the rebels have burned the farms, there the soldiers will have to grow the crops. It will need to be done.

"Spears to plows," you say. But Espada does not say anything. "You should go back to the camp. You will be needed there to take care of the rebels."

Once more that stiff bow that costs the general so much of his pride. “Take care,” you call after him. “The streets are not safe.”

You think about having him assassinated. One disgruntled townsman with a bow. But then you would have to replace him. And besides, it is better to humiliate him in this way. You can take his life whenever you wish. And you have other matters to attend to. Greba for one. Where has he gone? What is he up to? He is outside. Why?

You consider. You have sent agents out to look for him, but so far none have found any news. But they have all reported. None have disappeared. None are dead. You hold a scrap of paper in your hand. So much to think about.

Chapter Sixty-Three
Escape

Koreb

The tall man is struggling to keep up.

"Here, let me help you." But he pushes you away.

"Where are we going?" you ask. Not that it matters. As long as it is away from Saco and from Greba.

"I'm going back for them."

"Who?" And now he stops and turns to you.

"Who are you anyway?" he asks.

"I am Koreb. I am from the City of the Sun."

"Why are you here?" He scowls suspiciously.

"I'm looking for someone."

"Who? Why?"

There is no use, you will have to tell him. "I am a heretic." As if that explains everything.

"Wait," says the tall man. "I know who you are. You're the one who sent me here with those Alaba and Ennet."

"Yes, that's right. And before that, I sent you with a boy. Mukito. Do you know what happened to him?"

Bidann, you remember his name now, shakes his head. "I handed him over to the wine merchant like you said. After that, I don't know. Why do you want to know?"

"Someone is trying to kill him."

"I guessed that when you paid me to take him out of the City. I guess someone is trying to kill Alaba too? What's so special about the boy? Who wants him dead, and why have you come after him?" Bidann stands upright. He points the spear towards you. "It's not you that wants him dead, is it? You better answer me. I won't let you harm the boy or Alaba."

"I'm not here to harm the boy. I'm here to keep him safe. I…"

"You what?"

"I owe that to him. The guard caught me and I told them where he is, or where I sent him anyway."

"Tortured you, did they?" says Bidann and once more starts to use the spear as a crutch. "How did you get out?"

"No," you admit. "They never tortured me. They did not need to." You look away. "And we were both taken by the guards. How did we escape?"

"Good question," says Bidann. "I'm not sure how we got out."

"Me neither," you tell him. "I don't know why my cell was left open. Or why there was no else there."

"I'm not sure I can trust you," says Bidann. "I'm grateful for saving my life. I'm pretty sure I would have died back there if you had not come. I still might. But this all seems very odd."

"It is," you agree. "I think I can trust you though. Those wounds are not fake. And I think you should trust me too. I could have killed you or left you to die."

"But maybe you want me to tell you something. You've already said you told the guards about the boy. And you've not told me who it is that wants him dead, or Alaba come to that. I think you know more than you're telling."

The moon is beginning to rise. "Come on, let's keep moving," you say. "We don't want to get caught. I'll tell you what I know. It's not much really."

"All right," says Bidann. "But head for those trees. I want to find Ennet and Dova. And the girls."

Who is Dova? And who are the girls? One of them must be Alaba. Are you leading Greba to them? But when you ask Bidann he says, "You tell me. You said you were going to tell me what you had been up to."

It seems he is not going to trust you and perhaps he is right to do so.

"You know I am a follower of the Whisperer. Anyway, a man came to our meeting. A little younger than me. I thought he wanted to know the Whisperer, and perhaps he did. But he was deeper in the dark than I knew. I thought he was my friend but he betrayed me."

"One of the twelve's spies."

"No, worse than that. One of the twelve. The Whip it was."

That takes his breath away. He turns and looks at you. "One of the twelve?"

"Yes, and now he is here in Saco."

"Here. Why here?"

"Because I told him that Mukito is here."

"And why does he want to kill a four-year-old boy?"

"I'm not sure," you tell him.

"You must have some idea."

"Sometimes," you tell Bidann, "it is better not to know."

Chapter Sixty-Four
Riots

Hilketa

It was just as you expected. When there is no food handed out, the citizens riot. Or at least they try to. There are more townfolk than soldiers, many more. The rioters throw cobbles they dug from the street and use sticks. But the soldiers have swords and spears and shields. The rioters head towards the merchant quarter. The rich are not starving. The rich never starve. There they think they will find food.

Espada asks if he should stop them. You consider.

"No," you tell him. "Let them riot. Let them fight among themselves." You know eventually, they will turn on the citadel. And many of your men are looking for the rebels and for Greba. In the end, they will all die. It is inevitable.

You rise and go to the window. In the moonlight, you can see smoke rising. The town is burning. The smell of burning rises up from below. The noise of shouting and things breaking.

"Should we not stop this?" says one of the scribes.

"No, let them do our work for us. In the end, they will all die." You return to the high seat. "What news of him? Bring the governor."

It is some moments before he is brought to you. He lies on the ground before you. He is still wearing his robes, but they are dirty and dishevelled. He says nothing but waits for you to speak.

"You are Perdona, governor of Saco."

"Yes, great one," he says.

"But you have been negligent. You have allowed heresy to grow here."

Perdona says nothing. It was not a question.

"Are you a heretic?"

"No, great one."

I ask you the same question. You do not answer. But you do not say no.

"Tell me about Greba."

"What do you want to know?" he says.

"When did he come here?"

"About a month ago, great one. Perhaps longer."

As long ago as that? How did he get here and back so quickly? Has he used the dark portals? You make a note to inspect them. You motion to one of the scribes, Astani, and whisper to him to find the portal. You tell him not to use it. But you hardly need to. No one, not even the twelve wish to use those dark portals. Who knows where they lead? It is rumoured that to pass through them is to perish in Vatu's darkness and to be reborn. No one will even touch them unless they are compelled to. Still, it amuses you to watch the colour drain from the scribe's face and for him to reply, "It will be as you command, great one." He is wondering if you know that he is in the pay of Kong. Of course, you know.

"What did he want here?" you ask Perdona.

"I did not question him, great one. He did not share his plan with someone as humble as myself." You kick the governor hard when he speaks.

"Of course you did not question him. But he questioned you. What did he ask you?"

"He wished information, great one. About heretics."

"And what did you tell him?"

"Nothing, great one. I had nothing to tell him. There are no heretics here."

You smile. You know that Greba would not let this stand.

"No heretics you say, but even as we speak, the town is rioting."

"In the silk sheds some believe in the Spinner, the Weaver and the Cutter."

"And what did Greba say when you told him this?"

"Nothing. He was not interested. He was not interested in those types of heretics."

"In who then? In Sig or Cera?"

"No, great one. In another."

"In who?"

"In the Whisperer, great one."

Ah, now you stop. “In the Whisperer? Why was he interested in the Whisperer?”

“The ways of the twelve are above someone as humble as me, great one.”

Again you kick him hard. “Tell me what he wanted.” Perdona looks at you. “Yes, you should fear him,” you tell the governor. “But he is not here and I am. You should fear me more.”

“He is looking for a child,” the governor says.

“A child?”

“Yes, great one. A boy child. Brought here by heretics. By a follower of the Whisperer.”

“And where did he find him?”

“He did not. Or not that I know.”

You sit again. So what is Greba up to? What is he looking for? “Where did he look?”

“One of the scribes will be able to tell you.”

“Who? Bring him here!”

When the scribe is brought, he bows but does not abase himself. Instead, he hands you a scroll.

“What is this?” you ask.

“It is the information that the great one asked for.”

“And you have kept it?”

“By accident, great one. I made two copies and forgot to give him both.” Again he bows.

“You tried to keep this from me?” You turn to the governor.

“No, great one,” he replies. “I knew nothing of this. Only that the scribe was consulted. The great one had no wish to share what he was looking for.”

“And he has not been back since?”

The governor hesitates and then speaks. “He has not been back to the citadel. He has his own people here. But he has been seen.”

You look down the list of names and there you see it. She has not even thought to change her name. You know who she is. It was you who gave her name to Kong. It was you who betrayed Greba and Utas. Now you see her name again and smile. So this is where Greba has hidden her.

“General, get an escort. I will have to go into the city.”

“But great one, it is not safe. There are riots,” Espada protests.

“Are you unable to do your job?” you ask. “Can you not keep me safe? Am I unable to go about my business?”

“No, great one,” says the general. “I will gather the escort at once.”

"See that you do. I do not wish to be kept waiting."

You have no shame marching through the town to the woman whose life you destroyed.

"I did nothing," you say, but we both know you are lying. I am everywhere. You cannot hide from me. But you have no shame and you march on to the house on the list. This, you are certain, is where you will find Greba. You were never as smart as you thought.

The soldiers make two lines and push the crowd apart to let you pass. Espada is by your side. His hand is on the hilt of his sword.

"Are you nervous, General?" you ask him.

"No," he says and turns to look you in the face. "But I am prepared."

"For what?"

"For anything." He is still proud. "The crowd may turn on us."

But the crowd do not. They shout and plead with you to send them food. They push against the guard trying to get close to you. But they do not throw cobbles nor fight with the soldiers. They are calling out with hands cupped and pleading. They are beggars. They are broken. When the time comes to slay them, they will fall like sheep. That is what you think of them. They are sheep for the slaughter.

The way to the house is twisting and narrow. The shacks here are made of wood, not stone. The crowds have not followed you. Dull faces stare at you from low doorways. Hungry faces. Angry faces. Fearful faces. Why does seeing those faces bring you joy? Do you like to be hated? Does it make you feel strong?

When you reach the hut where Unead lives, you stop and look. It is mean and low, like all the others here. It is in poor repair. You think the roof must leak when it rains. A guard raps at the door, but there is no reply. "Open it." The guard pushes the door open and you step inside.

If you had thought to find Greba here, you are disappointed. He is gone. If he was ever here. There is no one here. The house is cold and there is no fire. The ashes have been swept from the hearth. They have gone.

"Fetch the people from nearby."

They are brought to stand before you. They all look down and are afraid. Some of them are weeping.

"Tell me who lives here."

"A woman. Unead. She is a weaver. There is an old woman Canna and a boy Mukito that live here."

"Where are they?"

There is a murmur and then someone speaks. "They have not been seen for two moon rises. No one has seen them."

"So they have gone! Where? Where have they gone?" Can they have escaped? Anger and frustration rise inside you. "And a man, about fifty years old, has anyone seen him?"

"There was a man," says a girl. "A foreman from the weaving sheds. Brau."

"Where does he live?" Can they be there? You send the guards to fetch them. You will wait here. Could this Brau be Greba? Is that possible?

No one moves while you wait. The prisoners stand and look down. None will look at you.

"Light a fire," you say. It is cold in the hut. You walk around looking for some clue as to where they have gone. There are no clothes or cooking pots. They have left here and you do not think they will come back.

When the guards return, they come empty-handed. "No one is at that house. Brau has been gone for about three moon rises. He lives alone. No one knows where he has gone."

So this Brau is known to the town. He is not Greba. Who is he then?

You look again at the girl that spoke. "Come forward," you say, and she wraps her arms around herself as she steps towards you. Still, her eyes are kept low. She is young. "What is your name?"

"Injutil."

"How do you know Unead?"

"I am her shuttle girl at the loom sheds."

"How long have you worked with her?"

"About four years? Since she came here."

"Where did she come from?"

"From the City of the Sun, great one."

"And the boy? She came with the boy?"

"No, she found the boy abandoned and took him in." How generous of her, you think.

"And how long have you known Brau?"

"He's a foreman at the sheds. I've known him since I worked there. About eight years."

"So where have they gone?" You had instructed that no one

should leave, but it seems that your prey has already fled. It seems as if they have escaped. But to where?

"I don't know," says Injutil. "Brau has had eyes for Unead for a long time. We used to tease her. But she did not encourage him."

"So why would she go with him now?"

"When you are starving, things change," says the girl. That is true.

"So you think he is with her?"

"The last time I saw Unead, she was with him. She had no rice and it is possible that he did." That made sense. She has gone with him to get food.

"One last thing. This Brau, was he a heretic? Did he follow the Spinner, the Weaver and the Cutter?" The girl shifts uneasily. "I am not here to punish you. I am here to find him."

"Everyone follows the three sisters in the sheds. No one believes in it. It's just superstition. But Brau didn't follow them." When she says those words, can she not see the sisters pulling her thread from the weave? The Cutter stands ready.

"Who did he follow?" you ask. "Did he follow the one we do not speak of?" You mean me. You mean the Whisperer.

"No," says Injutil. "Not that I know of."

"Then who?"

The girl looks around the hut. She is afraid, but not of you. What is she afraid of?

"Tell me," you say. And she can see that if she does not she will die.

"The hunter," she says and makes his sign. As she does, a dart flies through the air and catches her in the throat. There is uproar. The guards start to search for where it came from. A blowpipe falls to the floor and a man tumbles. He has taken poison. He is dead. The girl Injutil is lying on the floor and cannot breathe. The Cutter breaks the thread.

Chapter Sixty-Five
Loss

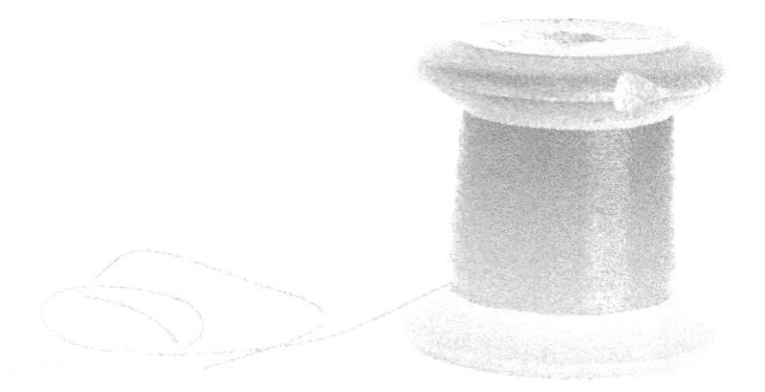

Ennet

He is still moving too fast. How can he expect you to keep up? You are not as young as you used to be.

"Slow down," you call to him.

He waits. "We need to keep moving. We need to find them. We need to catch them before they get to Saco."

"And then what?"

Utas looks at you. "Then we kill the soldiers." Is it not obvious?

You laugh. "One man and an old woman against five soldiers." But you know Utas is not an ordinary man. Something causes a chill when he speaks of killing. You cannot help but believe he will do it. You make my sign. And when you do, you know I am with you. "May the mercy of the Whisperer be with you." When you say those words Utas stops.

I speak to him. And you hear my voice. "This is not the way."

"Then what is the way?" he asks me. "I must save her."

But he is wrong. It is her that will save him, and everyone else. "You cannot save her," I tell him.

"I must try." And he is thinking of another time when there were others he could have saved and did not.

You go and take his arm. But he shakes free. "Stay here if you will. I am not going to stop." And what use would one old woman be anyway?

"Is she really your daughter?" you ask him.

"Yes," he says. And puts all doubts from his mind. "She is my daughter and I must save her."

"The Whisperer brought her to me," you tell him. "The Whisperer will save her if she needs saved. You must trust him."

Your words are wise, he should listen to you, but he does not. Nor will he listen to me.

"I would kill a thousand men to save her." Can you not see? You can save no one by killing.

"I do not doubt it," you say. "There was a time when I would have killed to save my daughter. But it was only one man I needed to kill. It was my master. I had thought he loved me. I thought he loved my daughter too. Our daughter. But he took her from me and sold her. That night he slept and in his room. He slept soundly without care. It was nothing to him. I was nothing. I had a knife. I thought I would kill him and then myself after. I held that knife as he lay sleeping. Could he not even see what I wanted to do to him?"

"Did you kill him?" His voice is surprisingly gentle.

"I wanted to." Tears are in your eyes. Tears that have been there for all those years. "I wanted to."

"What stopped you?"

"He did. The Whisperer. He can and told me that there was a better way. He promised he would take care of my girl. That this would be made right. He told me that it would not help. Revenge, he said, is never enough. And in the end, it would damage me more even than losing my child."

"Was he right?"

"Sometimes. I think so. Sometimes I am still angry. Sometimes I wish I had pushed that knife into his throat, or into his brain through his eyes. Sometimes I dream of it. What if I had? What would have happened then? It would only be what he deserved. But other times I thank the Whisperer. He gave me life and hope. He helped me earn my freedom and helped me keep myself. He tells me my daughter is grown and well. I ask him if she is happy. Yes, he tells me. Although she thinks of you often. I would like to meet her, I tell him."

"What does he say to that?"

You smile wryly. "He does not answer all our questions. And sometimes he tells me, it is better to find the answer yourself."

"And did you?"

You nod that wise head of yours. You are not so old really. "I think he could have answered me. But he was right. It was better that I answer that myself. I am not sure I have answered it right. But this is what I think. Maybe I have met her. How would I know? Every woman I meet, I think to myself; that could be her. And so I think everyone I meet could be her. I try to treat everyone I meet as if they are my missing daughter. That way if I ever do meet her, I know that I will have treated her as I should."

"Except the men," he says and laughs.

"Except the men," you agree. "But I said try. I never said I manage to treat everyone like that. I am sorry if I have not been kind to you."

"No, you have been very kind to me. I did not mean it like that. It's just that so many of this world's ills can be laid at the door of men."

"Yes, so many. But not all of them. And if men are what they are, then we are partly to blame for that too. After all, we made them."

"The Whisperer made them," he says.

"Well I promise you, Whisperer or not, we have plenty to do with it. I have my own memories of bearing a child and I've been to plenty of other birthings. It might not be all down to us. But trust me, we do our part."

"And the Whisperer made you too, and all the others," Utas says. He stops. "The Whisperer came for me too. Not in the way you tell it. But he came and led me from darkness. Sometimes I forget what he has done and turn to it."

You nod. "Me too. I think we all must. Otherwise, there would not be so much darkness in this world."

Now you stand up. You are rested and together you walk on towards Saco.

"She is my daughter," he says. "There must be something I can do. What can I do?"

Trust me, I tell him. "Yes," he agrees. "I will do that."

Chapter Sixty-Six
Honesty

Koreb

The big man seems to know where you are going but needs your help. Even using the spear as a staff he is struggling to walk. It is amazing that he can walk at all with those wounds. His breathing is laboured. From time to time he tries to push you away. But he needs your help even if he is too proud to admit it.

"We will never catch them," Bidann says. He is breathing heavily. What could you do if you did anyway?

"Do we know where they are going?"

"Not really. I think they are going back into the forest. I cannot think where else they would go. Or why he is taking them there."

You can. You think perhaps Greba is taking them somewhere to kill them in the dark. But that can't be right. Why did he not just kill them in the safe house?

"Perhaps he is using them to find the bandit camp?"

"Perhaps," agrees Bidann.

"Should we head there? If you know where it is you can lead us there."

Bidann bites his lip uncertainly. "It does not make sense. I suppose that could be it. But why take all of them? Why not just get one of them to go? And why with only a handful of soldiers?"

"We should be grateful that he has. It is the strangest thing to just leave us."

Bidann has caught his breath now and starts to walk again. He is wincing in pain but still looks around warily. You are climbing to the brow of a small hill. When you near the top Bidann crouches and begins to crawl. "We don't want to be silhouetted against the sky. We don't want to be seen."

You crouch low with him. As you lie at the top of the hill you look over a moonlit valley. Fields of mulberry line a road and a river. On the next rise are some barns.

"Look," says Bidann. And you follow his gaze. There is a group of people pushing a cart along the road, but no sign of Greba or those with him.

"Perhaps we should speak with them and ask if they have seen anyone."

Bidann considers. "You should go, I'm not sure a half-naked and half-dead man is the best introduction. You should go and I will be close by."

"I'm sure there will be no trouble. They look like ordinary people but they might have seen where Greba is going." As you say these words, you doubt them. If Greba had seen them, he would have killed them. Wherever he is going, he does not want anyone to follow. But what else is there to do? You walk down into the mulberry bushes and then stand tall and shout.

"Hey!" you wave your arms in the air and walk towards them. They stop and look at you as you approach. There are three of them. Four if you count the child that is with them. A tall man about your age stands and looks at you warily.

"Just stop there, friend," he says. "Who are you and what do you want?"

"I'm... My name is Koreb. I've just come from Saco. I'm looking for someone."

"Oh yes? Who?"

"I want to ask if you've seen any soldiers come this way."

"Soldiers? Why are you asking?" The man seems even more on edge now.

"Look, I don't have any weapons," you say and open your coat. "Do you mind if I come closer?"

"I think we'd mind very much," says the man. "Stay where you are. We do have weapons so you better not come any closer."

"All right." This is not going well. You put your hands on top of your head. "Do you mind answering my question? Then you can be on your way and I can be on mine."

Then the smell hits you. Smoke. Turning to the horizon you can see the glow of fire and sparks drifting up into the starlit sky. "What's happening over there? What's happening over the hill?"

"More questions. Soldiers I would guess. Looks to me as if

they're burning down a farm. What does it look like to you?"

You make my sign in the air. "May the Whisperer lead them to safety."

To your surprise, the man lowers his weapon and makes the same sign. "All right, come closer. But I warn you, if this is a trick, the Whisperer takes care of his own."

Does he? You wonder, but have I not taken care of you? Are we not all yours, you ask me. Do I not take care of you all? I reply.

One of the women hands you some water to drink. You bow and say thank you.

"You're from the City of the Sun," she says. "I can tell by your accent and your dark skin."

"Yes, I am," you agree. It is an accent she also has, and her skin is darker than yours. "What brought you here from the centre of the world?"

"None of your business," says the big man. The woman puts her hand on his arm.

"Hush, Brau. He is only making pleasantries." Is that what you are doing? She continues. "I came here to work in the weaving mills. I have gained my freedom but…"

"Yes, for many the city is not a happy place. A new start. I understand."

"Is that why you are here?"

You shake your head. "No, I came to find a boy. Or at least that's why I left the City of the Sun."

"Your son?" she asks.

"No," you tell her. "I'm not sure who he is. When I lived in the City of the Sun, people would come to me to send children to places that were safer for them."

"I understand," says the woman. "So this boy was one of them."

"Yes. But certain people found out where he had been sent and I came to warn those that had him. If I could. It seems absurd now. Thinking I could help."

"What happened to the boy?"

"I don't know. It seems that I came in vain, or perhaps it was well that I did. The man I sent him to and gave money to, abandoned the child. Left him to die. I guess that he is dead. When I found out, I was angry. But it is probably for the best. Those that seek the child would not be gentle."

The man draws his sword suddenly and points it to you. He shouts, "I can see you, come out now or I'll kill your friend." He is very quick and you do not have time to move before the sword is at your throat.

"You may as well come out, Bidann. If they have seen you then there is no point in hiding."

Bidann stands up. He is not far from where you are sitting. He grunts and climbs to his feet using the spear as a staff.

"No weapons, you said. Throw that away and come here."

"Please," you say. "We mean no harm. He needs that to walk." But Bidann thrusts the spear into the earth point down and strides proudly towards us. You know how much pain his pride costs him. "Can I go and help him? He is injured. Or let one of the women help him."

"No," says the man. And so Bidann walks to us.

"I know you," says Bidann. "You're Brau. I know who you are." And he makes the sign of the broken arrow. The sign of the bandit god.

"Well, I don't know you. Who are you?"

"Bidann. I am a wagoner. I've brought you plenty."

"Let me see your face." Here Bidann pushes his hair back. "You look a mess. What happened to you? No wonder I never recognized you. Not much of a ladies' man now."

"Always a ladies' man," says Bidann and turns to the two elderly women grinning and bows.

"Well," says the woman who has not spoken yet. "I can see why. Next time you bow, make sure your robe is closed."

Bidann pulls his robe closed. His embarrassment causes everyone to laugh.

"I'm sorry, mother," he says. "You find me not at my best. My name is Bidann and what are you two charming ladies called?"

"I'm Canna. And this Unead."

"We have food," says Brau, "come and eat. We were just about to eat."

"Thank you," says Bidann. And we sit as the women go about making rice. The boy sits on Brau's lap while we speak.

First Bidann tells how he was captured by bandits and then by guards and then how you escaped.

"That makes no sense," says Brau. "Why would they just let you walk out? Why was the place deserted?"

"It is not just a guardhouse," you tell them. "It was a safe house belonging to one of the twelve. That is why I was there."

"One of the twelve," says the woman, Unead. "Which?"

"I don't know," says Bidann. "No one mentioned the twelve when I was there. How did you know that?"

Tell them. Tell them everything, I whisper to you.

"It was one of the twelve that seeks the boy. The Whip. When I came to Saco, he followed me and took me prisoner."

The woman, Unead, stops and comes to you. She looks at you puzzled. "Yes, Greba. And what is your connection to him? I can see that you are like him."

"I am his son. Not his son. But the son from one of his past lives. He came to me, and I thought he was my friend. But he was not. He is not to be trusted."

Unead is shaking. No wonder, you think. The Whip is the most fearsome of the twelve. "You should show them," she says to Brau. "You should show them the bodies."

"All right," says Brau. "You asked about soldiers, come and see this."

When Unead speaks of bodies, you fear that they are all dead, that Alaba is dead. But when you walk along the path, Bidann leaning on your arm, it is not their bodies you see. Six soldiers lying in a ditch with barely a mark on them.

"I think their necks are broken," says Bidann as he kneels beside them.

"He could have done this," you say, remembering his awful strength. "He could have killed six soldiers without breaking a sweat. This is him."

"And these, I think, are the guards that took us to Saco," Bidann continues. "This makes even less sense. Why would he kill his own men?"

But you know the answer. "Witnesses, he wants no witnesses. He has three prisoners with him."

"Yes," says Bidann, "Dova, my woman, and her daughter, and Alaba."

"Who is Alaba?" asks Unead.

"She is a girl that shines with a light," says Bidann. "I brought her from the City of the Sun. Koreb asked me to. When we lived at the bandit camp, a guy called Utas came. He said she was his daughter."

"Was she?"

"She might have been. When he arrived he had this stone that glowed like the moon. He was a strange guy. He looked weak, but I have never seen a better fighter."

"We should go back to the cart," says Brau. And everyone nods but still stands looking at the dead, lost in their own thoughts.

"We should take their weapons," says Bidann. "It is likely we'll need them. And if no one objects, I'm going to take some of their armour and clothes. You should too." He is looking at Brau and at you as he says this.

"No," you say. "I will be no use in a fight."

"I don't believe that," says Bidann. And he hands you the sword. It nestles in your hand as if it belongs there.

Chapter Sixty-Seven
Retreat

Hilketa

There is no point in staying here. Greba is gone. Unead is gone. The child, the boy is gone. Whatever you hoped for is now out of reach. As you return to the citadel, the crowds shout and throw stones at your chair. The guards struggle to hold back the rioters. It is time. The city must burn.

"General," you call. "Take me to the camp." The column changes direction and heads to the gates. The crowd follows you, calling out at you. What do they expect you to do? Did they think you had come here to save them from famine? Surely they know the dark lord better than that. And if they know why you are here, then why would they do anything else but rebel?

Espada comes to your side. He is riding a pale horse. "What are your orders?" he asks.

"Close the gates. Let no one leave. Has the citadel been evacuated?"

"What of the prisoners?"

What prisoners? Does he mean the governor? You want to tell him to kill them, but they may still be useful. "Bring them too."

There is a tent set up for you. It is large and comfortable. A slave brings you wine. It is better than the wine offered at the citadel, much better. You set yourself and await the return of Andors and Astani. When they arrive they are out of breath. Andors has a graze on his forehead where he has been struck by a stone.

The side of your tent has been rolled up and to the south, you watch the quarter moon in the sky. A brazier of charcoal is set beside you. Wine, warmth and the moonlight, you feel peace returning to you.

"You have heard that the woman, Greba's woman, is gone."

"Yes, great one."

"Gone with another man."

"Yes, great one. We have asked about him and looked at the records. It seems he has lived here for many years. He is a foreman in the weaving sheds."

You hide your impatience. You already know all of this.

"Yes, yes, I know. What else?"

"It seems he is a heretic."

"Go on."

"He is a follower of the hunter or the bandit god. It seems that he has been involved in smuggling in the past. Small-time stuff, but he is a follower of the broken arrow."

"So is that where he has gone?"

"It is likely. It is thought he has family in the farms around Saco. That is usual for petty smugglers. They do not let others into their bands. It is mostly family."

"And where is this farm?"

"We are still investigating, great one."

You bite your lip as you consider. It is almost time to act. If you wait then things might go awry.

"How many farms are there? Can we not send men to them all?"

"There are around twenty collectives, great one. More, many more if you include the villages of runaways and bandits. There are many homes hidden in the forest." The scribe shifts uneasily.

"Go on, what is it?"

"Reports have started of the plague. The fiery rings have been seen on faces of the dead. The sickness has started."

It seems that you cannot wait. Once the plague starts there is only one cure.

"Where?"

"So far only in the city."

"And the gates are secure?"

"Yes, Espada has followed your orders. All his men have been withdrawn. The gates are held. No one leaves."

"What about the safe house? Are there any other ways out?"

"We hold the safe house. Perdona says there is a tunnel out of the citadel. We have also brought the dark portal."

And any other treasure too, no doubt. No doubt the two scribes will manage to lose much of the citadel's treasures. Or find them, depending on how you look at it. It is all ready for your order. What will you order? There can only be one order to give. You know full well what must happen now. It is too bad. You would have liked to find out more about what Greba has been up to. Still, it cannot be helped.

"How soon will we know where this Brau has gone?"

"It is difficult to say. No one seems to know. And it is hard to get information now that riots have started. We may never find out that way. We have some men placed amongst the smugglers, but many of them have left."

There is no point in waiting. But it is frustrating.

"And no sign of Greba?"

"No, great one. No one knows where he is. He has made no contact with the general or any others. His men seem to all be gone, or dead."

"Dead?"

"Yes, there were some dead in the safe house and we found others at a roadside. It may be that Greba is dead too."

Unlikely, you think. If Greba was dead, Vatu would be calling to you to return. There is no point in delaying.

"Very well, set the town on fire. Let Saco burn. Give Espada the order."

It is almost time to leave this town.

Chapter Sixty-Eight
Prisoners

Greba

Outside the walls of Saco, you follow as the guards lead you back to where they found the prisoners. The woman Dova is clinging to one of the guards. Perhaps she is hoping to gain his favour. She keeps turning back and looking at you, then whispering in his ear. The guard pushes her away. He looks back at you. He is hoping you are not watching, but of course, you are. You see everything, as do I. The two girls are walking side by side; your granddaughter and the prostitute's girl. You cannot see her face. She is still wearing the hood. Perhaps you should have hooded all the prisoners. That would have stopped the whore throwing herself on the guards.

There is no one else here. Just you, the guards and the three prisoners. Now the whore is weeping. She thinks you will have her killed, that you will have them all killed. Her crying is annoying. You wish she would stop. You almost want to kill her just make her stop.

"Put a hood on the other two prisoners," you call out. And the guards halt to follow your orders. Dova flinches as the hood is put over her face, but at least now her cries are muffled. The other girl does nothing except hold Alaba by the hand. You want to tell them to take her hood off. You want to see her face again. Why do you not? What is it that makes you stop?

"All right, let's get going," you say. Your voice is harsher than ever.

Now that the prisoners are hooded, the guards need to lead them.

They stumble as they walk over the rough ground. Dova falls to her knees, and one of the guards helps her up. He is not gentle. Now the group is slower than ever. The moon will be gone before you reach the forest.

"Head down to the road," you tell them. "The going will be easier." It does not matter if you are seen. It is a risk you will have to take. Hilketa has arrived with the rest of the army. He must not find your granddaughter. You will keep her safe. This time you will not let them harm her. This time you will save her. You will defy them all.

"As you command, great one," says the captain. And now you are pushing your way through the mulberry bushes. They are draped in webbing. Strands of cobwebs cling to your clothes and hair. Then you push out onto a track heading out towards a barn standing on the hill.

"Can we follow the track?" you ask.

"Yes, great one. The forest should not be too far beyond that barn. If we walk to the barn we should see the forest from there."

"Good," you say. You have all that you need now. The time for you to act is soon. You should have acted sooner. There is a stream running across the track. The ford is high. The stepping stones are covered by rippling water.

"We need to cross here," says the captain. "After this, the road leads straight there."

"Thank you, Captain," you reply. "Have the children carried across."

"It would be as easy to carry them all," says the captain. And you nod in agreement.

The guards lift the children in their arms and carry them across the stream. The water comes up to their knees. Dova is the last to cross. She shrinks into the guard that is carrying her and wraps her arms around his neck as if she is a bride being carried over the threshold. Now you walk across. The current is strong and the water cold after the rains. On the other side, the guards are trying to dry off. One has taken his boots off. They have put their spears down and now is the best time to do it. The prisoners are gathered together to one side. Why do you hesitate? Surely now is the best time to do it. You wonder then if there is no other way. I tell you there is. I tell you that they do not need to die. But you are not listening. You have made up your mind and will not change it. The guards are laughing together and one of them throws his wet boot at another. It is time.

You have done this a thousand times and more. The six of them, even with spears at the ready, would be no match for you. You walk up behind the captain and twist his neck. It snaps and without a word, he falls to the ground.

"What—" the next guard protests but he too is dead almost instantly. One turns towards you and you strike him hard in the face, driving his nose bone into his brain. The soldier sitting on the ground starts to scramble away. It is a simple matter to kick his vertebrae with enough force to shatter them.

"Why?" asks one of the remaining soldiers. But you do not tell him why. You give no explanations. You continue your task. You slay all of them. It is so easy and so quick. Now there is no one to speak of her. No word will get to Hilketa or Vatu about your daughter. He will not discover that she is alive. Your heart is racing now as you grab the last of them and twist his neck. It snaps beneath your grip. All done. Once they were your men, now they are dead. They pledged to give their lives for you and now they have. Why then does it bother you? That look of betrayal in their eyes. They were fools. They put their trust in darkness.

You check each one and roll them to the side of the track. You close their eyes. Why do you do that? You say it is the least that you can do. But does that stare make you uneasy, that look: startled and afraid.

The prisoners have not spoken nor moved. They are huddled together on the ground. They have heard the noise of the struggle.

"Stand up," you tell them. Then you go over and take off their hoods. There is fear in Dova's eyes, defiance in Sifyre's. What is in Alaba's eyes? You cannot tell. The light from her face shines on the dead.

"Why have you killed them?" she asks you.

You do not answer, but instead, untie the prisoners' hands. "Don't try and run away," you say. "If you do…" Here you indicate the dead soldiers. You need say nothing else.

"I won't run. I promise," says Dova.

"Good," you tell her. "Now follow me."

Chapter Sixty-Nine
Over the Hill

Greba

The woman is still whining. You find it so annoying. It is grating on your nerves. Still, if she has been caring for Alaba then you cannot kill her. Not in front of her. Be patient. There will be a time for everything and besides, this is a thing you do not need to do. It is a thing you should not do. But then there are so many things that you should not have done.

"I have promised you nothing," you tell me. "I will do whatever I want."

But I am right. You know you have killed too many. You are not the bloodiest of the twelve, but you know you should never have killed anyone. It is too late for that, you say. I tell you it is not. It is never too late.

The girls are walking ahead, and they are still holding each other's hands. Alaba is brave. She has not cried or complained. Her face now uncovered is radiant. You long to take her and tell her it will be well.

"There is no need to worry," you say. But none of the prisoners seem to hear. They are walking slowly up the track to the top of the hill. "It will not be long until we are safe."

The woman, Dova, turns and looks at you. "Safe from what?" she asks.

"Safe from being caught and found. I will set you free. I will take you back to where you were. Then you can go. You will need to go and find somewhere to hide."

When you say the words it comes to you. You cannot just send a woman and two children out into the darkness. There are other dangers. Vatu is not the only danger. You do not wish Alaba to die.

"Keep going," you say when the woman pauses to catch her breath.

"The children need to rest," she says.

"There is no time for that."

"Why? Who is following us?"

"No one. No one is following us."

Dova starts to walk again. Alaba follows her. Now it seems as if Alaba is leading the way. The other girl, Sifyre is being led by the hand. Alaba shines like a candle in the darkness. Perhaps you should put her hood back on, you think. But you cannot bring yourself to do it. You follow after. Watching to make sure no one is following.

As the road reaches the top of the rise, Alaba stops and waits. Dova is looking at something and raises a hand to her face. What can they see?

Standing there beside them you look over to the forest. It is as the guard said; it is not far away. In the dip stands a farmhouse and a barn stands on the top of the hill. It is built on the slope and is three stories high. Each story has an entrance and further down the slope is the next one. In the top story, the loft, there is grain and hay. In the second there are stalls for the animals, cows mostly, and below that there is space for their waste. It is gathered and put on the fields. Everything is arranged. You can hear the cows calling.

But it is not the barn they have been watching. They are looking at the edge of the forest. There is an army there, an army of bandits. There must be thousands of them. You did not think there would be so many.

"Who are they?" you ask.

"That is Condito," the woman tells you. She points to a wagon and on the wagon, there is a bright light.

"What is that?"

"I don't know," she tells you. "A man brought it. It is a stone that shines like the moon. His name is Utas. He says he is Alaba's father. But she does not know him."

At the sound of that hated name, you feel bile and anger rise within you. He is here. He will seek to take her from you. And yet what other choice is there? Who else will protect her?

"Where is he? Where is Utas?" You look down from the hill and search for his face. But you are too far away, and even in the light of the moon, the moonstone and the light from Alaba's face, it is too dark. It is too far away to see.

"Where is he?" you ask again.

"He will be at the camp," says Dova. "He is a prisoner."

You cannot believe that Utas would have let himself be taken by bandits. It makes no sense. There are too many bandits. You cannot fight them all. Not without calling on Vatu for aid. You can see that many have bows. Others have cudgels. They are poorly armed. Even with their great numbers, they cannot hope to stand against Hilketa's soldiers. They will be massacred where they stand. You cannot just send Alaba to them. They will be unable to keep her safe.

"Come here," you say to her. And she does as you command. She looks at you. What is she thinking? Do you wish me to tell you? I can tell you.

"Yes, tell me," you say.

"She is not afraid, but she pities you. She sees that you are broken and hurt. She sees what I see."

"Does she know who I am?"

"No, but it does not matter. She will heal you if you will let her."

But you cannot see what she will heal you of. You cannot see that you are broken and hurt. What nonsense, you think to yourself.

"I have no need for healing."

But still, Alaba has that look on her face. The light shines from her.

"I have no need," you tell her again. "I will keep you safe." But your words are hollow and empty. You cannot keep her safe. But do not worry, I will keep her.

"I want no harm to come to her." But I do not promise that. Which of us has passed through life with no harm? And would not to do so be the greatest harm of all?

You have been spotted. Alaba's light on the hilltop cannot be hidden.

"Come," you tell them. "Let us go down."

Chapter Seventy
Downhill

Greba

There is no point trying to hide. There are sentries posted. You will not be able to avoid being seen. And besides, you want to speak to whoever is chief down there. You walk down the track and the children and the woman follow you. They do not speak to you. What would you say to them anyway?

"Keep up," you tell them.

When you are halfway down, a sentry steps forward. "Who are you?" he asks.

You motion for the girls and the woman to step forward.

"These are some of yours," he says. "They got lost and now they want to get back."

The rebel looks at Alaba. "Who is she?"

"She was with us at the camp," says Dova. "She was with the woman Ennet and with Bidann." She does not say Bidann is dead.

"He's not Bidann," says the rebel, gesturing towards you.

"No, he's not," Dova agrees.

"Who is he then?"

"Just some old guy we met on the road," says Dova. "And this is my daughter."

"You've come to the wrong place," says the rebel. "You should head back into the forest."

"All right," says Dova. "If we can head back to the forest then that's fine. We'll go back to camp and wait for Bidann. Is he here?"

"No," says the rebel. "Not that I've heard of." He glances around, and hidden in the field you spy about ten others. They have their bows pointed at you. You could kill them all but not without putting Alaba in danger. "All right, head down to the farm. You might get something to eat there. Then head out."

"Thank you. That would be good. We're very hungry." Dova bows her head and gathers the children. You follow her. Why did she not betray you, you wonder. She was smart not to try. It would have ended badly for her.

The guards follow you. They do not trust you. Still, they have promised you food.

"So what is up with the girl?" he asks. "Why does she shine?"

"It is the work of the Whisperer," you say.

When you reach the bottom of the hill, you are stopped again. A slice of bread is handed to each of you. You break yours into two and give it to the two children. You are not hungry. Alaba thanks you for the bread and Sifyre bows stiffly. You would have given it all to Alaba, but you know that she would have split it with her friend anyway.

"You come with us," a guard tells you.

"I need to stay with the children," you reply.

"You need to do as you are told," replies the guard.

"I should bring the child with me. The one that shines. Your leader will want to see her."

The guard considers but then nods. "Very well."

"Can't the others come too?" asks Alaba. She is looking back at Sifyre.

"Go on," says Sifyre, "we'll wait for you here. We'll meet you here."

You also wonder if you should insist that the two others come with you. But there is no need. You had wanted to lead them to the forest and set them off to take Alaba far away from here. But it is too late for that now.

"Come along, we need to go now."

You are led towards the glowing moonstone that you saw as you walked down the hill. Some men are sitting around the stone arguing about something.

"Here is the man," says the guard, and pushes you forward. "I brought the girl back too. You know, the one that stayed with Bidann."

To your surprise, the men all rise and bow, but not to you. They are bowing to the child.

When they rise, a bald man asks her, "Who is this man? Do you know? How did he get a hold of you?"

"We were caught by soldiers. They killed Bidann and took us to a city. This man helped us get free."

"How did you do that?" he asks you.

"With help," you reply, and now you make the sign of the broken arrow. The bald man nods. It seems you have guessed right, they are followers of the hunter.

"Have you come to help us?" he asks.

"Yes," you tell him. "The guards are in Saco in great number. It is likely they will raze the city to the ground. If they know that you are here, they will come. You must prepare."

"We know all this. Thank you for bringing the girl to us. Go back and get something to eat. You will need to fight soon enough. We all will."

It is madness to fight. There are more bandits here than soldiers. But the soldiers are better armed and better trained. If the bandits retreat to the forest and pick off the villages and towns one by one, they might hold out. But even that is unlikely.

"You should let me stay. I can help."

"Why should we do that when we do not even know your name?"

The bald man has turned away. Does not even wait for your answer.

"Please, listen!" you say. But he does not and the rebel takes your arm. You could fight now, but not even you could kill them all. You are led away, back to where Dova and Sifyre are waiting.

Chapter Seventy-One
Tangles

Unead

Men only ever think to fight. It is how they solve all their problems. A woman cannot think that way. A fight is almost always something that they cannot win. How can you possibly win? You take the boy Mukito from Canna and hold him tight. When he is grown will he also be a fool like all the others? Will blood stain his hands?

"You should leave the weapons here," you say. Not that either Brau or the two strangers are listening. Men never listen to women. They do not even answer you. "If you are carrying weapons, then when you meet whoever did this they will kill you."

You know who killed the soldiers. You can feel it. He is near. Greba. You whisper his name. You find that it brings you no pleasure. Once you were certain that you loved him. You gave him a child. You lived with him. He showed you kindness. But now when you whisper his name your heart is filled with fear, not love.

If he has come for you then you will go with him. You will go back to the City of the Sun, even if you know that would be your death. Is that why he is here? It was he who told you to run. If danger came you should leave.

"Tell me nothing of where you would go," he had said to you as you lay in his arms. "It is better I know nothing, that way I will not follow after you."

"It will never happen," you had told him. "I will never leave you. I cannot live if not with you."

But he had sat up and looked at you. "If you should die, it would destroy me. You must be safe. You must do as I say."

"Very well, husband," you told him. "I will do as you command." Always, you did as he commanded.

When you first saw the strangers, you were shocked. You thought he had come. The older one, Koreb, is so like Greba. If you were to guess he is a little older, but still the likeness is remarkable. And it has been years since you saw him. Greba could have aged, and your memories could have faded. But it is not him. When you looked in Koreb's eyes, there was no madness there. It is not him.

The younger one, Bidann, tells his story. You listen. He is telling you about a child that glows in the night. He is telling you about being taken a prisoner first by bandits and then by Vatu's soldiers. He is telling about how the other one, Koreb, set him free and how they must find the woman Dova, and two girls.

"How did you get free?" asks Brau.

"Koreb should tell that tale," says the tall man. And now it is the one that looks like Greba's turn to speak.

"The Whisperer set me free," he says. "He opened the door to my cell, and the prison was empty. He led me to Bidann, and led us here."

"Convenient," says Brau. He is still suspicious.

"Yes," agrees Koreb.

"What were you doing in a cell? You're not from here."

"He's from the City of the Sun," you say. "He has the same accent as me. Why did you come here?"

"I can vouch for him," says Bidann. "I knew him before. He's a priest of the Whisperer or a follower at least. It was him that gave me the glowing girl, Alaba. And the other one, Mukito."

You hold the boy tightly. "I found him in the street abandoned," you say. "I don't see how you can be so sure it's him."

"I brought him here from the City of the Sun," says Bidann. "It's about a month's journey. I know him all right."

You look down at the child. There is nothing special about him. He is just a child.

"I was given him to smuggle out of the city," continues the one so like your lover, Koreb. "His parents are from the court."

"Why would they want to send him away then?" you ask. "It makes no sense. Why not foster him out to someone in the city? Who is he?"

"I am not certain," replies Koreb.

"Then tell us what you know."

Brau rises. "I'm not sure we have time for this."

It may be that he is right. But you cannot let it go.

"Who is he?"

"I think he may be the child of the High Priest of Vatu." When you hear those words, you feel a chill in your heart. A child of Utas.

"How is that possible?"

"I don't know, I only know that Greba, the Whip, is searching for the boy. I think he wishes to kill him."

"And the girl? Is she also his child? Does Greba wish to find that child too?" So many questions.

"I don't know. I only know about the boy. Who can know all the plans of the darkness?"

"Then we should go." You turn to Brau. "Where should we go? We need to get far from here. We cannot stay here."

"We should leave the boy with Koreb and Bidann. We should let them take him and run," says Brau.

"No, I can't. I can't leave him." Because you love him. Because he is yours.

"It would be for the best."

But you are shaking your head. No, you will not leave him. His thread and yours are woven together.

"We need to escape."

"The Whip would find us," says Brau. He takes your hand. "But if it is what you want, then so be it. Perhaps we can be safe for a while."

"I will come too," says Koreb.

"What about Alaba, and Dova and Sifyre?" says Bidann. "I'm not giving up on them. If you want to go with the others, fine. I'll go on myself."

For all the tall man's talk, he is weak and still struggles to walk. You look at Brau.

"It may be that our paths are the same, at least for a while," he says.

Canna takes the boy from you. "Either way, we should be moving."

"You're right," says Brau. "I'm just not sure where we should be moving to. I had thought we would go hide at the farm over the hill. But I'm not sure that's safe anymore."

"We should go back to Saco," says Canna.

"No," says Koreb, "that's where the soldiers are. I'm pretty sure that would be a bad idea."

"We can't stay here forever. We need to decide."

"We go on," says Koreb. "But be careful. Whoever killed those soldiers is still out there."

Brau starts to push the wagon along the track. "Sit on the cart," he says to Bidann. "You're not in the best of shape. We can push you for a while."

But Bidann shakes his head. He limps on using his spear as a staff. Mukito runs over to him and takes his hand. The tall man smiles at him.

You help Brau push the wagon. It seems that more than just Mukito's thread is woven with yours. You make the sign of the Weaver to show your gratitude. Let the Cutter come when she will. You have made a pattern that you are content with.

Chapter Seventy-Two
In Camp

Koreb

Bidann seems so much better. You had thought he would die. And now, even if he is limping a bit, he is keeping pace easily with the rest of you. The boy, Mukito, it is him. It is the son of the high priest of darkness. The disgraced one. The one that Vatu seeks.

The Whisperer will protect him, you say. Yes, I will protect him. Right up until the end. I healed Bidann, but his shoes are ill-fitting. That is why he limps. Now he is as strong as you, almost. You do not know how strong you are.

How awkward the sword feels at your hip. It keeps banging against you as you walk. What, you ask, does the Whisperer wish from me now?

I wish only the best for you. Only the best. Do you even know how to use the thing? You have never used one before. It will not protect you. Only I can do that. You let your hand fall to the hilt. How strange it feels. It is as if it has changed you completely from a man of peace to something else entirely.

What if I should die? you ask me. And the only promise I can give is that you will die someday. How can I protect the boy? you say. But you cannot do that either, one day he too will die. That is the nature of life. What if we are attacked and killed? Do you not see? Wearing the sword makes attacking and killing fair, it is as if you have joined with their game. There are rules now, and killing someone armed is not the same as killing someone unarmed. It is only fear that makes you wear the sword. Let go of your fear. It will do you no good.

The other man, Brau, he also has taken a sword. The three men are armed, even Canna the old woman takes a knife.

There is little talk now. The boy sits on the cart. Unead is trying to get him to sleep. It does not matter.

"We should turn around and leave," you say. "We should leave this place. There is no point in staying."

"I won't leave my home," says Brau.

"It is too late for that. Saco will be ruined. It will burn to the ground. The soldiers will kill everyone. We should go as far as we can." It is not you who speaks. Unead is holding Brau's hand. "We should go and start again somewhere else. There is no point in staying and fighting if we all die."

"I won't leave Dova," says Bidann.

"There is nowhere else to go, anyway," says Brau. "We can either follow the track back to Saco or head onward. Even to get to the forest we need to head on. If it's not safe at the farm then we can go on into the forest. We'll find somewhere."

You look back. There is a red haze in the distance. Saco is burning. And from over the hill comes the glow of fire and a thick pall of smoke. It seems that you will need to go forward. Besides, you can see some soldiers coming towards you along the track.

"Looks like we're not going anywhere," you say.

"They look like rebels," says Brau. "We'll be fine. Let me speak to them."

"All right. So what do we do now, just wait for them?"

You do not have to wait long. Canna is muttering something under her breath. You cannot quite make it out. It is either a complaint about men and war or a prayer to some god that you do not know. It is not a prayer to me, but I hear it. And the Weaver comes to answer.

The soldiers halt and call out to your band. Brau steps forward. He is making the sign of the broken arrow.

"What brings you here then?" asks the first soldier.

"I'm getting out of Saco. Looks like I got out just in time. I'm headed for the farm over the ridge."

"That's ours now. We're there, all of us."

"All of us. I never got a message." The rebel does not seem to care.

"So can we go on?" Brau asks.

"If you like," says the rebel. "But we need to take you. The camp is crowded and you'd be better to move on. There's no food or shelter there. Not for you and not for them. You and the two men can fight with us. But the women and child should move on."

"Where should they move to?"

"Not my problem," says the soldier.

"I think I should stay with them," says Brau.

"We'll see once we get to the farm. Condito will decide. Or one of the others." The rebel looks at Bidann. "I know you," he says. "I'm sure Condito will want you to stay."

Bidann peers at the rebels. "Yes," he says. "You were at the camp. Tell me, has Dova come this way?"

The rebels whisper to each other. "Yes, she's at the farm. For now anyway. She came in with two children, that glowing one that stayed in your hut and her own girl. They came with some old guy."

When you hear those words you know that it is Greba he speaks of. Greba is waiting for you at the farm.

"Come along," says the rebel. "We'll take you to them."

There is no real choice but to follow. Bidann is still too weak to fight and you have never held a sword in your life. Besides, it is where you should go. You should be getting as far away as possible.

When you get to the farm, you are amazed to see how many rebels are there. There must be thousands of men.

"Wait here," says the rebel. "You come with us." The last is addressed to Brau. The rest of you stay and wait.

"Is there anything to eat?" Canna asks one of the bandits, but they do not answer. There is food in the cart, but it is better to keep it hidden. Otherwise, the bandits would take it from you. You look around to see if you can see Greba, but there is no sign of him here. The camp is vast, it is possible he is close.

"Can you see the children? Or your wife?" asks Unead.

"She's not my wife," he says. But she is not here anyway. Bidann turns to one of the bandits. "You! I know you. You're one of Condito's men. Tell me where Dova is. Or better, go and bring her here."

"I don't take orders from you," says the bandit.

"The hell you don't," says Bidann. "You know me well enough to know that if you don't I'll ram a spear up your backside. Go on. Get her and bring her here!"

"Big talk," says the bandit. "You look half dead."

"Even half-dead, I could eat you alive."

"All right," says the bandit. "But not because you say so. It's better to keep the prisoners together."

"Prisoners." Bidann snorts. "Sure, whatever you say. Now go get her and bring her here."

The bandit spits on the ground. He wants to fight, but leaves to fetch Dova.

"You could have just asked," you say to him. But Bidann is sitting on the ground and does not answer. You can tell he is in pain. "Turn over and let me look at your wounds."

When Bidann rolls over, you lift his shirt to look at the arrow wounds. They look sore and red, but there is no smell, nor is there any fresh blood or pus. Whoever healed him did a good job. A better job than you could have done.

"Let me sleep," says Bidann. "I am tired."

It is probably for the best. You leave him and walk over to the child and the two men. The boy comes and sits beside you. What a strange little creature he is. So silent. He looks at you with dark eyes. "It will be all right," you say, uncertain if the words are for him or for you.

Chapter Seventy-Three
The Other Side

Utas

The old woman is keeping you back. But you wait for her. Somewhere out there Alaba is alone or worse. Who has taken her? You will find them and save her. Now that the trees are thinning out, now that you are near the edge of the forest, you slow your pace. Who knows who you will meet?

You wait again and she catches up with you.

"Any sign of them?" she asks.

You point to the dry needles on the forest floor. There are spots of blood, Bidann's blood. You can see it in the dim light.

"Is that his blood?" she asks. "I hope he's all right."

"He is probably dead," you say. "He has lost a lot of blood. Without the proper help, he will die."

"I hope not," says Ennet and makes my sign. "May the Whisperer preserve him. Why have they taken him anyway?"

"Because he was with Alaba. They will not want to leave any trail behind. If he lives then he may have information."

"Information about what? For who?" Good questions, you think.

"About the rebels, and about Alaba."

"I don't think he knows much about that. Bidann is not a bandit or a rebel. And he knows as much about Alaba as I do. Which is nothing. Other than that glow, she's just an ordinary girl. Poor thing, she'd have been better off without it."

"Perhaps," you say. And you wonder if it is true. "But she does glow, and only the Whisperer knows why."

You start moving again, moving slowly over the forest floor.

Ennet follows you. "Is she really your daughter?" you ask.

"Yes," you say. "I am certain, or at least as certain as any man can be."

"Where is her mother?"

"Dead."

"Oh, poor thing." And you wonder who she means, Alaba or Irid. Not that it matters. They are both poor things. "What happened?"

But now is not the time to think of these things. Darkness takes the thoughts. You will not think about it now.

"Hush," you say. Ahead you can see a farm.

"Do you think they have taken them there?" Ennet asks.

"I don't think so," you say. "Look, there are guards there, but not soldiers, they are bandits." And then you see. The whole army of rebels is here. There is Condito standing by the wagon with the moonstone shining.

"We should go round them," Ennet says. "I don't want to get caught up with them again."

But there is no choice. "They may have caught the patrol," you say. "They may have them as prisoners or killed them. We need to go and look. Besides, the tracks lead that way. If we are going to follow them, we need to follow them."

"So what now?"

There is only one thing for it. There are too many to avoid, and it is better to approach them openly than to be caught sneaking around and risk getting a stray arrow in the gut.

"Maybe you should stay here," you tell Ennet.

"Sure," she says. "Then if you get captured I can raid their camp and rescue you."

The old woman always did speak her mind. But she's right, she may as well come with you. Condito will be more likely to listen to her anyway.

As you get closer you see that the rebels have found food at the farm. They are mostly sitting around eating. Mostly they are eating meat from slaughtered cattle. They are cooking it over small fires.

"Hey," you shout. And wave your arms in the air. "Any for us?"

You do not recognize any of the rebels. It seems that the bandit camp was only one base. There are many more than those at the camp. There must be thousands of rebels here. You had not thought there were so many.

"Where do you think you are going?" one of the rebels says.

"I want to speak to Condito," you reply. "We're looking for Bidann."

"Condito is at the farm. Never heard of Bidann."

You wonder if the bandit will stop you, but you walk on and he lets the two of you pass.

Ennet is looking around for any sign of them.

"Do you think they are here?" she asks again.

"No, probably not."

"Can you still see the trail?"

"No, not now that all this lot have trampled though."

"So we've lost them."

"Maybe, I guess they would be going to Saco. That is the only city near here."

"Maybe we should just go round then. We can just leave this lot to get on with it."

"That's not how it works. This is an army. They are not going to let us just walk out of here. Not without Condito's permission anyway."

"Do you think he will let us go?"

"Only if there is something in it for him."

"Like what?"

Why does she always ask so many questions?

"We could spy on Saco for him. That's the only way he'll agree to let us go."

"All right," she says. "But be careful. Condito is smarter than he looks. I mean he's more than just a thug."

Yes. You will need to be careful.

There are more men with Condito. You do not recognize them. They look dangerous. Some are big, bulky men while others are small and mean looking. Each of them is wearing the sign of the broken arrow. They are better organized than you expected. You see that the camp is divided into sections. There are fewer women than you thought there would be, and no children. Where has Condito sent them? This is not a rabble, this is a fighting force. You have underestimated them.

"Condito," says Ennet, as she walks into the light of the moonstone.

When the bandit chief turns and sees the two of you walking toward him, he scowls.

"What are you doing here? The women and children are to return to the camps. And why is he not in chains?"

"We are looking for Bidann," Ennet says smoothly. "There has been a raid by soldiers. We think they are from Saco. He should be told. They have taken Dova."

"He's not here," says Condito. "He's better off without that whore anyway. Did they find the camp?"

"No, I don't think so," says Ennet. "We came across them in the forest. They took Dova. But I got away. I went back for him and followed them. They came this way."

"We've not seen any patrol," says Condito. "We've just arrived here a few hours ago. We've collected food, but that's all. A few of the farmers tried to stop us."

You wonder what happened to them. But do not ask. You can guess. Condito is not merciful.

"We need to find them," says Ennet. "They have the children."

"Well, they haven't come this way. Go back to the camp. There's nothing you can do but get in the way."

"I wonder where they would take them," Ennet says. "Saco perhaps."

Don't overplay your hand, Ennet, you think.

"Probably," Condito says, and shrugs.

"Let us go there, and see."

"And what then? Do you think you can spring them out? Go back to the camp."

"I could spring them out," you say. He turns and looks at you. He is thinking of when you bested him with only your bare hands. "I could go. Then I can tell you what's happening there."

"I already know what's happening at Saco," Condito says.

"And what is that?" you ask. But Condito only taps his nose.

"Seems to me that you don't know as much as you think," says Ennet. "You didn't know that a patrol had been through the forest. You didn't know that they came this way. Right under your nose. Seems to me you don't know anything. I can tell you now they're waiting for you. I can see you're ready to fight, or at least think you are. The more you know, the better. You should let us go and see, then we'll come back and tell you."

But Condito is not listening. He has turned away and motioned to some of the bandits.

Ennet looks at you. But you shake your head. There are too many. It is a fight they cannot win.

Chapter Seventy-Four
Mother

Unead

The big man is snoring now and the other man is sitting with Mukito. You should rest too. You are so tired. Canna is worried. She has good cause to be afraid.

"It will be all right," you tell her.

"Will it?" She is not looking convinced. "The Cutter comes for us all in the end."

"Then all we can do is follow the Weaver until then," you reply and make the Weaver's sign.

They all three of them are here and bow to me. Then go on with their dance.

"The Weaver has plenty of tricks of her own," says Canna. And that is true. The Weaver laughs at Canna's words. Only I can hear.

"If we could see her pattern we would not think so," you reply. It seems you have more faith in her than you thought. You sit and think of the pattern of your own life and the threads in them. You think of Irid and hope her thread is bright in the weave. And Greba. You do not forget him. What a tangled mess it seems. Greba, Irid, Brau, Mukito, Canna: all tangled together with your own. And those two others.

You walk over to the older one. He is indeed like Greba.

"Tell me more about the boy," you say. "He has lived with me only for a few years."

"I don't know anything really," the old one replies. "I was given him by someone from the inner court. I don't know much. But the man could not help gossiping. He said the boy was the son of someone important and of the girl kept prisoner. A secret prisoner of the dark tower. He hinted more than he said."

"So you think he is the son of the high priest?"

"I am certain of it. Or certain that the eunuch thought he was."

You turn to Mukito and look at him. You can see no likeness to Irid. But yes, he could be the son of Utas. Those eyes for one thing. His skin is not as dark as Utas' or Irid's. But then he has spent his summers away from the Valley of the Sun. And when you look at him you feel your heart leap.

"What happened to the girl?" you ask. Your voice is flat and toneless. You give nothing away.

"She is dead. That is what the eunuch said. Sacrificed to Vatu. She was a prisoner."

So Irid did not escape. Perhaps she did not even escape the City. But at least she lived long enough to have a child. Strange that after those years with the high priest, it is only after she fled that she had a child. If Mukito is Irid's child, that is. The dark tower is full of so many secrets. Even if Utas is the father, then the mother may be someone quite different.

"It does not matter," you tell yourself. It does not matter who the child's mother and father are. You loved him before and you will love him still. Even if he is not Irid's child, you will love him.

"Come," you tell Mukito and hold out your hand. He takes it and you hold him. "Are you tired?"

The boy shakes his head.

"You have been a good mother," says Koreb.

"I am not his mother." But if not you then who is?

When Brau returns, he looks weary. The guards let him through. You wish you had been able to go with him and hear what the bandit leader, Condito, had to say.

"What is wrong?" you ask.

"Nothing. It is just that we cannot stay here. We will have to leave soon."

You are relieved that is all. It will be much better to leave. You had worried that you would not be allowed to leave. You want to leave before you find Greba. If he is here. If you met him, you do not know what will happen. What will happen to Mukito and to Brau? It is better not to find out. What will happen to you? You are not certain. But you think you know. You will follow him as you have always followed him, even if he leads you back into the darkness.

"When will we leave?" you ask.

Brau moves to speak but is interrupted by Bidann. "I'm not leaving before I find Dova," says the tall man. "You can go if you like, but I have come for my wife. If she is here, I am not leaving without her."

"Very well," says Brau. "But we need to leave." The tall man walks on into the camp, leaving you all behind.

"If we are quick we can be gone before the fighting starts," says Brau.

Koreb lifts the boy onto his shoulders and Brau and Canna push the cart and you head towards the trees. Keep going, I tell you. Keep going until you are safe. Keep going until you are far from here. The sound of battle drives you on. It is days and days before you stop. There is a house lying empty in the woods. Brau pushes the door open. There is no one there. You will be safe here, for a while.

Chapter Seventy-Five
Strike

Greba

When you return to the others what can you say? "We should leave," you tell Dova. "You should take the girls and leave."

Bandits come. "Are you Dova?" they ask the woman.

"Yes," she replies.

"Come with us. You and the girls."

"Why?"

The bandit grits his teeth. He wants to hit her for asking. "None of your business."

But surely it is.

"What about him?" asks one of your guards, and points at you.

"What about him? He's your problem."

"Where are you taking them?" you ask.

This time the bandit does strike out. Or tries to. He swings a clumsy blow at you. And you step inside the arc of his swing. The anger inside you will not let you stop. You crash your forehead into the bridge of his nose and send him sprawling back. Blood runs down his face. The other bandits are too shocked to move. You step forward over the fallen man. For all his bravado he is slight and scrawny. "I won't ask again, where are you taking them?"

"There's a man there who says the woman belongs to him. And the girl."

"Bidann?" asks Dova. "Is his name Bidann? I thought he was dead."

"No, he's not dead. He's looking for you."

"No," you say. "We should get away."

But Dova is not listening. The tall man is walking towards her and Dova is running to embrace him.

Chapter Seventy-Six
Burning

Hilketa

From the citadel you can smell the smoke. Saco is burning now. All of it. The flames are high and tinged blue. The fire started in the silk sheds. The dye works were next and then the loom halls. Who started them? You gave no order to start the fire, but you would have soon. It is time for the city to burn. Your soldiers spread the fire to the houses of the poor first and then to the houses of the rich. There is more for them to steal there. The poor have almost nothing. It is almost not worth burning them out. They are like rats. Somehow some of them will survive, no matter what.

"It is time to leave," says Astani. The flames are unlikely to reach the citadel. It is built of stone, not wood. It will not burn easily. Still, the smoke has made the air thick and hard to breathe. Everything is ready. The sedan is waiting for you. But still, you cannot take your eyes from the fire. You are thinking of another time and place.

"Very well," you say and sit in the chair. Now you are lifted up and the escort begins to make its way to the gate. You will leave by the north gate, from the citadel rather than go through the town. That way will be easier. A guard will remain to keep the townsfolk out of the citadel, but you have things to do now.

"Where is Espada?" you ask an aide.

"He is getting things ready."

"And we will be ready to move soon?"

"I think as soon as you arrive in camp. The vanguard is ready."

"And he is certain this is where they are?"

"Yes, it is the only place that none of our patrols have returned from."

Yes, that will be where the rebels are. "How many?"

"We don't know great one, but it will make no difference. We will kill them all." But you know that some will escape. There is always some. How is it that some always escape? And you think of me. Is that your doing, Whisperer? And if it is, why not save them all?

"You see," you tell me. "You are as much to blame as I am. You could save them all but you don't."

You are wrong though, I do save them all. When their role is over, they leave the stage. How many will leave the stage this moon round, you ask me.

Espada is waiting in the camp. He dismounts from his pale horse that seems to fade in the moonlight.

"Is everything ready?" you ask him.

He bows low. You have taught him to fear you, and he has learned well. "We can leave now. Great one."

"I shall take your horse," you tell him. The sedan will be too slow. On horse, you will be able to keep up and to see more.

He does not argue, but you can see his mouth pressed hard shut as he bows. "As you wish. There is another prepared."

No doubt there is, but Espada will not have prepared a horse for you as fine as his own. "You may take that one," you tell him, and again he bows. He is such fine sport. You might decide not to kill him. Not yet at any rate.

The horse is as fine as you expected. You can feel its strength beneath you. It is strong-willed but follows well. You clap the horse on the neck. The skin is soft and fine.

Espada arrives beside you, his horse is bay coloured with white fairing. It is passable. It is taller than the pale horse.

"Move out," Espada shouts, and the column starts to trudge along the road. You goad the pale horse into a trot and follow along. Espada follows a length behind you.

Chapter Seventy-Seven
Salvation

Utas

What are you thinking, Utas? There is so much anger within you. You blame me for all of this.

"Why is it that you always desert us?" you ask me. But I have never deserted you.

"I have tried to follow you, but still things end this way."

Did you think that if you did what I asked then everything would be easy? That is a promise I never made. I promised only that it was the right thing.

"You can save us! Why will you not save us?"

Here in the camp you will be slaughtered when the fighting starts. You watch as the army of Vatu lines up on the hilltop; there are so many. This can only end one way. At the top of the hill, a dark mass of soldiers lines the crest. They are holding torches. How many of them are there? You can see Hilketa on his horse. What is he thinking as he looks down on the rebels? He is thinking only of death.

And then you see Greba walking towards you. Alaba is with him. And the others. Dova, Bidann and Sifyre. It seems that they are all here.

Ennet runs to Alaba and hugs her. Dova is talking to Bidann. You are surprised that he is alive.

You see Greba and shift, ready to attack. He stops just a few feet away and you stare at each other.

"You should be dead," he says.

"Why are you here?"

Greba looks around at Alaba. She is his grandchild. That is why he is here.

"I will keep her safe," you tell him.

"You did not keep her safe before."

Alaba runs up and takes your hand. She smiles up at you. Then she hugs you.

"I will keep you safe," you tell her.

Greba turns and walks away.

"Where are you going?" you shout.

"Back to the darkness," he replies.

Chapter Seventy-Eight
Time

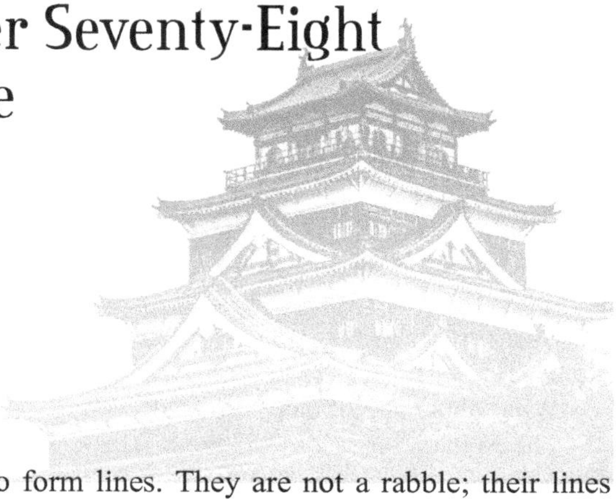

Utas

The rebels rush to form lines. They are not a rabble; their lines are straight. They cannot hope to win, but they will not die without a fight. They cannot win. The soldiers charge down the slope. Each of them carries both a lantern and a spear. They surge against the rebel lines like a dark tide. The rebels fall back but hold, at least for a while. The line buckles and bends. The rebels are pushed back, and the fallen are trampled underfoot.

"Push back, push back," is the shout. And the line holds. Hilketa is riding at the rear.

When I look he is gone. Where are you, Erroi?

He is with you. "Come with me," Erroi says to you.

"Who are you?" asks Bidann.

"I have come to save you," Erroi says. "Come with me. I will take you from the fight."

"I'm not afraid of a fight," says Bidann. "I'm not afraid of anything. I'm going nowhere."

"I'm too old to run any further," says Ennet. "If this is the end then it's about time."

"I can't leave Bidann. I can't leave him again," says Dova, and Sifyre holds tight to her mother's hand.

"Very well," says Erroi. He turns to you again. You want to argue, to beg them to come. But there is no time.

"Please."

But no one is listening. They will not come.

"You cannot make them," Erroi tells you.

* * *

He leads you from the fight. He leads you out to edge of the forest. Your wagon is there waiting.

"Go now," he tells you.

You see Utas, I have not deserted you.

"What of the others? What of the old woman and the giant and his family?"

Erroi says nothing but takes Alaba in his arms then passes her to you. "Take her away," he says. "Keep her safe."

Erroi, do you remember that the child was not yours, but that you were hers. Now Utas is hers too. Perhaps one day the whole world will be hers.

"Come with me," you say to the child, and Alaba takes your hand.

"What about the others?" she asks.

"The Whisperer will save them, Erroi will save them," you say. Then together you turn towards the forest and run. Erroi has gone. Where will he go now? Who will he save next?

Chapter Seventy-Nine
Victory

Greba

You have returned to the darkness. It fills your heart. The child is not yours. Only death and destruction can fill the emptiness, you say. But I tell you it will not. I tell you that only love can do that. I tell you that you should love and be loved. You should let love fill you. Even now you should let love fill you.

We spoke once before. We will speak again, and again until you listen.

The mulberry fields are now burning. Groups of rebels are coming out of the fields, mostly archers. They gather in small pockets and fire into the back of Hilketa's soldiers. Espada sends a small group to chase them off. It is enough to let the rebel line begin to advance, to push back.

Now the line is moving back and forth. The grunts of warriors and the clash of iron rings in the air. The dying scream out and then are silent. The light of the moonstone shines brighter than a summer day. Then it happens, the line is broken. The rebels start to run or fight in small pockets. Hilketa and Espada ride into the camp. Hilketa is looking for Alaba. He is standing in his saddle looking around but he does not see her. He sees someone else. He sees Utas.

"This way," he says and turns to catch Utas as he runs for the forest along with so many other rebels. He rides forward but then comes a voice. Your voice.

"Halt!" and at the sound of your voice, the soldiers halt. You step forward. The soldiers follow your command. Greba. You stroll coolly up towards Hilketa. "You're late," you say.

"I came as soon as I could," says Hilketa. "I had things to do. Where have you been? What brings you here?"

You do not answer. Instead, you reach up and grab Hilketa's leg. With a quick sudden twist, you throw him to the ground. "You're on my horse," you say and mount up. You can see Espada smirking. It seems Hilketa has not made himself popular. You are not surprised.

Looking around you can see the fighting going on. But it's over. Now it's just a slaughter. They will not escape. None of them will escape. You gesture to Espada and with a nod, a detachment is sent to cut off the rebels' retreat.

It is a blood bath. There is no escape.

"Vatu will be pleased," says Hilketa.

It is then that you see him. He is standing beside the moonstone. Erroi. At first glance, he looks more like a farmer than a warrior. But he moves like a dancer, and his sword strikes flesh with every stroke. No one can stand against him.

Hilketa sees him too.

"You should kill him," he says.

And what is that you feel? Is it fear? You know that you cannot defeat him.

You call back all the divisions. You must take him, even if the whole army is destroyed. Archers surround him, arrows fly but not one strikes him. With a gesture he makes them fall at his feet.

Ringed by the whole army, there is nowhere for him to go. He cannot escape.

The moonstone shines brighter and brighter. You step down from your horse and lift the blade from your side. He smiles as you approach. The whole army will watch. You remember when you last fought, so many years ago.

"Surrender," you tell him, "you are surrounded and you cannot win."

Erroi smiles. And you run at him. If he will kill you then so be it. He parries your thrust with ease, and you spring back to avoid his returning stroke. He is still better than you. It is you who cannot win. But neither can you retreat. Pride will not let you.

You put on a good show, you use every trick that ever he taught you. Here before all of your men, you will be defeated. It is not fear you feel, it is shame. He is playing with you. How can he still have so much power? Why will the dark one not come to you and aid you? But it is always this way. You have seen it many times; the darkness always betrays those who follow it.

You have been fighting for some time now. The soldiers are silent; they have stopped their assault on the rebels. They know that you are beaten. They have seen that you cannot win. Erroi has won. He has defeated the darkness. The rebels have slipped away into the forest. Utas, your granddaughter: they have found safety in the trees.

You are glad. It is better this way, and now you bow your head and wait for the killing stroke. Who knows, perhaps this time, you will stay dead. Perhaps Vatu will not drag you back to life, back to him, back to the darkness.

But the stroke does not come. The moonstone shines so bright your eyes feel as if they are burning. You are blinded. Then there is a noise like thunder, the earth shakes. And then a blast of air and heat and light and rock. You are thrown to the ground. You are bleeding from your nose and ears and eyes. You turn and retch, black blood comes from your mouth. How long do you lie on the ground before you can stand? How long before you can see and hear? When finally you can see, what a sight for you.

Erroi is gone and you live. You are the first to stand. You can see Hilketa still lying on the earth. He will live, but he also is lying in blood and vomit. All of your soldiers are lying like scattered pins, like broken twigs, like dying leaves. Many of them are dead, some are moving. If the rebels returned now, they could kill them all. As you walk across the devastation, you find so many dead. Is Unead amongst them? You look everywhere. Every woman's corpse you turn over but you do not find her. There is one old woman; when you see her face you are certain it is familiar. But you cannot think where you have seen her before. You say a silent prayer to me. Keep them safe. Let them live. I promise that I will. I promise when the time comes I will take them to me as I take them all.

The Cutter is here, she is cutting the threads of so many, but the Weaver is also here and she spreads the tapestry she has made. It is very beautiful. And the Spinner passes new threads to her and the game begins again. It will play over and over. I will not save you, but it will play over and over until you all save yourselves.

What is written cannot be unwritten.

Epilogue

How long has it been? You sit in the wagon thinking back on that day. If only, you say to yourself. But how could it have ended any differently? How could you have changed it? How could you have saved anyone that would not be saved?

You have been running ever since that day. You and Alaba. I have kept you from him, from Vatu. But it has been no use. She has grown, but she has grown sick and ill. Each summer, the Sun brings her back to health and then slowly fades away. Where can you hide? You are so tired.

You glance backward into the wagon. Alaba is hidden well. There is not even a glimmer of light to be seen.

So many memories. They hover in the air around you.

"Is this the victory you promised me?" you ask. And I listen to your words. Is this not enough? To live and to wait for me? Be certain I will come. Be certain I will send him. From the corner of your eye you see him. Erroi. But you are not ready. You turn away and ride on.

Glossary

Alaba: Daughter of Utas.

Andors: A scribe.

Astani: A scribe in the service of Kong.

Bidann: A wagoner.

Brau: A foreman at the weaving shed.

Caester: A guard.

Canna: A nurse to Mukito.

Condito: A bandit.

Dova: A prostitute and mother of Sifyre.

Ennet: An old woman, follower of the Whisperer, guardian of Alaba.

Espada: A general in the army.

Ezena: A bandit woman.

Gaesta: A bandit.

Garra: A bandit, brother to Gaesta.

Injutil: A draw girl at the weaving shed.

Ivre: A wealthy man in Saco.

Koreb: The heretic priest.

Mukito: Son of Utas.

Perdona: Governor of Saco.

Sifyre: A bandit child.

The Gods

Cera: Goddess of food.

Sig: The hunter god.

The Spinner: The weaver's god of creation.

The Weaver: The weaver's god of life.

The Cutter: The weaver's god of death.

Motoni: The god of fire.

The Whisperer: The god of forgiveness.

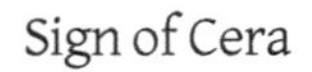
Sign of Cera

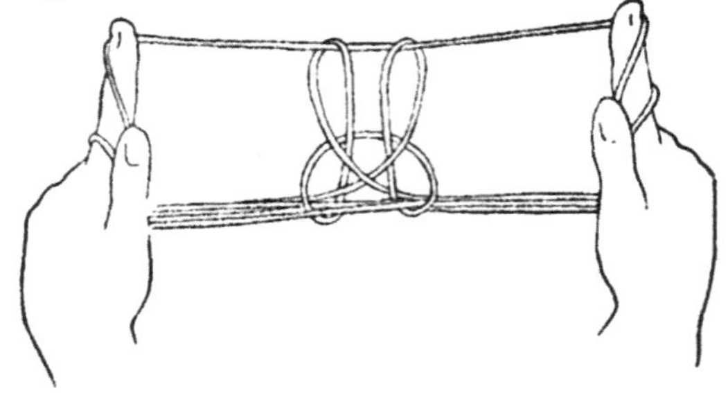

Sign of the Hunter

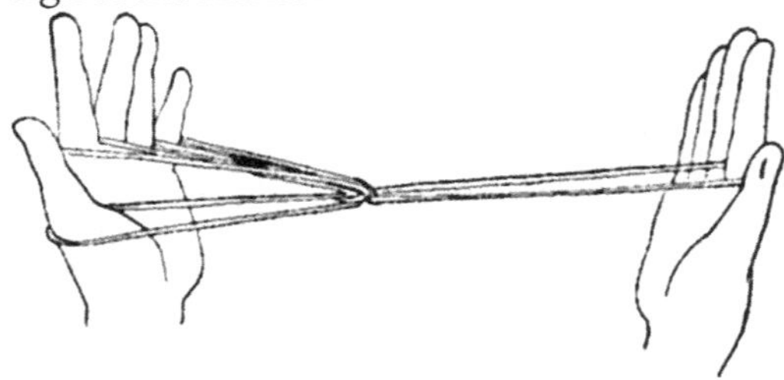

Sign of the Weaver

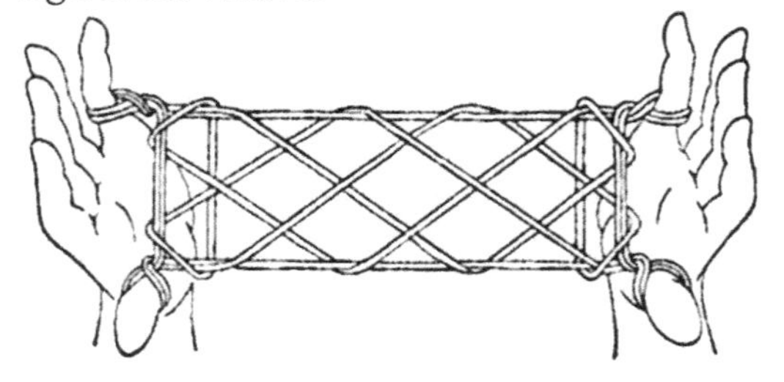

Sign of the Spinner

Sign of the Cutter

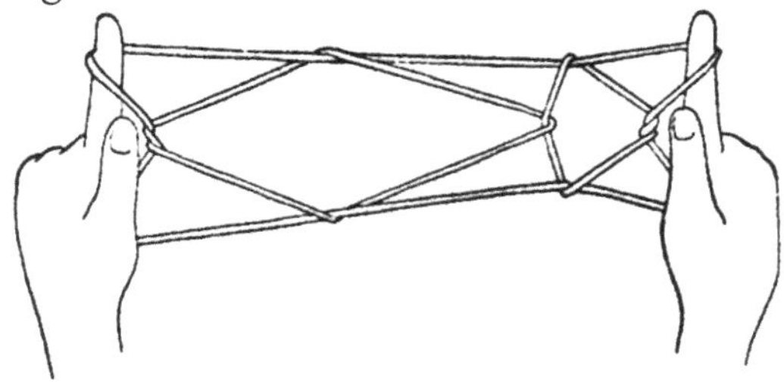

Sign of Motoni, the fire god

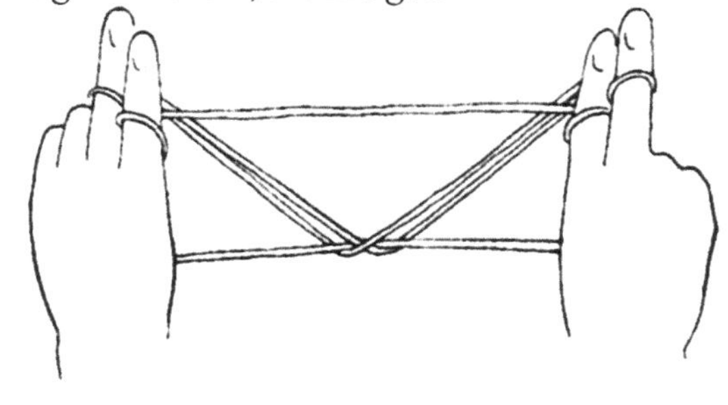

Sign of the Whisperer

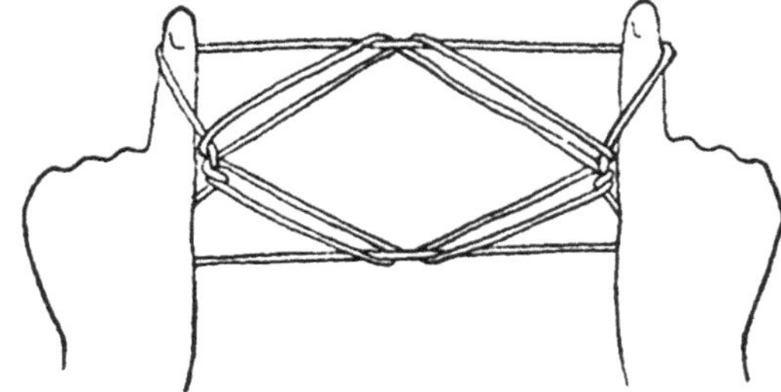

Acknowledgements

A big thank you to all that helped encourage me along this journey. Thank you to Catherine and all at Brain Lag books. Special mention to Iseult, Valorina, Chris, Tom, Steven, Elisabeth and everyone else that helped support me. A special mention to the International String Figure Association for all of their excellent information about string figures. To Andreas for help explaining how to tell the time from the moon, instead of just howling at it. Apologies for any that I have missed.

David Rae is the author of the Sun Thief trilogy, a dark fantasy series that deals with issues of redemption and forgiveness. He is an award-winning writer of short stories, flash fiction and poetry. His work has appeared in numerous magazines, anthologies and online.

David lives in Scotland and grew up in a world where workers spill out of factories, a world where fog and smoke shroud all kinds of creatures, a world where ruined castles, factories and houses are haunted by ghosts, gangs and memories. He lives in a world where witches have been burned at the cross and martyrs have been hung on the Gallowgreen.

He is married and has four lovely children and now lovely grandchildren. And he continues to read and to write and marvel at the world he lives in.

Crowbait is the final book in the Sun Thief Trilogy together with *Crowman* and *Crowtower*, also available on Brain Lag.

Ingram Content Group UK Ltd.
Milton Keynes UK
UKHW012129060323
418151UK00010B/144